ORGANIZED CHAOS PART 4: DESTRUCTIVE
TRANSCENDENCE

by

Brandon S. Todd

FOA (Freedom Over All)
OCU (Organized Chaos Universe)

Spec-Script   704-685-6885

ORGANIZED CHAOS PART 4: DESTRUCTIVE TRANSCENDENCE

FADE IN:

INT. INTRODUCTION - PREAMBLE CREDITS - MORNING

- CAVEAT LECTOR -

EDGAR ALLAN POE, a very popular American author, believed in a unique philosophy that advocates a concept called "DESTRUCTIVE TRANSCENDENCE". Destructive Transcendence is the belief that in order to return to original unity, the PHYSICAL WORLD and the SPIRITUAL WORLD must BOTH be DESTROYED.

With regard to the INDIVIDUAL - DESTRUCTIVE TRANSCENDENCE means that to achieve their own sense of happiness, one is willing to DESTROY themselves; vice-versa.

The 4 Stories Herein are meant to be Filmed strictly with 70MM 'IMAX' Cameras AND 65MM 'Panavision' Cameras:

                                          CUT TO:

COPYRIGHT AND CREATIVE DISCLAIMER(S):

Copyright 2024 Brandon S. Todd

All rights reserved. No part of this publication may be reproduced, stored in a retrieval system, or transmitted, in any form or by any means, electronic, mechanical, photocopying, recording, or otherwise, without the prior permission of the author.

Disclaimer:

This content may include explicit material. Reader discretion is advised. The intention is not to offend but to provide a fictional story. Proceed only if you are comfortable with potentially sensitive content.

Any similarities to real people, real places, and/or real events are entirely coincidental.

FADE IN:

INT. THE DACROPOLIS - DAY

                                      LOCATION: OLD HELL

                                        TIME: UNKNOWN

THE DEVIL didn't create HELL...

--GOD DID--

ANGELS who serve THE BEING (God) are slaving over hot fires within a DIVINELY MONUMENTAL MONOLITHIC STRUCTURE. GOD's HELL is populated with the most abominable of horrors...the worst being the STAINED human souls; those destined for EVIL.

Mindless, monstrous REAPERS (Dark Seraphim) incessantly fly and hover around THE LIGHTSMITHS, as security, guarding them as they work. Trained, divinely influenced SMITHS among other arts, these ANGELS are forging weapons in the belly of HELL, even beyond the SEVENTH CIRCLE, TRILLIONS OF MILES beyond...

...The place is fueled by the screams of the damned, those sinners who renounced God through their rejection of repentance. Tortured endlessly, continuously by FALLEN ANGELS who are now nothing more than deformed Demonic-Monsters -

Metals are rolling through instruments, melted, scorching. The viscosity of the lava-like metals is absolutely beautiful. RINGS are forged, formed, and fed in the pits of THE DACROPOLIS; they are instruments of PEACE and of WAR.

Two RINGS: 'THE LIGHT RING' and 'THE DARK RING' - The RINGS of CHAOS:

Weapons made in pure balance and equilibrium, respectively containing the supernatural powers of both sides, the LIGHT and the DARK. Yet...ARE THE RINGS EQUAL?

CUT TO:

YEAR: 2049 AFTER-DEATH

We now see a broad glimpse of NEW HELL in all its GLORY - and we zoom in on its RULER, MICKEY MORENO MONTANA in his ANGELIC new form, now with him having banished the tyrannical SATAN and replaced him by GOD's WILL.

MICKEY, immortally young as his youthful adult-self, has on a glowing white kingly outfit with gold emblems and supernatural markings all over it. He has on no shoes as his feet are consumed by HELLFIRE. He, too, has a CROWN made of GOLDEN FIRE, with the utmost serious look on his still scarred face, the look of a MAN destined to rule HELL with an Iron-Fist.

> MICKEY MONTANA
> (narrating from
> the future in NEW
> HELL on the
> THRONE)
> - What a wicked web we weave. Look at the wrath we wrought. The pain, the hurt. Was it worth it? The Light pulls me, US, as does the Darkness. Before this time, in a time before time, the weapons of Light and Darkness manifested into physical form. RINGS of CHAOS, capable of great or terrible things. THE DARK RING allows for the control of Dark Matter, telekinesis, telepathy, and all the powers of Darkness. To balance the equation, THE LIGHT RING was created. It holds the power of 5 suns, granting its host flight, heightened strength, allowing them
> (MORE)

                    MICKEY MONTANA (cont'd)
          to create energy while also
          providing invulnerabilities to
          DARK MAGIC. Both are weapons of
          tremendous power. I know this
          because I am supposed to know
          this. IT IS MY FATE.

                                               CUT TO:

HELL, old or new, still has SEVEN CIRCLES, spanning for
nearly 5 trillion miles, total:

There's no water.

There's no food.

There's no oxygen.

There's no salvation.

There's only darkness, and the utter absence of The Lord God
Almighty. All that is felt by the souls of the damned, and
the spirits of the beastly Angels, is God's PERFECT torment.

- GOD IS LOVE.

- NO LOVE IS THE WORST PAIN.

- GOD'S ETERNAL ABSENCE AWAY FROM THE SOUL IS THE TRUE HELL.

                                               CUT TO BLACK:

"There is no terror in the bang, only in the anticipation of
it." - ALFRED HITCHCOCK

ACT I. BANG!!!

CHAPTER I - THE GOOD OLE DAYS

                                               FADE IN:

INT. THE "BLACK" CABIN - MORNING

                              LOCATION: EL PUEBLO,
                              CALIFORNIA (LOS
                              ANGELES)

YEAR: 1887

A BLACK MAN, and his WIFE, sit at a TABLE...

They're praying. Not over food, for they have none. This CABIN is not theirs...it's simply a "rental" for SLAVES who work for the AMERICAN RAILROAD COMPANY.

They lay tracks throughout America and travel to the locations to do so. MR. JOHN HENRY is the best of the best at it, yet still, he's treated as an outcast, a second-class citizen.

The COUPLE are simply praying for MERCY from GOD -

The MAN is JOHN HENRY. Not the myth, THE MAN himself - JOHN is shiny bald, almost supernaturally muscular, and has a strong jaw covered with shaped up facial hair.

He's in his early 30s - wearing tattered blue-jeans and a sleeveless beige flannel, exposing his hammer-waving arms. The WIFE is JANE HENRY, she is nearly as beautiful as EVE was in the GARDEN of EDEN, even living under such monstrous conditions. She's blacker than a bruised berry, exquisitely built, lovely as a sunrise.

JANE, in her late-20s, has gorgeous long hair wrapped up in a bun covered with a black bandana, and she's wearing a red shirt with tight-knit black pants on - it's one of her only outfits. She and JOHN are the epitome of AMERICAN STRUGGLE.

They live in precarious, and rather divided times. They live as INDENTURED SERVANTS among a White class that would gut them at any given chance but instead want to see them struggle.

As MR. JOHN HENRY prays, he cries tears of silence; he can't show them as a man. He doesn't complain in front of JANE. He keeps the hurt to himself. She is resilient, classy, and stubborn. She sticks with her man, no matter what. No food is no matter to her.

She knows he'll get something to eat BY ANY MEANS NECESSARY.

                                                    CUT TO:

EXPOSITION:

The contest between JOHN HENRY and the steam-drill was something black folk made up to ease their minds of the real tragedy. Like, Jonah and the whale.

JOHN HENRY didn't smash steel with his mighty HAMMER in a contest against a steam-drill. He was simply an outcasted hard worker who rose up valiantly against oppressive White folk. He raced not against machines or time, but against his own species.

There was no happy ending for MR. HENRY or his beloved WIFE.

JOHN HENRY could handle his HAMMER better than any man could handle any tool. It wasn't a weapon or even a tool to him. It was simply an extension of himself.

He used it every day, and even at night as he lay beside JANE, he would imagine working with his awesome HAMMER - it was more than muscle-memory, more than routine, it was a WAY OF LIFE for him. Even more so, a way of coping.

JOHN HENRY didn't win anything on earth. Rather, he accumulated a heavenly wealth that was to be passed on. He did die...not from exhaustion in a race against a steam-engine, but from LOSS and a broken heart.

Despite the fabrication of MR. HENRY's battle and subsequent death, best believe, the HAMMER was VERY REAL. "BANG!, BANG!, BANG!" was the only sound it made. It only needed to be made once for people to know whose hammer it was.

                                                    CUT TO:

INT. THE "BLACK" CABIN - CONTINUOUS

JOHN gets up. He stands tall.

His HAMMER lies against the wall of THE CABIN - it is composed of the heaviest iron, with a magnificent gleam, and a more than sturdy wooden handle. The HAMMER is the greatest of tools, ready to do work.

MR. HENRY grabs his tool, and prepares himself for the day ahead.

He takes a deep breath.

                   JOHN HENRY
JANE, I will get us out of this situation, soon. I'll figure it out. When I do, we'll have a true wedding. We'll wear all-white, have the piano playing in the background, we'll say our vows in a CHURCH. We'll do it right, honey. I just got to work these numbers down with BIG BO.

                   JANE HENRY
           (rubs JOHN's cheek)
We don't need a CHURCH, or a piano, or anything else to be HUSBAND and WIFE. We just need each other. I love you, JOHN HENRY, more than anything in the whole wide world and nothing, NOBODY, can change that.

                   JOHN HENRY
           (hugs his WIFE
            tightly)
You're all I need, too, baby. You got me and I got you. My hands, though, they're getting tired. My HAMMER, it's getting weary.

                   JANE HENRY
           (comforting)
JOHN HENRY, I believe in you. And, I believe in God. You let the HAMMER do the work, let it work until it's a nub if you have to. YOU JUST DON'T GIVE UP, no matter what. You make sure to come home
                    (MORE)

                    JANE HENRY (cont'd)
          to me. We'll make a way,
          regardless.

                    JOHN HENRY
               (turns and nods
                his head)
          Yes, ma'am. Who loves you, baby?

                    JANE HENRY
               (smiling wide)
          You do. Always have.

                    JOHN HENRY
               (winks at JANE)
          I'll come back with some food. I
          promise.

                    JANE HENRY
          You just come back to me in
          one-piece, you hear? I'll do some
          fishing over yonder in the pond
          and conjure up something myself,
          so you don't worry about that.

JANE smiles at JOHN. He blows her a kiss, she blows him one.
And, he heads off to work, feeling much better from his
wife's ostensible optimism.

                                        CUT TO:

EXT. THE "OFFICE" - LATER

THE "OFFICE" is not a modern day setup. It's a tent, with
supplies, water, food, things of that nature. However,
BLACKS cannot use it.

They must fend for themselves with all the surrounding
elements that may or may not be available.

After walking the 2-mile stretch to the makeshift "OFFICE",
JOHN enters.

                                        CUT TO:

INT. THE "OFFICE" - CONTINUOUS

MR. HENRY has to take his orders from the manager BIG BO, the whitest, meanest, most country man in the US-of-A. JOHN doesn't even look him in the eye, nor does he speak to him.

BIG BO speaks very loudly. He's in his early-40s - fat, bald, bearded, a drunkard, and he's racist as hell. And, just about all the other workers are all the same - in fact, JOHN is the only black on the team, he's surrounded by WHITE MEN, everyday all-day, year-round. HIS ONLY PEACE IS JANE...

...He's allowed to be with her, as long as he does his job and keeps his mouth shut.

The intention from THE WHITE MEN is to keep his morale up, because he's the best man they've got. They know JOHN has to have something to hold onto.

Yet, even so, HE HAS SOMETHING TO ALSO BE TAKEN AWAY -

MR. HENRY simply stands in silence, awaiting BIG BO's orders.

     BIG BO
  Well, well, well...if it ain't
  JOHN HENRY! Boy, I'll tell you
  what, we're putting your ass to
  work today! We're laying a
  quarter-mile of track today...or
  shall I say, more correctly, YOU
  ARE LAYING A QUARTER MILE OF TRACK
  TODAY, good sir.

JOHN keeps his composure, but he grips his HAMMER with all of his might...his hands start sweating, and his blood boils with anger.

He's not only ready to do it. HE WANTS TO DO IT.

     BIG BO
  You may leave...but, before you
  do, what do we say?

                    JOHN HENRY
                (keeping his cool)
            Yes, boss. I'm on it, boss.

                    BIG BO
            - Good Boy.

MR. HENRY exits the tent...

                                        CUT TO:

EXT. THE WORKSITE - DESERT AREA - MORNING

JOHN HENRY is working like his life depends on it - in fact, it does. He strikes the HAMMER down on the makeshift RAILROAD with all his strength. He pauses after so many hits and wipes the withdrawing sweat from his brow.

A WHITE MAN, JIMMY THE OVERSEER, rides up to JOHN on horseback -

JIMMY THE OVERSEER, mid-30s, has long blonde hair and a full beard and moustache. He's missing one leg yet still able to work. He has on a 19th Century Military uniform (Civil War Era). JIMMY has a shotgun and a bull whip on him -

                    JIMMY THE OVERSEER
                (scowling at JOHN
                  HENRY)
            What are you pausing for, boy,
            huh?

                    JOHN HENRY
            Just pacing myself, JIMMY. I don't
            want to have a heatstroke, is all.

                    JIMMY THE OVERSEER
            Is that right? It's only the
            morning, JOHN, wait til' the
            scorch hits us today - you might
            think about TRYING to quit.

                    JOHN HENRY
            Quitting was never an option.

                    JIMMY THE OVERSEER
               No, it wasn't. Not for scum like
               you. Now get to work, you lazy
               sum-bitch! This day's no different
               than any other. YOU WILL WORK.

There're a few workers in the vicinity of JOHN HENRY, not
all of them are bigots, either. A WORKER, MR. KNOX (a white
man), swings a much smaller hammer about 20 feet away from
JOHN. MR. KNOX is also an INDENTURED SERVANT to THE COMPANY.

MR. KNOX is a slim yet brawny old man (early-50s) with a
face full of stubble and spring blue eyes - he's sunburnt,
working away with his hammer alongside JOHN HENRY.

                    MR. KNOX
                  (swinging away,
                   raising his voice)
               Hey, JOHN! How goes it?

                    JOHN HENRY
               It goes how the wind blows, MR.
               KNOX! How's it hanging for you?

                    MR. KNOX
                  (smirking,
                   sweating)
               Despite the heat, it's shriveled
               and in my gut.

                    JOHN HENRY
                  (laughs out loud)
               No kidding, KNOX. My wife would
               leave me forever if that happened
               to me.

                    MR. KNOX
                  (swinging the
                   hammer to strike)
               Yep, that's the way the cookie
               crumbles ain't it? Speaking of
               which, how is your old lady?

                    JOHN HENRY
                  (gets in the
                   groove, yells
                   back)
                       (MORE)

                    JOHN HENRY (cont'd)
          As beautiful as ever, she could be
          better, though. WE could be
          better. But beggars can't be
          choosers, you know.

                    MR. KNOX
          Ain't that the darn truth.

                    JOHN HENRY
          Yessir, MR. KNOX. Yessir.

JIMMY THE OVERSEER rides back JOHN's way again.

                    JIMMY THE OVERSEER
          You got a hamster in that brain of
          yours, JOHN? If you keep talking
          on the job today, I'll have your
          ass on a chain-gang in TEXAS
          before you can swing that hammer
          again. No more work, no more WIFE,
          no more nothing.

JIMMY strikes a nerve in JOHN HENRY that he's never struck
before.

JOHN turns, raises his HAMMER and points it at JIMMY THE
OVERSEER in a powerful way.

                    JOHN HENRY
                (as solemn as a
                 vow)
          Never mention my wife again,
          JIMMY, or it will be your end.

                    JIMMY THE OVERSEER
                (eyes bulging in
                 surprise)
          Is that so, big man? Say that
          again, so I can relay it to
          BIG-BO. Pretty please, say that
          again or anything like it.

JOHN HENRY keeps his peace and doesn't talk back, realizing
he's already made a grave error.

                    JOHN HENRY
            My apologies, JIMMY, I-

Like a disturbed wasp, JIMMY dismounts his horse and
approaches JOHN on foot with a sawed-off shotgun in his
hands.

                    JIMMY THE OVERSEER
            You thought you'd back-talk today,
            huh? What do you think this is? Do
            you really think that piece of
            flesh in that piece of shit CABIN
            is your wife? She's no different
            than one of them heifers down
            yonder on the ranch. You are no
            different than a monkey at a
            CIRCUS. Except we don't even gotta
            feed you!

JOHN HENRY grips his HAMMER with all of his strength, and he
thinks for a moment. Just a moment.

MR. KNOX senses the eruption occurring in JOHN - any man
knows the look when another man has had his fill. KNOX, in a
rush, proceeds toward JOHN and JIMMY in an attempt to simmer
down the two.

It's too late.

                    JOHN HENRY
                (grits his teeth,
                 shakes his head)
            You had this coming, OVERSEER.

                    JIMMY THE OVERSEER
            Had what coming you son-of-a--

Before the OVERSEER can finish his derogatory sentence, JOHN
HENRY swings his HAMMER in full-force and breaks JIMMY's
neck like a twig with it (his head nearly comes off of his
body). The other men on the line, the HENCHMEN, see this act
of violence and they run to tell BIG-BO the manager.

                    MR. KNOX
                (saddened)
            JOHN...what have you done?

                    JOHN HENRY
               (breathing heavy,
                stunned by his
                own actions)
          I couldn't resist.
               (snaps back to
                attention)
          Run, KNOX! While you still can.
          The swarm will be here any time
          now.

                    MR. KNOX
               (smiling,
                sinlessly)
          There's nowhere to run to. I
          reckon I'll ward off this
          so-called swarm with you. Got
          nothing better to do, after all.

                                        CUT TO:

As soon as KNOX concludes this utterance, a small army of
HENCHMEN and ENFORCERS, led by BIG-BO, started jogging
and/or walking very fast to JOHN HENRY and MR. KNOX, in a
raging fury like a hive-minded group of monsters with
weapons in-hand.

                                        CUT TO:

JOHN HENRY lets his shimmering HAMMER, now covered in blood,
hang downward beside his right leg. BIG-BO confronts the
HAMMER swinging WORKER.

                    BIG BO
               (with a violent
                tone)
          Now, JOHNNY-boy, what's the
          matter? Did JIMMY say something
          not to your liking?
               (walks up closer
                to see JIMMY
                nearly headless)
          Dammit to hell, you nearly
          decapitated him!

                    HENCHMAN
               (spits chewing
                tobacco)
          I told ya, boss.

BIG-BO puffs a mighty big cigar, almost nervously.

                    JOHN HENRY
          BO, he's been talking shit to me
          for the last 10 years I've been
          with this company. I don't want
          any more trouble, I just had to
          settle up with him. He was talking
          about my WIFE.

                    BIG BO
               (gripping his belt)
          Even a FREE-MAN can't commit
          murder, son. You're one notch
          above being a slave. You had no
          right to retaliate against JIMMY.
          He's my best OVERSEER. You just
          cost me a lot of production money,
          you know that?
               (smiling
                vengefully)
          And you technically don't have a
          WIFE. Once again, you gotta be a
          FREE-MAN to have one of those. So
          your whole thang you got going on
          right now, it's null and void.
          What about you, MR. KNOX? Are you
          feeling resistant today? Just
          know, resistance is futile.

MR. KNOX picks his HAMMER up and holds it with both arms in
a tactical fashion -

                    MR. KNOX
          No, BO. I'm feeling FREE today.

                    BIG BO
          2-against-6. Guns-versus-Hammers.
          You sure you don't want to
          reconsider those odds?

                          JOHN HENRY
                BO, listen-

                          ENFORCER
                BOSS, can we get this over with,
                already? JIMMY's going to smell
                soon out in this heat.

                          BIG BO
                      (points to the
                       OVERSEER)
                Get 'em to the cool-house, boys,
                put the poor bastard on ice.
                Telegram his wife and kids of this
                terrible, terrible tragedy.
                      (to JOHN HENRY)
                There's nothing to hear, JOHN.
                NOTHING. You've committed a crime
                on my property, on my line. I'm
                judge, jury, and executioner out
                here. But I still got to follow
                the law. The law says if an
                indentured servant commits a
                murder, they are basically
                dead-on-arrival - something to
                that effect. And MR. KNOX, you're
                an accomplice to this here crime,
                I bear witness.

JOHN HENRY and MR. KNOX look at one another, with a
certainty, and they each nod their heads in a silent
agreement.

                          BIG BO
                      (to the HENCHMEN
                       and ENFORCERS)
                Kill 'em. Kill' em GOOD.

JOHN raises his shoulder and winds it backward, and he
throws his HAMMER with all of his strength at HENCHMAN #1.
The HAMMER hits the MAN directly in the face, smashing his
skull into his brain.

MR. KNOX sprints in a circular motion directly toward the 2
ENFORCERS, ready to strike like a TIGER in the JUNGLE.

CUT TO:

JOHN HENRY's HAMMER falls past the group of WHITE MEN.

They group of WHITE MEN raise their REVOLVERS and take aim -

JOHN doesn't even really need it. He jukes the multiple gunshots from the other HENCHMEN, grabbing one of them by the throat with his bare hands - JOHN HENRY raises HENCHMAN #2 off of his feet and twists his neck to the breaking point. MR. HENRY drops the man like a sack of bricks and he falls as limp as a dish-rag.

CUT TO:

MR. KNOX is not quite as able as JOHN HENRY but he still manages to incapacitate and eliminate one of the ENFORCERS with his HAMMER. He plunges ENFORCER #1 in the stomach, then raises the HAMMER up breaking the ENFORCER's CHIN instantly and shattering the man's teeth. ENFORCER #1 shakes, shrivels, and seizes to DEATH.

MR. KNOX goes to hit the other ENFORCER - but he's not quite quick enough. ENFORCER #2 aims his revolver at KNOX and unloads the CHAMBER like a true COWBOY, a quick western hand.

              JOHN HENRY
            (in disbelief)
      KNOX, no!

KNOX tries to catch his breath but his lungs fill-up with blood and he basically begins to drown in his own fluids.

JOHN does a barrel-roll to his HAMMER. He picks it up and stands ever so swiftly, only to bring it around with all of his might to HENCHMAN #3, striking the MAN in the ribs where his heart is. JOHN lands such a blow that it stops the man's heart.

CUT TO:

ENFORCER #2 reloads his revolver like a pro.

He stands back, with BIG-BO using him as a human-shield, and the ENFORCER takes shot after shot at JOHN HENRY -

JOHN, quicker than a god, BLOCKS all 6 bullets with his HAMMER.

                    BIG BO
               (pats the ENFORCER
                on the shoulder)
          Block this.

ENFORCER #2 ducks in front of BIG-BO.

BIG-BO, with his fully sawed-off SHOTGUN, sprays two shots at JOHN HENRY one-after-the-other. He doesn't miss. JOHN takes shells to the chest and stomach, hurt badly.

BIG-BO puts two more shells in his SHOTGUN and walks right up to the suffocating MR. KNOX - he blows his head off with one shot, it looks like a tomato getting smashed with a lightning bolt.

                              CUT TO:

                    BIG BO
               (to the ENFORCER)
          Is JOHNNY-boy still kicking? If
          so, put him out of his miserable
          existence.

ENFORCER #2 cautiously goes up to JOHN HENRY with his revolver pointed at his head -

He hovers over the fallen MAN. JOHN's eyes are closed and he seems to be not breathing.

                    ENFORCER 2
          I think you got 'em, BOSS. No
          signs of life.

                    BIG BO
          Put two more into his chest and
          one in his head. Then, we'll go
          visit that pretty little "WIFE" of
          his for a petty fuck. She'll
          become the local trough from now
          onward.

JOHN HENRY jolts awake after hearing such a threat.

He bends his knees toward his chest and uses his hands and arms to jump back up, like a ninja, with his HAMMER still in his possession. He does it so quickly that it's difficult for the ENFORCER or BIG-BO to register the movement.

CUT TO:

          JOHN HENRY
     (with absolute
      ANGER)
   No more!

JOHN raises the HAMMER up and then brings it down with all the GRAVITY in the world, right upon the ENFORCER's skull - smashing the man's neck-bone into his spine, crushing both.

ENFORCER #2 falls to his knees, almost unrecognizable as his eyes have rolled into the back of his head.

JOHN HENRY doesn't even pick up his revolver, no. He walks toward BIG-BO with a calmness, with righteous indignation.

BIG-BO runs toward his OFFICE.

          JOHN HENRY
     (with sarcasm)
  Where you going, BOSS? Anymore
  dogs you wanna sic on me? To MY
  HAMMER, you all are just nails!

BIG-BO nears the OFFICE and unluckily, for JOHN, JANE HENRY herself appears from the adjacent side of the OFFICE - she and BIG-BO are many yards away from JOHN.

JANE has innocently brought some fire-cooked fish for JOHN to eat so he didn't have to work on an empty-stomach.

          JANE HENRY
     (in awe, shocked
      at the sight of
      JOHN's bloody
      flannel)
  JOHN? What - what's happened?

                          JOHN HENRY
                JANE, get out of here, now!

                          BIG BO
                      (to JANE)
                Freeze! Don't you move a muscle,
                dear, or I'll shoot the soul out
                of your body.

JANE drops the platter of fish.

BIG-BO wrangles her by the neck and places her in front of
himself, to create a barrier between he and JOHN.

JOHN places his hand out, waving it down as a gesture for
BIG-BO to drop his SHOTGUN.

                          JOHN HENRY
                BO, don't do this. Don't shoot
                her!

                          BIG BO
                Call me "BOSS", and I'll think
                about it. No. No. Call me
                "MASTER". And drop the God-blessed
                HAMMER, now!

JOHN HENRY puts the HAMMER down on the ground, gently.

                          JOHN HENRY
                Okay. MASTER, please, put the
                SHOTGUN away. Please, don't shoot
                my WIFE.

                          BIG BO
                      (throws the
                       SHOTGUN down to
                       the side)
                That's much better, JOHNNY-boy.
                And I'm not going to shoot her.
                      (pulls a steel
                       blade from his
                       back)
                I'm going to cut her throat.

                          JOHN HENRY
                     (reaches out,
                      sprints to BIG-BO
                      and JANE)
               NO!

BIG-BO slices JANE's throat wide-open, with his steel blade,
like it's nothing at all. Blood spews out of her jugular -
BO lets her fall to the ground. JOHN approaches his dying
WIFE, and grabs hold of her and cradles her.

                          JOHN HENRY
                     (holding JANE,
                      swaying back and
                      forth almost
                      helpless)
               Baby, stay with me. Don't leave
               me, please. It's okay, it's all
               right. I'll get you some help.

                          BIG BO
               I told you to reconsider.

BIG-BO's reinforcements arrive. The SHERIFF and his GOONS on
horseback. JOHN HENRY cries tears of pure pain. He's
bleeding out from the SHOTGUN blasts, yet he's as furious as
ever now - JANE's life leaves her abruptly, infuriating MR.
HENRY even further.

                          THE SHERIFF
               BO, I heard you're having some
               serious issues with your WORKER. I
               came as soon as I heard.

                          BIG BO
                     (relieved)
               Word travels faster than light.

                          GOON 1
                     (walks up to JOHN
                      HENRY)
               Get up, boy.

JOHN looks upon his WIFE one last time.

                    THE SHERIFF
               (to JOHN)
          Are you deaf, dumbass? You heard
          the man, GIT!

                    JOHN HENRY
          Sheriff, I--

                    THE SHERIFF
          Did I say you could talk, son? You
          think BO's bad? I'm your worst
          nightmare's nightmare. Just zip
          it, and zip it good - or we'll
          beat your ass to death right here.
                    (prepares
                     handcuffs)
          Hands behind your back, now -

                    JOHN HENRY
               (keeping his honor
                and holding his
                tongue)
          Yes, Sir.

JOHN rises and puts his hands behind him. The SHERIFF and
GOON #1 put the handcuff restraints on JOHN's wrists.

                    BIG BO
          Be mighty careful, SHERIFF. That
          abomination murdered several of my
          men like they were butterflies.

                    GOON 1
          Is that a fact?

The SHERIFF signals to his GOON. The GOON hits JOHN HENRY
over the back of the head with his GUN, knocking him out
cold. Really it's the blood-loss that makes him lose
consciousness. The GUN-BUTT doesn't help one bit, though.

                                              CUT TO:

EXT. THE RIVER-DOCK - DAY

JOHN HENRY awakens. He's now on a RIVER-DOCK, with his feet and wrists tied. He's not blind-folded. We hear distored indistinguishable speech from BIG-BO, the SHERIFF, and GOONs #1 and #2 -

                    GOON 2
    ...he killed all your boys with a
    goddamn HAMMER?

                    BIG BO
    Yes, he did, OFFICER. A crying
    shame, ain't it?

                    THE SHERIFF
    Well, he can drown with that
    HAMMER, then. Stand the bastard
    up.

GOON #1 helps JOHN HENRY up onto his bound feet.

The WHITE MEN make MR. HENRY hop to the edge of the RIVER-DOCK.

The two GOONS tie big BRICKS to HENRY's feet.

                    GOON 1
    Any last words, boy?

                    JOHN HENRY
    God will not be kind to EVIL in
    the day of judgment.

                    THE SHERIFF
      (to his GOON)
    Gag his fucking mouth shut.
      (points to the
       water)
    Now MR. HENRY, you're either going
    to jump off this DOCK, or I'm
    going to shoot you off of it.
    That's the only choice you have,
    right now.

Without hesitation, JOHN HENRY turns around on the DOCK and faces the hateful WHITE MEN.

He looks up at the sky one final time.

Then...JOHN HENRY JUMPS OFF THE DOCK, tied, bound, and gagged.

                              CUT TO:

The 2 large BRICKS follow JOHN HENRY into the deep RIVER. They scrape the DOCK and plunge downward into the water. The WHITE MEN all put their guns up and share a sinister laugh. They wait patiently, eyeing the bubbles that float to the surface. They wait until the bubbles stop -

                    THE SHERIFF
          Where's the HAMMER?

                    BIG BO
                (dragging the
                 HAMMER onto the
                 DOCK)
          Here, SHERIFF. I need help with
          this thing! It's heavier than my
          ex-wife.

                    GOON 2
                (assists)
          I got you, BO.
                (amazed)
          No wonder he was able to do such
          damage with this thing. It weighs
          a ton!

                    THE SHERIFF
          Ah, quit your whining. Throw it in
          there with the murdering piece of
          shit.

                    BIG BO
                (sips from a pint
                 of whiskey)
          So long, JOHNNY-boy. See you on
          the other side -
                (pours some
                 whiskey into the
                      (MORE)

                    BIG BO (cont'd)
        RIVER)
- Probably sooner rather than later.

                                    CUT TO:

BIG-BO and GOON #2 manage to toss the HAMMER into the RIVER with JOHN HENRY.

A CROW sits perched atop a neighboring TREE - watching the drowning of the GREAT JOHN HENRY. The MAN, the MYTH, the LEGEND -

We zoom in on the blackness of the CROW's EYE and enter it.

AND WE CUT TO:

<u>INT. 2 BEDROOM HOME - NIGHT</u>

                                  LOCATION: LOS ANGELES

YEAR: 2012

In the BASEMENT, a MAN, a junkie, prepares a spoonful of HEROIN.

- He loads up 2 syringes with the DOPE.

He injects himself, passing out almost immediately - in a state between LIVING and DYING, as high as a bald-eagle on Mount Everest.

The MAN is MAJOR DALE MANHUNTER - the MAN is 6'2, 190 lbs., Caucasian but olive-skinned, in his early 50's. He has a wiry goatee with no moustache. He has sky-blue eyes and a sunken in face with a few lesions on it.

MAJOR is out of shape, in the state of a HAS-BEEN who never could-be. A fleshly shell of wasted potential.

                                    CUT TO:

After doing the 2 injections in each arm, MAJOR slaps his veins in the right and left appendages, making the DOPE hit harder. He goes into a state of narcoleptic slumber, overtaken by the heroin -

A sound is heard, someone opens the BASEMENT door, walks down the steps to MAJOR.

                    NICK MANHUNTER (MAJOR'S SON)
              (taking baby steps
               down the
               staircase)
          Dada? Dada?

The DOPE is still out on a brown folding-table, the bag wide open.

NICK MANHUNTER, MAJOR's 3-YEAR-OLD SON, enters the BASEMENT area after descending the stairs. NICK MANHUNTER is between being a baby and a kid - golden haired with a bowl cut, wearing overalls over a red long sleeve shirt.

The CHILD has brown eyes that sparkle. NICK MANHUNTER is the essence of innocence -

                    NICK MANHUNTER (MAJOR'S SON)
          Wh - What you doing, Dada?

                              CUT TO:

                    MAJOR MANHUNTER
              (eyes flickering,
               rolled in the
               back of his head)
          Aah. Oh. Oh, no.

Unbeknownst to MAJOR, the DOPE is laced with FENTANYL.

- NICK goes to shake his dad's arm to wake him up.

He doesn't awaken.

The very young child sees the bag of HEROIN - and the 2 NEEDLES with product residue still in them.

                              CUT TO:

NICK MANHUNTER does the unthinkable - yet it's what any
CHILD would do.

                    NICK MANHUNTER (MAJOR'S SON)
        You got sugar? Wow!

The young boy touches the open bag of fentanyl laced heroin.
Tragedy strikes like an atom-bomb.

                    NICK MANHUNTER (MAJOR'S SON)
         (lets out a
          hurtful cry)
        I feels funny!

                    JANICE MANHUNTER
         (from up the
          stairs in the
          HOME)
        NICKY! Where are you, son? MAJOR,
        did you leave the BASEMENT
        unlocked again!?

The 3-year-old starts crying an awful cry, one of pain, one
of terror.

                    JANICE MANHUNTER
         (walks down the
          stairs)
        Oh, DEAR GOD! No!

JANICE MANHUNTER - MAJOR's WIFE (late 40s, gray-haired, 5'6,
ruggedly beautiful) - sees the evilest sight; her baby boy
has overdosed on fentanyl.

He touched the bag, ate raw heroin, dying within moments.

The WIFE sees her bloated, purple, nonresponsive child lying
on the BASEMENT FLOOR.

                    JANICE MANHUNTER
        MAJOR! Wake up - NICK - NICK is
        sick!

MAJOR is a mute due to the drugs. He can't even move.

                    MAJOR MANHUNTER
                (speaking
                  gibberish)
            Yeah. Yeah, I can do that. One
            second -

                    JANICE MANHUNTER
                (races upstairs
                  with NICK in her
                  arms)
            Oh, God in heaven.
                (begins
                  asphyxiating)
            I can't, I can't see, I---

Before even reaching the top-stair, JANICE MANHUNTER
succumbs to the topical-saturation of the fentanyl, fainting
with her now dead child in her arms.

She reaches out, there is NOTHING, there is NO ONE -

                                        CUT TO:

THE NEXT MORNING:

We see nothing but BLACK from MAJOR's perspective until his
eyes start to open - we see things from MAJOR MANHUNTER's
POV:

                    MAJOR MANHUNTER
                (awakens from his
                  high to DEATH)
            NO! NICKY-boy - JAN, what - what
            in god's name, NO!

MAJOR MANHUNTER sees his WIFE and his CHILD overcome with
rigor mortis, stiff as the hardwood floor of his home. He
panics, going into utter SHOCK -

                    MAJOR MANHUNTER
                (holding his wife
                  and son)
            Please, Jesus, no. Please, God,
            this can't be -

MAJOR MANHUNTER pleads to the Heavens.

AND WE CUT TO:

EXT. BRODY BARNES' MANSION - LOS ANGELES - MORNING

MAJOR MANHUNTER pulls up to a MANSION in LA - that of BRODY BARNES, himself. KINGPIN, BOSS, SUPERVILLAIN.

MAJOR exits his 2004 CADILLAC DEVILLE. He walks through the pathway to the FRONT DOOR.

He's met by 2 MEN in BUSINESS SUITS - VITO TEDESCO (white, green eyes, mid-40s, medium length blonde hair, light beard and moustache) and GERALD NIXON (black, brown eyes, mid-40s, fade haircut, stubble on face) - who stop him on the path.

                  VITO TEDESCO
      Whoa, whoa, whoa. What's your
      business, here, man?

                  GERALD NIXON
      - You have any earthly idea whose
      property you're on?

                  MAJOR MANHUNTER
      Name's MAJOR. MAJOR MANHUNTER. I
      need to see MR. BARNES, urgently.
      It's a critical situation. I think
      ONLY he can fix it.

GERALD nods at VITO.

VITO peeks his head inside the entrance of the MANSION -

                  VITO TEDESCO
         (raising his voice
          so BRODY can hear)
      Hey, BOSS, we got a stray out
      here, he's asking specifically for
      you!

                    BRODY BARNES
                (from inside the
                 MANSION)
            Let him in.

                    GERALD NIXON
            All right, buddy. You're good to
            go. But first, I need to search
            ya. Standard procedure.

GERALD pats MAJOR down, all over his person. GERALD locates
a PISTOL firearm at MAJOR's back.

He also finds his wallet, and scopes it out, too.

                    GERALD NIXON
                (curious as a cat)
            What are you, a cop?

                    MAJOR MANHUNTER
            Not quite. I'm a BAILBONDSMAN and
            a BOUNTY HUNTER.

                    VITO TEDESCO
                (returning from
                 the FRONT DOOR)
            Is that so? Well, well, well. You
            must be hot shit around the CITY,
            huh?

GERALD returns MAJOR's wallet to him. MR. NIXON holds on to
the PISTOL, though -

                    MAJOR MANHUNTER
                (with a tad of
                 humility)
            No, not really. I'm a regular guy
            like any other.

                    VITO TEDESCO
            You may enter. Meet him in his
            OFFICE, to the left. Oh, yeah, and
            BAILBONDSMAN - keep it short and
            simple. BRODY's got a ton of work
            to get done, understand me?

                    MAJOR MANHUNTER
                 (with his head low)
            I understand, sir.

MAJOR enters the premises. GERALD shuts the door as MAJOR
goes in.

                                        CUT TO:

INT. BRODY'S OFFICE - MORNING

BRODY BARNES - mid-50s, no facial hair, muscle-bound,
athletic - is in a BLACK TANKTOP, WHITE SLACKS, and BLACK
DRESS SHOES - dressed most fashionably. He has on a couple
of GOLD RINGS, one on each hand.

MAJOR MANHUNTER has taken a seat in front of BRODY's oakwood
desk - BRODY is puffing a gigantic COHIBA CIGAR, to die for.

                    BRODY BARNES
                 (welcoming)
            - MR. MANHUNTER. What can I do for
            you, my friend? - First off, would
            you like a COHIBA?

                    MAJOR MANHUNTER
                 (fearful)
            No, sir, MR. BARNES. Thank you for
            the offer. What I came here for is
            something of the utmost
            importance. I made a mistake
            yesterday - it could cost me
            everything. It HAS cost me
            everything, really. I need your
            influence to prevent me from going
            to jail for the rest of my days,
            sir.

                    BRODY BARNES
            - What have you done, MR.
            MANHUNTER? You are a BOUNTY
            HUNTER, are you not? Is your
            current immunity not sufficient?

MAJOR MANHUNTER
(cries several
heavy tears)
My - my WIFE and CHILD died yesterday, sir. It, it was my fault! I've really screwed up. My kid, he found me in a haze, my product was laced with fentanyl, he got it in his system - he was a goner before I even snapped out of my high, as was my dear WIFE. I - I - I had to bury them below the BASEMENT! I'm at a loss for words. I'm -

BRODY BARNES
(relighting his
COHIBA, puffing
away)
This is very serious, MAJOR. But I think I can handle it - you will not be harassed by the POLICE. You will not be questioned by them. Your WIFE left you, all right? She took your CHILD with her. They went to MEXICO.
(brushes his hands
together)
Ta-dah, problem solved. You have my sincerest condolences, my friend. But don't beat yourself up! It wasn't you who did it, no. It was the rotten piece of shit dealer who sold you fentanyl, see? Don't be too hard on yourself. Adapt, adjust. Most pertinently, MOVE ON. I know it's hard, but you must move forward and repent.

MAJOR MANHUNTER
(wiping away more
tears, sniffling)
Yessir. I will try. So, I won't be reprimanded in any way.

                    BRODY BARNES
          MANHUNTER, it's as if it NEVER
          even happened. Your slate is
          clean, as far as I'm concerned.
          The LAW can't do anything to you
          over this, starting now.

                    MAJOR MANHUNTER
               (as sad as can be)
          Thank you, MR. BARNES. It's an
          honor to be in your presence. I
          appreciate your wisdom, I truly
          do. I will get out of your hair
          now, sir.

                    BRODY BARNES
               (lets out a manly
                giggle)
          I have no hair. Be free and be
          gone. Oh, and take a COHIBA,
          MAJOR. It'll make you feel right
          as rain.

Still downtrodden, MAJOR takes the COHIBA from BRODY.

                    BRODY BARNES
          Ah, I almost forgot. I have a job
          for you.

                    MAJOR MANHUNTER
          A job? What kind of job?

                    BRODY BARNES
          The kind that pays, MAJOR. You'll
          be instrumental to my cause, if
          you take it.

                    MAJOR MANHUNTER
               (sits back down)
          All right, I'm all ears, MR.
          BARNES.

AND WE CUT TO BLACK:

CHAPTER II - MICKEY BROWN EYES

FADE IN:

EXT. BASKETBALL COURT - DAY

LOCATION: COMPTON

YEAR: 2010

MICKEY MONTANA, DRE FERRARA, MICHAEL CARTER, and YOUNG NATHAN TOWNHALL (Michael Carter's son) and YOUNG FREEDOM FERRARA (Dre Ferrara's son) are all enjoying the bright Spring Day in Sunny COMPTON, CALIFORNIA.

MICKEY is modest, composed, and has a bulletproof demeanor. He's a 29-year-old COMPTON MULATTO - handsome, smells of money, and has looks that could kill a dame.

MICHAEL CARTER is a black man in a white man's body; he's tall, slender, has some tattoos, and a pearly white smile. CARTER is a good father. His son, NATHAN TOWNHALL (Carter's true last name), is as innocent as a first snow. He's 5 years old at this time - a BIRACIAL young boy with DISABILITIES (Cerebral Palsy and Asthma). Yet his disabilities do NOT stop him in anyway. NATHAN is as persistent as they come.

DRE FERRARA is a short, stubby BLACK MAN with dreadlocks and not a tattoo to speak of. DRE is humble and he's a gentle soul, especially to his SON. DRE's a good friend and an exceptional father to FREEDOM.

YOUNG FREEDOM FERRARA, also 5 years of age, is AFRICAN AMERICAN, with very dark skin. He's a bright kid, very smart, and a born leader. FREEDOM is skinny but eats like a horse. He's COMPTON born, and has the respect of a MAFIOSO CHIEFTAIN, even as a boy. FREEDOM treats NATHAN like a TRUE BROTHER. The two children are inseparable. The two BOYS idolize their respective fathers, sure - but MICKEY MONTANA is THE MAN to them, they fear him, love him, and respect him.

DRE, CARTER, and MICKEY MONTANA are about as best of friends as MEN can be - their bond is unbreakable, and that bond has bled into the lives of FREEDOM and NATHAN. MICKEY is childless, so he treats those two young boys like his very own.

The BASKETBALL COURT is crowded, but the group of boys and men have a section all to themselves; there are many basketball goals across the court.

                YOUNG FREEDOM
          (dribbling the
           ball)
      Uncle MICKEY, can you dunk?

                MICKEY MONTANA
          (holds his hands
           out to catch the
           ball)
      Pass it to me, let's find out.

YOUNG FREEDOM throws MICKEY the basketball. He dribbles it several times. MICKEY stands still in place, almost charging up to gather his "hops".

Running from the 3-point line, MICKEY lunges toward the hoop and jumps practically from the Free-Throw line like Michael Jordan himself.

MICKEY MONTANA dunks the ball like it's 2+2---

The KIDS, his "Nephews", go crazy, as do his friends in DRE and CARTER.

                YOUNG NATHAN
      Goddamn, Unc!

                MICHAEL CARTER
          (slaps NATHAN
           upside the head)
      Boy, watch your mouth, or I'll
      wash it out with soap, again.

                YOUNG NATHAN
      All right, deddy, damn, sorry.

>   DRE FERRARA
>   (to MICKEY)
>   You do realize you just about
>   dunked exactly like Michael Jordan
>   did from the free-throw, right?
>
>   MICKEY MONTANA
>   (passes the ball
>   to CARTER)
>   What can I say, man. It's all in
>   the hips.
>
>   MICHAEL CARTER
>   Just don't dunk on ME like that,
>   and we'll be just fine.
>
>   MICKEY MONTANA
>   I don't know. I'm feeling frisky.
>   How about a game of "Carolina"?
>
>   DRE FERRARA
>   All right, I'm down for that. I'm
>   warmed up. FREE, NATE, ya'll get
>   out of bounds or go to another
>   goal, we're about to get rough.

MICKEY, DRE, and CARTER initiate their game of CAROLINA - rules are simple:

It's a basketball match done 1 vs. 1 at a time, up to a certain score between a few competitors. The scorer stays in the game. Whoever is scored on steps to the side and the next man enters the court to contend the scorer - the cycle continues and repeats. You can play with up to 5 people.

FREEDOM and NATHAN proceed to start playing at another goal, as young kids would, amateur and purely for FUN (DRE and CARTER knocked up their "baby mamas" around the same time).

FREEDOM and NATHAN chase one another around on the rocky terrain of the basketball court, paying no mind to the world or its surroundings.

NATHAN has a little trouble, as he is inflicted with CEREBRAL PALSY and ASTHMA - FREEDOM doesn't use his full

energy to play with NATHAN, he takes care to not be rough
with his BROTHER FROM ANOTHER.

                        CUT TO:

EXT. BASKETBALL COURT - LATER

NATHAN runs as fast as he can to catch FREEDOM.

They, without thought, stumble onto the court and interrupt
a GANG'S Basketball game. The GANG is comprised of 5
members. NATHAN hits their ball and it goes flying away from
the GANG'S Game. These men are barely in their 20s, all of
them. They're dressed in RED gym attire - they're BLOODS.

                    BULLY #1
              Hey, little Nigga, you gon' get
              that ball, ain't you?

FREEDOM and NATHAN stop dead in their tracks, voiceless,
afraid to speak to the intimidating MEN.

                    BULLY #2
              What, are ya'll dumb? You're
              supposed to respond to an adult
              when he speaks to you, you know
              that, right?

NATHAN jogs to get the BASKETBALL. He picks it up and takes
it to the leader of the GANG, politely. FREEDOM stands
quietly -

                    BULLY #2
              Attaboy. Good job. You listen when
              spoken to.
                    (jabbing at
                    FREEDOM)
              What about you, kid? You got any
              RESPECT for your elders?

                    YOUNG FREEDOM
              Not for a bum like you.

The GANG, all, stop what they were doing. The ball dribbles
a few times, then stops and rolls.

                    BULLY #1
                (shakes his head)
            You got a really big mouth. A
            pretty mouth, too. We're PIRU,
            youngin'. You just broke the
            number one rule. What's your
            penance?

FREEDOM and NATE back away gradually from the GANG in an
attempt to get back to their fathers and MICKEY. In a flash,
a couple of the GANG Members appear behind the two kids.
They grab NATE by the shoulders, holding him completely
still as BULLY #2 overpowers FREEDOM.

                    BULLY #1
                (to BULLY #2,
                 concerning
                 FREEDOM)
            Hold down Mr. Trash-Talk, here.

                    YOUNG FREEDOM
                (hands on him,
                 struggling)
            Get your hands off of me.
                (panicking)
            DAD, MICKEY, Help!

As soon as YOUNG FREEDOM utters these words, he's
man-handled. The 2 BULLIES go to work on the child. BULLY #2
keeps him held to the ground while BULLY #1 punches the
young kid in the FACE a FEW times, KNOCKING MANY of his
TEETH out - severely damaging his mouth and jawline.

FREEDOM can't defend himself from the strength of the young
adult men. NATHAN is defenseless against them, too. The
BULLY goes for that NEXT PUNCH, one that could end a person,
and right before it strikes, MICKEY, DRE, and CARTER all
three tackle the 2 BULLIES down, going to work on them.

A quasi-RIOT ensues. It's not a riot, though, it's just a
lot of ass-kicking happening all at once, led by MICKEY
MONTANA.

                                              CUT TO:

MICKEY grabs BULLY #1 by the neck and elbows his larynx, disposing of him quickly with one single blow, without killing him. DRE uppercuts one of the GANG MEMBERS, hitting him with a combination of punches. CARTER pulls a GUN on the GANG as they try to run.

                    MICHAEL CARTER
          Hold it! You gentlemen aren't
          going anywhere until you answer
          for trying to harm my family.
                (to DRE)
          Get FREE to a HOSPITAL, man. Me
          and MICKEY got this handled.

The 5 GANG MEMBERS stand solemnly still now. They show their bellies, at the drop of a hat.

DRE picks up his boy, protectively hovering over him, he carries him down the street en route to the HOSPITAL. The TRIO have no cars, so, DRE has to walk -

No matter the situation, no cops will be called.

MICKEY punches the BULLY who punched FREEDOM's teeth out until his face is a bloodied pulp of fleshly matter, yet the man's still breathing...suffering while he does it, now.

                    MICKEY MONTANA
                (gestures to be
                 handed the gun)
          Let me see the tool, CARTER.

CARTER voicelessly obeys.

                    MICKEY MONTANA
                (thrilled AND
                 pissed off)
          We're going to play a game. Not
          basketball, no.

MICKEY cocks open the revolver to check its ammo count.

                    MICKEY MONTANA
          Full chamber. This, my friends, is
          American Roulette.

MICKEY, without warning, flips the chamber inward and points the GUN at the BULLY lying on the ground, emptying the CHAMBER on him...

WE HEAR: "BANG, BANG, BANG, BANG, BANG, BANG!"

...the BULLY is NOT shot even one time. MICKEY simply fired 6 bullets around his head in a circular manner, to frighten the bastard. The BULLY pisses himself from the bullets whizzing by his head at such close range. Not to mention the ringing ears.

Sometimes humiliation, fear, and intimidation work better than outright violence.

The GANG act like cowards after MICKEY showed his ass. They cannot even look him or the kids in the eyeball. They tuck-tail and go on their way, away from the BASKETBALL COURT.

MICKEY puts the gun away, knowing he's accomplished establishing total dominance; he may not have been able to prevent FREEDOM'S injuries, but he was able to prevent further harm from coming to the boy.

                       MICKEY MONTANA
                (with a passionate
                 voice)
         If I ever catch you boys on this
         court or even near it, again, I'll
         kill every single one of ya. Now
         be gone.

The "BLOOD GANG" MEMBERS quietly continue in the other direction, whispering in their minds and sighing under their breath. They're beaten animals.

                                        CUT TO:

```
                                                                    41.


EXT. BANK - DAY

                                        LOCATION: WEST LA

                                        YEAR: 2012

TIME: 1:11 PM

MICKEY MONTANA, DRE FERRARA, and MICHAEL CARTER (each in
their early 30s now) wearing their respective PRESIDENTIAL
MASKS - (OBAMA, CLINTON, and GEORGE BUSH) - invade a BANK
with their guns in-hand and bags strapped to their backs.

                                        CUT TO:


INT. THE BANK - CONTINUOUS

MICKEY enters theatrically as do the others, but all is not
well.

                    MICKEY MONTANA
            Hello, my fellow Americans! Your
            Presidents are here! WE ARE THE
            ELITE -

7 GUARDS hop up from behind the counter of the BANK, and
take aim at MICKEY, DRE, and CARTER. There aren't supposed
to be GUARDS there -

                    DRE FERRARA
                (attempts to take
                 cover)
            It's a HIT!

                    MICHAEL CARTER
                (stunned)
            What the Fu-

MICHEAL and DRE both get hit consistently and
simultaneously, they both react too late.

Not MICKEY, he's already on the other side where the
shooters are.
```

The SHOOTERS stop firing, thinking they've gotten their targets.

                    MICKEY MONTANA
                (roaring)
           Aarh!!!

MICKEY disarms the lead SHOOTER, and fires two shots from the gun into 2 more of the SHOOTERS' heads.

He breaks SHOOTER 1's neck, twist his head completely around.

3 of the gunners are deceased now.

SHOOTER 4 lunges at MICKEY and gets jaw broken, his teeth kicked into his brain.

SHOOTER 5 tastes MICKEY's blade; he gets severely injured by the knife work of MICKEY. SHOOTER 5 is the one who shot DRE FERRARA - SHOOTER 5 is MAJOR MANHUNTER.

SHOOTER 6 gets gutted.

SHOOTER 7 stands in awe of this 'ANGEL OF DEATH' in The Flesh.

                    SHOOTER 7
                (puts his hands up)
           Woah! Lis--

MICKEY bitch slaps the SHOOTER all the way across the BANK.

MONTANA jolts up to the man and picks him up off his feet by the neck.

SHOOTER 7 reaches at MICKEY, resisting - in doing so, he rips MONTANA's OBAMA MASK halfway off his face...

                                        CUT TO:

                    MICKEY MONTANA
           Who is responsible for this--this
           CHAOS!? Tell me, and I'll let you
           die quickly!

                    SHOOTER 7
                  (pissing himself)
            B - BRODY...

MICKEY pulls his blade once more, and stabs the man directly
in the Adam's Apple, and rips the knife downward exposing
the man's guts to the open air...

...MICKEY gets saturated with blood. He's "Blood Drunk",
totally enraged. MAJOR MANHUNTER, still breathing
laboriously, looks upon MICKEY in devastational awe. A
mindless beast of a man who's lost the only brothers he's
ever known.

                    MICKEY MONTANA
                  (checks on his
                   brothers)
            DRE? CARTER?
                  (sees they're dead)
            NO!

Discovering that DRE and CARTER have been murdered on this
botched job, MICKEY exits the BANK, to an ARMY of LAW
ENFORCEMENT, bloodied and mad at the entire world -

                                        CUT TO BLACK:

FADE IN:

                                        72 HOURS LATER:

EXT. THE CARTER RESIDENCE - MORNING

MICKEY, severely wounded, walks up to the door of his dead
friend's HOME, where his wife and child are. He doesn't
stay, rather he leaves his WILL and 3 LARGE DUFFEL BAGS with
precisely 1.2 MILLION DOLLARS in them, all 20s, 50s, and
some 100s.

CUT TO:

HEAVEN CARTER - a fit, pretty, 20-something black woman -
answers MICKEY's knock...she sees no one there, only the
bags, the Will...no explanation. She doesn't even know where
her man is, that he is perished.

She's bound to know. MICKEY didn't wanna push it on her although he's partly responsible.

HEAVEN CARTER takes the bags and the WILL into the house.

CUT TO:

INT. THE CARTER RESIDENCE - CONTINUOUS

HEAVEN reads MICKEY's WILL aloud, hearing HIS voice. We hear HEAVEN's voice at the beginning then it bleeds into being MICKEY's voice.

                  HEAVEN CARTER
- Dear Heaven,

This is my Will. Please, Forgive me. US, really. I didn't intend for this to happen. I'm dead and gone now. Leave the BOYS the house, and the bags are also for FREEDOM and NATHANIEL. They're just as much brothers as DRE, MICHAEL and I were - ARE. Ya'll are all my family. And the money is to see the boys through when they get of age. I hope you respect my wishes and do as I've written. I'm sorry, HEAVEN.

Sincerely,

MICKEY

HEAVEN opens the bag and witnesses all the cash.

She knows something bad has happened.

She sighs, and nearly passes out.

CUT TO:

EXT. MICKEY'S MOTHER'S (ELVIRA'S ESTATE) - MORNING

LOCATION: BALTIMORE, MARYLAND

MICKEY MONTANA, very much wounded, stands at the doorstep of the last person he'd ever expect to be around...his MOTHER: ELVIRA.

He knocks 3 solid times, shaking the door as well as the area around it; the knocks can be heard all over the heavily guarded property.

Though heavily guarded, MICKEY MONTANA got past them all, wounded and all....

...Before any guard can respond, ELVIRA herself answers the door. She's thin, pale-white, blonde-and-gray haired, dressed in a gown with house-slippers on.

> MICKEY MONTANA
> (falls to his
> knees right at
> the threshold)
> - Mom. Help me.

> ELVIRA
> (with a cold-tone)
> If you die on my door-step and the spooks come here, I'll hand your body right over to them just like I did your father's.
> (throws a small
> white-towel to
> MICKEY)
> Get the hell up, get inside.

MICKEY stands with nearly all his strength...

...He enters the threshold and passes out cold -

> ELVIRA
> You Little Sh--

The door slams shut.

CUT TO:

INT. MICKEY MONTANA'S HOUSE/COMPTON-FLASHBACK - MORNING

The year is 2010...

...MICKEY awakens to his alarm clock set at 4:44 AM.

He tidies up his room-area, which is already pretty neat as is, then he cleans up himself: shower, shave, deodorant

He puts on his regular outfit: a white V-neck T-shirt, fitted black pants (Dickies), and some athletic shoes (Nikes)

All we see is this done in fast-motion, sprawled out/cut shots, til' MICKEY exits his room-area, shutting the door behind him.

CUT TO:

EXT. COMPTON STREET-FLASHBACK CONTINUED - DAY

It's now 7:00 AM precisely, and MICKEY is walking casually down his COMPTON street...

...His phone rings.

              MICKEY MONTANA
          (answering his
           cellular)
    Yeah.

We hear just muffled speech, as MICKEY listens and continues walking onward.

              MICKEY MONTANA
    Listen, I don't give a damn if
    you're nervous---

It's DRE and CARTER on the other-line, MICKEY'S compadres, fighting over the phone to speak to him.

More Muffled Speech can be heard through the phone, unintelligible.

                  MICKEY MONTANA
        The job isn't til' 11 on the dot.
        That's when the drop's happening.
        We have 4 hours. Trust me, we got
        this. I'm on my way now - I've got
        everything covered. Just be ready.

A quick "MMM, MMM, MMM" is heard, almost like KENNY from 'SOUTHPARK'.

                  MICKEY MONTANA
        "What MASKS?", you say. Been
        thinking about that - with this
        being our first job, I want to go
        theatrical. I've had this idea in
        my head...

                                        CUT TO:

<u>INT. ELVIRA'S ESTATE - DAY</u>

CUT BACK TO 2012:

MICKEY has been laid out in a pseudo-coma for 7 days. He's awake and coherent, bandaged from head-to-toe, looking half-man/half-mummy.

He and ELVIRA are sitting in the living-room of her ESTATE.

                  ELVIRA
            (not shocked)
        So, you've become a bank robber?

                  MICKEY MONTANA
            (aching, favoring
             his ribs and
             torso)
        WAS a "bank robber".

MICKEY has a glass full of SCOTCH (no ice) in front of him - he sips it.

ELVIRA
(sipping a vodka
martini)
Same difference, MICKEY. Hell, I'm just glad you never came to me for any money.

MICKEY MONTANA
Not as glad as me. I did well for myself, actually.

ELVIRA
Doesn't impress me even one tiny bit. My question of the day is, why did you come back here? Why'd you come back HOME?

MICKEY MONTANA
Nothing heals a man's wounds like his mother's voice or his childhood home. And honestly, I was in a shitstorm. Baltimore is another world from LA. Plus I need your connections.

ELVIRA
Tell me so I can go ahead and arrange it.

MICKEY MONTANA
Get me on board a private charter to AMSTERDAM. And you'll never have to deal with me again, mom. I've never been there. Nobody will know me there. It'll be a perfect situation. I'm a dead man here in AMERICA. I killed BRODY BARNES.---

ELVIRA gulps down the rest of her vodka martini -

ELVIRA
YOU KILLED BRODY BARNES? How did you manage that?

48.

MICKEY MONTANA
I've fought a lot in my day, I'll admit. I've kicked so much ass that my feet stink. But I only beat BRODY out of pure luck. That was the toughest bastard I've ever scrapped. He kicked my ass north, south, east and west. Had a blade in my boot. BAM, hit him wear it hurts. Then I unloaded nearly a whole clip into him.

ELVIRA is none to impressed with what her son has told her. Everyone worth knowing knows of BRODY BARNES.

MICKEY MONTANA
If I leave the country, I don't think the 'ORDER' will come for me. His sociopathic sons won't think twice if they know what's good for them. AMSTERDAM is my best chance at both living and being FREE. You know it as well as I do. YOU OWE ME THIS, MOM.

ELVIRA
Consider it done. I had no idea it was this bad. That's not me giving you sympathy, that's me telling you how fucking stupid you are. Just as hot-tempered, spontaneous and off the cuff as your sperm donor of a father. You'd be him if you did cocaine.

MICKEY MONTANA
Speaking of off the cuff - leave him out of this. I'm tired of hearing your references to the "great" -

ELVIRA snaps her fingers and wags her index, saying:

"Don't you say his fucking name, MICKEY. Don't you Dare."

She makes herself another vodka martini -

                    MICKEY MONTANA
          OK. Well, back to the subject of
          you helping me. I do thank you.

                    ELVIRA
               (sips the martini)
          My driver will take you to the
          airport when your passport, ID,
          and ticket are ready.
               (sits her drink
                down)
          But MICKEY MORENO MONTANA, you
          better never peek your head back
          at this house, ever again. I say
          that with LOVE. I don't want to
          see you end up dead, another
          criminal slain as a statistic.
          I've seen how that works, up close
          and personal. PROMISE ME, SON.
          When you get to AMSTERDAM, you'll
          lay low and let the dust settle.

MICKEY finishes his drink - he stands up from the chair
across from his MOTHER. He nods at her in a yes-manner,
signaling he respects her wishes to never return home again.

                    MICKEY MONTANA
          Thank you. I'm going upstairs to
          rest. I'll need it.

                    ELVIRA
               (rolls her eyes)
          Yes, you will, your wounds are
          leaking like a faucet. You bled
          out on my favorite chair, damn
          you. Stop right where you are,
          don't move.

...ELVIRA gets up and approaches her only son. As frustrated
as she is, she still cares for her boy. She lifts the loose
gray t-shirt he's wearing to see the multitude of fresh
wounds.

It's UNNATURAL. IT'S SUPERNATURAL that MICKEY's still able
to stand, walk, and talk. Clinically he was dead...only to
live again.

CUT TO:

> ELVIRA
> (getting teary
> eyed)
> What did they do to you?

> MICKEY MONTANA
> ...They made me stronger.

MICKEY'S mother is nursing his wounds. She's taken the bandages off and his rubbing, dabbing, gently touching the many wounds with a sanitized white-rag. MICKEY is in hellish pain. But, oddly enough, the wet rag feels good to his wounds.

He feels a light breeze of air touching the blood, flesh, and muscle. MICKEY's been given enough pain-medicine to put down any other man. But he's drinking with the painkillers. The pain is that SEVERE. He simply needs rest.

ELVIRA dips the blood-soaked rag in the bowl of fresh warm water. She rings it out and proceeds to dab some more on other wounds.

> MICKEY MONTANA
> How long's it been since I left home? I don't even remember, honestly.

> ELVIRA
> (gingerly nursing
> MICKEY's wounds
> with the rag)
> It's been too long. If I had to calculate, I'd say you left for CALIFORNIA on your 18th birthday, from what I recall.

MICKEY winces and groans at the pain. ELVIRA is shocked by the way his wounds look. She had an "underground" doctor come by and fix him up (take out the bullets, sew shut his fleshly wounds, etcetera) -

ELVIRA's doing the rest.

MICKEY MONTANA
I remember now. It was my 18th birthday. I was itching to leave, now that I think back on it. I just knew CALI was the answer.

ELVIRA cleans a few more areas on MICKEY's back.

ELVIRA
Did you find what you were looking for, son? Was it worth it in the end?

MICKEY MONTANA
It was, after all. I did my dirt, yeah. But I also learned to be a self-sufficient man. I became a leader. People feared me, respected me, and loved me in COMPTON. But I never found what I was looking for, actually. That being FREEDOM. The only freedom I would know in COMPTON was my friend DRE's son. Little FREEDOM FERRARA.
(sheds a tear)
- I knew I was getting greedy. We should've called it quits, and they'd still be alive for their kids. I was selfish to keep taking jobs from that son-of-a-bitch BRODY.

ELVIRA puts the blood-drenched rag in the bowl. And walks around to face her son.

ELVIRA
Listen, son. What's done is done. There's no going back. There's just not.

MICKEY MONTANA
I know it. I know it. But those kids are going to grow up without any kind of a father figure because of what we did. DRE and CARTER deserved better. They
(MORE)

                    MICKEY MONTANA (cont'd)
          deserved to have a family. Me, I
          deserve Hell. Nothing more,
          nothing less.

                    ELVIRA
               (gets out the
                first-aid
                supplies)
          Nobody deserves Hell, MICKEY.
          Life's too short for that. Give
          yourself a break. Don't put that
          on your conscience. Those men who
          ran with you, they knew what they
          were doing. They knew the risk.
          YOU LET THAT SHIT GO. I need you
          to be focused. I need you to go
          upstairs and rest. We'll have the
          traveling necessities for you in
          no time. My people are quick. I'll
          pour you another scotch, knock it
          out and count some sheep. You are
          safe here. Trust me.
               (bandaging MICKEY)
          If you think AMSTERDAM is the key,
          then, come Hell or highwater,
          we'll get you there, okay? Stop
          worrying. Quit the anxiety. Quit
          the pity-party. It's not going to
          help me or you.

ELVIRA dresses the remaining stitched areas on her son's
upper body after having thoroughly cleaned them.

                    ELVIRA
               (lightly pats
                MICKEY on the
                shoulder)
          All right, you're as good as new.

ELVIRA hands her son a fresh glass of SCOTCH - no ice.

                    MICKEY MONTANA
               (with gratitude)
          I sure did miss you, mom. THANK
          YOU for all that you're doing.

                          ELVIRA
                    (cold and distant)
          You didn't miss me. You needed
          help or you were going to die.
          There's a difference.

                          MICKEY MONTANA
          Well, either way, I'm still
          grateful for you.

ELVIRA walks out of the room, quiet as a mouse. MICKEY pays
no mind. He knows how his mom is, she's the coldest person
he's ever known...

...MICKEY chugs his scotch, it hits the painkillers like
cold-water to a hot frying-pan, giving the man a sincere
burn in his chest and true sedation, the pain floats away as
the liquor flows through his system.

MICKEY lies back and he's out like a lamp.

                                                  CUT TO:

EXT. FLORIDA - MONTANA REALTY CO. - MORNING

                                        LOCATION: MIAMI

2 DAYS LATER -

The recuperating MICKEY MONTANA, his fingernails painted
black, is wearing his black trench-coat, a black-tee-shirt,
a fedora, and some CHUCK TAYLORS with blue-jeans, as he
stands outside of his demolished birthright -

MONTANA REALTY COMPANY, along with numerous other business
endeavors, is shut down, boarded up, destroyed.

The sign of the business is hanging off the hinges. The
doors are open, homeless people sit outside of the place
underneath the shade of the roof.

                          MICKEY MONTANA
                    (balls his fist up)
          What a waste. Dammit to hell.

About 30 yards down the street, there are STREET PREACHERS praising GOD, stopping civilians in the middle of the street.

MICKEY expresses grimace at the MONTANA REALTY CO. building, wiping his hands of it - he moves on, pacing down the street toward the PREACHERS.

CUT TO:

> PASTOR FAROK
> Repent ye or perish, the choice is yours my Black brothers and sisters. We are the REAL Jews, can ya dig it?

MICKEY stands before the STREET PREACHERS with his hands in his pockets.

> MICKEY MONTANA
> (stops in front of the PREACHERS)
> What are ya'll selling besides Snake Oil?

> DEACON JONES
> What was that, young blood?

> MICKEY MONTANA
> (blunt)
> You heard me.

> PASTOR FAROK
> We ain't selling nothing. We are showing people to The WORD of GOD, that's all. There's nothing to sell, The Word is its own Power. The Word was with God, The Word was God - my brother, you look like a new Jew! We are your brothers.

> DEACON JONES
> Yessir, we have no problem with a black man in BLACK. You are black, ain't you?

55.

                    MICKEY MONTANA
          My father was CUBAN. They ARE
          Black. My mom is as white as one
          of those clouds in the sky,
          though.

                    PASTOR FAROK
          It's all about your father's
          lineage, young blood. He sowed the
          seed. You know what you are, at
          heart?

                    MICKEY MONTANA
          A Mutt.

                    DEACON JONES
          No! -

                    PASTOR FAROK
          You an Israelite.

                                        CUT TO:

                    MICKEY MONTANA
          Well, well, well - there's a first
          time for hearing everything. An
          Israelite? I'm no more a Jew than
          that piece of gum on the sidewalk.

                    STREET PREACHER 1
          Are you calling PASTOR FAROK a
          liar, my brother?

                    STREET PREACHER 2
          PASTOR FAROK and DEACON JONES
          CAN'T lie. They are divinely
          inspired. Who the hell are you to
          say otherwise, huh?

                    PASTOR FAROK
          At least take a flyer, young
          blood. Ponder on your heritage, if
          you will. No harm, no foul.

MICKEY pulls his hands from his pockets, revealing his
ink-black fingernails.

This SHOCKS the STREET PREACHERS to their very core.

CUT TO:

                DEACON JONES
    Whoa, whoa. You paint your nails,
    man?

                PASTOR FAROK
        (to MICKEY)
    That's of the devil!

MICKEY snatches the flyer from the preachers with the speed of a gunslinger in the wild west.

                MICKEY MONTANA
    I'll take your flyer, but I don't
    have to explain myself to
    fellow-SINNERS. I am what I am -
    accept it or get out of my way.

                STREET PREACHER 1
    You ignorant piece of -

                PASTOR FAROK
        (to STREET
         PREACHER 1)
    - Let the man pass. He's going to
    hell, anyway. That's self-evident.
    He's got to buy him some mascara
    and glitter.

MICKEY balls up his fist yet he contains his righteous indignation.

The STREET PREACHERS make way for MICKEY - he walks past them peacefully without incident.

When he skirts by, he spits on the ground to let them know what he thinks of their two-faced antics. The other civilians, enthralled with the preachers, are all eyes and ears; totally immersed in their "sermons".

MICKEY moves on - he puts the brochure in his trench-coat

pocket; genuinely interested in the racial lineage rhetoric the PREACHERS were yapping about.

                              CUT TO:

EXT. LA CITY STREET - DAY

CUT BACK TO 2010:

"JOB #1"

MICKEY, DRE, and CARTER are cruising down a LOS ANGELES STREET in an AMBULANCE with the sirens roaring in hot pursuit of some Loot. This will be there very first job. The AMBULANCE, they stole off a HOSPITAL-lot without any problems.

                              CUT TO:

INT. AMBULANCE - CONTINUOUS

MICKEY, DRE, and CARTER are wearing MASKS...they have on SLASHER MASKS. The men have on wardrobes unique to their respective "characters": (MICKEY is MICHAEL MYERS), (DRE is FREDDY KRUEGER), (CARTER is JASON VOORHEES).

The trio of would-be robbers have with them a more than disposable, expendable asset of a DRIVER up front as a charade, dressed as a PARAMEDIC.

Traffic moves out of the way of the AMBULANCE at will, giving the DRIVER a clear path. The DRIVER pulls into a grocery-store parking lot and immediately kills the sirens.

                    DRE FERRARA
                 (tightly gripping
                   his weapon)
            I can't believe you fools talked
            my black ass into this.

                    MICKEY MONTANA
            Quit your whining, DRE. You like
            money, don't ya?

DRE nods while wearing his FREDDY KRUEGER' MASK.

                    MICHAEL CARTER
        Then that's what we do, we think
        about the money, stay focused, and
        nip this shit in the bud.

The AMBULANCE DRIVER says, "We've Made It!" - loud and clear, and the vehicle comes to a halt.

                    MICKEY MONTANA
           (laughs)
        This is gonna be fun!

                              CUT TO:

EXT. LA SHOPPING-CENTER/GROCERY-STORE PARKING LOT - DAY

This shopping area is vast, lots of stores right on top of each other. The AMBULANCE is in the GROCERY-STORE PARKING LOT, close to a 'WELLS FARGO' BANK - near the bank's ATM. This ATM is about 40 yards away from the AMBULANCE in the GROCERY-STORE PARKING LOT.

                              CUT TO:

EXT. WELLS FARGO ATM DRIVE-THRU LANE - DAY

A 'LOOMIS' ARMORED TRUCK DRIVER is delivering 100,000 cash to the ATM of the 'WELLS FARGO'. There's no traffic in the drive-thru. The 'LOOMIS' TRUCK pulls up to the ATM.

The SOLO 'WELLS FARGO' DRIVER carries 2 moneyboxes (each holding precisely 50 GRAND) with a 'loader' all by himself to the ATM, jamming to some music (headphones in), without a care in the world, like it's just another day.

                              CUT TO:

INT. AMBULANCE - CONTINUOUS

The DRIVER knocks on the roof of the AMBULANCE in the cab-area. MICKEY knows that's their go-ahead.

                    MICKEY MONTANA
                (like a leader,
                 stern)
            Take cover and cover me, on my
            move.

DRE says: "All right, MICKEY, let's do this."

CARTER says: "Let's make it happen, captain."

The three men speedily exit the AMBULANCE, in their SLASHER COSTUMES.

                                        CUT TO:

EXT. THE AMBULANCE - CONTINUOUS

DRE and CARTER are totally undetected and unnoticed amongst the pool of people and proceed to the left and right of the AMBULANCE, machine-guns in-hand to their sides.

MICKEY is right behind them. He surveys the situation. MICKEY has a propane-tank in his hands with a 9MM pistol tucked in his waistband.

He, DRE, and CARTER watch the ARMORED TRUCK DRIVER - hawkishly. They patiently wait and observe.

                                        CUT TO:

EXT. GROCERY-STORE PARKING LOT - MOMENTS LATER

MICKEY watches like a lion would his prey on the African plains...all while DRE and CARTER are on standby, ready to pounce as well.

Nobody gives two shits about the AMBULANCE, the COSTUMES, the MASKS, none of it. You'd think this was normal...in this part of LA, it pretty much is.

                    MICKEY MONTANA
                (a little let down)
            These idiots only brought one guy?
            There's supposed to be
            three...overkill it is.
            Theatricality is everything.

MICKEY MONTANA, cold as ice, sprints toward the 'WELLS
FARGO' ATM DRIVE-THRU LANE and throws the half-empty
Propane-Tank right under the ARMORED TRUCK...

- It lands perfectly under the TRUCK.

...The DRIVER takes out one earbud as he heard the metal
clank.

                    ARMORED TRUCK DRIVER
                (alarmed)
            What the hell was that?

                                            CUT TO:

                    MICKEY MONTANA
                (laying down on
                 his belly)
            Gotcha -

MICKEY takes aim and shoots his pistol at the Propane-Tank,
we hear: "BANG!!!"

The DRIVER jumps in shock at the explosion. He immediately
leaves the money and runs the other way trying to avoid
damage, headphones still blasting music.

The ARMORED TRUCK DRIVER isn't quick enough - he gets caught
in the flames. He's engulfed by them.

The TRUCK, because of the explosion, jumps into the air
about 4 ft. It moves a bit in the air from the force, and
lands directly on the DRIVER's flame-covered body.

                    MICKEY MONTANA
                (admiring the
                 scene)
            Holy Chicken Biscuits!
                (signals his
                 partners)
                        (MORE)

                        MICKEY MONTANA (cont'd)
              DRE, CARTER, get the loot. Let's
              hit it, boys!

                        MICHAEL CARTER
                   (sprinting to the
                    ATM)
              You got it, man. I'm on it.

                        DRE FERRARA
                   (observes the
                    fiery damage)
              Damn!

DRE and CARTER each pick up a moneybox and they sprint back
to the AMBULANCE. MICKEY gets into the back of the
AMBULANCE, nothing in-hand; he leads DRE and CARTER
naturally. The money, despite the explosion, is UNHARMED.

DRE and CARTER follow behind MICKEY and take a seat in the
AMBULANCE with the moneyboxes.

Sirens can be heard blaring around them.

The DRIVER cuts on the sirens in their respective AMBULANCE,
and they proceed to haul ass back to MICKEY's SAFEHOUSE.
THEIR AMBULANCE blends in like all the others. The lights
indistinguishable from all the rest.

"JOB #1" COMPLETE.

- Sloppy, yes, but complete.

                                                 CUT TO:

INT. MICKEY'S HOUSE - MORNING

                                        - NOVEMBER 2010

MICKEY is sitting at his dinner table, enjoying a bowl of
cereal.

His cellphone rings:

MICKEY MONTANA
Hello?

BRODY BARNES
MICKEY MONTANA.

MICKEY MONTANA
This is he. Who's speaking?

BRODY BARNES
This is BRODY BARNES. Do you know who I am?

MICKEY MONTANA
Y - yes, I do. Everybody worth a damn knows who you are, respectfully, sir.

BRODY BARNES
(laughs a bit)
I have work for you and your men, if you're interested.

MICKEY MONTANA
We - we're highly interested. What did you have in mind?

BRODY BARNES
Meet me at my HOME, alone, at 25052 SEASHORE DRIVE, in 1 hour. I'll provide the details when you arrive.

MICKEY MONTANA
Yes, sir, will do.

MICKEY hangs up, as does BRODY.

MICKEY dials DRE, directly after hanging up with BRODY.

MICKEY MONTANA
DRE, tell CARTER I think we just got a promotion. I'm meeting with BRODY BARNES.

DRE speaks through the phone with muffled speech.

                          MICKEY MONTANA
                Yes, THE BRODY BARNES. I'll call
                you when the meet is done.

MICKEY hangs up with DRE. He eats a bite of his cereal,
smiling like a fat kid with a birthday cake -

CUT TO:

INT. THE AIRPORT - MIAMI, FLORIDA - MORNING

- 2012

MICKEY MORENO MONTANA (with a forged TICKET, PASSPORT, and
ID) has entered a MIAMI AIRPORT with 2 medium sized FLIGHT
BAGS, one in each hand -

He comes up to the HOSTESS of the AIRPORT at the counter:

                          FLIGHT HOSTESS
                How may I help you, sir?

                          MICKEY MONTANA
                    (smiling)
                Yes, miss, I have a FIRST-CLASS
                TICKET to AMSTERDAM -
                      (hands the HOSTESS
                       the TICKET)
                How are you today?

                          FLIGHT HOSTESS
                I'm doing very well, thank you.
                      (looks at the
                       TICKET INFO)
                - MR. HANCOCK - your TICKET has
                been certified and your flight
                will be departing in 1 hour, give
                or take. You may proceed to your
                terminal, sir.

MICKEY nods like a gentleman to the YOUNG LADY -

                          MICKEY MONTANA
                Thank you, kindly. This is my
                dream. Wish me luck, stranger.
                      (winks to the
                                                    (MORE)

64.

                    MICKEY MONTANA (cont'd)
               HOSTESS)
     AMSTERDAM, here I come.

                    FLIGHT HOSTESS
          Good Luck! May you enjoy your
          flight and your stay in AMSTERDAM,
          stranger.
                    (winks right back
                    at MICKEY)
          You'll do just fine there.

MICKEY walks away, like a SMOOTH CRIMINAL - he heads toward
his waiting section; all in the search for his dream
location: AMSTERDAM -

                                             CUT TO BLACK:

CHAPTER III - METALLIC SCREAMS

FADE IN:

YEAR: 2024

LOCATION: COMPTON, CALIFORNIA

This COMPTON community...it is a cesspool of ORGANIZED
CHAOS. The Ghetto, projects, Hood, whatever you'd like to
call it. COMPTON is the Mecca of madness. The Sun sets
differently in the city, the blood flows differently...

...Gang-Bangers roam, pillage, steal, kill, all in the name
of a "set". Rather than BANG, a couple of kids in the city
of COMPTON are striving for greater things. They record
music, and refrain from the Gang life...

There's a CIVIL WAR unfolding in COMPTON, at this point in
time; between 2 KINGS (KING RED and KING BLUE).

WE WITNESS - FAST CUTS:

- 2 MEN in RED throwing a MAN in BLUE off the top of a 4
story ROOFTOP, to the ground until he smashes like a
pumpkin.

- A MAN in BLUE shooting a MAN in his own HOME while taking a shower. Bullets penetrate the SHOWER-CURTAIN, the man flails and seizes until he meets DEATH.

- A MAN in RED is getting his haircut at the BARBER. His eyes are closed, he's comfortable. A MAN in BLUE enters the SHOP, he gestures to the BARBER to move; the MAN in BLUE slits the throat of the MAN in the BARBER CHAIR, like it's a stick of butter.

WE PAN OUT to a SKY-VIEW of COMPTON:

AND WE CUT TO -

INT. MICKEY'S OLD HOUSE - FREEDOM'S STUDIO/RESIDENCE - MORNING

LOCATION: COMPTON

                                        - OAKLAND STREET

It's 2024, the YEAR OF THE LORD.

The sun has yet to rise on this CALIFORNIA morning - FREEDOM FERRARA (Black) and NATHAN TOWNHALL (Biracial), both 19 years of age, are in THE STUDIO of their HOME (MICKEY's OLD HOUSE), recording freestyles over beats.

They are both dressed unassumingly; FREEDOM, with black-painted fingernails, is wearing a forest-green t-shirt, NATE is "rocking" a white one. FREEDOM has on Chuck-Taylor retros, slack-laced, gum-bottoms with gray Dickie-pants. NATHAN has on black gym-shorts, sporting Air-Jordan 20s, all-black...

...FREEDOM has dreadlocks. NATHAN has a fresh-fade, his hair the texture of a white person's - FREEDOM FERRARA is 6'2, dark skinned, muscular, has long arms/reach. His grainy dreads hang to his shoulders.

He has steel-platinum teeth, all throughout his once shattered mouth. FREEDOM has an AMERICAN FLAG GAITOR-MASK on as he raps. He has several tattoos on his body, arms, and hands - none on the face.

NATHAN TOWNHALL is light-skinned, 5'10, scrawny. His teeth are porcelain white. One of NATHAN's arms is longer than the other due to his condition. He has no tattoos.

The two 19-year-olds are the sons of the deceased DRE FERRARA and MICHAEL CARTER, respectively. NATHAN was given the last name "TOWNHALL", as that was his grandmother's maiden name.

CUT TO:

INT. MICKEY MONTANA'S HOUSE/THE RECORDING STUDIO - MORNING

FREEDOM boldly raps into the microphone:

                FREEDOM FERRARA
        (in the booth)
- Masochistic, fatalistic, futuristic. Movie clips, cameras attached to the rifles. Silver ingrained in my Bible, teeth, too, we need food. I eat crews. I fuck boos, I suck boobs. Titties, yeah, COMPTON is my city. The one right beside LA, where people kill for bargains, or just nada. Botch ya, Chris Bosh ya. Chicken shits, sandwiches. Pop the eyes out ya head. TRY TO SEE THE FAKENESS MYSELF. You ain't got no vision. You fucking flamers...I'm a master of ceremonies, myself, red belt wearing pelts. She snorted it all, the snow did not melt. I hope they're feeling what I felt, when I thought about hanging myself with a belt. Niggas wanting to kill me, because I painted my nails black, Jesus has returned and He's bringing Hell back.
        (pauses, nodding
         head)
Whoo!

NATHAN looks at FREEDOM from the computer desk outside of the soundproof booth. He gives him two thumbs up, yelling, "I GOT IT!"

NATHAN TOWNHALL is FREEDOM FERRARA's ENGINEER (he helps him to record and works out all the kinks). They're still BROTHERS, even as they've grown and aged.

Their BOND is that of family, stronger than ever. FREEDOM is NATHAN's caretaker and payee, as NATHANIEL TOWNHALL receives DISABILITY PAYMENTS from the US GOVERNMENT - this helps the MEN keep a shelter over their heads, FOOD on the table, and their BILLS PAID.

They live together in MICKEY MONTANA's old HOUSE - a place of peace, space, and privacy. They've just built a legitimate, very clever STUDIO set-up: it has a black Styrofoam covered booth, with a new MICROPHONE that is attached to a stand, everything is professional and official for them, now, after MONTHS of trial-and-error.

- FREEDOM made it himself. NATHAN led him vocally.

NATHAN TOWNHALL can work a computer and engineer records, which is even a lot for him, but he's EVEN MORE limited physically now, as his CEREBRAL PALSY has gotten far more severe with age. He uses crutches to get around - his arms and legs are fragile, not very strong; but his hands work just fine for helping FREEDOM record music when they can. Regardless, FREEDOM and NATHAN are a solid TEAM.

MR. FREEDOM raps with ease. It's second nature...and NATHAN knows just how to tweak his sound.

- FREEDOM continues recording - his rhyming fades into a calm voiceover narration.

>   MR. FREEDOM
>   (narrating)
>   - I can hear the gnashing of teeth
>   in my sleep. I have sympathy for
>   the devil, even though he is a
>   lie. My father, God rest his soul,
>   was a thief. I went another route
>   in life, not following in his
>   footsteps. Me, I'm an artist, a
>   (MORE)

MR. FREEDOM (cont'd)
RAPPER at heart; a pure-blooded workaholic. I can spit in my sleep. I been rappin' since I was a chap; me and NATE record and put it on the internet with ominous album covers, no traces. No videos. No publicity; YET. We do it for the hell of it. One day, though, we're going to be SUPERSTARS. My Uncle MICKEY taught me how to rap, actually. My Dad, DRE, he couldn't rap like Unc. I miss both 'em so much. Dad is passed on. NATHAN's pops is dead, too. I look after him like he's my twin - NOBODY ELSE does. They say MICKEY is dead, too - but I refuse to believe that. I know he's still out there, somewhere, I can feel it. Hell, MICKEY MONTANA, at the end of the day, is unbeatable. For now, though, NATHAN is the only family I got. My MOTHER died in CHILDBIRTH I was told. NATHAN's MOM, she's hooked on drugs - we NEVER see her unless she needs a couple of dollars or a hot-meal, sadly. We got plenty money, food, and we have this house with our booth. Me and NATE don't BANG no more, despite the culture of COMPTON - we left that banging nonsense in the rearview when we became MEN. We used to get down, flags and all. I see how futile that lifestyle is, I know how brutal it can be. 'KING BLUE' and 'KING RED' are at constant war - you'd think the SECOND US CIVIL WAR was going on, but ONLY in COMPTON. We're locked in the city; although me and NATE don't BANG, we still have to pay our dues. I work 60 hours-a-week to make sure we're straight and that KING BLUE is paid off. The KINGS of COMPTON,
(MORE)

                    MR. FREEDOM (cont'd)
          the dueling leaders of the BLOODS
          and the CRIPS, are ruthless. Cops
          ain't safe, nobody is safe round
          here; especially rappers. But I'm
          not nobody. I AM FREEDOM. I keep a
          low profile - no Social-Media, no
          pictures, no license, no paper
          trails, no nothing. If I flaunted
          or got complacent, I'd be hunted.
          I already feel like they are
          gearing up - either way, LIBERTY
          has always had enemies.

MR. FREEDOM is still rapping at will, as NATHAN jams, smoking a fat blunt; the MEDICAL MARIJUANA helps NATHAN to function and stay semi-productive, despite his condition. He outgrew his ASTHMA, but just couldn't get over the Cerebral Palsy.

NATHAN TOWNHALL is a great engineer. He and FREEDOM record over well-known beats, and put them out for FREE, making no money. They're artists...and thanks to MICKEY, they're well-off.

MICKEY MONTANA made sure they were looked after before he left town. After both of the boys' fathers passed away, MICKEY left them with plenty: MONEY and THE DEED TO THE HOUSE (MICKEY made NATHAN's MOTHER - HEAVEN CARTER - SWEAR to give them what he had left).

MICKEY got out of town, FOREVER - mistaken for dead. However, he did all he could to ensure the boys were taken care of before departing.

FREEDOM and NATHAN, they're well off, but FRUGAL (FREEDOM is a penny-pincher, very wise with funds, a perfect PAYEE for NATHAN) - the boys have all they need and could want.

The HOME they live in is 3 Bedrooms, 2 Bathrooms. On the exterior, it looks like a typical COMPTON HOUSE, but inside, the guys have their culture together, a CULTURE of their own design - one of CREATIVITY. The place is well-furnished, nicely lit, and has a masculine decoration about it.

Posters are all over the place of various movies: 'Jaws',

'Alien', 'Terminator', classics such as that. Then there's music posters of Lil Wayne, Wiz Khalifa, G-Eazy, Drake, and even COMPTON's own Kendrick Lamar. FREEDOM and NATHAN are film-buffs and music-heads.

They have VINYL cases on the walls - Jimi Hendrix, Eric Clapton, Bob Marley, J. Cole albums, etc., covering some of the interior of the home. The INTERIOR DESIGN is outstanding for two young bachelors -

FREEDOM narration starts bleeding back into him rapping, concluding his verse:

> MR. FREEDOM
> ...Basking in the robbing, see? Spent the last "Stimmy" at the Dollar-Tree. Bought a bunch of bullshit I don't need. Assassin's Creed. Really ballin', though, like Michael B. I'm Drakula, they still bitin' me. The world's sick of me living...nobody invited me. It's only the weed that's enticing me. And who am I kiddin'? Of course, the pretty women. They always kiss me first before I finish a sentence. Romanticism. She couldn't be chilla', get her a mink. Gotta make ya weakest link ya strongest link. FUCK WRITER'S BLOCK. Put bullets in ya ink. Yeah. Let the music tell you what to think. One year sober. I still need a drink, damn -

CUT TO:

FAST CUTS intertwined:

- FREEDOM BANGS a HAMMER at a CONSTRUCTION SITE.

- FREEDOM spars, BOXING, another young man.

- FREEDOM continues BANGING his HAMMER, doing construction.

AND WE CUT BACK TO THE STUDIO -

                    NATHAN TOWNHALL
               (smiling from
               ear-to-ear)
          You ripped it, bro! Good work.
          Let's master this -

MR. FREEDOM exits the booth, and he and NATE fist-bump,
knowing the tracks they have just recorded are "FIRE".

                    FREEDOM FERRARA
          - After you mix and upload
          everything, let me know, NATE. I
          gotta get ready for work. My shift
          starts soon. When I get off, let's
          go to the GYM -

                    NATHAN TOWNHALL
          You read my mind. I got some ideas
          for you when you hit the bag.
          Might even be able to get GUS to
          setup another sparring session.

                    FREEDOM FERRARA
          Already, BROTHER.

FREEDOM leaves the STUDIO area of the HOME as NATHAN fiddles
with the newly created music on the CPU.

CUT TO:

FREEDOM prepares his BOXING gear in his room, then he gets
ready for work.

FREEDOM is a BOXER, too - he works a JOB, he RAPS - in his
spare-time, though, he BOXES.

- BOXING, that is FREEDOM's true passion.

                                                  CUT TO:

EXT. CONSTRUCTION-SITE - FREEDOM'S JOB - MORNING

Working early, FREEDOM is slaving at a CONSTRUCTION-SITE, earning money, as per usual. He is doing trim work, pipefitting, he's carrying doors with glass windows up a few staircases - when it's called for, FREEDOM is bashing his sledgehammer against deteriorated brick walls, as the WORKERS are putting up new infrastructure on this site, first taking the old stuff down.

                    CONSTRUCTION WORKER
        You're putting in work, today,
        FREEDOM. You got me motivated,
        man.

                    FREEDOM FERRARA
        The money isn't going to make
        itself. Ain't that right?

                    CONSTRUCTION WORKER
          (working hard)
        Damn skippy.

The CONSTRUCTION JOB MANAGER whistles to his workers.

                    CONSTRUCTION JOB MANAGER
        All right, everyone, it's
        lunchtime. Eat well, restore your
        energy. We have a lot more work to
        do.

The WORKERS, including FREEDOM, discontinue their activities, preparing to grub.

CUT TO:

FREEDOM sits at the edge of the CONSTRUCTION-SITE, elevated observing things from above, his feet dangling down, as he eats 2 ham sandwiches with lettuce and tomato.

The CONSTRUCTION JOB MANAGER places his hand on FREEDOM's shoulder, startling him - he jumps.

                    FREEDOM FERRARA
        - You scared the hell out of me,
        boss.

                    CONSTRUCTION JOB MANAGER
          Sorry, kid, didn't mean to give
          you a start. Just wanted to let
          you know that I appreciate your
          hard work and dedication to the
          company. I'm giving you a $1.50
          per hour raise, starting next
          week.

                    FREEDOM FERRARA
               (chomping on his
               sandwich)
          Wow! Thank you, sir. That's very
          much appreciated. I - I'm happy to
          be here working for the company. I
          really thank you for looking out
          for me. You have put me to work,
          kept me busy. I'm extremely
          thankful.

                    CONSTRUCTION JOB MANAGER
          Think nothing of it, kid. Every
          man's gotta get paid. You've
          earned it. Now, we're clocking out
          early today; 1:30 PM. You'll still
          get a full day's pay, though, no
          worries.

FREEDOM nods, chewing his food.

                    FREEDOM FERRARA
          Whatever works for you, works for
          me.

                    CONSTRUCTION JOB MANAGER
               (shakes FREEDOM's
               hand)
          Good man. Keep it up, FREEDOM.
          Keep up the good work.

                                        CUT TO:

EXT. THE DRIVEWAY - DAY

MR. FREEDOM owns a 1996 CHEVY IMPALA with 13' inch rims. It is purple, and customized modestly. NATHAN TOWNHALL, owns a 2017 POLAIRS SLINGSHOT, blue-and-black; all-stock.

They're the guys' toys; their only real luxury to take them away from the madness of COMPTON.

>   MR. FREEDOM
>   We racing? Or can your lil'
>   SLINGSHOT even keep up with the
>   beastly IMPALA?

NATHAN cranks up the POLARIS, and takes off out of the DRIVEWAY, no helmet.

>   NATHAN TOWNHALL
>   (racing onward
>   laughing)
>   Let's see!
>
>   FREEDOM FERRARA
>   (yelling into his
>   hands at NATHAN)
>   We'll race to the FOOD MART -
>   then, let's ride in the IMPALA to
>   hear these new tracks!

NATHAN acknowledges FREEDOM from afar as he races on.

MR. FREEDOM urgently gets his IMPALA going and swerves away from his residence, chasing NATHAN's SLINGSHOT. The BROTHERS storm off.

>   CUT TO:

EXT. COMPTON ROAD - AFTERNOON

FREEDOM and NATHAN are cruising around COMPTON in FREEDOM's IMPALA, listening to the new music -

A plain-vehicle, with red-and-blues, flags FREEDOM and NATHAN down from the rear.

                    FREEDOM FERRARA
                (to NATE)
            Dammit! We're being pulled by a
            FED, man.

                    NATHAN TOWNHALL
                (nervously)
            Oh, hell.

With no license or proper registration, FREEDOM pulls to the
curb, getting himself situated and ready for anything.

A FEMALE FED walks up to the driver's side -

FREEDOM rolls down the window:

                    AGENT GRACE
                (with a happy tone)
            FREEDOM ERICO FERRARA - how the
            hell are you doing, man?

AGENT GRACE is 5ft10 and caramel skinned - in a federal
uniform, wearing a bulletproof vest, a holstered pistol on
her hip. She has medium-length bouncy hair. Her eyes are
yellowish with a green tint. She's very lovely -

                    FREEDOM FERRARA
            Um, who are you, lady? What have I
            done?

                    AGENT GRACE
                (excited)
            It's SASHA. SASHA GRACE -

                    FREEDOM FERRARA
                (gets out of his
                 CAR)
            Oh, my God! SASHA. How have you
            been?

FREEDOM hugs SASHA.

NATHAN also gets out on the other side of the vehicle:

                    NATHAN TOWNHALL
          We're hugging plain clothes 12,
          now, FREE?

                    FREEDOM FERRARA
          SASHA, this is my best-friend,
          NATHAN. He and I grew up together.
          We're roommates these days.
          NATHAN, this is SASHA, my
          ex-girlfriend.

NATHAN limps around to the trunk area with the help of his
crutches.

                    NATHAN TOWNHALL
                (with his hand out
                 to shake)
          Hello, SASHA. It seems our mutual
          friend, here, forgot to ever
          mention you.

NATHAN and SASHA shake hands:

                    AGENT GRACE
          Same with you, NATHAN. I think
          FREEDOM's got a brick for a brain,
          he forgets to remember.

                    FREEDOM FERRARA
          So, I'm not in trouble, right?

                    AGENT GRACE
          Nope, you just need to get your
          tag updated, it's super expired.
          I'm going to let you slide on
          that. I spotted you down the road,
          put your plate code in the system
          - I knew it was you, though. You
          look the same as before, still
          handsome - I wanted to reintroduce
          myself. I'm a ROOKIE with the
          F.B.I now. You're one of my first
          pulls. Gotta practice on somebody,
          right?

                    FREEDOM FERRARA
          Damn, girl. A rookie F.B.I AGENT,
          huh? You always said you were
          going to get into Law Enforcment.
          Look at you go! Living your dream,
          there's no better way to live
          life, is there?

                    AGENT GRACE
          I appreciate the support, FREE,
          really. Well, it seems I pulled
          you in one of the busiest spots in
          COMPTON. I pulled you - because I
          want your number. I want to go out
          for a bite with you. Is that okay?
          I'll leave my badge at home. I
          just want to catch up.

                    NATHAN TOWNHALL
          My brother ain't going on no date
          with a FED -

                    FREEDOM FERRARA
               (to NATHAN)
          Brother, you don't speak for me.
          Be nice.
               (to SASHA GRACE)
          You got yourself a date, dear.
          What's a good day and time?
          Tomorrow, let's say at 4 PM or 6?

                    AGENT GRACE
               (innocently
                smiling)
          6 sounds perfect. Let's eat at the
          old BUFFALO WING restaurant we
          used to go to, huh? Give me
          another hug, FREEDOM. It's been
          too long. I really have missed
          you, you know?

FREEDOM bear-hugs SASHA:

                    AGENT GRACE
                (excitedly)
            - 6 O'Clock, CHARLIE's BUFFALO
            WING eatery, don't be late!

                    FREEDOM FERRARA
            I'll be there.

                    AGENT GRACE
                (flirtatiously)
            By the way, I like the
            black-fingernails.

                    FREEDOM FERRARA
            What can I say? I'm a ROCKSTAR.

SASHA smiles.

FREEDOM gets back in the IMPALA, as does NATHAN -

AGENT SASHA GRACE gets in her plain FEDERAL vehicle, she takes off from behind FREEDOM, then FREEDOM swerves off -

                                        CUT TO:

INT. FREEDOM'S IMPALA - CONTINUOUS

FREEDOM and NATHAN ride quite quietly -

                    NATHAN TOWNHALL
            So, you're dating a FED, now, man?
            A fool - all for the concha.

                    FREEDOM FERRARA
            No, NATE. Not for a piece of ass.
            For LOVE - I've always loved
            SASHA. She's the only girl, WOMAN,
            I've ever loved.

                    NATHAN TOWNHALL
            That's why I've never heard about
            her? How'd you keep her under
            wraps?

                    FREEDOM FERRARA
          It didn't last long. You never
          asked. And I'm not one to spill
          beans on my relations. Especially
          with one as beautiful as her.
          Leave it alone, man. She's special
          to me. FED or no, I'm going on
          that reunion date.

                    NATHAN TOWNHALL
                    (disappointed)
          To each his own. Just be careful,
          man. I bet she could fuck the legs
          off of a bed and the wheels off a
          car.

                    FREEDOM FERRARA
          Sex is for the animals. Pussy, my
          dear friend, is merely the devil's
          ham. What SASHA and I had was true
          love.

FREEDOM keeps driving focused and quickly. He cranks the
music up. HIS MUSIC...

CUT TO:

INT. MANHUNTER' BAIL-BOND CO. - DAY

- MAJOR MANHUNTER, still a BAIL BONDSMAN, sits at his desk,
passing in and out of consciousness, high on HEROIN...having
flashbacks. He's even more flawed than the convicts he deals
with AND puts away...

...MAJOR is still also a BOUNTY HUNTER along with being a
BONDSMAN. His now deceased father perfected this DUALISTIC
approach. MAJOR, to this day, does miserably at it - the
heroin surely doesn't help.

                    MAJOR MANHUNTER
                    (narrating, high
                     as a kite)
          I was a MAJOR in the Military.
          Ironic and repetitive because
          that's my actual first name. I had
          a pristine career til' the shit
                         (MORE)

MAJOR MANHUNTER (cont'd)
hit the fan. I got caught smuggling opium, and using it all at the same time. They discharged me dishonorably. I came back, but Dad was gone. He left the business to me in his will. I half-ass ran it when I started. I took up other jobs for bad people, KINGPINS and such. I stopped that, though. I just love the H now. My wife is passed away. My son is gone, too...the drug took them from me. Now I have nothing to live for but the drug. I never wanted this for myself. If I had beaucoup funds, I would just throw all this away and move to France - my father, way back, wanted me to take up the family business; he was adamant: I'm a MANHUNTER. He was proud to call me "MAJOR" after my supposed "service", even with the discharge the way it was. He was a real 'BOUNTY-HUNTER'. Me? I just transport the convicts. Couldn't hunt to save my life. Not with the aches and the sickness. It's incessant. MANHUNTER is my birthname. Family-name. I used to take pride in that name til' the Heroin got to me. I can't even sit up, much less do my job. Yet, somehow, I still find a way to continue on. I'm not THE MANHUNTER my father was by any stretch. Every-time I get the call, I dread it. Because I can't get high. That's the stone-cold truth. I wish I had the balls to go ahead and put a round through my skull, but I don't. I'm just letting the time pass, and I'm just passin' through this life...needle all the way in -

The MAJOR's phone rings...

He snaps awake from his slumberly high, and answers.

                  MAJOR MANHUNTER
        (into the phone,
         half-asleep)
    H - hello?

We hear indistinct mumbling on the other line.

                  MAJOR MANHUNTER
    - What? No. Yeah. All right. Got
    it.
         (hangs up)

The MAJOR gets up, stumbling a bit. He goes to the Bathroom of his office, and washes his face - this perks him up, awakens him while still allowing him to feel the "H" in his veins.

                            CUT TO:

<u>INT. THE STATION - LATER</u>

MAJOR MANHUNTER appears at the STATION to apprehend a couple of folks for transport.

                  MAJOR MANHUNTER
        (walks up to the
         desk, signs
          papers)
    You know who I'm here for. Send
    'em please. I got a life to lead.

                  OFFICER 1
    Adopt the pace of nature, sir. Her
    secret is patience.

                  MAJOR MANHUNTER
    You read that in a 'Self-Help'
    book?

                  OFFICER 1
    It's Emerson, you jackass.

MAJOR MANHUNTER, wholly angry by the sass, immediately grabs the OFFICER and slams his head into the table several times and then punches 5 of the man's teeth out.

Cops surround MANHUNTER and restrain him. He gathers himself.

> MAJOR MANHUNTER
> You imbeciles try to book me and you'll all be working in Rhode Island by next week! Now, bring me those convicts!

They back off, and so does he.

He gathers those ready for transport and leaves THE STATION.

CUT TO:

INT. MAJOR MANHUNTER'S VEHICLE - DAY

MAJOR MANHUNTER is escorting the felons in his COMPANY VEHICLE to their respective places.

The ride is silent til'...

> THUG 1
> How long you been doing this, cracker?

...MANHUNTER gives a death-stare through the rear-view mirror to the THUG.

He doesn't respond.

Suddenly, the cuffed MEN reveal their hands are free as THUG 2, with a metal wire, goes to strangle MAJOR MANHUNTER - there's no barrier between them.

> THUG 2
> (strangling MAJOR)
> He asked you a question!

MAJOR MANHUNTER stops the CAR. No one is around as they're on the outskirts.

The THUGS manage to break the rear car windows and jump out after hitting MAJOR in his head with several heavy blows.

They pull him out of the vehicle.

CUT TO:

EXT. STREET - CONTINUOUS

The THUGS drag MANHUNTER from his vehicle with simplicity.

              MAJOR MANHUNTER
    You pieces of shit! Let me go -

              THUG 1
    The last words of a Junkie wanna
    be cop. This here beating is from
    KING RED.

The THUGS beat the MAJOR nearly to death, by stomping and kicking him.

They do this for a couple of minutes til' he's bloody and black-and-blue.

                                  CUT TO:

The THUGS throw MANHUNTER's beaten body in a WASTEPRO Dumpster...

...Maggots, rotten food, and trash cover him as he inches closer to death.

              MAJOR MANHUNTER
        (barely able to
         speak)
    Some - somebody, help me.

                                  CUT TO:

INT. THE GYM - DAY

MR. FREEDOM is holding a punching bag steady for NATHAN.

NATHAN, disabled with his cerebral palsy, still favors his right side...

MR. FREEDOM is zoned out, as NATHAN races on as he also punches.

                    NATHAN TOWNHALL
           (punching
            repetitiously,
           and ranting)
We need to call my Mom, bro. You ain't called her in a year. Shame on you, FREE. I call her every two weeks, and she always asks me about you. Anyway, also we need -
           (punches more)
- We need to get the payment to KING BLUE.

                    MR. FREEDOM
           (snaps out of his
            daydream)
You haven't paid the KING yet? That was due at 10AM, NATE!

                    NATHAN TOWNHALL
           (eases off the bag)
Well, I didn't get it there. No problem. What's the worst that could happen? We've been late before.

                    FREEDOM FERRARA
We're on strike 3 with him! The 15K has to go there by 10AM now, or you know, he told us he'd "out" us.

                    NATHAN TOWNHALL
I just wanted to record, man. And I overlooked it. We'll go now. But, first, you hit the bag 100 times, 50 kicks, 50 punches. You
                      (MORE)

                    NATHAN TOWNHALL (cont'd)
                too stressed, bro. Hit the bag.

                    MR. FREEDOM
                    (goes to face the
                    bag to punch it)
                Aite.

MR. FREEDOM demolishes the punching bag, almost knocking
NATE back into the wall.

He is a skilled boxer. They both are, even NATE, despite his
disability.

                                        CUT TO:

THE GYM is nearly empty, yet the people in it do react.
FREEDOM calms down as to not show his ass.

GUSTAV BORZANO approaches the two YOUNG MEN - he is
FREEDOM's BOXING TRAINER.

                    GUSTAV BORZANO
                What's the raucous, boys? Is there
                some kind of trouble?

                    FREEDOM FERRARA
                No, GUS. We - we just got some
                stuff to handle in a bit. I wanted
                to pound the bag for a minute
                before taking care of things.

                    GUSTAV BORZANO
                You're hitting it wrong, FREE -
                don't attack with all your might.
                Make the bag come to you, finesse
                it, visualize the opponent. You
                know this, man!

NATHAN stands back, taking in the lesson GUSTAV is
attempting to demonstrate -

                    FREEDOM FERRARA
                (adjusts, becomes
                 pliable to the
                 bag)
            Yessir.

GUSTAV stands behind the bag, to give FREEDOM a sense that
he's hitting a person and not a bag. FREEDOM goes to town on
the punching bag while also trying to adapt to the method
GUSTAV is referring to -

                                        CUT TO:

                    GUSTAV BORZANO
            Good, good, kid. You still got it.
            This next match, for you, is going
            to be gold. You're a notch away
            from breaking through the AMATUER
            LEAGUE to the SEMIS. You're a
            rising star, as far as I'm
            concerned.
                (to NATHAN)
            - You keeping him sharp, NATE? You
            are the HYPE MAN, you know.

                    NATHAN TOWNHALL
            Trying to, COACH. But you know
            FREE, he's as stubborn as you are.

                    GUSTAV BORZANO
            The most honest thing I've heard
            all week. Ain't that the damn
            truth, though? I saw you hitting
            the bag, too, NATE - you got
            skill. You could knock out one of
            my other fighters with that type
            of swing, kid.

                    NATHAN TOWNHALL
            Oh, I know I could GUS. I know.

                    GUSTAV BORZANO
                (chuckles)
            Fast with the punches and
            arrogant, a lethal combo.

FREEDOM eases up on the punching - fatigue starts setting in on him.

                    GUSTAV BORZANO
          Are you going to make weight,
          FREE? You're still dieting, right?
          Jogging, hydrating with only
          water?

                    FREEDOM FERRARA
              (backs away from
               the bag and
               GUSTAV)
          You already know, COACH - I'm on
          it.

                    NATHAN TOWNHALL
          I think he takes it more seriously
          than you do, GUS. He's a champ,
          this guy. He'll be ready, come
          fight night. That's a guarantee.

                    GUSTAV BORZANO
          Great, that's what I like to hear,
          you guys. I'm appreciating the
          confidence. You two make a damn
          good team, you know that?

                    FREEDOM FERRARA
              (gives NATE a fist
               bump with his
               boxing glove)
          We're BROTHERS, of course we do -

                    GUSTAV BORZANO
              (straining a bit)
          I - I...

GUSTAV takes a knee in the boxing ring. He begins to sweat intensely.

                                                  CUT TO:

FREEDOM takes his gloves off, super worried -

                          FREEDOM FERRARA
                    What - what's wrong, COACH? Are
                    you good?

GUSTAV's veins are bulging in his face and head.

                          GUSTAV BORZANO
                              (red faced)
                    I can't breathe.
                              (pounds his own
                               chest)
                    Call 911, now.

GUSTAV keels over in the boxing ring. NATE gets out his
smartphone, calls the FIRST RESPONDERS with urgency -

                          FREEDOM FERRARA
                              (kneels down to
                               GUSTAV, holds him)
                    It's okay, GUS. It's all right,
                    just hold on! Help is on the way,
                    COACH. Don't you dare leave me.

As FREEDOM holds his TRAINER, GUSTAV lets out deep, dry
dying breaths - his HEART is giving out on him.

30 SECONDS LATER:

FREEDOM's TRAINER is NO MORE.

                          NATHAN TOWNHALL
                              (through the phone)
                    Yes, I need an AMBULANCE at
                    GUSTAV's GYM in COMPTON off of
                    CEDAR STREET. I need it,
                    yesterday!
                              (responding to the
                               voice on the
                               phone)
                    Our, my BROTHER's TRAINER, he's
                    had a heart-attack or something.
                    He's blue. He's - he's dying!

                          FREEDOM FERRARA
                              (crying painful
                               tears)
                    What, what the hell, man? He was
                              (MORE)

                    FREEDOM FERRARA (cont'd)
          just fine, healthy as a horse.
          What happened!?
                  (to GUSTAV)
          Don't leave me, GUS. Don't leave
          me alone.

                    NATHAN TOWNHALL
                  (to FREEDOM, hand
                   on his shoulder)
          You're not alone, FREEDOM. You
          never will be - we did what we
          could, bro. Let's let the first
          responders take care of this.

FREEDOM backs away from GUSTAV.

NATHAN consoles his dear friend, as best he can.

WE CUT TO BLACK:

INT. NATHAN'S SLINGSHOT VEHICLE - EVENING

Having left his IMPALA at the GYM - FREEDOM is driving
NATHAN's VEHICLE with him in the passenger. He is
maneuvering with utter awareness and quickness, in a type of
shock from seeing his BOXING TRAINER pass away so suddenly.

                    FREEDOM FERRARA
          The music isn't important. The
          boxing's not important. Seeing
          GUSTAV fade away like that makes
          me want to go see HEAVEN, right
          this second. That's where we're
          headed, okay?

                    NATHAN TOWNHALL
          - Let's go.

NATHAN puffs his INHALER twice.

                                              CUT TO:

INT. CHARLIE'S BUFFALO WINGS - EVENING

It's 5:55 PM - AGENT SASHA GRACE is seated, in a casual dress and comfortable women's shoes. She's dolled up.

She checks her watch.

                    CHARLIE
               (walks up to SASHA)
        What can I get you, SASHA?

                  AGENT GRACE
        I - I'm waiting for FREEDOM,
        FREEDOM FERRARA. Remember him?

                    CHARLIE
               (rubs his hands
                together)
        Ah, yes, MR. FREEDOM. How is the
        young man?

AGENT GRACE checks her watch again.

                  AGENT GRACE
        Well, CHARLIE, he's almost late,
        that's how. I'll take a 10-piece
        BUFFALO WING and a SALAD - when he
        gets here, we'll take a second
        salad; he'll give you his order.
        Okay? He should be here any minute
        now.

                    CHARLIE
        You got it, Ms. GRACE. 10-piece
        coming right up. Be patient, dear.
        Love always finds its way.

                  AGENT GRACE
        Oh. Uh, we're not in love -

                    CHARLIE
               (smirks)
        SASHA, I'm 63 years old. I've been
        running this here shop for 39 of
        those years. I know love on a
        woman's face when I see it. Can't
                    (MORE)

                    CHARLIE (cont'd)
          fool a fool.

                    AGENT GRACE
                      (blushing)
          I need a good pint of brew, too,
          CHARLIE.

                    CHARLIE
          You got it.

                                        CUT TO:

35 MINUTES LATER:

FREEDOM is late.

SASHA GRACE finishes her salad, nibbles on a buffalo wing.
She's now fed up.

                    AGENT GRACE
                      (chugs her beer)
          I've been ghosted. Jesus.
                      (to CHARLIE)
          I need the check, please.

                    CHARLIE
          He didn't show. Oh, well, that's
          on him, Ms. GRACE.

                    AGENT GRACE
                      (feisty)
          It's AGENT. AGENT GRACE.

                    CHARLIE
          Indeed - AGENT GRACE. You're with
          the F.B.I now? Congratulations!

                    AGENT GRACE
          Thank you, CHARLIE. I'm sorry for
          being confrontational. I'm just
          disappointed.

92.

                    CHARLIE
          A woman as pretty as yourself,
          abandoned on a date - you have
          every right.

                    AGENT GRACE
              (puts a 100 dollar
               bill on the table)
          Take care.

                    CHARLIE
          You, too, dear. And remember,
          it'll be all right. Don't worry.
          If it's meant to be, it'll happen.

AGENT GRACE leaves with her head stooped downward, her heart aching.

                                             CUT TO:

INT. FREEDOM'S BEDROOM - FLASHBACK - NIGHT

                                             YEAR: 2020

FREEDOM FERRARA and SASHA GRACE, young teens, lie with one another in the young man's bed. Their hands intertwined, making out.

                    FREEDOM FERRARA
          I love you, SASHA. With all my
          heart.

                    SASHA GRACE
              (endearing)
          I love you more.

                    FREEDOM FERRARA
          No. No. I love you more. More than
          the sun is from the farthest
          galaxy.

                    SASHA GRACE
          FREEDOM, you're my everything.
          I'll never give my heart to anyone
          else. I promise.

The two TEENS proceed to mingle, more romantically, smooching, caressing one another - they are deeply in love. They WERE -

                              CUT TO:

EXT. HEAVEN CARTER'S HOME - NATHAN'S MOM'S PLACE - EVENING

FREEDOM knocks at HEAVEN's front door: No Answer.

NATHAN, with his crutches, limps along to the back door, to peep inside. He sees nothing or no one, ostensibly.

                    FREEDOM FERRARA
                (from the front
                 door)
            Ms. CARTER? It's FREEDOM and NATE.
            Are you HOME?

                    NATHAN TOWNHALL
                (from the back
                 door)
            Mama! Open up. It's us!

No Response. This worries the YOUNG MEN -

NATHAN comes back around to the front.

FREEDOM kicks the door in, and he and NATE enter HEAVEN's HOME.

CUT TO:

INT. HEAVEN CARTER'S HOME - CONTINUOUS

The HOME is not very large, yet still it's a 3 BEDROOM, 1-and-a-HALF BATHROOM.

FREEDOM and NATHAN do not see HEAVEN when they enter.

They search the place for her. It's dark, it's quiet, it's ominous.

                    FREEDOM FERRARA
                 (checking the DEN
                  and BEDROOMS)
            HEAVEN!? You in here? It's us.

                    NATHAN TOWNHALL
                 (checking the
                  BATHROOMS)
            Mama. Where are you?

                                        CUT TO:

NATHAN finds his MOTHER in the HALF-BATHROOM - she has
Overdosed.

                    NATHAN TOWNHALL
                 (cradling his
                  MOTHER)
            What did you take!? Wake up!

FREEDOM storms to the BATHROOM, he sees the saddening scene
- he's helpless to help NATE's mom.

FREEDOM gets out his smartphone, calls the PARAMEDICS.

                    FREEDOM FERRARA
                 (into the phone)
            Yes, I'm at 387 FRANKLIN STREET,
            in COMPTON - there's an overdose
            victim here. She needs your help
            now! Please, hurry -
                 (the voice garbles
                  on other side of
                  phone)
            Okay, 10 minutes. Okay, we'll be
            here with her until you arrive.

FREEDOM is panicked, stressed to the T. NATHAN is
heartbroken.

                    NATHAN TOWNHALL
            FREE, she - she has no pulse, man.
            She's gone.
                 (howling somberly)
            No!

FREEDOM stands at the threshold, observing his BROTHER's pain, feeling the same - he stays strong, though, for NATHAN.

CUT TO:

EXT. HEAVEN CARTER'S HOME - EVENING

The PARAMEDICS have wheeled out HEAVEN's corpse from her HOME - they load her up in the AMBULANCE.

NATHAN's cheeks are flowing with tears.

FREEDOM's totally hurt - he's seen two people close to his heart dead on this day. He stops a PARAMEDIC.

              FREEDOM FERRARA
      Excuse me, what exactly caused the
      OD?

              PARAMEDIC
      - I'm not sure if you're aware,
      but this lady, she has HEROIN in
      her system. She has signs of
      FENTANYL overdose. She has track
      marks up-and-down her arms. She
      has marks between her fingers and
      her toes, too. Fentanyl is a death
      sentence. I'm so sorry for your
      loss, kid.

FREEDOM nods then attends to NATE, comforting him.

              FREEDOM FERRARA
      NATE, let's go, man. There's
      nothing more we can do. We - we
      got that meet, still.

              NATHAN TOWNHALL
        (defensive)
      Forget that meet, man. Forget it!

NATHAN shrugs FREEDOM away from him.

> FREEDOM FERRARA
> I know you're upset, bro. I get it. HEAVEN was just as much my mother, too. But KING BLUE expects us both, we're late.

> NATHAN TOWNHALL
> (nods, sniffling)
> Okay. Okay. Let's go.

CUT TO:

EXT. KING BLUE'S HQ - LATER

The brothers, FREEDOM and NATHAN, go up to the door of KING BLUE'S HQ after parking a block down the street.

The HQ has dozens of cameras at the top. The place is an architectural wet dream. It's magnificent, right in the middle of COMPTON. Blue and white all throughout.

KING BLUE is the leader of the LA CRIPS, as suggested by the name. His real name is RAOUL AZUL. He's shady looking, nefarious in the eyes.

KING BLUE, Black though he may be, is rich like a White-Man.

KING BLUE charges and taxes MR. FREEDOM and NATHAN for a lot of their income and inheritance - to maintain peace and prevent conflict, they pay up every time.

> GUARD
> (opens the peep-hole)
> What's the password?

> MR. FREEDOM
> White Rabbit.

The peep-hole shuts. The steel-door opens -

FREEDOM and NATHAN enter the HQ.

CUT TO:

INT. KING BLUE'S HQ - CONTINUOUS

The guys are accommodated by the GUARD and escorted to BLUE's OFFICE.

                    MR. FREEDOM
              (to the GUARD)
- We got the full 15 racks, man. Can we just leave it with you and dip?

                    GUARD
No. You gotta see the KING, his orders.

                    NATHAN TOWNHALL
              (under his breath)
Dammit.

                                CUT TO:

INT. KING BLUE'S HQ - MOMENTS LATER

FREEDOM and his brother stand before KING BLUE who's sitting in a actual throne eating grapes from a gold-bowl.

12 GUARDS stand ready for the would-be KING...

...KING BLUE has a dark complexion; he's BLACK and muscle bound. His hair is blue, in cornrows; he has a moustache and a beard, not fully grown out.

KING BLUE has face-tatts. Some of his front teeth are gold. He's a short man, only 5'8. He has on shiny rings, a couple of gold necklaces, and all blue attire from head to toe.

                  KING BLUE (RAOUL AZUL)
              (mid-discussion)
...What the hell do you think this is? A negotiation? You're giving me all of your money, everything you have, tonight! Or I am taking both of your heads and putting them on those walls as my trophies, ya got me?! Your MOTHER, NATE, she owed me over 100-GRAND.
                  (MORE)

                    KING BLUE (RAOUL AZUL) (cont'd)
          Didn't you know?

                    MR. FREEDOM
               (held back by KING
                BLUE's GUARDS)
          You motherfucker, you touch my
          brother and I'll -

                    NATHAN TOWNHALL
          My MOTHER is dead! What'd you give
          her, huh?

                    KING BLUE (RAOUL AZUL)
               (addressing
                FREEDOM and
                NATHAN)
          - You'll what, FREEDOM? You know
          our fathers, they were affiliated.
          I never told you that, huh? My
          father, GERALD NIXON, was a hitman
          for BRODY, as your father was a
          Heist-Man for him. Now, look at
          us. The beef is spreading into our
          relationship. You've been late,
          and late, and late. You've shamed
          me three times. I have a
          three-strike policy, and you good
          sirs just expired yours. And fuck
          your MOTHER, NATHAN, sincerely.
          She owed, she got her medicine.
          Just what the doctor ordered. No
          more borrowing, no more false
          promises, no more fiending for
          product.

12 more GUARDS start moving toward FREEDOM and NATHAN.

MR. FREEDOM signals to NATHAN to move away. FREEDOM goes to
fight all the men single-handed, while NATHAN backs far
away. NATHAN can hardly fight due to his disability.

KING BLUE's GUARDS confront FREEDOM, and the remainder move
toward NATHAN -

> MR. FREEDOM
> NO! Leave him alone!

With a temper like MICKEY MONTANA before him, MR. FREEDOM hooks, elbows, knees, dodges, and counters like clockwork -

He tries to surgically, precisely hurt all the men, implementing his BOXING TRAINING.

However, there are too many and they overpower MR. FREEDOM.

NATHAN pushes past the GUARDS and intervenes, trying to pull 2 of the men off of his brother. He can't. NATHAN starts having an ASTHMA ATTACK.

> NATHAN TOWNHALL
> (struggling to
> help FREEDOM)
> Get off of him, man! He don't know
> no better! I'm the reason the
> payment is late. Let him be.

At the utterance of this sentence, the wheezing NATHAN gets stabbed a few times in the lower region of the back and then in his one of his vital organs by KING BLUE himself.

It's a near fatal blow that drops the young man.

MR. FREEDOM, through the huddle of GUARDS, witnesses his brother get stabbed and flips his kill-switch.

> MR. FREEDOM
> (shocked,
> distraught)
> NO! NATE -

MR. FREEDOM manages to throw several men back off of himself.

He punches one's face in.

Kick's another's feet out and stomps his throat in.

He's able to kill one more by breaking his neck.

He's then restrained once more, for good.

                    KING BLUE (RAOUL AZUL)
                         (patronizing)
                    You - MR. FREEDOM, you were
                    brilliant! I should've made a
                    worker out of you rather than a
                    financier. You just signed your
                    own death certificate.
                         (signals the
                          remaining GUARDS)
                    Cuff him. Put blocks on his feet,
                    then dump him in the water. While
                    he's still breathing.
                         (concerning NATHAN)
                    Make an example of him. Feed him
                    to the dogs. I know they're
                    hungry.

The GUARDS start beating the living hell out of FREEDOM.

KING BLUE goes back to his THRONE and takes a seat, calmly.

                                                  CUT TO:

EXT. THE CANAL - LATER

A car pulls up to THE CANAL.

Three men exit the vehicle and then open the truck.

MR. FREEDOM is bound, tied, gagged - his hands in cuffs, his mouth duct taped. Rope is tied around his ankles as well as two cinderblocks.

No words. They just throw him in THE CANAL and drive off.

No one helps. NO ONE is there.

                                                  CUT TO:

EXT. THE WATER - CONTINUOUS

MR. FREEDOM is suffocating, drowning painfully.

He can't break free, and he can't swim upward due to the

restraints AND the blocks tied to his feet.

He struggles to the point of...dying...

                              CUT TO:

EXT. THE DREAM REALM - MOMENTS LATER

FREEDOM's life flashes before his eyes.

He sees his own birth, his own upbringing, everything both simultaneously and consecutively...

...MISTER FREEDOM even has glimpses of the Future. The terror, havoc, and tyranny to come. He can't make anything out of it. He merely senses the gravity of it all.

                              CUT TO:

                              3 HOURS LATER

EXT. THE CANAL - LATER

We see an orb of white light descend into the murky waters...

...Several or so seconds go by.

FREEDOM, still tied and bound, is basically thrown from the water onto THE DOCK area of THE CANAL.

                    FREEDOM FERRARA
                 (gagging, coughing
                    up water,
                    shivering)
             Um! Ummm! AaH!

FREEDOM is unable to speak due to the tape over his mouth and unable to see due to the fabric around his face covering his eyes.

He's bone drenched, shivering.

                              CUT TO:

The 'ORB' that saved FREEDOM exits the water, in behind him. The light fades, flying up far into the sky. There's something else on the DOCK with FREEDOM: it's AGENT ORANGE's PET CROW.

Neither Angel nor Demon...THE talking CROW is a creature with a connection to the spirit realm. He has found FREEDOM for a purpose.

                                        CUT TO:

EXT. THE DOCK - MOMENTS LATER

THE CROW takes the fabric away from FREEDOM's eyes.

The bird removes the duct tape from the YOUNG MAN's mouth.

FREEDOM is awed in seeing that a bird is the one to be helping him. THE CROW unties FREEDOM's hands and disconnects the cinderblocks from FREEDOM's feet, untangling the rope -

                    THE CROW
              (calming, hopping
               around FREEDOM)
          Hello, there. You were a bit tied
          up. Now you're free as a bird. Pun
          intended.

FREEDOM vomits up so much water up. It's disgusting. The water flows from his lungs, through his nose, all over the ground.

                    FREEDOM FERRARA
              (confused,
               breathing steam)
          A talking b-b-bird. I really have
          lost it.
              (passes out cold)

FREEDOM's perspective fades to black - he is down for the count.

                    THE CROW
              (scoffs)
          Not the "thank you" I was
          expecting, but oh, well. Gotta get
                    (MORE)

                    THE CROW (cont'd)
          you somewhere safe, my friend. But
          first -

THE CROW extends his WING. The bird reaches for FREEDOM's
RIGHT ARM and with its other wing the creature puts the
'LIGHT-RING' on FREEDOM's right MIDDLE FINGER. It's a
perfect fit.

- The LIGHT-RING is made of heavenly GOLD. It's a BAND, with
ANCIENT ARABIC engravings on it - the writing reads THE
LORD's PRAYER.

Power, glowing energy shields FREEDOM, encapsulating him in
pure light.

                    THE CROW
               (awed)
          I knew he'd be THE ONE for this.
               (looks up to the
                HEAVENS)
          Thank You, GOD.

THE CROW, as the energy grows around FREEDOM, puts his WINGS
on the YOUNG MAN and the two TELEPORT from the area -

                                        CUT TO:

INT. THE CROW'S NEST - THE LA HILLS - DAY

FREEDOM, his black nails now tarnished from the submersion,
lies within THE CROW's NEST. His outfit and shoes now dried
out on his body - both ragged, though.

It's a cave in the LA HILLS, near the HOLLYWOOD sign, where
the animal resides from time-to-time.

THE CROW has racked up various non-perishable foods, goods,
and other necessities. It's quite comfy in fact, considering
a "Bird" made it.

The bird gives FREEDOM nibbles of water and food from his
beak. He regains consciousness -

                    FREEDOM FERRARA
              (jolts awake)
          NATE!

                    THE CROW
              (flies back and
               perches)
          Woah! Listen, calm down.

                    FREEDOM FERRARA
          Where am I?! I've got to get back
          to NATE! He's alone out there -
          he...

                    THE CROW
          You're safe. You're safe. Breathe.
          Just Breathe, kid. It's okay.

FREEDOM inhales and exhales, slowly. He calms down.

He looks at his hands and his body, examining himself.

                    FREEDOM FERRARA
          I feel like I've been hit by a
          train, literally. But I can't
          remember as to why. It's all
          foggy. All I remember is not being
          able to take a breath. The water
          stinging my eyes and my nostrils.
          Then I went -

                    THE CROW
          - You went to THE DREAM REALM.
          Your spirit called to me. You are
          meant to be dead. Yet, here you
          are. Alive as can be, breathing
          and all.

                    FREEDOM FERRARA
          What are you?

                    THE CROW
          A bird. Nothing more, nothing
          less. My name is OPPIE. Now,
          FREEDOM FERRARA. The question
          really is, who are you? WHAT ARE
                         (MORE)

                    THE CROW (cont'd)
          YOU?

                    FREEDOM FERRARA
          I'm - I'm just a person. A person
          trying to get by. Trying to take
          care of my brother.
                    (gets up, anxious)
          I have to see about NATE. Look at
          me, sitting here talking to a bird
          that is supposedly talking back.

                    THE CROW
          You were attacked. You were thrown
          in THE CANAL, you drowned. What
          you are going to look for, it's
          not there. Your brother is gone
          now. I could only save you.

FREEDOM is hit with heavy flashbacks of the incident of his
drowning. It overcomes him like a shockwave.

                    FREEDOM FERRARA
                (weak, angered)
          Let me find out.

FREEDOM leaves the CROW'S NEST, using his hand as a crutch
against the cave wall, he stumbles out to the bright
sunlight. The sun nearly blinds the YOUNG MAN.

                    THE CROW
          Lord, grant me grace. And grant
          him STRENGTH.

OPPIE THE CROW flies and attaches itself to FREEDOM's right
shoulder, as he exits THE CROW's NEST.

                                              CUT TO:

EXT. LA TRAIL - MOMENTS LATER

FREEDOM walks. THE CROW talks.

                    FREEDOM FERRARA
                 (to THE CROW)
            What is it you want?

                    OPPIE THE CROW
            I, like you, want JUSTICE, my
            friend.

                    FREEDOM FERRARA
                 (limping, weak)
            Why are you resting on my
            shoulder?

                    OPPIE THE CROW
            Well, someone's got to tell you
            about your LIGHT-RING, right?

                    FREEDOM FERRARA
                 (looks at his
                  right hand)
            My what? LIGHT-RING, what's that?

                    OPPIE THE CROW
            A tool, to be used for good.
            Listen, kid, something is coming.
            A storm like you've never seen.
            But you - you can save this world
            from the Hell and the CHAOS that's
            approaching.

OPPIE THE CROW remains perched on FREEDOM's right shoulder -

                    OPPIE THE CROW
            You, you're one of the last hopes.

                    FREEDOM FERRARA
            I'm a nobody, man. I'm a rapper.
            I'm a boxer. A worker. I'm not a
            force for good. I'm not a savior
            of any kind, OPPIE -

                    OPPIE THE CROW
            That's your old life. That time is
            done. You will become a force for
            good. Not a savior, no - a
            WARRIOR. It's your FATE.

                    FREEDOM FERRARA
          All I want, right now, is revenge.
          I need to go to KING BLUE and
          avenge my brother. They, he killed
          NATHAN!

                    OPPIE THE CROW
          Revenge, my friend, is NOT
          justice. Revenge will bring you
          nothing but more pain. Trust me.
          Once you go down that path, it's
          very hard to turn back. Revenge
          can consume your soul, if you're
          not careful. Do flowers chase
          bees?

                    FREEDOM FERRARA
          We'll see about that. I'm going to
          end KING BLUE and his whole
          operation, tonight.

FREEDOM begins shadowboxing - OPPIE leaps from FREEDOM's
shoulder, flying above him.

As FREEDOM shadowboxes, he swings his RIGHT HAND and the
LIGHT-RING activates - a huge burst of LIGHT-ENERGY pushes
its way out of the RING, hitting the dirt then trees,
creating a path of FIRE. The fire doesn't spread, though.
Still, FREEDOM realizes he has a tremendous power.

CUT TO:

                    FREEDOM FERRARA
          Whoa. What is this thing, bird -
          really?

                    OPPIE THE CROW
          One of GOD's greatest creations.
          Forged in HELL, millions of years
          ago by ANGELS - known as
          LIGHTSMITHS. The LIGHT-RING is the
          ultimate tool. It's your purpose
          to have it, or else you would
          still be dead in that CANAL, being
          fished out by the authorities.

                    FREEDOM FERRARA
                (inquisitive)
            Can I use it against KING BLUE?

                    OPPIE THE CROW
            You have FREE-WILL, kid. I mean,
            for god's sake, your name is
            FREEDOM - you can do whatever you
            want with this power. Just know,
            the Lord giveth, the Lord can
            taketh away, too. Do what you
            will, kid. The choice is all
            yours. The LIGHT-RING is yours.
            Just don't turn to the darkness,
            don't give in. That's all I ask of
            you -
                (ascends)
            - Goodbye.

                    FREEDOM FERRARA
                (melancholy)
            Goodbye, bird.

THE CROW, having flown upward, fades into spiritual black smoke, disappearing from the scene.

FREEDOM feels the power within.

The LIGHT-RING syncs itself to FREEDOM's brain, heart, and central nervous system - he looks forward. His head held high; FREEDOM takes flight. The LIGHT-RING has given FREEDOM knowledge as well as power.

MR. FREEDOM ascends into the sky, uncontrollably. This is FREEDOM's first flight -

                                        CUT TO:

INT. KING BLUE'S HQ - DAY

KING BLUE, in mid-speech to his GOONS, relaxes in his THRONE.

> KING BLUE (RAOUL AZUL)
> The situation between I and KING RED, it's getting more tense and intense by the second. I've lost dozens upon dozens of MEN, soldiers. This is a WAR, it's all out. I don't think we'll ever achieve a legitimate PEACE. Gentlemen, this may be COMPTON's end. I -

FREEDOM FERRARA, in his worn-out civilian clothes, crashes into KING BLUE's HEADQUARTERS through the roof/ceiling using the LIGHT-RING - pure LIGHT invades the HQ, crumbling the top part of the HQ. Brick, ceiling debris, glass, it all comes falling hitting the GOONS and even KING BLUE -

FREEDOM lands on his feet, in his Chuck Taylors, in the HQ, in the middle of the GOONS.

CUT TO:

> FREEDOM FERRARA
> (breathing heavily)
> I'm sorry, did I crash your meeting, RAOUL?

> KING BLUE (RAOUL AZUL)
> (points to FREEDOM)
> You. You're supposed to be in the CANAL!
> (to his GOONS)
> Who is responsible for this, which one of you idiots didn't tie the bricks right!?

> FREEDOM FERRARA
> I died, last night, BLUE. Thanks to you. I'm back, though!

> KING BLUE (RAOUL AZUL)
> (to his GOONS)
> Get him. I want his head on a plate.

3 of the GOONS dominatingly walk towards FREEDOM.

He reacts - as does his LIGHT-RING.

                  FREEDOM FERRARA
        You motherfuckers.

FREEDOM swings with his RIGHT HAND (his ring hand), causing a giant fist made of LIGHT to appear. It knocks the 3 GOONS through the HQ wall in separate holes.

                  KING BLUE (RAOUL AZUL)
        Whoa! What the hell have you got
        there, FREEDOM, huh?

                  FREEDOM FERRARA
        Your end.

                  KING BLUE (RAOUL AZUL)
        Shoot him -

The other GOONS raise their pistols, firing upon FREEDOM.

FREEDOM simply holds up his right hand, stopping the BULLETS coming toward him from all the angles. The bullets fall to the ground -

                  KING BLUE (RAOUL AZUL)
        Where did you get these remarkable
        gifts?

                  FREEDOM FERRARA
        From GOD.

                  KING BLUE (RAOUL AZUL)
        Is that so? God is dead. Just like
        you're about to be.

                  FREEDOM FERRARA
        No, no, no. You all are the dead
        men.

                  KING BLUE (RAOUL AZUL)
            (to his MEN)
        This idiot thinks he's a
        superhero!
            (to MR. FREEDOM)
                (MORE)

                    KING BLUE (RAOUL AZUL) (cont'd)
               What, are you going to do,
               superhero? Kill us all with your
               newfound abilities?

DIVINE LIGHT surrounds FREEDOM's body - he starts to
overheat, as the LIGHT-RING makes him literally begin to
light up. His eyes become fiery, his fists do, too.

His body is scorching, supernaturally, and without intent -
the RING sends energy all throughout his body and
extremities. However, FREEDOM's clothes do not burn.

                    FREEDOM FERRARA
                         (strongly)
               I'm not going to kill you. But I
               also don't have to spare you.

                    KING BLUE (RAOUL AZUL)
               - From what? You going to shine us
               to death?

                    FREEDOM FERRARA
                         (charging up
                          atomically)
               From this.

FREEDOM shines like a human sun -

His body is now completely flowing with supernatural energy;
he can somewhat control it now.

                    KING BLUE (RAOUL AZUL)
                         (coming to a
                          realization)
               Oh, shit.

FREEDOM lets out a mega-burst of LIGHT POWER, causing KING
BLUE's HQ, and all those therein to be caught in an intense
blast. The explosion rocks the place - the HQ is eaten by
FIRE, from the inside and the outside.

                                                  CUT TO:

EXT. KING BLUE'S DECIMATED HQ - CONTINUOUS

KING BLUE and most of his ARMY are now deceased.

FREEDOM stands in the debris field of what used to be KING BLUE's HQ.

FREEDOM's LIGHT ENERGY goes back into his body, he regains his power balance, his homeostasis.

The YOUNG MAN notices his newly gifted LIGHT-RING is flashing -

FREEDOM FERRARA has a supreme VISION (his eyes roll into the back of his head, becoming solid LIGHT). This VISION has been given to him by the LIGHT-RING. It's telling him something...

- MR. FREEDOM pauses. He reaches in his pocket, getting out his AMERICAN-FLAG GAITOR/FACE-MASK. He puts it on.

...Almost possessed, FREEDOM levitates out of the scorched debris and takes flight away from the scene as the FIREFIGHTERS, PARAMEDICS, and COPS arrive to the destruction.

CUT TO BLACK:

CHAPTER IV - THE HUNTER OF MEN

                                        FADE IN:

EXT. THE STREET - NIGHT

MAJOR MANHUNTER is borderline deceased - he's been lying in garbage for hours, right on the verge of dying. His mind is not yet gone though.

He hears someone...SOMETHING.

                    MAJOR MANHUNTER
                (gasping deathily)
            Is - is someone there? Please,
            help me.

114.

CUT TO:

EXT. THE ALLEY - NIGHT

MAJOR MANHUNTER lies nearly dead, completely defeated in a mess of foul garbage that smells like pus and a dead body combined; unimaginable grime and filth merging with his blood, flesh, and bone.

He reaches his hand out one more time, in a gesture that someone, anyone, will help him...

...Today's the day -

- TIME STOPS. FATE CREEPS CLOSER TO MAJOR MANHUNTER. The ALLEY lights flickering, the wind breezing heavily, voices echoing through the radio-waves. SOMETHING enters our world that is not human.

This THING walks through a portal that suddenly emerges. The creature walks from the OTHER SIDE of the portal onto the EARTHLY PLANE, slowly, elegantly, almost limping down the ALLEYWAY with the help of a wooden walking-stick.

The PORTAL closes as quickly as it opened.

> THE DEALMAKER
> (demonically)
> At long last. Is that a call for help? It's like music to my ears. I've seen this moment for an eternity. I've seen your potential for as long as I've been alive. You called for help, and I've arrived, MAJOR MANHUNTER.

The creature, gripping its staff, is oddly handsome. He has on an all-white business suit that's tailored. He's pale - his eyes are large and WHITE. His hair is long and blonde.

His nails are lengthy. His garb is illusionary. His suit is only buttoned with one button on his blazer. His tie is black-and-white, made of a pattern.

The creature is a representative of LUCIFER. This creature

is THE DEALMAKER, merely an extension of SATAN - his EARTHLY PROJECTION, if you will.

The teeth of the monster are vampirical as he smiles, BLACK GOO foams in his mouth. He has unnaturally pointy white shoes.

There's even a fractured, glowing BLACK halo hovering above THE DEALMAKER's head.

His white eyes are made of pure hellfire - full of light, with pupils full of utter darkness. The creature is of unnatural power. He's THE MASTER OF THE FALLEN. This DEALMAKER has come to Bargain -

> MAJOR MANHUNTER
> (dying, sweating blood)
> Please, I'm hurt, real bad, man. I've been in this dumpster for a long time - I - I can't move. I was left here like this. Please, do something, sir. If you'll just give me a hand, I can pull myself up, I just know it.

> THE DEALMAKER
> (smirking)
> Okay, I will. But, first, we must - chat. I need reassurances. I need complete compliance from you, MAJOR. Do You Understand?

> MAJOR MANHUNTER
> (disturbed)
> Who are you?

> THE DEALMAKER
> (arrogant)
> - I DESTROY when I create. I AM what haunts the angels. I AM what confuses the children. I AM what fuels the fire. I AM the darkest of the dark, the destroyer of worlds, the thief of souls, the killer of all that is innocent. I
> (MORE)

                    THE DEALMAKER (cont'd)
AM HE, THE DEVIL.

                    MAJOR MANHUNTER
                (convinced)
            I'm not even surprised, actually.
            I'll take help from
            whoever...Goddammit, get me out of
            here! Y - you see God's not here
            to be with me...if what you have
            to offer is so much BETTER than
            show me -

THE MAJOR coughs septic blood. His breath is getting more
and more gentle, fleeting.

This DEVIL knows his next move. MANHUNTER just wants out of
the filthy dumpster and rid of his deathly injuries, no
matter what he has to do.

The decisions and motivations were already cemented;
MANHUNTER's FATE was sealed from the day he was born. He had
a choice, and he made it EONS ago. THE DEALMAKER's gestures,
ITS antics are simply theatrical formality at this point.

                    THE DEALMAKER
                (angelically, with
                 false nurture)
            You see, little one? How THE
            FATHER abandons us? He forsakes
            us. He shows not one trace of
            Himself to anyone except those He
            chooses to spoil. I will correct
            this mistake, sir. I was with you
            in all that CHAOS. I was with you
            when you killed, when you ate,
            when you slept. I've seen your
            ability far before My Father did.
            He's so "busy", that he forgets my
            Power!
                (switches to
                 demonic voice)
            They say I lose...yet, before I
            do, I gain so much. I change what
            is meant to not be changed. I
            empower those with no power.
            There's no good in this world, or
                        (MORE)

116.

>   THE DEALMAKER (cont'd)
>   even the universe. We're all just
>   in motion. Humanity is constant,
>   like time. You people fuck like
>   rabbits and give me all the filthy
>   souls I need to do my work. I'm
>   not trying to prove my worth to
>   THE FATHER. I'm trying to show him
>   how obsolete His work is. I KNOW I
>   LOSE. I DESERVE TO. All He
>   deserves is to be made a fool of.
>   He can't change minds anymore than
>   I can. But, perhaps I can change
>   THE SITUATION just enough to show
>   His foolishness. MAJOR...I'm here
>   to grant you your wish. Not only
>   am I going to get you out of this
>   dumpster. I'm going to provide you
>   with more power than you've ever
>   been able to even dream of. All
>   you have to do is accept my offer.

Before taking his last breath, MAJOR confides in the creature.

He says: "Yes, I accept."

Then we hear a death-groan.

>   THE DEALMAKER
>   (in MAJOR's face)
>   Are you ready, MANHUNTER?
>   (backs away)
>   Let the fun begin...

Standing near the WASTEPRO dumpster, THE DEALMAKER slams his wooden staff to ground, proceeding to chant a dark spell.

Metallic Light beams from the dumpster where MAJOR MANHUNTER lies.

Grinding of metal, scraping of metal, twisting of flesh, and MAJOR's god-awful screams are heard in the ALLEY-WAY.

Time is frozen there in that specific location as THE

DEALMAKER does his dirty work and transforms the MAJOR into something more than sinister: "THE MANHUNTER"

CUT TO:

EXT. THE ALLEY - NIGHT

THE DEALMAKER stands over his new MONSTROUS creation - holding a BLACK ring in his hand. This is the DARK-RING. MANHUNTER breathes like an ox...

                    THE MANHUNTER
                (unseen)
       - What is thy bidding, my MASTER?

                    THE DEALMAKER
       Behold. DESTRUCTION incarnate. I
       grant to you: the DARK-RING.

The DARK-RING floats from THE DEALMAKER's palm, landing itself onto MAJOR MANHUNTER's shadow, on his left middle finger.

- The DARK-RING is a HELL-BLACK BAND with a small BLACK STONE in it. The DARK-RING has divinely ingrained text on it in ANCIENT GREEK, written in the shiniest silver.

                    THE DEALMAKER
                (slams his staff)
       Make me proud, MANHUNTER. Make
       them hurt. Make them bow. Make
       them want to die. And, by any
       means necessary, find the
       LIGHT-RING and destroy its bearer
       - then, I will finally rule this
       world.

THE DEALMAKER converts himself into black smoke, disappearing from the scene.

MAJOR MANHUNTER is no longer human. He's a MONSTER, still lurking in the shadows, WE CAN'T SEE his new form yet.

CUT TO:

EXT. ALLEYWAY - NIGHT

MAJOR MANHUNTER is changed, completely. He's made of METAL. His flesh is gone - his head looks like a silver skull.

He has blue lights in his eyes, his eyeballs are gone.

He has 6 horns popping out the top of his head.

He's muscular, robotic, void of a soul - a platinum demon. He's more machine than man, now. He looks at the DARK-RING on his left-hand, with wonder.

              MAJOR MANHUNTER
        (impressed)
  What is this?

He extends his left arm out - the DARK-RING explodes with dark energy into the ALLEYWAY wall, blowing it to pieces. He smiles wide, exposing diamond-black teeth.

              MAJOR MANHUNTER
        (laughing
         robotically)
  Damn!

MAJOR MANHUNTER grabs a green poncho out of a trash-pile in the ALLEYWAY. He places it on himself, putting up the hood to cover his new METALLIC form.

                        CUT TO:

INT. KING RED'S UNDERGROUND BASE - NIGHT

KING RED is a BLACK MAN; taller, built quite stocky - no jewelry. He has lighter skin. He has green eyes. He has tattoos all the way up on his neck, extending from his stomach. He's got on a RED DICKIES' suit and red sneakers with red shoestrings. KING RED's hair is made of short, RED twists. He has pearly white clean veneers for teeth.

One of KING RED's SOLDIERS stands guard at the DOOR at his UNDERGROUND BASE -

There are three slow metallic knocks at the DOOR. KING RED's SOLDIER peeps through the peephole.

                    KING RED'S SOLDIER
          What's the password?

                    THE MANHUNTER
          Revenge.

                    KING RED'S SOLDIER
          We got an intruder! -

The DOOR is obliterated by blue light energy - a laser blast eviscerates the door.

                    KING RED (ARTO MILLS)
                (stands up from
                 his THRONE)
          What the hell is going on!?

MAJOR MANHUNTER enters KING RED's BASE - he slings the green poncho off of him. The men in the base experience pure horror at the sight of this skeletal robot, unable to even shoot their weapons out of complete fright.

He has a steel smile. He sees everything in infrared - targeting his targets.

With robotic tentacles that jump out of his body (from his legs, shoulders, arms), he grabs every GUARD in the ROOM.

MAJOR flexes his left-hand holding the DARK-RING, he balls his fist up; KING RED is snatched up off of his THRONE, telekinetically. His feet slightly drag the ground - MAJOR grips KING RED tighter, lifting him off his feet, high above his metallic head.

                    KING RED (ARTO MILLS)
          Who - WHAT ARE YOU?

                    MAJOR MANHUNTER
          I am decimation. I am
          resurrection. I AM - THE
          MANHUNTER.

121.

THE MANHUNTER snaps KING RED's neck like a twig without even touching him. The machine leaves the KING paralyzed AND still breathing. KING RED's eyes blink rapidly, the suffering written all over his now pale face.

                                        CUT TO BLACK:

We then hear (but not see) SCREAMING, horrific mutilation, all by the hands of THE MANHUNTER.

CUT TO:

INT. THE LA MUSEUM - AFTERNOON

FREEDOM walks into the LA MUSEUM, draped in a quasi-disguise, as to not be noticed -

He has on a big, long brown trench coat and a hat with sunglasses covering his face - his pants are torn and ripped, his shirt stained. He has on his trashed CHUCK TAYLORS. FREEDOM also, trying to be anonymous, has on his AMERICAN FLAG GAITOR/MASK, covering the bottom half of his face.

The LIGHT-RING glows on his right middle finger. The object begins pulsating. It becomes magnetic and literally pulls FREEDOM in a direction towards the back of the LA MUSEUM.

                      FREEDOM FERRARA
               (quietly)
     Whoa. Where are you taking me, you
     stupid RING?

Suddenly the LIGHT pours into the building as the LIGHT-RING glows supernaturally. The RING stops FREEDOM in front of a glass cage holding a HAMMER, of all things. The RING keeps glowing and pulsing with energy, as if it's calling out to this HAMMER -

                      FREEDOM FERRARA
               (reading the
               GLASS-CAGE tablet)
     "This HAMMER belonged to the
     mythical JOHN HENRY. The man who
     beat the steam-drill in a contest
     of wills. JOHN HENRY is a folklore
                    (MORE)

                    FREEDOM FERRARA (cont'd)
          hero, representative of heroism
          and willpower. He showed his
          fellow African-Americans that they
          too could overcome the odds. JOHN
          HENRY's HAMMER is a strong
          American symbol. JOHN HENRY stood
          up to the steam-drill and
          conquered it. He died battling it
          in the ultimate contest - but even
          in death, he has glory. The HAMMER
          was his tool, an extension of
          himself - it is rumored to weigh
          more than 2 MEN. Legend has it
          that no mortal, ordinary man can
          lift it. Found in 1892, the HAMMER
          signifies what men are capable of,
          even against relentless,
          formidable machines."

FREEDOM, after reading the tablet, succumbs to a severe
headache. He has a VISION - he sees the torment, the
enslavement, the corruption that JOHN HENRY had to face in
OLD AMERICA.

He sees JOHN HENRY's true death with his own eyes.

                                        CUT TO:

                    MUSEUM WORKER 1
                (to FREEDOM)
          Sir, we do not allow vagabonds
          into the MUSEUM. You also are
          disturbing our customers with your
          "light-show". I must ask you to
          leave, please.

FREEDOM doesn't respond. His mind is overwhelmed by the
Vision.

The LIGHT-RING forces him to step toward the glass-cage and
put his right-hand out to touch the glass.

                    MUSEUM WORKER 2
          Sir, did you not hear my
          colleague? You are not welcome
          here. This MUSEUM has fashion
                        (MORE)

122.

                    MUSEUM WORKER 2 (cont'd)
              standards and rules. If you do not
              leave right now, I will have to
              get the MANAGER and call the
              POLICE.

As soon as FREEDOM makes contact with the glass, the CAGE
shatters into thousands of pieces. The LIGHT-RING compels
FREEDOM to grab hold of the historical HAMMER.

As he takes hold of the tool, a giant blast of LIGHT bursts
out from the HAMMER and breaks through the roof and ceiling
of the MUSEUM -

                    MUSEUM WORKER 1
                     (to the MANAGER)
              We need to call 911, NOW!

The MUSEUM MANAGER begins to walk toward the spiraling
situation.

                    MUSEUM MANAGER
                    (turns a corner,
                     stands stunned)
              This is ridiculous, get that
              beggar out of -

LIGHT pours into FREEDOM's soul.

He starts physically changing - his clothes begin peeling
away in a fiery storm of transformation.

The LIGHT-RING synchronizes with the HAMMER, causing a type
of instantaneous metamorphosis.

MR. FREEDOM is consumed by THE LIGHT. His perception is of
nothing but LIGHT, flowing all around him everywhere and in
everything.

                                                CUT TO:

We Hear: "BANG!!!"

The MUSEUM ceiling collapses in some 30 yards at the other
end.

Lo and behold, THE MANHUNTER himself appears in the MUSEUM, crashing the scene. The MUSEUM spectators fill with anxiety and fear at the sight of this tall, bulky, sentient MACHINE-BEING in their presence.

THE MANHUNTER stands his ground - he extends his arm, pointing a finger at the TRANSFORMING FREEDOM FERRARA.

CUT TO:

                THE MANHUNTER
          (with a darkly
          robotic voice)
You! You hold the LIGHT-RING - my Master will be pleased. Give it to me OR die.
          (reads FREEDOM's
          mind)
Ah, FREEDOM FERRARA. 19 Years Old. COMPTON born and raised. An ORPHAN. Pathetic.
          (shouts to the
          VOID)
This is my opponent, MASTER? This weakling - just like his FATHER.

                FREEDOM FERRARA
          (shaking, flexing,
          on his knees)
What - how do you know my FATHER?

                THE MANHUNTER
Because, kid, I'm the one who murdered him - when I shot him, he squealed like a RAT. DRE FERRARA was a bum, a low-life thief who deserved to die. Killing him was a pleasure!

                FREEDOM FERRARA
          (overcome with
          emotion)
N - no.

Grabbing the HAMMER has caused a drastic reaction in FREEDOM FERRARA, not to mention the CHAOS of emotions that he is feeling after this heavy revelation.

The HAMMER becomes shiny, shedding its rust. The TOOL mutates into a DIVINE HAMMER - stronger than steel, more durable than a diamond. It morphs into a beautiful piece of craftsmanship:

- FREEDOM's transformation merely intensifies.

- THE MANHUNTER, with his head cocked to the side as he observes, is actually impressed by this abrupt CHANGE in FREEDOM FERRARA.

FREEDOM's skin turns blue, as do his dreadlocks.

His eyes turn milky white.

A RED CAPE forms across his shoulders, down his back.

An "F" appears on his chest.

White stars manifest themselves on him - on his chest, stomach, and forehead - ingrained in his skin.

Red and White stripes form on his stomach and on his lower back.

A bright golden HALO reveals itself atop his head.

And WHITE ANGEL WINGS made of pure LIGHT sprout from his back, through the red cape.

His jeans repair themselves. His CHUCK TAYLORS are turned into tall RED BOOTS.

His hands are covered with skin-tight Red Gloves - the glove on the right-hand forms under the LIGHT-RING. The AMERICAN-FLAG GAITOR merges itself with FREEDOM's face, transforming from fabric to a hardened faceguard that shield his mouth and nose.

The LIGHT-RING in collaboration/combination with the HAMMER has allowed FREEDOM to create a whole new projected image of himself, all through mental and spiritual effort.

SECURITY GUARDS surround both FREEDOM and THE MANHUNTER with their pistols drawn -

                    THE MANHUNTER
                 (surrounded by
                    SECURITY GUARDS)
               You all are in my way. This is
               between me and him - move or you
               will be moved.

                    GUARD LEADER
               Stand down or be fired upon.

                    MUSEUM GUARD
                 (surprised)
               What - what is that thing? A - a
               MACHINE?

THE MANHUNTER's blue laser-eyes flare up - he spins his head
360 degrees while shooting blue laser beams out of his eyes.
The 7 Surrounding SECURITY GUARDS are decapitated with
rapidity - heads roll in the LA MUSEUM.

FREEDOM reaches out, unable to stop the killings.

                    MISTER FREEDOM
               Everyone, get out of here, now!

FREEDOM stands tall.

The HAMMER in his left hand.

The LIGHT-RING on his right hand. FREEDOM regains his
health, strength, acuity, everything in a matter of moments.

                    MISTER FREEDOM
                 (to THE MANHUNTER)
               You, you killed my FATHER? What in
               the Hell are you?

                    THE MANHUNTER
                 (charges FREEDOM)
               I'm not the one to the fuck with,
               that's who.

As THE MANHUNTER flies with ferocity at MISTER FREEDOM, the
young man swings his newly acquired HAMMER -

When he strikes this machine-like entity, it takes

significant damage. It goes flying across the MUSEUM
interior, through panes of glass-cages, crashing directly
into a wall at full-speed.

                              CUT TO:

FREEDOM flaps his ANGEL WINGS and charges in the air at THE
MANHUNTER head-on, with god-speed.

THE MANHUNTER dodges FREEDOM, flipping its body in a split
second.

The HAMMER slams into the MUSEUM wall causing the entire
building to shake, to its foundations.

                    THE MANHUNTER
          Think Fast, hero.

THE MANHUNTER crawls backwards up to the ceiling and one of
his robotic arms turns into a BLASTER, raging with BLUE
ENERGY. THE MANHUNTER shoots from the ceiling, hitting
FREEDOM dead-on in the chest.

FREEDOM crashes through the floor, greatly affected by the
energy blast. The BLUE PLASMIC ENERGY burns strong making
the hole in the MUSEUM floor even larger.

                    THE MANHUNTER
                (hissing,
                  snake-like)
          You don't want to give me the
          LIGHT-RING? I'll take it from your
          dead body!

                              CUT TO:

THE MANHUNTER winds up his DARK-RING, balling his left fist
up - with it, the creature creates a BLACK ENERGY field, a
shield. THE MANHUNTER walks toward the hole in the floor,
preparing a defense -

                              CUT TO:

His HALO golden and illuminated, FREEDOM FERRARA rises from
the bottom level of the MUSEUM like a speeding bullet, with
the HAMMER and his LIGHT-RING activated. MISTER FREEDOM's

fist is saturated with glowing heavenly LIGHT. He hits THE MANHUNTER with all his power -

Still, though, FREEDOM is unable to penetrate the DARK-SHIELD created by THE MANHUNTER. The creature takes the hit and goes flying backward across to the other side of the building.

FREEDOM shoots another straight stream of heavenly-LIGHT energy at the monster, hitting the DARK-SHIELD again and it crashes through the MUSEUM wall into the CITY-STREETS of LA.

        CUT TO:

EXT. CITY STREET - METROPOLITAN AREA - AFTERNOON

THE MANHUNTER crashes into a vacant WHITE VAN, piercing it, he zooms through the other side of the VAN into a brick wall of a BANK - his DARK-SHIELD disables.

FREEDOM ascends into the air, as the LIGHT-RING swoops him off of his feet, taking him to face his opponent mano-a-mano.

     MISTER FREEDOM
  You're the threat that I was
  warned about. Who are you? Who is
  your MASTER?

THE MANHUNTER floats to his feet, squaring himself up. He reaches out with the DARK-RING, balling up his fist, activating the weapon -

     THE MANHUNTER
  Oh, oh, oh. I'm a lot more than a
  threat, boy. You can call me THE
  MANHUNTER. And my MASTER - well,
  let's just say, he's not of this
  world, this much I know. Now,
  catch -

THE MANHUNTER was merely distracting MISTER FREEDOM -

A forcefully levitating SCHOOL-BUS full of high-schoolers comes out of nowhere, smashing directly into MISTER FREEDOM

- he gets caught in the grill. The SCHOOL-BUS is being pushed by THE MANHUNTER's DARK-RING telekinetically.

The BUS crashes into a WASTEPRO TRUCK's TRAILER/HOPPER with FREEDOM in the front of it, causing an explosion.

CUT TO:

THE MANHUNTER flies into the sky - to examine the ground from the air.

                      THE MANHUNTER
        Not the wisest, I see.

FREEDOM pushes the BUS off of himself, falling onto one knee. He sees that the BUS is full, the flames are spreading about to consume the HIGH-SCHOOL STUDENTS.

FREEDOM shakes his head to regain his focus.

He uses all of his newfound strength, flipping the BUS on its wheels, on its normal side. FREEDOM then pries open the DOORS to the vehicle, he steps inside -

                      MISTER FREEDOM
                (to the students)
        Come on, everyone, hurry! I need
        you all to exit, to the best of
        your ability, before this thing
        catches fire completely -

THE MANHUNTER swoops down like the Grim Reaper, carrying MISTER FREEDOM away from the BUS.

The injured students are able to evacuate the fiery BUS, thanks to FREEDOM's efforts. His and THE MANHUNTER's battle resumes, as they strike one another with all their energy, going tit-for-tat.

CUT TO:

THE MANHUNTER puts FREEDOM in a headlock, choking the dear life out of the young man.

The villain then grabs MISTER FREEDOM by the cape, proceeding to swing him like a crash-dummy, far up into the

sky until the young man involuntarily rushes through a
CORPORATE BUILDING, near the top floor.

MISTER FREEDOM goes through the building, flying out of the
other side, breaking the windows due to the force.

AND WE CUT TO:

THE MANHUNTER approaches the CORPORATE BUILDING where
FREEDOM entered. The technological creature, harnessing his
DARK-RING's power, fires a BLACK-BLAST of DARK-MATTER into
the CORPORATE BUILDING, evaporating an entire floor of
civilians and workers.

>					THE MANHUNTER
>				(sing-songy)
>			Tsk, tsk. Superhero. Superhero.
>			Superhero. Look what you have
>			done!
>				(wrathful)
>			The thing about a hero is, no
>			matter how powerful they may be,
>			they can't be everywhere at once.
>			Isn't that right?

In mid-air, MISTER FREEDOM examines the destruction on
display. He gets teary eyed - the pain is unbearable.
FREEDOM aggressively attacks THE MANHUNTER, uppercutting the
minion with his HAMMER.

FREEDOM then brings his HAMMER downward, crushing it against
the metallic skull of THE MANHUNTER being - this causes the
machine-man to plumment to the cement. FREEDOM flies with
all of his might to strike THE MANHUNTER with the power of
the LIGHT-RING in tandem with JOHN HENRY's HAMMER -

THE MANHUNTER, temporarily, is incapacitated.

MISTER FREEDOM advances - swinging his HAMMER, violently. He
swarms the machine-creature with several intense blows. THE
MANHUNTER is weakened by the HAMMER, plus the LIGHT-ENERGY.
FREEDOM's ears are ringing, he's zoned out, focused only on
the ENEMY. THE MANHUNTER is down on his back - FREEDOM rears
back his HAMMER once more and ROARS.

                    MISTER FREEDOM
               (raises the HAMMER
                for a killing
                blow)
          This, this is for my FATHER, you
          son of a b-

Many, many POLICE SQUAD CARS have arrived at the scene -

MR. FREEDOM pauses; he doesn't strike THE MANHUNTER with the
kill blow:

                    POLICE OFFICER 1
               (pointing a gun at
                FREEDOM and THE
                MANHUNTER)
          FREEZE!

                    POLICE OFFICER 2
          KINETICS, stay where you are, do
          not move, or we will use lethal
          force!

FREEDOM snaps out of his trance. He realizes the gravity of
the situation, now.

ADVANCED MILITARY TEAMS have shown up to the pandemonium as
well.

                                                  CUT TO:

MISTER FREEDOM realizes the consequential nature of the
circumstances. He drops the HAMMER, puts up his hands,
backing away from THE MANHUNTER - FREEDOM's form changes
back to HUMAN. His HALO and ANGEL WINGS disappear.

He's half-naked, with only his damaged blue-jeans and his
AMERICAN-FLAG MASK (now fabric again) on still - everything
about him goes back to normal.

His skin is black again, his eyes become their typical
color, his CHUCK TAYLORS are ragged, his toes sticking out
of them.

The HAMMER lies on the ground - MR. FREEDOM grips his right
fist into a ball, the LIGHT-RING still flowing with

insurmountable energy.

THE MANHUNTER's platinum machine form recedes back into his body, his power withdraws into the DARK-RING - this awes the authorities. He becomes HUMAN again, dressed in his work-attire he was wearing before striking the deal with the DEALMAKER. MAJOR MANHUNTER puts his hands up, getting down on his stomach -

MAJOR has a giant human smile across his face - one of villainy.

MISTER FREEDOM falls to his knees, with his hands behind his head.

                    FREEDOM FERRARA
    I - I only wanted to help. I
    didn't mean for any of this to -

                    POLICE OFFICER 3
    - Shut your pie-hole and get your
    ass up, right now.

FREEDOM stands -

                    MAJOR MANHUNTER
              (maniacally
               giggling)
    Hahaha!

POLICE OFFICER #1 aims his gun at THE MANHUNTER, point-blank, while standing over him:

                    POLICE OFFICER 1
    What are you laughing about? Wait
    a second, MAJOR MANHUNTER? Is that
    you?

                    MAJOR MANHUNTER
              (on his stomach,
               chin to the
               ground)
    The one and only, you bet your
    sweet, pickled ass.

                    POLICE OFFICER 1
               (into his comms,
                to the other
               OFFICERS)
          Code-33, we have a BAIL BONDSMAN
          in our custody, how shall we
          proceed?

                    MAJOR MANHUNTER
               (cocky)
          - Don't forget, I'm a
          BOUNTY-HUNTER, too.

A pause. The MILITARY LEADER comes from behind the POLICE
OFFICER, armed with an automatic weapon -

                    MILITARY LEADER
               (to POLICE OFFICER
                  #1)
          Bail Bondsman or no, if he's
          KINETIC, take all the precautions
          necessary. Don't be blinded. We
          have to treat him like all the
          others -

                    POLICE OFFICER 1
          Yessir, understood.
               (to THE MANHUNTER)
          Put your hands behind your back,
          now.

                    MAJOR MANHUNTER
          And here I thought I was going to
          get some special treatment - I'm
          practically one of you!

The OFFICER, with help, slaps cuffs on MAJOR MANHUNTER,
lifting him off the ground onto his feet -

                    POLICE OFFICER 3
               (smacks MAJOR
                upside the head
                with his PISTOL)
          You're a KINETIC piece of trash;
          we saw what you did. YOU killed at
          least 40 people in that building
                         (MORE)

>   POLICE OFFICER 3 (cont'd)
>   up there! You fucking scumbag.
>
>   MAJOR MANHUNTER
>   It wasn't me; it was the
>   metallic-man, I tell ya. Do I
>   really look like I could do
>   something like that, fellas?
>
>   POLICE OFFICER 2
>   (spits at MAJOR's
>   feet)
>   Get him and that other FREAK out
>   of my sight.
>
>   CUT TO:

The COPS, the MILITARY MEMBERS, they suffocate FREEDOM with
their numbers, arresting him immediately - he doesn't resist
one bit.

The COPS have arrested MAJOR, too. The authorities try to
take the DARK-RING off of THE MANHUNTER - it will not move a
microinch, it won't come off.

They also try to remove the LIGHT-RING from FREEDOM; it
comes right off of him. They place it in a special
POWER-CONTAINER. It takes FIVE MEN to lift FREEDOM's HAMMER
- they contain it, too.

FREEDOM is placed in a MILITARY VEHICLE.

MAJOR is put in the back of a highly advanced POLICE
CRUISER.

The authorities take their new prisoners away from the
CHAOS:

                                              CUT TO:

INT. PRESS-CONFERENCE - CITY HALL - EVENING

Over a dozen reporters in front of a podium in CITY HALL -
there are other observing citizens standing behind the
reporters, curiously.

The REPORTERS are going back-and-forth with the DISTRICT ATTORNEY, YELENA STEIN -

MADAME D.A YELENA STEIN is snow white, blonde, fairly tall at 5'9 - she has rosy cheeks. She's dressed in a pantsuit, with tall heels on that make her appear even taller. She has on lipstick, and her nails are glossily painted.

                    THE D.A - YELENA STEIN
          (mid-sentence,
           into the
           microphone)
...I'm not running for reelection but, even so, I have a job to do until I leave office. We are still going to prosecute both KINETIC individuals to the fullest extent of the law. We will not tolerate such unchecked power in the great state of CALIFORNIA. These beings, they do not deserve due process - look at the damage they caused. The lives lost because of their recklessness and near omnipotent strength. There's no place for it, especially in LOS ANGELES. We have a responsibility to tame these KINETIC persons. Their abilities, they're enough to scare God. We'll see to it that these beings never see the light of day, again. Justice will be served -
          (points to a
          REPORTER)
Now, to your questions. Shoot.

                    REPORTER
Where did these KINETIC beings come from? Are they even human?

                    THE D.A - YELENA STEIN
We are still investigating the specifics. I expect to have more information very soon. From what we understand, right this moment, is they're both CALIFORNIA
                    (MORE)

                              THE D.A - YELENA STEIN (cont'd)
                    CITIZENS, one an Angeleno, the
                    other a Comptonian; they somehow
                    became KINETIC through unnatural
                    means. That's all I can say, for
                    now.
                              (points at another
                               REPORTER)
                    Next question -

The REPORTERS get antsy. D.A YELENA STEIN works the room -

CUT TO:

INT. THE JAIL - SUPER-CELL SECTION - NIGHT

THE MANHUNTER is being held in THE JAIL in the SUPER-CELL
SECTION, awaiting sentencing and punishment.

MAJOR MANHUNTER is near the end of the section.

                              THE MANHUNTER
                              (looking at the
                               CAMERA in his
                               CELL)
                    Nice setup. But do you all think
                    this place can hold me? We shall
                    see.

                              MYSTERY INMATE
                              (in a thick
                               RUSSIAN accent)
                    And who might you be, my arrogant
                    friend?

The VOICE of the MYSTERY INMATE comes from the SUPER-CELL
beside THE MANHUNTER - this MYSTERY INMATE lurks in the
shadows, not visible.

                              THE MANHUNTER
                    I'm an APEX PREDATOR, that's who.

                              MYSTERY INMATE
                    Hmm? Interesting - are you an ally
                    or foe?

136.

                    THE MANHUNTER
          Neither. I'm the end of worlds.

The MYSTERY INMATE appears from the SHADOWS of his CELL to
reveal himself...

...He is THE EUTHANIZER/DR. VLADIMIR MILSTEIN.

                    DR. VLADIMIR MILSTEIN
                      (with a pure
                      RUSSIAN accent)
          That's some tough talk coming from
          a MAN in a cell.

                    THE MANHUNTER
          I am NO MAN. I AM THE MANHUNTER.

                    DR. VLADIMIR MILSTEIN
          Quite a name. I am THE EUTHANIZER.
          Formally, DR. VLADIMIR MILSTEIN.

MAJOR goes to the front of his SUPER-CELL, to talk through
the small opening and to hear better.

                    MAJOR MANHUNTER
          You - you're that mad scientist
          from NEW YORK CITY. You were
          defeated by-

                    DR. VLADIMIR MILSTEIN
                      (interrupts MAJOR)
          No, not defeated. DELAYED. That
          was a minor hiccup, if you will.

                    THE MANHUNTER
          Coming from a guy who was
          outsmarted by a Shih-Tzu.

                    DR. VLADIMIR MILSTEIN
          THE LITTLE-MAN is not just a
          Shih-Tzu, my friend. He - he is
          the KEY to the Future. He and I,
          we have unfinished business - I
          will meet him again, and I'll have
          my vengeance upon him and the CITY
          of NEW YORK, you'll see. Don't
                         (MORE)

                    DR. VLADIMIR MILSTEIN (cont'd)
discount me.

                    THE MANHUNTER
You're a glorified vet, then, huh?
What, you couldn't pay the bills,
so you took up villainy?

                    DR. VLADIMIR MILSTEIN
Supervillainy, actually. And
prodding me, good sir, will not
get you out of here.

                    THE MANHUNTER
No, no, it won't. But it'll get
one of the GUARDS down here to try
and shut me up. Then, then I will
get the hell out of here.

                    DR. VLADIMIR MILSTEIN
How so?

                    THE MANHUNTER
I have a WMD on my left middle
finger. The DARK-RING - I can read
your mind, doctor. I can smell
your fear.

                    DR. VLADIMIR MILSTEIN
Don't confuse my concern for fear.
I, like you, am just biding my
time. I fear nothing. I fear no
one. My heart, my goal in life, is
to find that Shih-Tzu before it's
too late. Nothing else matters.

                    THE MANHUNTER
                (using telepathy)
You've nearly perfected THE BANE
ALGORITHM, and you need that dog's
corpse to get it done.

                    DR. VLADIMIR MILSTEIN
Very good. I'm impressed. This
DARK-RING, where did you discover
it?

                    THE MANHUNTER
                (observing the
                  RING)
            It's a gift from THE UNDERWORLD,
            let's just say. It has given me so
            many abilities - my opponent is no
            dog, either. He, too, has a RING -
            the yin to my yang. I need his
            RING, then, only then, can I
            unleash HELL on this EARTH.

                    DR. VLADIMIR MILSTEIN
            See, me, I'm a realist. I don't
            believe in Hell. I believe in
            science.

                    THE MANHUNTER
            Well, you should believe in Hell,
            EUTHANIZER. IT BELIEVES IN YOU.

                    KINETIC SUPER-CELL GUARD
                  (loudly)
            Shhh! Shut up you two or I will
            gas the both of you.

                    THE MANHUNTER
            Raymond Brockman, lives at 2247
            Airline Avenue. Your wife is
            pregnant. Your bills are late.
            Your boss is considering firing
            you -

                    KINETIC SUPER-CELL GUARD
                  (gets close to the
                   SUPER-CELL)
            If you don't shut the hell up,
            I'll -

THE MANHUNTER activates his DARK-RING - he extends his ARM
to grab the GUARD. When he seizes him, he drains the GUARD
of his life-force. MAJOR MANHUNTER starts morphing, again,
into his ROBOTIC METALLIC FORM - the GUARD turns into a pile
of bones, there's the smell of burning flesh, hair, and shit
in the KINETIC SECTION now.

THE MANHUNTER blasts the SUPERCELL to pieces, breaking open

the DOOR like its cellophane. A fiery explosion happens - startling even THE EUTHANIZER.

15 GUARDS with KINETIC PREVENTION WEAPONRY open fire upon THE MANHUNTER, with nearly zero effect.

The MACHINE-BEING slaughters them like cattle. THE MANHUNTER darts upward through the ceiling AND roof infrastructure with utter intensity - the backup GUARDS and OFFICERS reach the hole in the ceiling with their guns pointed upward.

THE MANHUNTER vanishes from the scene.

>   DR. VLADIMIR MILSTEIN
>   (with his head
>   down)
>   Ha-ha-ha. So, the end has begun -

                                             CUT TO:

INT. THE COURTHOUSE - KINETIC COURT - NIGHT

FREEDOM has a lawyer present (a PUBLIC DEFENDER): CARISSA BRONTE - there's no jury, no spectators. He holds his front-triple-cuffed hands in a prayer position, whispering to GOD ALMIGHTY. Even his ankles are cuffed.

CARISSA BRONTE goes through procedure for KINETIC proceedings. She's a poteat young White lady; only 5'5. She has silky brown hair - she's dolled up with makeup. She has on a business skirt, with a dressy blouse. She's even wearing a female tie.

The JUDGE, wide awake, looks upon MISTER FREEDOM very cautiously and closely. JUDGE HARRIS is a powerful dark-skinned Black woman who means business - she has long, natural hair that shines in the light. She's built like a brickhouse. She's got on a traditional black JUDGE's robe. Her nails are blue.

>   JUDGE HARRIS
>   (stoic and stern)
>   - Let it be known to the
>   DEFENDANT; this is merely a
>   sentencing hearing for the
>   accused. What do you have to say
>   (MORE)

                    JUDGE HARRIS (cont'd)
          for your client, MS. BRONTE?

                    CARISSA BRONTE
          Ma'am, FREEDOM FERRARA has been
          accused of superhuman KINETIC
          activity, destruction of public
          property, and vigilantism, among
          other charges. I ask the COURT to
          consider lessening the sentence,
          if MR. FERRARA agrees to
          cooperate.

                    JUDGE HARRIS
          The COURT denies that motion. The
          defendant will be COMMITTED to
          LIFE-CONTROL, where he will spend
          the rest of his life. If he
          displays any type of SUPERHUMAN
          KINETIC ability within those walls
          there, he may face DEATH. Is that
          understood, MS. BRONTE?

                                             CUT TO:

The WALLS, FLOOR, the JUDGE's STAND, the TABLES all begin to shake in the COURTROOM, as if an earthquake is occurring.

Randomly, the DOORS to the COURTROOM are barged open with BLUE LIGHT ENERGY - THE MANHUNTER bursts into THE COURTROOM.

FREEDOM stands up, shocked by THE MANHUNTER's ARRIVAL...

...MR. FREEDOM reaches out to the air with his cuffed hands - calling for his HAMMER.

                    THE MANHUNTER
          ---Death is here, madam.

THE MANHUNTER rushes JUDGE HARRIS, destroying her with one motion -

                    FREEDOM FERRARA
                         (pleading)
          No!

CUT TO:

INT. THE LABORATORY - LOS ANGELES - CONTINUOUS

THE LIGHT-RING is being held magnetically in a very high-tech bulletproof examination container within the LA LAB -

However, SCIENTISTS are attempting to dissect FREEDOM's HAMMER - they have it under a UV LIGHT on a high-tech table. Suddenly, the HAMMER starts shaking on its own. Then, ZOOM, BOOM, BANG!!! -

The HAMMER roars through the LAB WALLS, breaking through at the speed of LIGHT.

The RING attempts to leave the LAB but is unable. It simply ricochets back-and-forth in the container. The HAMMER leaves the LAB like a shooting star -

                    SCIENTIST 1
                (astonished)
        What the...?

                    SCIENTIST 2
                (in awe of the
                 huge holes in the
                 WALLS)
        We've now got a lot of explaining
        to do to DR. BROOM.

                    SCIENTIST 1
        Make sure the RING is secure -

                    SCIENTIST 2
        The contraption seems to be
        working. It's still there. It's
        trying to get out, but can't -

                    SCIENTIST 1
        Good, let's keep it that way. Now
        where in the hell is the HAMMER
        going?

CUT TO:

INT. THE COURTROOM - NIGHT

In a matter of seconds, FREEDOM's HAMMER enters THE COURTROOM.

THE MANHUNTER is walking toward CARISSA BRONTE.

In the nick of time, the HAMMER gets into FREEDOM's hand - he transforms in a split second, in his AMERICAN-FLAG uniform, RED BOOTS, AMERICAN-FLAG MASK, RED GLOVES, everything minus the LIGHT-RING. His golden HALO and white ANGEL WINGS reappear, too.

FREEDOM breaks his handcuffs and anklecuffs with pure brute strength.

THE MANHUNTER goes to claw at CARISSA. Before the creature can harm her, MR. FREEDOM stops the creature's swipe by grabbing his wrist, stopping him from killing the attorney.

              THE MANHUNTER
          (notices there's
          no LIGHT-RING on
          FREEDOM's hand)
    Hmm. Where's the LIGHT-RING?

              MR. FREEDOM
    I don't need it to stop you, this
    time.

              THE MANHUNTER
    You may not need it, BUT I DO.

MANHUNTER starts to overpower FREEDOM -

              MR. FREEDOM
          (to his lawyer)
    Run, now!

THE MANHUNTER hits FREEDOM with all of his strength with his other arm and hand - knocking him through several layers of walls.

CARISSA runs with all her might -

                              CUT TO:

INT. THE COURTHOUSE HALLWAY - CONTINUOUS

AGENTS in the COURTHOUSE have various weapons, prepared to take the heat to THE MANHUNTER - one of the agents is SASHA GRACE.

Some agents have assault rifles. Some have shotguns. SASHA has a measly pistol sidearm.

- The bullets merely ricochet off of the MONSTER.

THE MANHUNTER charges the many AGENTS - there are about 20, all firing upon MAJOR. He relaxes his two METALLIC arms; BLUE WHIPS appear from his wrists. He winds them up, whipping the ground and ceiling, simultaneously, causing caustic, blue-tinted flames to consume the interior of the COURTHOUSE HALLWAY. THE FIRE RISES...

CUT TO:

...MAJOR MANHUNTER, as he flexes his newfound HELLWHIPS, starts mutating. His form takes on a WOLF-like appearance.

BLUE LIGHTS appear in his arms, legs, hands, and feet - his teeth get sharper.

His ears grow to look like a wolf's, yet he maintains his humanoid ROBOTIC structure - THE MANHUNTER now has a tail made of steel. His shiny-black teeth grow two huge K9 FANGS.

THE MANHUNTER grabs 2 AGENTS with his HELLWHIPS - incinerating them, instantaneously. He then shoots blue beams from his eyes, terminating more of the defenders; some of them run away, horrified.

- THE MANHUNTER withdraws his blue HELLWHIPS back into his arms.

CUT TO:

AGENT SASHA GRACE, bravely, unloads her recessive pistol, failing to do much of anything to THE MANHUNTER - the bullets bounce off of him, unable to penetrate.

The MONSTER walks up to her. He raises his huge, muscular, supernaturally technological arm to swing at AGENT GRACE.

She flinches, shuts her eyes at the sight of THE MANHUNTER - before he can meet her with a deathly slap, MAJOR's SILVER ARM is caught by MR. FREEDOM.

MR. FREEDOM saves AGENT GRACE, standing in front of her, he shields her - his ANGEL WINGS fluttering.

                    AGENT GRACE
                 (surprised by the
                  save, to FREEDOM)
        Who are you?

                    MR. FREEDOM
        The guy who just saved your ass,
        now get out of here before he
        tears this pl-

ROOKIE AGENT GRACE scatters far away from the ongoing battle.

THE MANHUNTER uppercuts FREEDOM with his free arm. MISTER FREEDOM gets catapulted into the ceiling and out onto the roof.

He adapts very fast. Jumping back down through the hole to confront MAJOR MANHUNTER.

MR. FREEDOM comes down with his HAMMER, nailing MANHUNTER into the FLOOR, several feet.

                    MR. FREEDOM
        You bastard. I have my HAMMER,
        you're going down!

THE MANHUNTER elevates by levitating. He gets on even ground with FREEDOM once again.

                    THE MANHUNTER
        And, I have CERBERUS -

                    MR. FREEDOM
        What is th-

From behind, FREEDOM is grabbed by the THREE-HEADED Demon-Dog: CERBERUS, of mythological legend.

Like MAJOR MANHUNTER, CERBERUS is very ROBOTIC - yet the creature has a fleshly composition underneath all of the METAL. It's huge. The THREE-HEADED DOG has red eyes, it is fueled by HELLFIRE. The main head of the monster grabs FREEDOM and doesn't let go; the other two heads participate in the mauling.

CERBERUS man-handles MR. FREEDOM like he's silly putty.

The HELLISH CREATURE slams FREEDOM to the ground, raises him up to hit the ceiling - it does this several times, as FREEDOM yells at the top of his vocals.

CUT TO:

                    COURTHOUSE AGENT
        Holy Mother of God.

THE MANHUNTER runs against the COURTHOUSE HALLWAY walls - racing toward the agents who have stayed to fight him.

He, like the machine he is, eliminates them with great power and physicality, near effortlessly.

CUT TO:

MR. FREEDOM lunges off of his back, kicking the beastly machine-ANIMAL off of himself. He swings his mighty HAMMER to the main head, knocking the MONSTER nearly 25 yards away from him all the way down the COURTHOUSE HALLWAY - it hits the wall, cratering it, at a ridiculous velocity.

MISTER FREEDOM refocuses on THE MANHUNTER, chasing him down - as he gets to him, MAJOR turns around faster than hell, grabbing FREEDOM by the throat.

FREEDOM hits MANHUNTER's arms with his own, with very little luck.

                    AGENT GRACE
              (with a SHOTGUN
               in-hand)
        Let him go, NOW.

MANHUNTER squeezes FREEDOM's jugular even tighter. MR. FREEDOM gasps, lethally.

                    THE MANHUNTER
              - Or what, you little bitch?

                    AGENT GRACE
                      (furious)
                   To hell with this.

AGENT GRACE runs up to THE MANHUNTER, squeezing the SHOTGUN
trigger while pointing the weapon square at the back of the
CREATURE's head. It actually does minor damage, taking a
small chunk out of it; but the chunk is replaced with more
platinum, THE MANHUNTER can regenerate.

MANHUNTER drops FREEDOM - MR. FREEDOM falls flat, nearly out
of breath. He coughs up blood, it saturates his MASK, coming
out of the small openings on it.

                                        CUT TO:

CERBERUS reestablishes its footing and awareness -
proceeding to roar its way down the COURTHOUSE HALLWAY to
meet its MASTER, THE MANHUNTER.

                    THE MANHUNTER
                     (to CERBERUS)
                   Get her.

Salivating black-blood, CERBERUS charges AGENT GRACE -

FREEDOM fights his way to his feet. Stunned but fully
prepared for WAR. He flies forward like an ARCHANGEL at his
opponent(s). He throws his HAMMER at MANHUNTER, injuring the
machine.

Then MR. FREEDOM grabs CERBERUS before it can harm AGENT
GRACE - he takes the DEMONIC DOG through the CEILING/ROOF
with tremendous force.

CUT TO:

EXT. COURTHOUSE ROOF - MID-AIR - CONTINUOUS

FREEDOM goes for the tail - he then whips the ANIMAL around,
around, and around, gaining more gravity; MR. FREEDOM slings
CERBERBUS into the concrete ground of the LA CITY STREET.

The mythological ANIMAL descends underground, severely hurt by FREEDOM's supernatural toss.

CUT TO:

INT. THE COURTHOUSE HALLWAY - MOMENTS LATER

THE MANHUNTER, seeing FREEDOM's magnificent HAMMER, attempts to pick it up - AGENT GRACE is awesomely terrified at this sight.

>   MAJOR MANHUNTER
>   (struggling to
>   pick up the
>   HAMMER)
>   C'mon. You will work for me, now.

The HAMMER glows, flashing light on-and-off - as if it's calling out to FREEDOM and disobeying MANHUNTER.

CUT TO:

THE MANHUNTER tries and tries again to pick up the HAMMER, with no success. He struggles so badly that the floor of THE COURTHOUSE HALLWAY starts to cave in due to his weight, his feet flexing, and the HAMMER's magical ability preventing ANY DEMONIC being from accessing its POWER -

CUT TO:

>   MAJOR MANHUNTER
>   Damn it to hell! Screw it.
>   FREEDOM, you're a dead man!

THE MANHUNTER leaps through the ceiling/roof, making another tremendous hole in the upper COURTROOM infrastructure.

- AGENT GRACE looks up to the sky through the hole, trembling with fear. More AGENTS pour into the COURTHOUSE HALLWAY, zooming past her, chaotically.

CUT TO:

EXT. THE COURTHOUSE ROOF - NIGHT

The sky is thick with gray overcast, cloudy. Thunder and lightning stir about.

MANHUNTER and FREEDOM look at one another with death-stares, facing each other one-on-one.

THE MANHUNTER charges MISTER FREEDOM, hitting him in the stomach with his steel-tail - FREEDOM spits up more blood. The force drives him through one of the higher buildings of the COURTHOUSE.

CUT TO:

EXT. COURTHOUSE BUILDING #4 - NIGHT

FREEDOM fixes himself. He appears from BUIDLING #4, brushing his shoulders off of cement, brick, the works.

He calls for his HAMMER, mentally, it comes to him speedily, in a matter of seconds. The HAMMER lights up, extravagantly.

CUT TO:

THE MANHUNTER flashes toward FREEDOM, showing up above him a couple of feet.

MAJOR proceeds to reverse uppercut him with both fists and arms - beating him to the ground.

CUT TO:

EXT. LOS ANGELES CITY STREET - CONTINUOUS

Slightly incapacitated, FREEDOM struggles subsequent to meeting the ground after such a blow. THE MANHUNTER isn't letting up - the MONSTER proceeds to punch MR. FREEDOM over-and-over. Then, CERBERUS recalibrates, tag teaming with its MASTER, and both CREATURES try to tear MR. FREEDOM to shreds -

CUT TO:

FREEDOM, on his back, holding on for dear life, reaches out his hand to the FULL MOON.

                    FREEDOM FERRARA
      Lord Jesus, Forgive me.

MR. FREEDOM, due to the combination of MANHUNTER AND CERBERUS, lets out a dead man's yawn - a climactic breath exits his mouth. FREEDOM DIES in this MOMENT.

                              CUT TO:

                    MAJOR MANHUNTER
          (to the now
           deceased MR.
          FREEDOM)
     I may not be able to pick up the
     HAMMER, kid. But I guarantee you,
     I WILL FIND THAT LIGHT-RING. I
     promise you; I will find it. And
     NOBODY will be able to stop me!
     There are 215 bones in the human
     body and there are 9.3 BILLION
     people on this Earth this very
     second. I will break every single
     goddamn human bone there is and
     build a throne on their empty
     corpses. I will utterly destroy
     them. There will be no life. There
     will only be HELL.

THE MANHUNTER and CERBERUS, who can also fly, leave the scene through the LOS ANGELES NIGHT-SKY - they leave FREEDOM's breathless body on the CITY STREET.

FREEDOM, due to losing so much life, is drained of his power. He takes on his regular form, as the HAMMER leaves his grip, rolling over onto the asphalt. It then blasts itself into OUTER SPACE toward the HEAVENS - out of sight, out of mind of the witnesses.

CUT TO:

Out of all the FIRST RESPONDERS, AGENT SASHA GRACE spots MR. FREEDOM first. She identifies him, as soon as she sees him, now that he's in HUMAN FORM.

                    AGENT GRACE
                   (shocked)
              F - FREEDOM! Oh, my God.

AGENT GRACE, followed by other OFFICERS, PARAMEDICS, and
MILITARY MEMBERS, tries to give FREEDOM CPR, unsuccessfully.
He is dead -

                    AGENT GRACE
                   (looks up to the
                    HEAVENS and weeps)
              No. Please, don't go. Stay with
              me.
                   (cradles FREEDOM)
              I - I love you, FREEDOM. Come
              back!

AGENT GRACE's VOICE cracks and echoes, simultaneously,
filled to the brim with PAIN, GRIEF, and SADNESS.

                                        CUT TO:

INT. THE LOS ANGELES MORGUE - LATER

MR. FREEDOM lies on a metal slab, lifeless, motionless.

The MEDICAL EXAMINER addresses AGENT GRACE -

                    MEDICAL EXAMINER
              - Being a KINETIC BEING, AGENT
              GRACE, his skin simply isn't
              penetrable with man-made tools. I
              can't even perform a proper
              autopsy, ma'am.

                    AGENT GRACE
                   (stressed)
              Jesus Christ in Heaven; FREEDOM,
              what happened to you?

She sheds one last tear. It lands on FREEDOM's lips,
slipping into his mouth -

AGENT GRACE covers FREEDOM back up with the white sheet,

puts her hand on his chest, saying her goodbyes. She exits THE MORGUE.

CUT TO BLACK:

CHAPTER V - LIBERTY LIVES

                                                  FADE IN:

EXT. THE CENTER OF COMPTON - MIDTOWN - NIGHT

THE MANHUNTER lands in MIDTOWN with CERBERUS leashed with his HELLWHIP -

MANHUNTER raises his voice as loud as he can to the community members, specifically the drug addicts, criminals, gang bangers, etc. They look upon the MACHINE-BEING, frightfully.

                 MAJOR MANHUNTER
                (announcing)
    Hello, CITIZENS. I have a
    proposition.

                 GANG BANGER
                (pulls a pistol,
                 holding it
                 sideways)
    What the hell are you, man?

                 THE MANHUNTER
    Me? I'm your GOLDEN-TICKET,
    friend. Now listen up. To all you
    would be misanthropes, you
    outcasts of COMPTON, I'll give you
    ALL what you want, right fucking
    now. All you have to do is pledge
    allegiance to me - be my eyes,
    ears, informers, my WARRIORS. I
    need you to find a tool for me. In
    return, I'll give you all the
    money, drugs, and POWER you could
    ever dream of.

                          DRUG ADDICT
                    Prove it. And you might just have
                    a deal, freak.

THE MANHUNTER activates his ELEMENTAL POWER -

He works a dark miracle. There's nothing more terrifying
than a miracle.

He turns old raggedy NEWSPAPER floating through the COMPTON
STREETS into CASH-MONEY.

An ALCOHOLIC is sipping water. THE MANHUNTER turns the MAN's
water into MOONSHINE.

He impresses mostly all the people with his deathly wonders.
They submit in a jiff. He, in place of KING RED's and KING
BLUE's "monarchy", erects a THRONE of BONES, leaving the
witnesses in awe -

                          THE MANHUNTER
                    Bow and take a vow to me AND me
                    ALONE, and wonders, for you all,
                    will never cease. I assure you.

                          DRUG ADDICT
                       (mystified)
                    Wh - Who are you?

                          MAJOR MANHUNTER
                       (snarling)
                    - THE MANHUNTER.

CUT TO:

The COHORTS bow, solemnly taking a vow to THE MANHUNTER -

AND WE CUT TO:

Over 5 dozen POLICE OFFICERS, FEDERAL AGENTS, and NATIONAL
GUARD MEMBERS arrive to MIDTOWN COMPTON in ARMORED VEHICLES:

With CERBERUS on a leash, THE MANHUNTER turns his head,
looking over his steel back, at his opponents and
dissidents. He turns his body all the way around to face
them.

Igniting his DARK-RING, creating a massive BLUE ORB of energy covered in BLACK LIGHTNING, THE MANHUNTER lets loose a more than powerful energy blast at the DEFENDERS - the blast consumes them all in a bluish, fiery explosion that causes absolute destruction; it looks as if a NUKE has gone off in COMPTON, there's a mushroom cloud and all. More RESPONDERS appear - THE MANHUNTER and CERBERUS charge them with all they've got.

WE CUT TO BLACK:

EXT. MANHUNTER'S STRONGHOLD - COMPTON - AFTERNOON

                                      3 DAYS LATER:

MANHUNTER sits on the THRONE of BONES - his ROBOTIC STRUCTURE is stronger than ever. He now RULES this STRONGHOLD in COMPTON with a METALLIC FIST.

An INFORMER walks up to MANHUNTER's makeshift THRONE:

                     INFORMER
     MANHUNTER. I have discovered where
     they are keeping the so-called:
     "LIGHT-RING".

                  THE MANHUNTER
        (with a deeply
         demonic tone of
         VOICE)
     Good. Where is it?

                   INFORMER
     Deep underground, at the EINSTEIN
     RESEARCH LABORATORY, MASTER. The
     scientists, they are working on
     harnessing its power. They are
     getting very close, my LORD.

THE MANHUNTER reads the INFORMER's mind, as to find the exact location of the LIGHT-RING -

                    MAJOR MANHUNTER
               (rises up from his
                BONE THRONE)
          I see.

MANHUNTER takes flight and bursts through the atmosphere.
He's now on a MISSION.

                    INFORMER
          Wait! What about my payment!?

THE MANHUNTER is gone like the breeze before the man even
finishes his request -

AND WE CUT TO:

INT. THE EINSTEIN LAB - UNDERGROUND - MOMENTS LATER

THE MANHUNTER plunges deep UNDERGROUND, reaching the
EINSTEIN LAB where the LIGHT-RING is, in a matter of
moments.

The SCIENTISTS collectively look at the supervillain in
absolute HORROR. Then they ALL collaboratively SCREAM at the
top of their lungs. THE MANHUNTER tears them all to pieces,
one by one, with agility beyond human belief -

                    THE SCIENTISTS (COLLECTIVELY)
               (running around
                like chickens
                without heads)
          Aaaah!!!

MAJOR MANHUNTER decimates the SCIENTISTS like they're petty
prey.

CUT TO:

THE MANHUNTER walks up to the BULLETPROOF GLASS holding the
LIGHT-RING -

He grabs the glass with one hand, pulses BLUE ENERGY,
destroying the container. Glass explodes everywhere.

MANHUNTER takes possession of the LIGHT-RING, holding it in his left palm, caressing it; laughing as he does it.

                    THE MANHUNTER
             (caressing the
             LIGHT-RING)
      There, there, my precious. There,
      there.

                                    CUT TO:

INT. THE MORGUE - AFTERNOON

FREEDOM FERRARA lies in the METAL CONTAINER at THE MORGUE -

A chilling wind swirls through the place.

Miraculously, MISTER FREEDOM's HAMMER bursts through the MORGUE DOORS into the METAL CONTAINER holding FREEDOM, leaving jagged edges all around it -

The HAMMER enters the darkness of FREEDOM's temporary lying place. Next thing WE see is a bolt of PURE LIGHT ENERGY expand and expand until FREEDOM returns to life. He hops out of the METAL CONTAINER, HAMMER in his right hand - he's READY for WAR. He once again sees the LIGHT all around him.

- MR. FREEDOM morphs into his AMERICAN FLAG themed SUIT. His ANGEL WINGS even larger, his HALO more golden than ever before.

The HERO jumps with all of his willpower through the CEILING/ROOF of THE MORGUE. He escapes the mighty grip of DEATH -

CUT TO:

EXT. COMPTON - CITY STREET - MANHUNTER'S STRONGHOLD - EVENING

It is SNOWING. Yes, snowing, apocalyptically, in COMPTON, CALIFORNIA (a heavy mixture of snow AND nuclear-ASH) - the GRAY flakes shower the CITY STREET. The ashy snow is so chunky yet so unnatural.

THE MANHUNTER, his mind totally twisted and mutated, now evolved into a more monstrous cybernetic demon - (still with the head of a wolf yet he's taller and bulkier, and has even more blue energy coursing through his metallic armor) - is sitting on his now golden HELLFIRE THRONE of BONES; the men, women, and children he has held captive are famished, thirsted, and completely fatigued -

THE MANHUNTER has spikes coming out from his shoulders, back, and forearms. His metallic tail is even lengthier, too.

THE MANHUNTER has defeated all of the POLICE, FEDS, NATIONAL GUARD TROOPS, and the defenses that came to the aid of COMPTON - he has taken the community siege.

MANHUNTER's minions (those who have willingly sworn allegiance to him at the sight of his power), those HUMANS who chose to serve him, keep all the captives in line and in cages. THE MANHUNTER, on his THRONE, sips a gold diamond filled goblet full of TEARS.

One of the creature's subservient minions approaches his THRONE -

                    MINION 1
             (breathing steam,
              possessed by
              darkness)
      The sun sets on your victory,
      MANHUNTER. May we indulge in more
      of what you have provided us?

                  THE MANHUNTER
             (swaying his hand)
      Yes, you may - ingest all of it
      that you can, my friend.
             (toying with the
              LIGHT-RING,
              speaking to it)
      What power do you hold?

                                    CUT TO:

MINION 1 begins eating, what looks to be, sugar from a bag. It's really cocaine -

MINION 2 begins snorting, what appears to be, brown sugar from its bag. It's really heroin -

Other MINIONS begin breaking down common food, drink, and organic consumable products that have been transformed into DRUGS by THE MANHUNTER.

He has used his elemental powers to transubstantiate common goods into the most powerful of substances, all for his criminal and addict minions to partake in.

Also, those who are still in COMPTON who have not been taken hostage, have also had their foods, drinks, water, everything, laced with crack, cocaine, heroin, promethazine, LSD, MDMA, you name it - even their medications have turned into hard drugs.

                              CUT TO:

                THE MANHUNTER
             (DARK-RING starts
                glowing, flashing)
         What? What is it, RING?

THE MANHUNTER questions his DARK-RING, almost nervously -

Out of nowhere, far down the CITY STREET, away from the STRONGHOLD, walks MISTER FREEDOM. "F" on his chest with his AMERICAN FLAG theme costume, his cape swinging behind him, his HAMMER in-hand.

The LIGHT-RING, full of DIVINE POWER, escapes from THE MANHUNTER's grasp ever so quickly - THE RING speedily races toward MR. FREEDOM. He opens his hand with his palm facing the sky - the LIGHT-RING then calmly puts itself onto FREEDOM's hand; it has CHOSEN him again.

MR. FREEDOM stops in the middle of the snowy street - he flexes his ANGEL WINGS. His HALO grows brighter with HEAVENLY LIGHT.

He extends his HAMMER to THE MANHUNTER in a threatening gesture.

> MR. FREEDOM
> (with righteous
> indignation)
> MANHUNTER! You say you took my
> father's life. I've come to repay
> the debt. As you can see, I am
> still very much alive!

> THE MANHUNTER
> (worrisome)
> Freedom...Lives.
> (to his cohorts)
> Get that - that MAN. And, for the
> sake of all that is unholy, get me
> that RING back!

> MANHUNTER'S COHORTS (IN-UNISON)
> Yes, my Lord.

A small ARMY walks from the STRONGHOLD down the COMPTON CITY STREET toward MISTER FREEDOM -

> MR. FREEDOM
> (winds his HAMMER
> back)
> Fine, have it your way.

FREEDOM throws his HAMMER at full speed straightforward toward the many minions and henchmen - the HAMMER literally bursts through the men's fleshly bodies, ripping them apart as it travels forward towards THE MANHUNTER's THRONE.

The MINIONS separate, scatter as they see the HAMMER mutilate their fellow henchmen.

The HAMMER finally reaches MANHUNTER's face - the MONSTER holds up his ringed hand and stops the HAMMER dead in its tracks, telekinetically, right before it hits him in the face.

CUT TO:

THE MANHUNTER, mystified, goes to grab the HAMMER -

FREEDOM calls back the HAMMER, it ZOOMS back into his

possession, zigzagging, taking down even more of the cohorts.

      THE MANHUNTER
    (dog-whistles)
 CERBERUS - destroy him!

The giant three-head cybernetic demon-DOG comes from out of its hideaway on the CITY STREET. The animal walks slowly behind the remaining MINIONS.

The MINIONS attack MR. FREEDOM all at once. CERBERUS stands dominatingly in the middle of the CITY STREET, swiping its giant paws against the snow-covered road.

      MR. FREEDOM
    (powering up)
 Rah!

      CERBERUS
    (viciously
     growling)
 Grrrr -
    (salivating dark
     matter, breathing
     fire)

LIGHT ENERGY exudes from the LIGHT-RING, creating a limited explosion of divine energy. The MINIONS are absorbed by the LIGHT, immediately incinerated; their flesh ripped from their bodies, their bones turned to piles of ash -

THE MANHUNTER, and even CERBERUS, cover their faces because the LIGHT is too bright, it's almost blinding.

      THE MANHUNTER
    (to CERBERUS)
 Attack!

The fleshly robotic CERBERUS growls like a demon from hell, it charges MR. FREEDOM with all its power -

      MR. FREEDOM
 Come on, I want you to do it. I
 want to you to do it. C'mon!

The giant CERBERUS' and its THREE-HEADS go to gnaw on FREEDOM.

MR. FREEDOM raises his HAMMER upward to reach the animal's middle head's jaw. He hits the creature with all his might - the blow breaks the MIDDLE HEAD's neck, turning its head 180 degrees, disabling CERBERUS.

MR. FREEDOM, as the DEMON DOG squeals like a stuck pig, SMASHES the other two HEADS of CERBERUS with his HAMMER, murdering the hellish monster. CERBERUS is absorbed back into HELL, its body boils and disintegrates - it's black blood drenches the snow AND drips from MR. FREEDOM's HAMMER...

CUT TO:

THE MANHUNTER
(stands up from
THRONE)
No. This can't be - he's-

MR. FREEDOM
I'm here to take back my CITY, MANHUNTER. This ends, NOW -

THE MANHUNTER
(pointing his
finger at MR.
FREEDOM)
Yes. Yes, it does. I'll just have to kill you better this time, huh?

...MR. FREEDOM flies at full speed like a cannonball at THE MANHUNTER and his THRONE.

THE MANHUNTER rises off of his throne into the air to contest FREEDOM - the two clash, collide, and proceed to battle with absolute ferocity.

CUT TO:

EXT. COMPTON - CITY STREET - MANHUNTER'S STRONGHOLD - EVENING

MISTER FREEDOM is attacked by THE MANHUNTER in the air - as they meet (as equals in power), a huge energy explosion is created, causing great damage to the COMPTON area.

FREEDOM attacks with a BOXER's methodology - he swings on MANHUNTER with a ferociously aggressive uppercut, making the beastly entity fly upward far in the sky.

FREEDOM then flies toward his opponent like a missile, HAMMER as ready as can be.

              THE MANHUNTER
           (thrilled at the
            action)
    Give me the RING, FREEDOM -

              MR. FREEDOM
           (swings a right
            hook)
    I'd rather burn in hell!

              THE MANHUNTER
           (blocks the punch)
    That can be arranged.

FREEDOM, after being blocked by MANHUNTER's DARK-RING, comes around with all of his strength, swinging his HAMMER - he hits MANHUNTER's head so hard, it comes off of his body.

THE MANHUNTER then falls to the ground from far up in the sky - his body lands near his head.

FREEDOM levitates downward to meet his seemingly defeated enemy.

                                      CUT TO:

              MR. FREEDOM
           (disturbed)
    What the...?

THE MANHUNTER's metal head is oozing black fluids - DARK MATTER.

Suddenly, the black blood from his head becomes stringy and starts reattaching from a distance to his body - it's horrifying.

THE MANHUNTER is not dead.

                  THE MANHUNTER
            (stands up, fixes
            his head onto his
            body)
     Is that all you've got, boy?

THE MANHUNTER activates his DARK-RING, telekinetically grabbing various guns (pistols, shotguns, and automatic machine guns) with his mind.

- The MONSTER holds the weapons in the air by both his right and left sides, in an unbalanced row - THE MANHUNTER, with his DARK-RING, pulls the many triggers of these weapons, without even touching them physically, firing upon MISTER FREEDOM, unrelentingly.

- MR. FREEDOM, with his LIGHT-RING and HAMMER synchronized, blocks every single bullet and projectile fired at him - using pure LIGHT-ENERGY.

CUT TO:

FREEDOM blitzes THE MANHUNTER, attempting one more death-blow with his HAMMER -

THE MANHUNTER blocks the HAMMER this time, there's a pause between the two -

MANHUNTER does a winding back-fist, nailing FREEDOM in the face, knocking him back some 30 yards against the snowy landscape; he slides on the slick ice, shaken.

CUT TO:

MISTER FREEDOM dusts the snow off of himself, regaining his stance.

THE MANHUNTER grabs a military vehicle, like it's a softball, and throws at FREEDOM with the speed of a major league baseball pitcher.

MR. FREEDOM strikes his HAMMER downward as the VEHICLE enters his personal space - the HAMMER is able to smash the VEHICLE in HALF; the two halves go flying behind FREEDOM. His CAPE flails in the cold wind.

CUT TO:

FREEDOM picks his head up and realizes THE MANHUNTER has sprinted toward him.

The CREATURE reaches FREEDOM in a heartbeat, grabbing him by the neck, picking him up off of his feet -

              THE MANHUNTER
      I could crush you, kid. Now give
      me the RING or I will rip it off
      of you. I will open the gates to
      HELL. The devil will have his day
      and his due!

              FREEDOM FERRARA
      You want this RING? This power?
      Here, have it, see if you can
      handle it -

While still being choked and held off of his feet, FREEDOM drops his HAMMER - he reaches with his left hand, proceeds to take off the LIGHT-RING. He holds his left hand out with the LIGHT-RING in it, offering it up to THE MANHUNTER.

The MONSTER gladly takes it.

              THE MANHUNTER
         (turns his back on
         FREEDOM)
      Very good. Now, watch your city
      die, this whole world, just like
      my wife and child did.

THE MANHUNTER puts the LIGHT-RING on the middle finger of his right-hand, symmetrically opposite of the DARK-RING -

As soon as he puts the LIGHT-RING on, a PORTAL opens up above him in the sky.

When MAJOR puts on the LIGHT-RING, FREEDOM has visions - visions of MAJOR MANHUNTER's entire life up until this point. He sees all of his pain, grief, heartache, and he sees how MAJOR accidentally killed his own wife and kid - it breaks MISTER FREEDOM's heart, hurts his soul.

CUT TO:

Demonic Seraphim start trying to claw their way from HELL into EARTH's plane in COMPTON, up above.

MANHUNTER holds his two fists up in a champion stance, pouring LIGHT-ENERGY AND DARK-ENERGY into the atmosphere, allowing HELL to encroach onto the worldly dimension -

> FREEDOM FERRARA
> Is this what your wife would want!? Is this what your kid would want from his father!? Think MAJOR - it's not too late to end this CHAOS.

> MAJOR MANHUNTER
> I have a MASTER, now. I serve him and him alone. These RINGS, they're the key. I've been in Hell for far too long on this Earth. It's time for you all to feel my pain - FREEDOM is a lie. Hell is the only absolute, the only constant.

> OPPIE THE CROW
> (voiceover in FREEDOM's mind)
> Remember, FREEDOM, the LIGHT-RING is merely a tool. The HAMMER is just an extension of yourself. You yourself are the weapon.

MR. FREEDOM rises up from his knees - he holds his HAMMER up, pointing it to the HELL PORTAL. HEAVENLY LIGHT flows from the HAMMER in a wide spray - the LIGHT confronts the HELL PORTAL, forcing it to collapse in on itself.

The demonic angels and demons attempting to enter Earth are

coerced back into HELL. The PORTAL is destroyed in a matter of moments, thanks to FREEDOM's FAITH and OPPIE's motivational push -

                    CUT TO:

Fire rains from the sky.

THE MANHUNTER increases his power output, to no avail. The PORTAL is sealed.

          MAJOR MANHUNTER
     You - you fool! What have you
     done?

          FREEDOM FERRARA
          (points his HAMMER
            at MANHUNTER)
     You think you know HELL? You know
     nothing. Time to be destroyed,
     MAJOR.

FREEDOM FERRARA slams his HAMMER into the snow-covered CONCRETE -

A humungous earthquake like crack appears in the ground.

It lines up with THE MANHUNTER, going from FREEDOM to the MONSTER.

Spontaneously, another PORTAL to HELL opens up in the GROUND directly under MAJOR MANHUNTER's feet. MANHUNTER is paralyzed, oddly enough - he cannot move a muscle or limb.

CHAINS from HELL rise up, wrapping themselves around MANHUNTER's cybernetic wrists and feet.

          FREEDOM FERRARA
     Can you feel it? The sulfur, the
     brimstone, the HELLFIRE?

          THE MANHUNTER
     You have no power here! I AM THE
     MANHUNTER - I, I cannot be
     defeated. I-

The METALLIC SKIN of MANHUNTER proceeds to MELT, revealing his humanly body, as the HELLFIRE raises up to meet him.

FREEDOM does one last slam of his HAMMER on the ground.

This causes MAJOR MANHUNTER to be dragged to HELL by clawing demons, ghosts, dark angels, and the like - the beings rip THE MANHUNTER to pieces and shreds, absorbing him into the hellish dimension.

The Dust Settles...

...FREEDOM is victorious, having slain the supervillainous MANHUNTER for good -

CUT TO:

Having observed this victory through satellite footage, the remaining COMPTON DEFENSE FORCES move in on the STRONGHOLD to discontinue the elemental drug saturation that has occurred and to arrest MANHUNTER's darkly MINIONS -

Sirens whinny through the air, COPS, FEDS, CIA AGENTS, NATIONAL GUARD TROOPS, ARMY SOLDIERS, the works move in.

MR. FREEDOM looks behind him and sees the forces incoming.

He turns his head back around, holds his HAMMER up high, and proceeds to take off from the scene - MR. FREEDOM takes flight, his red cape waving in the air like an AMERICAN-FLAG.

> COMPTON DEFENSE FORCE
> (to the MINIONS
> and ADDICTS)
> Freeze or we will open fire!
> Surrender, now!

The MINIONS and ADDICTS comply, as the HOSTAGES and CAPTIVES are finally FREED - LIBERTY has returned to COMPTON.

CUT TO:

INT. THE JAILHOUSE INFIRMARY - LOS ANGELES - NIGHT

The D.A, YELENA STEIN, is in the INFIRMARY of the LA JAILHOUSE -

She is attending to ARTO MILLS (KING RED) - she's visiting him, her hand around his hand as he lies on a stretcher.

              THE D.A - YELENA STEIN
        (concerned)
  It's okay, my sweet BROTHER. It's
  going to be just fine; FATHER will
  have you rehabilitated in no time,
  I promise. I'm - I'm getting you
  out of here, right now.

YELENA STEIN wheels KING RED's stretcher out of the INFIRMARY ROOM into the JAILHOUSE HALLWAY -

              JAILHOUSE GUARD
        (alerted)
  Madame D.A, where are you taking
  MR. MILLS?

              THE D.A - YELENA STEIN
        (clicks tongue)
  He has X-RAYS to get done. I'm
  taking him to the other side,
  myself, OFFICER.
        (with an attitude)
  Is that all right with you?

              JAILHOUSE GUARD
  - I reckon so. I'm just a guard,
  you're the D.A.

              THE D.A - YELENA STEIN
  Yep. Mine is bigger than yours.

The D.A wheels KING RED into the ELEVATOR - inside the ELEVATOR is CARISSA BRONTE (FREEDOM's PUBLIC DEFENDER).

              THE D.A - YELENA STEIN
        (clears her throat)
  Hello, CARISSA.

                    CARISSA BRONTE
                  (questioning)
            What are you doing, YELENA?

The ELEVATOR doors seal shut -

                    THE D.A - YELENA STEIN
                  (reaches from
                   behind her back)
            - What has to be done.

YELENA pulls a syringe from her behind her -

She forcefully injects CARISSA BRONTE in the neck; in the
syringe is POTASSIUM CYANIDE. It kills the LAWYER instantly,
her sight fading to complete blackness.

                    THE D.A - YELENA STEIN
            Easier done than said.

                                        CUT TO:

EXT. BLACK MERCEDES VAN - JAILHOUSE PARKING LOT - CONTINUOUS

YELENA STEIN loads KING RED into the back of a BLACK
MERCEDES VAN.

There are several ARMED MEN in the back who jump out before
ARTO MILLS is loaded up - the ARMED MEN get into tactical
formation; they have submachine guns on their person.

CUT TO:

                    THE D.A - YELENA STEIN
                  (whirls her finger
                   commandingly)
            Fellas, you know what to do.

                    GUNNER LEADER
                  (in RUSSIAN)
            Yes, ma'am. We're on it -

                                        CUT TO:

INT. JAIL - SUPERCELL AREA - NIGHT

At the end of the HALLWAY of the SUPERCELL AREA of the LA JAILHOUSE, a massive explosion transpires, breaking the brick wall into crumbs.

> GUNNER LEADER
> (enters the
> building in the
> lead, speaking
> RUSSIAN)
> Let's go, let's go!

GUARDS jump into action only to be slaughtered by the RUSSIAN GUNNERS.

CUT TO:

INT. SUPERCELL #4 - VLADIMIR MILSTEIN'S CELL - CONTINUOUS

Sirens are crying throughout the JAILHOUSE, yet no backup arrives in time. The LEAD GUNNER approaches SUPERCELL #4, that of DR. VLADIMIR MILSTEIN aka. THE EUTHANIZER -

> DR. VLADIMIR MILSTEIN
> (in RUSSIAN)
> To whom do I owe the pleasure?

> GUNNER LEADER
> (speaking RUSSIAN)
> Your daughter, sir. She has sent
> us. It is time - time to create
> some CHAOS.

The LEAD GUNNER pulls out a special device that disables the SUPERCELL's ELECTRIC BARS, then, they use a specialty tool that slices through the STEEL BARS underneath - the soldier hands THE EUTHANIZER his white, ghoulish GHOST MASK:

> DR. VLADIMIR MILSTEIN
> (pauses, holds his
> MASK)
> My GOD, how long I've waited for
> this day. Where is my daughter
> now, SOLDIER?

THE EUTHANIZER looks deeply into his MASK - he puts it on.

                    GUNNER LEADER
    Right outside, Doctor. Come with
    us -

                    DR. VLADIMIR MILSTEIN
        (rubs his hands
         together)
    Oh, goody.

THE EUTHANIZER himself escapes the SUPERCELL and the LA JAILHOUSE. He and the RUSSIAN GUNNERS exit through the hole in the brick in the back of the HALLWAY -

                                CUT TO:

EXT. BLACK MERCEDES VAN - JAILHOUSE PARKING LOT - NIGHT

VLADIMIR MILSTEIN opens the back doors to the BLACK MERCEDES VAN all to see his 2 CHILDREN (half-siblings, different MOMS) with his own eyes - YELENA MILSTEIN (the D.A) and ARTO MILSTEIN (the injured KING RED).

                    THE D.A - YELENA STEIN
        (pleased)
    Father, thank God.

                                CUT TO:

INT. BLACK MERCEDES VAN - JAILHOUSE PARKING LOT - CONTINUOUS

VLADIMIR MILSTEIN has entered the BLACK VAN - two of the GUNNERS go up front to drive the VAN and the other to be an ENFORCER for the MILSTEINS. The remainder of the RUSSIAN GUNNERS spread out and go their separate ways.

                    DR. VLADIMIR MILSTEIN
        (hand on YELENA's
         cheek)
    My sweet, sweet girl, how have you
    been?

                    THE D.A - YELENA STEIN
                   (speaking RUSSIAN)
               Never better, Father. Never
               better.

                    DR. VLADIMIR MILSTEIN
                   (in RUSSIAN)
               My God, what's happened to your
               brother? Is he stable?

                    THE D.A - YELENA STEIN
               He's stable, dad. He just needs
               your skillset. We have no time to
               waste. We need to get him to
               safety, immediately.

                    DR. VLADIMIR MILSTEIN
                   (kisses his son's
                    cheek)
               I'll fix him, I swear it, if it's
               the last thing I do -

THE EUTHANIZER, THE CORRUPT D.A, and KING RED all ESCAPE the
JAILHOUSE PARKING LOT and in turn, they head away from LOS
ANGELES -

                                             CUT TO:

INT. LOS ANGELES FBI HEADQUARTERS - DAY

AGENT SASHA GRACE sits at her computer desk, typing away on
a report for what has been deemed the "INFINITY EVENT" - in
which the HELL PORTAL manifested in COMPTON.

                    AGENT GRACE
                   (bored, sipping
                    COFFEE)
               I need a break.
                   (pops her hands
                    and fingers)
               This report is hell.

AGENT GRACE hears a "BANG!" noise outside, like a JET is
close by -

However, it's no jet, no. It's MR. FREEDOM flying through LA. He appears outside the FBI HEADQUARTERS' WINDOW right in front of AGENT GRACE -

MR. FREEDOM is unmasked, yet he has on his RED CAPE, "F" on his chest, RED GLOVES, HAMMER in his HAND - sans the LIGHT-RING (which was consumed by HELL, its home).

                    AGENT GRACE
                (lovingly)
        FREE?

FREEDOM grins at SASHA - he then blows her a kiss.

She acts as if she "catches" the Kiss...

                    FREEDOM FERRARA
                (through the
                 window)
        See ya around, SASHA. I love you
        with all my heart -

                    AGENT GRACE
                (standing at the
                 window)
        I love you more, FREEDOM. I always
        will.

...FREEDOM flies upward, up, up, and away far into the atmosphere. A rapper, a boxer, a worker, an earner - a HERO.

                                          CUT TO:

<u>EXT. THE SKY - LOS ANGELES - DAY</u>

MID-CREDITS' SCENE:

MISTER FREEDOM, in his divine AMERICAN-FLAG costume and with his supernatural HAMMER, soars through THE SKY in LA, giving hope to the people -

                                          CUT TO:

- A BUILDING-TOP -

...WE PAN OUT FROM MR. FREEDOM INTO A SNIPER SCOPE...

He's being watched.

We see a mysterious long-haired MAN, in a black leather trench coat with black military pants on and a thick matching bulletproof vest, on top of a BUILDING holding this SNIPER RIFLE, pointing it at MR. FREEDOM...

...He reveals himself from behind the scope.

It is MICKEY MONTANA - now in his 40s; a giant-SCAR, monstrous looking, stretching across his face.

                MICKEY MONTANA
           (inquisitive, to
            himself)
    Man was not meant to fly. Don't
    get too comfortable, NEPHEW.

MICKEY straps the SNIPER RIFLE to his person, exiting the frame.

MICKEY MONTANA is BACK.

                                    CUT TO:

<ins>INT. THE MORGUE - NIGHT</ins>

POST-CREDITS' SCENE:

The mutilated, chewed up corpse of NATHAN TOWNHALL lies on a metal slab, covered in a plastic sheet. It's eerily silent in THE MORGUE.

A wind breezes into THE MORGUE, the plastic sheet lightly flails.

A clicking sound can be heard, like, wood tapping the floor.

THE DEALMAKER himself, like a physical shadow in a beastly form, walks up to NATHAN's swollen, purple dead body - he rips the plastic sheet off of him and puts his wicked pale hand to his forehead:

                    THE DEALMAKER
                  (authoritatively)
            Rise. I command thee -

NATHAN's mouth opens wide...

...THE DEALMAKER pours the powers of DARKNESS into his
lifeless body.

NATHAN TOWNHALL is revived in an instant, wheezing severely
- something's not right with him. He's zombified, smelling
of dead flesh; his is eyes are solid white, glowing. NATHAN
balls up his fists, his head held upward. He screams to the
top of his lungs.

                    NATHAN TOWNHALL
                  (hurting severely)
            What the fuck!?
                  (to THE DEALMAKER)
            Who - who are you?

                    THE DEALMAKER
                  (confident,
                   gravely voice)
            - The Man with a masterplan. A
            Serpent with a purpose. I am your
            MASTER now.

                    NATHAN TOWNHALL
            What happened to me? What is this,
            where am I? Answer me!

                    THE DEALMAKER
            You were a victim of a tragic
            circumstance, my friend. However,
            sometimes, victims can become
            VICTIMIZERS.
                  (grins)
            That's who you are from now on:
            THE VICTIMIZER. You - you will see
            to it that this, uh, MISTER
            FREEDOM...this SUPER-ANGEL is
            terminated. Eternally.

THE DEALMAKER slams his witchy staff -

NATHAN becomes possessed, convulsing.

WE SEE FROM BEHIND THE TWO:

Glowing blackness permeates THE MORGUE. The darkness consumes NATHAN TOWNHALL, torturing his resurrected soul - even though we don't see, we can hear chaotic commotion as he begins morphing into something...UNHOLY.

- NATHAN TOWNHALL is no more.

- There is only THE VICTIMIZER now.

          THE VICTIMIZER
     (breathing
      beastily, unseen)
  Yes, my MASTER.

AND WE CUT TO BLACK:

un·leash

[un·leSH]

VERB

unleashed (past tense) · unleashed (past participle)
release from a leash or restraint:

"we unleashed the dog and carried it down to our car" · "the failure of the talks could unleash more fighting"

cause (a strong or violent force) to be released or become unrestrained:

"the failure of the talks could unleash more fighting" · "his comment unleashed a storm of protest in India"

                        ACT II. CAPTAIN
                        BREEDLOVE UNLEASHED

CHAPTER I - AFTERMATH

                                 FADE IN:

177.

INT. TRICKEY'S CHILDHOOD HOME - NORTH CAROLINA - EVENING

YEAR: 1989

LOCATION: HICKORY, NORTH CAROLINA

TRICKEY BREEDLOVE's MOTHER, a beautiful, frail, tiny white woman with short dyed red-hair, MARJORIE BREEDLOVE, is cooking SUPPER for her curly-headed Mulatto son prior to going to CHURCH -

TRICKEY's UNCLE, NEIL (his MOM's BROTHER), is at the HOME, too, watching 4-Year-Old TRICKEY as MARJORIE cooks. This is TRICKEY BREEDLOVE's CHILDHOOD HOME -

NEIL looks like a hippy. He has smoker's teeth, long black hair, a beard and moustache, dressed in a boilersuit (coveralls) with a camo hunting jacket over it.

CUT TO:

INT. THE LIVING-ROOM - TRICKEY'S CHILDHOOD HOME - EVENING

NEIL is in mid-conversation with his NEPHEW:

              UNCLE NEIL
    - In the HOLY BIBLE in JUDGES 3:31
    it says, SHAMGAR THE JUDGE
    slaughtered over 600 PHILISTINES,
    by himself, all with an OX-GOAD.
    Can you believe it? He delivered
    ISRAEL from tyranny and CHAOS.

              YOUNG TRICKEY
    How did one man do that, UNCLE
    NEIL? How could one man kill 600
    giants?

              UNCLE NEIL
    The answer to that question,
    TRICKSTER, is FAITH. With belief
    in GOD, anything's possible. If a
    man believes in the CREATOR as
    higher than himself, he can do the
    impossible - scripture says so.

YOUNG TRICKEY
So, did SHAMGAR go against all 600 PHILISTINES at one time?

UNCLE NEIL
No, not exactly. See the PHILISTINES had taken over ISRAEL. They built checkpoint-like entries into the KINGDOM, basically roadblocks, you know? What SHAMGAR did, he was an expert with an OX-GOAD, he went to each checkpoint the giants had setup and took out each and every PHILISTINE at each checkpoint. You understand?

YOUNG TRICKEY
Wow, UNCLE NEIL. That's so cool. He was basically a superhero!

UNCLE NEIL
Yes. I guess he was, NEPHEW. You have a point. The real point of the story, though, is that any man, if he believes in GOD can do exactly what SHAMGAR did - we can take on THE ADVERSARY and we can create miracles with GOD's blessing, through His WILL.

YOUNG TRICKEY
SHAMGAR must've been really tired afterward, huh? He survived, didn't he?

UNCLE NEIL
(pats TRICKEY on
the head)
You bet; he was. He had to have been so. Faith gives a man the strength he needs to move forward. He survived because of his FAITH -

CUT TO:

                    MARJORIE BREEDLOVE (TRICKEY'S MOM)
               (from in the
                KITCHEN)
          Supper is ready, TRICKEY, NEIL,
          get it while it's hot!

TRICKEY gets up from the recliner, adjacent to his UNCLE, and races into the KITCHEN -

                    YOUNG TRICKEY
               (genuinely
                grateful)
          Thanks, MAMA!

INT. THE KITCHEN - TRICKEY'S CHILDHOOD HOME - CONTINUOUS

                    MARJORIE BREEDLOVE (TRICKEY'S MOM)
               (smiling at her
                kid)
          You're very welcome. Now, wash
          your hands, son.

                    UNCLE NEIL
          Thank you, MARJORIE. Wow, you made
          spaghetti and meatballs - mom's
          recipe? It sure smells like it.

                    MARJORIE BREEDLOVE (TRICKEY'S MOM)
          Yep, NEIL. Right out of her
          cookbook.

                    UNCLE NEIL
          Nice. Thanks, sis. Really - I'll
          be back on my feet in no time,
          you'll see. I won't be eating off
          you too much longer. God's going
          to bless you.

                    MARJORIE BREEDLOVE (TRICKEY'S MOM)
               (admiring her
                healthy son)
          - He Already Has. Look at my son.
          He's happy, I'm happy. I'm so
          looking forward to going to your
          CHURCH, brother. I think getting
          TRICKEY into church is the best
                         (MORE)

                    MARJORIE BREEDLOVE (TRICKEY'S MOM) (cont'd)
          thing I could do for him.

TRICKEY, after having washed his hands, sits at the wooden
dinner-table in the middle of the KITCHEN. NEIL washes his
hands, and he also takes a seat. MARJORIE sits at the head
of the table -

                    UNCLE NEIL
          Let's say GRACE. TRICKEY, would
          you do the honors?

MARJORIE and NEIL bow their heads over their respective
praying hands.

                    YOUNG TRICKEY
          I sure will, UNCLE NEIL.
               (bows his head
                over his
                intertwined hands)
          God is great. God is good. Please
          LORD JESUS, bless this food. By
          your Grace are we saved. I thank
          you JESUS, everyday. AMEN -

                    UNCLE NEIL
          That was a very good prayer,
          kiddo. Very thoughtful of you.
               (surprised)
          You've got the gift of prayer.

                    YOUNG TRICKEY
          I learned it at school! In our
          YMCA after-school program, before
          we eat our snacks, we say that
          prayer. I have it memorized. Cool,
          right?

                    MARJORIE BREEDLOVE (TRICKEY'S MOM)
          Very cool, son. Let's dig in.

NEIL, MARJORIE, and TRICKEY proceed to grub on the
home-cooked dinner -

                                                  CUT TO:

EXT. THE ROAD - NEIL'S TRUCK - EVENING

NEIL is driving his black TRUCK down THE ROAD, with MARJORIE in the passenger seat and YOUNG TRICKEY in the backseat.

It's quiet.

NEIL stops the TRUCK at a road sign.

                    UNCLE NEIL
           (hollering loudly)
AaH!

               MARJORIE BREEDLOVE (TRICKEY'S MOM)
           (jumps)
What the heck, NEIL!?

                  YOUNG TRICKEY
           (grabs NEIL's
            shoulder)
UNCLE NEIL, are you all right?

NEIL giggles, continuing to drive.

                    UNCLE NEIL
           (jokingly)
The sign back there said, "YIELD", so I yelled at it.

MARJORIE lightly punches NEIL in the shoulder.

               MARJORIE BREEDLOVE (TRICKEY'S MOM)
           (laughing)
You idiot.

                  YOUNG TRICKEY
           (chuckling)
You're not right, UNCLE NEIL.

                    UNCLE NEIL
Another joke. A MEXICAN, he and his wife had just moved to AMERICA, and they couldn't speak English very well. The roads here were a challenge for them, too. One day, the husband is driving like Jeff Gordon down a busy road.
                    (MORE)

                    UNCLE NEIL (cont'd)
          He gets a call from his wife. She
          says, "Honey, are you okay?". He
          says, "Si". She says, "Thank God",
          I'm watching the news and there
          showing some dumbass driving down
          the road going the wrong way! The
          husband says, "I know, I'm passing
          hundreds of them!".

MARJORIE shakes her head, looking out the window. She's humored, trying to act like she's not.

TRICKEY belly laughs in the backseat.

                    UNCLE NEIL
               (goofy)
          Now that's funny right there. I
          don't care what nobody says.
          That's funny.

WE CUT TO:

The exterior of the TRUCK as it travels down THE ROAD. NEIL, MARJORIE, and TRICKEY are on their way to CHURCH -

                                        CUT TO:

INT. NEIL'S CHURCH - EVENING SERVICE - EVENING

                                        LOCATION: NEWTON,
                                        NORTH CAROLINA

TRICKEY, NEIL, and MARJORIE sit comfortably in their pew, amongst the CONGREGATION, taking in the fiery sermon from PASTOR JOHN BOYD -

The PREACHER is a giant WHITE MAN. He's obese, no hair on his face. He has a slick parted hair style, wearing thick glasses. He's sweating profusely as he makes declarations in this HOUSE of GOD.

                    PASTOR BOYD
               (mid-sermon)
          - Most folks just don't get it, do
          they? They think SATAN is a myth!
                    (MORE)

                        PASTOR BOYD (cont'd)
A myth, for God's sake. You know
what the name SATAN means? It
means THE ADVERSARY - "SATANA" is
the word used in classical
Septuagint Scripture. He doesn't
want anything for you, except your
permanent death, destruction, and
to be bound in HELL without the
presence of GOD. That's all the
devil wants for you, people! He's
the thief, the killer, the
destroyer of souls. He can't
create anything, yet he wants to
be GOD. SATAN hasn't had an
original thought since the book of
GENESIS, you see! He's a fraud, a
plagiarist, a fiend who wants to
be king. He's a NOBODY trying to
be somebody, how about that?

CUT TO:

                        YOUNG TRICKEY
                    (being as quiet as
                     can be)
Mama, can I have a piece of gum,
please?

                        MARJORIE BREEDLOVE (TRICKEY'S MOM)
                    (whispering)
I don't have any, son, sorry - all
I have are peppermints. Ask your
UNCLE, see if he's got a piece.

                        YOUNG TRICKEY
                    (nudges NEIL)
UNCLE NEIL, can I have a piece of
gum, please?

                        UNCLE NEIL
Sure thing, TRICKSTER.
                    (hands TRICKEY a
                     couple pieces of
                     gum)
Now pay attention to PASTOR BOYD,
                        (MORE)

UNCLE NEIL (cont'd)
he's REALLY preaching tonight.

YOUNG TRICKEY
(contented, starts
chewing gum)
Yessir.

CUT TO:

PASTOR BOYD takes notice of YOUNG TRICKEY in the CONGREGATION - MARJORIE notices it, as does NEIL.

PASTOR BOYD
See, folks, SATAN is a TRICKSTER. He defies GOD with every fiber of his being. Since he can't create anything, he feeds off of GOD's divinity to create unholiness. You want to know what's unholy? This may be off topic, but it's the daggum truth! The mixing of the tribes is one of the pinnacles of unholiness. MISCEGENATION, that's one of the greatest sins in the eyes of GOD.

MARJORIE has her guard up - NEIL's eyes are wide open, almost in shock.

PASTOR BOYD
By mixing of the tribes, I mean the mixing of races. It's EVIL! Evil, I tell ya. Black men should not have sexual relations with white women, for starters-

Some people in the CONGREGATION gasp - we hear: "Ah!" amongst some of them.

PASTOR BOYD
Also, little black boys should not play with little white boys. Black girls shouldn't be friends with white girls. It's SCIENCE - and it's in the scripture. The mixing of the tribes, THE RACES, is an
(MORE)

184.

                    PASTOR BOYD (cont'd)
          absolute abomination. We see these
          new kids being born, with white
          mamas and black daddies - IT AIN'T
          RIGHT, I'll say it! Mixed babies,
          mixed kids, they are abominations
          before GOD.

NEIL starts sweating bullets.

MARJORIE holds tight to her son.

TRICKEY is frightened by the message, he's an apt
4-year-old, he knows what's being said.

NEIL stands up, pointing his finger at PASTOR BOYD -

                    UNCLE NEIL
          You are wrong, PREACHER!

                    MARJORIE BREEDLOVE (TRICKEY'S MOM)
                (in shock, pissed
                 to the limit)
          Dear God, help us.

The CONGREGATION is wholly surprised by NEIL's intervention
in the sermon. This CHURCH is one of totality - uniformity,
compliance.

                    UNCLE NEIL
                (filled with angry
                 passion)
          Sis, get your stuff, hold tight to
          TRICKEY, WE ARE GETTING THE FUCK
          OUT OF HERE, right now!

                    PASTOR BOYD
          NEIL, what do you think you're -

                    UNCLE NEIL
                (rushes past the
                 pews with
                 MARJORIE and
                 TRICKEY)
          I - WE are leaving, that's what,
          PASTOR BOYD. And I'll never come
                         (MORE)

                          UNCLE NEIL (cont'd)
                     back here again. Period.

                          PASTOR BOYD
                     - Suit yourself. Now, folks, back
                     to the good ole message I was
                     providing.
                              (undecipherable
                               dialogue)
                     ....

CUT TO:

INT. NEIL'S TRUCK - CHURCH PARKING LOT - CONTINUOUS

NEIL starts his TRUCK in a fury -

TRICKEY has on his seatbelt in the backseat.

MARJORIE sits, heartbroken, in the passenger.

NEIL proceeds to exit the CHURCH PARKING LOT, so fast that his tires scream, smoke is produced in the evening-air.

MUSIC is playing on the RADIO -

                          YOUNG TRICKEY
                              (curious)
                     UNCLE NEIL, I been meaning to ask
                     you: what kind of music is playing
                     on your radio?

                          UNCLE NEIL
                              (turns to face his
                               NEPHEW)
                     It's called "DARKWAVE", TRICKSTER.
                     Do you like it?

TRICKEY nods in a yes manner with a small smile, jamming to the music. Tears stream down MARJORIE's face. NEIL sees this and is shattered, focusing on his NEPHEW in the rearview mirror.

                    UNCLE NEIL
              (to his NEPHEW)
     - It's 1970s and 1980s European
     rock-n-roll. A mixture of
     punk-rock and synth-rock; a darker
     style of rock that came about,
     hence the name.

                    YOUNG TRICKEY
              (innocently)
     So awesome -

The DARKWAVE MUSIC is cut up by NEIL, as he and MARJORIE gloomily sit up front -

The TRUCK engine spews decibels, sounding like thunder.

                                             CUT TO:

INT. WASTEPRO TRUCK - NORTHWEST FLORIDA - DAY

                                        YEAR: 2018

LOCATION: WEWAHITCHKA

TRICKEY BREEDLOVE - 33-years-old, very athletic, tattooed, biracial and tan-skinned, with very long curly black hair - is hauling tail in the WASTEPRO TRUCK that he crushed his grandfather, CAPTAIN KARL NOOSE, in.

TRICKEY's wearing a WASTEPRO VEST and muddied, bloodied workpants and work boots, having risen out of the grave and killed NOOSE's gang of subordinates.

He makes the truck go as fast as it'll go.

Yet TRICKEY hasn't anywhere to go. He drives, nonetheless. He zooms off of CAPTAIN NOOSE's PROPERTY.

No one attempts to stop TRICKEY. No one chases him. He's killed off all the threats and the police are nowhere in sight.

                    CAPTAIN BREEDLOVE
                  (driving, shedding
                    tears of PAIN)
              - They got my baby. They - they
              got my wife! What am I gonna do?

TRICKEY drives right over a fence that's blocking his route.

                    CAPTAIN BREEDLOVE
                   (crying, agitated)
              This is a nightmare. Wake up,
              TRICKEY. Wake up!

TRICKEY looks into the rearview mirror and into the TRUCK camera. No one is around him.

He finally reaches a perpendicular intersection; he sees he's on the RURAL HIGHWAY. TRICKEY comes to a full stop at the stop-sign.

He reads the road signs:

- PORT ST. JOE: 30 Miles
- PANAMA CITY: 60 Miles
- DALKEITH: 10 Miles

TRICKEY reads the last of the road sign.

                    CAPTAIN BREEDLOVE
                   (pressing the gas
                      pedal)
              Dalkeith? My UNCLE NEIL. He has to
              still be there.

TRICKEY takes off, straight through the RURAL HIGHWAY, right toward DALKEITH...

                                              CUT TO:

INT. MEXICAN DEPARTMENT OF DEFENSE BASE - MOMENTS LATER

LOCATION: MEXICO CITY, MEXICO

...A young, very attractive MEXICAN woman, in a gray blouse and skirt, with glasses and military decoration on her attire walks in high heels through a BASE of the MEXICAN DEPARTMENT OF DEFENSE. She's a D.O.D WORKER -

She is holding several files in her left hand. Her heels click as she walks -

She arrives at the CONTROL-ROOM. She enters, files in-hand.

CUT TO:

INT. CONTROL-ROOM (MEXICO D.O.D) BASE - CONTINUOUS

The D.O.D WORKER seals the door shut behind her, we hear a vacuum sound as it closes.

In the CONTROL-ROOM are many military members, collecting and cyphering through surveillance data and intel.

Leading the military group is GENERAL NINO ESTEVEZ (tall, athletic-build, olive-skinned, late 30s). Dressed in full military garb, decorations, and outfit, to the shine on his shoes, not a speck on his tie. The GENERAL's uniform is black-and-red, he's dressed in complete POWER; he has on black gloves. He even has on a red-and-black CAPE.

The GENERAL has all black hair that is slicked back, fully. He has no facial hair, with a black military-hat, with red-trim, on top of his head. GENERAL NINO ESTEVEZ has a scar that stretches across his face - he has a dark tattoo-like bandage on top of the scar, it resembles war-paint.

The scar is courtesy of CAPTAIN TRICKEY LAMAR BREEDLOVE...

                    D.O.D WORKER
               (attentative,
                speaking spanish)
       GENERAL, senor. I have located a
       significant energy surge in
       NORTHWEST FLORIDA. It's not
       mechanical. It's organic.

...GENERAL NINO ESTEVEZ stands in the center of the CONTROL-ROOM, powerfully, with his hands behind his back, fist in-hand.

> GENERAL NINO ESTEVEZ
> (curiously)
> Do the Americans know about this?

The GENERAL turns around to face the D.O.D WORKER -

> D.O.D WORKER
> (subservient)
> No, Senor. I believe they have ignored it. I've heard no chatter or feedback from them, which, I must say, is odd. The signal I have for the energy source is currently on the move as we speak.

> GENERAL NINO ESTEVEZ
> (interested,
>   speaking spanish)
> On the move, you say?

> D.O.D WORKER
> Si, GENERAL. You told me to report any anomalies north of the border. This is an irregularity which I've never seen before. The ENERGY...it's off the meter.

> GENERAL NINO ESTEVEZ
> (hyping himself
>   up, commandingly)
> Get our best technical staff in here, immediately. I want a top-notch crew. I need more intel and I need that intel vetted to perfection - I want facial recognition of the target, on the move or no.

CUT TO:

EXT. AMERICAN AIRSPACE - DAY

A MEXICAN DRONE invades AMERICAN AIRSPACE, tracing the energy signal. It flies at MACH speeds to the target.

CUT TO:

INT. CONTROL-ROOM (MEXICO D.O.D BASE) - CONTINUOUS

> ANALYST
> - GENERAL, we got a precise ID on the energy signature!

> D.O.D WORKER
> Senor, the US I.D database is giving us a TRICKEY LAMAR BREEDLOVE.

TRICKEY's picture appears on the huge monitor within the CONTROL-ROOM...

...GENERAL NINO ESTEVEZ gets a spark in his eye.

> GENERAL NINO ESTEVEZ
> (tenses up, straightens himself)
> Well. Mierda, it's him! This will be more than fulfilling. Two birds, one stone. I'll be guaranteed to get my promotion to PREMIER after securing this KINETIC and seizing his power for the greater good of MEXICO, but I'll also avenge my son as I torture him. I'll give him his big surprise. Prepare The JAGUAR QUEEN and the HAMMERHEAD. We'll do a search and secure on this asset. Mobilize our resources, prepare yourselves - tomorrow, we're going to AMERICA.

GENERAL ESTEVEZ' smiles wide, his eyes lit up by the COMPUTER MONITER - looking at his TARGET: CAPTAIN TRICKEY BREEDLOVE

CUT TO:

EXT. THE RIVER CAMP ROAD - DAY

LOCATION: DALKEITH, FLORIDA

TRICKEY BREEDLOVE is rushing in the WASTEPRO TRUCK, speeding:

The forestry of DALKEITH is quaint, quite beautiful. Greenish bushes and high pine trees cover beyond both sides of the roads. Crickets are chirping, birds are singing. There's a stillness on the ROAD. Not another vehicle coming or going from TRICKEY's location.

TRICKEY's only focused on getting to his destination. He's not panicking, though. Keeping his wits about him, despite the shock he's experiencing. He's on a straight RIVER CAMP ROAD leading to LESTER'S LANDING. His speed is 85 miles per hour...

...BLOOD LEAKS OUT FROM THE BACK OF THE WASTEPRO TRUCK - mixed in with garbage juice so it's hard to tell that it's human blood (more black than red) - the smell of the compacted nearly full garbage-hopper has merged with the smell of the corpse of CAPTAIN KARL NOOSE that is crushed within in it.

CUT TO:

EXT. NEIL'S CABIN - LATER

TRICKEY goes slow down HAZELNUT LANE at LESTER's LANDING.

He gently pulls the WASTEPRO TRUCK up at the top of the DRIVEWAY of his UNCLE NEIL'S CABIN.

TRICKEY, shaking, eyes bloodshot red, tired beyond his limits, musters up enough will to exit the WASTEPRO TRUCK.

He walks down the driveway in his bloodied WASTEPRO VEST and dirtied, torn up military fatigue pants; his boots squelching with mud and water.

TRICKEY on the verge of collapse, but he wills himself on -

CUT TO:

A MAN, beer gut, short and stubby (full beard), pokes his head out of NEIL'S CABIN. He sees TRICKEY and his head jumps back. He turns around and YELLS very loudly to where even TRICKEY can hear:

BARO
(burps, rubs his
belly)
Hey, NEIL! There's some Hawaiian dude walking down your DRIVEWAY!

TRICKEY lights up a little bit. He KNOWS HIS UNCLE IS ALIVE and THERE. He looks up to sky, almost giving a look of "THANK YOU" to the Heavens.

TRICKEY stops in the driveway as not to be imposing. Delirious, he leans against NEIL's WHITE-WORK-VAN - leaving bloody handprints.

CUT TO:

UNCLE NEIL
(from inside the
residence)
A Hawaiian dude? Who the hell? Get the dogs away from him, now-

BARO
(to NEIL)
I'm on it.
(whistles)
RAMBEAU, RENA, all you mutts get back NOW.
(questioning)
Who are you, bud? What do you want?

The DOGS immediately obey BARO, and scurry away from TRICKEY after being so curious like cats. TRICKEY'S UNCLE, NEIL NOOSE, walks out on the porch of the CABIN. He raises his hands up in excitement. He doesn't quite see the blood all over his NEPHEW.

      UNCLE NEIL
    (running down the
     steps of the
     porch, arms open)
 - The prodigal nephew returns! -

TRICKEY is beat to shit. Bleeding out. Bordering on unconsciousness. NEIL goes to hug TRICKEY like a MAN, like a BEAR. NEIL is now a rugged and gray-haired white man - skinny yet athletic, in his late-50s.

      CAPTAIN BREEDLOVE
    (soft spoken,
     weakly)
 Uncle. UNCLE NEIL - it's you.

TRICKEY BREEDLOVE passes out and nearly falls flat on the concrete until his UNCLE catches him mid-drop. NEIL notices the bloody handprints on his WORK-VAN...

      UNCLE NEIL
 BARO! Get your lard ass down here
 and help me get this
 son-of-a-bitch in the house, right
 this second.
    (seriously, to
     TRICKEY)
 Jesus, NEPHEW, you're colder than
 a snowman sipping on a milkshake
 in a snowstorm. What have you
 gotten into, man!?

      BARO
    (shocked, rushes
     down the
     porch-steps)
 You got it, NEILY, I'm on it.

...The two men take TRICKEY's right and left arm, respectively, and carry him from both sides on their shoulders. His red-stained work boots drag the ground. The WASTEPRO is nearly lifeless.

NEIL and BARO, with care, get TRICKEY into the house. They shut the door.

                              CUT TO:

INT. NEIL'S CABIN - DAY

The two men take TRICKEY into the KITCHEN. NEIL leaves BARO to hold his full weight and slings EVERYTHING off of the kitchen-table.

NEIL immediately helps BARO get TRICKEY on the table. He grabs a first-aid kit out of the cabinet.

                    BARO
          What do you need, man?

                    UNCLE NEIL
               (using scissors to
                cut TRICKEY'S
                VEST off)
          I need you to pray. I've never
          seen a man this badly wounded in
          MY LIFE, BARO. I haven't seen this
          kid in a over a decade and he's
          dying on me.
               (slaps TRICKEY's
                face)
          You stay with me, TRICKEY! You
          hear me, son!

                              CUT TO BLACK:

CHAPTER II - THE CAPTAIN THAT COULD

WE BLEND INTO:

INT. MILITARY BASE - SAN ANGELO, TEXAS - MORNING

YEAR: 2013

COMMANDER FELICIA FACTOR - a redbone biracial woman - is in her early-30s, muscular, with piercing green-eyes and long blonde hair. She stands as the leader of a SQUADRON of SOLDIERS - there are 20 SOLDIERS in this STRATEGY ROOM, located in the SAN ANGELO MILITARY BASE in TEXAS.

We hear the almost hypnotic whooshing of the ceiling-fans:

                COMMANDER FELICIA FACTOR
           (mid-lecture)
    - Ladies and Gentlemen, this will
    be as COVERT a mission as can be.
    There will be no backup, no
    air-support, no cavalry. If we
    fail as a unit, we will perish as
    a unit, understood?

One of the SOLDIERS raises a hand -

                COMMANDER FELICIA FACTOR
           (points to the
             SOLDIER)
    Yes, CORPORAL BATES?

                CORPORAL BATES
    Are we 100% certain that GENERAL
    ESTEVEZ is going to be at the
    COMPOUND?

Another LEADER-SOLDIER, LIEUTENANT MOVAK KILGORE, walks to COMMANDER FELICIA FACTOR's side -

LIEUTENANT MOVAK KILGORE is extremely built and quite tall at 6ft5. He's Hawaiian, late-30s, has a tight military crew cut. His eyes are brown, he's clean-shaven.

                LIEUTENANT MOVAK KILGORE
           (arms folded)
    Our intel suggests he will be
    present at the FAMILY COMPOUND,
    yes. We will hit them with all we
    got. Even if he's not there, this
    mission is imperative on a
    logistical level - we need to shut
    this place down. We storm it, we
    seize it, we find out what the
    MEXICANS are really up to. These
                    (MORE)

                    LIEUTENANT MOVAK KILGORE (cont'd)
          people have nukes; and reports
          have shown they're kidnapping
          AMERICANS and experimenting on
          them, NAZI-style.

                    COMMANDER FELICIA FACTOR
          GENERAL ESTEVEZ is as much
          MILITARY as he is a CARTEL BOSS -
          in MEXICO, the two factions are
          intertwined, inseparable. PREMIER
          MADARO isn't running MEXICO,
          people - the GENERAL is.

Another SOLDIER raises their hand; it's TRICKEY BREEDLOVE
(in his late-20s at this point).

                    LIEUTENANT MOVAK KILGORE
          SOLDIERS, we have a Navy-man
          tagging along on this mission.
          He's a newly christened CAPTAIN
          among his own. This frogman is
          going to help us get the job done.
          He may be a CAPTAIN in his branch,
          but don't get it twisted.
          COMMANDER FACTOR and I still have
          command superiority on this here
          mission. With us, CAPTAIN
          BREEDLOVE will be logging in some
          much-needed COVERT ARMY hours so
          he can be of even better use to
          our blessed NAVY.
                (nods to TRICKEY)
          CAPTAIN BREEDLOVE, you may speak.

                    CAPTAIN BREEDLOVE
          Are we to take out EVERYONE in the
          building? What about gathering
          more intelligence from the
          relatives, workers, and ESTEVEZ's
          subordinates?

                    COMMANDER FELICIA FACTOR
          CAPTAIN, SOLDIERS, if you see
          JESUS CHRIST himself in that
          COMPOUND, you blow his ass to
          smithereens. If it moves, kill it,
                        (MORE)

                    COMMANDER FELICIA FACTOR (cont'd)
          that's an order. That's the
          MISSION - the intel will always
          keep coming. The main objective is
          to severely obstruct this new
          CARTEL-government and find out
          what secrets they're harboring in
          that FACILITY. We can call it a
          FAMILY-COMPOUND all day long. It's
          a government facility, though, and
          it MUST be shutdown, no matter the
          cost.

                    CAPTAIN BREEDLOVE
               (obediently)
          Yes, sirs - understood.

COMMANDER FELICIA FACTOR and LIEUTENANT MOVAK KILGORE
adjourn the STRATEGY-MEETING.

The SOLDIERS, including CAPTAIN BREEDLOVE, arise and gather
their gear: weapons (guns and knives), Teflon-vests,
helmets, the WORKS...

CUT TO:

EXT. MEXICO HIGHWAY - NAYARIT - NIGHT

...A small CONVOY of the 22 AMERICAN SOLDIERS maneuvers
through MEXICO at a speedy pace. There are BLACK SUV
vehicles and MILITARY TRUCKS carrying the troops to their
target(s).

They all have automatic weapons in-hand, with PISTOLS on
their sides, they have grenades on their person. Their
automatic guns have scopes with green, red, and blue lasers
on them.

- CORPORAL BATES is sweating bullets.

- COMMANDOR FACTOR is hyping herself up in silence.

- LIEUTENANT KILGORE has murder in his eyes.

- CAPTAIN BREEDLOVE has the look of a MAN on a MISSION - a

look of Dedication and Commitment to the task at hand. He's polishing his KNIFE.

                          CUT TO:

                    COMMANDER FELICIA FACTOR
                      (breaking the
                       silence)
               Who are we?

                    SOLDIERS IN TRUCK (IN UNISON)
               We are not to be fucked with!

                    LIEUTENANT MOVAK KILGORE
               I didn't quite catch that, who are
               we!!?

                    SOLDIERS IN TRUCK (IN UNISON)
               We're the last thing the ENEMY
               will ever see on this Earth!

The LEADERS' energy uplifts the several SOLDIERS in the back of the TRUCK in the Front of the CONVOY.

They proceed to check their magazines, bullets, scopes - they're preparing not for battle, but for WAR -

                          CUT TO:

EXT. THE ESTEVEZ' COMPOUND - NAYARIT - LATER

All CHAOS has broken loose at the ESTEVEZ' COMPOUND -

The AMERICANS are firing their weapons with rapidity, unrelentingly. The MEXICANS, the ESTEVEZ' ARMY, don't stand a chance.

WE CUT TO:

TRICKEY BREEDLOVE finagles his way to the TOP of the ESTEVEZ' COMPOUND as his fellow troops lay down heavy fire, suppressing the enemy.

                          CUT TO:

TRICKEY enters a ROOM, unaware of what's behind the door. He's ready, though.

> CAPTAIN BREEDLOVE
> (sees one TARGET, pointing his RIFLE)
> Get down! Drop your weapon now.

NINO ESTEVEZ's 16-year-old son is awaiting the AMERICANS in this ROOM. He has an AK-47. He lets it rip upon TRICKEY.

> EMMANUEL ESTEVEZ (NINO'S SON)
> (spraying his AK)
> To hell with you, GRINGO!

CUT TO:

TRICKEY BREEDLOVE does a barrel-roll to avoid the gunfire. He accomplishes dodging the bullets, by a camel hair. TRICKEY then, on his side, unloads his ASSAULT RIFLE upon the 16-year-old EMMANUEL ESTEVEZ, killing the BOY instantly - blood splatters behind the kid onto the WALL. A couple of the bullets hit him in the face.

TRICKEY BREEDLOVE regroups, mentally - checking his ammunition count, making sure he's fit to take on more of the MEXICANS. He stands over the dead BOY, NINO's son - he sees the corpse is just a youth. It sickens TRICKEY.

The SOLDIER turns around, only to see the boy's FATHER in his near presence.

GENERAL NINO ESTEVEZ fires his .357 REVOLVER at TRICKEY - hitting him twice, but only flesh-wounds. TRICKEY gathers his balance, pulls his MILITARY BLADE, and slices the GENERAL clear across the face, leaving him bleeding all over the ROOM FLOOR - TRICKEY stabs the GENERAL in the chest -

We hear NINO gasping for air, subtly.

AND WE BLEED INTO:

INT. SPARE BEDROOM - NEIL'S CABIN - NIGHT

TRICKEY, borderline deceased, stirs about, almost as if he's having a seizure. He's mutating...

...His eyes roll into the back of his head. A DIVINE SEAL appears on TRICKEY's FOREHEAD in what looks to be ARABIC CALLIGRAPHY. His UNCLE NEIL stands back on the other side of the ROOM, in absolute awe.

TRICKEY grips NEIL'S hand until it starts crunching and popping - NEIL jerks his hand away from his NEPHEW.

Suddenly, supernaturally, TRICKEY'S various bandaged, bloodied, leaking wounds heal instantly. Blood and puss move backward and reverse their way back into his body.

- Bullets pour out of some of wounds, thudding metallically on the tile-floor. TRICKEY's pigmentation begins turning light blue. His body's muscles constrict, his muscle fibers start showing. His fingernails turn black and grow wildly. TRICKEY's teeth grow, all of them, becoming FANGS - creating a wicked looking almost permanent smile.

NEIL is in shock at this sight, with a pale expression on his face. He prays, then-and-there to God. He lets go of TRICKEY'S hand, kneels, and BARO walks into the room dead-panicked by the commotion.

After the wounds heal on TRICKEY, he then subconsciously begins to levitate above the bed...out of nowhere, LIGHTNING STRIKES through the roof and ceiling of the CABIN - TRICKEY'S body acts as a conductor of electricity.

It courses through his NOW blue VEINS, white and blue EYES, and bluish SKIN.

TRICKEY...has TRANSFORMED. His muscle mass has grown denser yet a lot more slim - he's skinny now and you can clearly see his many muscles bulging in his blue skin.

He's SKY-BLUE, his FANGS are white as cotton and sharp as nails. Even his tattoos have disappeared. He still has a mane full of hair, though. In fact, it's even a bit longer now.

                    BARO
              (hidden, with fear
               in his voice)
          Dear God -

                    UNCLE NEIL
              (grabs TRICKEY'S
               hand once more)
          Nephew? Are - are you okay?

                                        CUT TO:

TRICKEY explosively jolts awake, he sits up slowly, looking around the ROOM.

                    CAPTAIN BREEDLOVE
          UNCLE NEIL? It's you!

                    UNCLE NEIL
              (happy as can be)
          Damn right, kiddo, it's me. You
          found me. What's the word
          thunderbird?

                    CAPTAIN BREEDLOVE
              (smirks, shakes
               his head)
          I feel like a new MAN.

                    UNCLE NEIL
          You should, you look like the
          leader of the Blue-man group now.
              (gestures to BARO)
          Get the mirror, man. Let him
          see...

Bullets lie scattered on the ground at the feet of NEIL and TRICKEY. TRICKEY stands and holds the mirror to his face.

                    CAPTAIN BREEDLOVE
          Oh, no. W-what's happened to me? I
          look like...a MONSTER.

TRICKEY sets the mirror down, horrified by his bluish
appearance, not to mention the ARABIC SEAL now etched into
his forehead. His uncle and BARO are equally disturbed by
it. It's not natural looking, whatsoever. He looks, alien.

                    UNCLE NEIL
          TRICKEY, you're my family. I am
          here for you, NEPHEW. But you've
          got to fill me in on the bad news
          bears of all this. You SELF-HEALED
          in a matter of seconds. You've
          undergone some kind of mindfuck
          metamorphosis. What the hell, man?
          We were preparing dinner before
          you showed up to my doorstep
          bleeding out. Now I have 4,000
          Dollars worth of Roof damage
          because the GOOD LORD saw fit to
          strike you with lightning. God in
          Heaven, just saying all that, I
          need a fat joint.

                    CAPTAIN BREEDLOVE
          I-I feel like, like I've never
          eaten a bite of food in my entire
          life. I feel thirstier than a
          vampire at midnight, NEIL. Food
          and drink first, then I'll talk.

                    UNCLE NEIL
                (pulls out a fat
                 joint from his
                 coat pocket)
          What do you fancy, TRICKSTER? You
          name it, I'll cook it -
                (lights the joint)
          Whatever you want to eat, it's all
          yours, buddy. We gotta get some
          food in you, BLUE or NOT.

                    CAPTAIN BREEDLOVE
          General Tso's Chicken, like you
          used to make for all of us.
          Please, man? And a glass of
          Ice-water.

                          BARO
            Water's coming right up.

                          UNCLE NEIL
            Give me 45 minutes, I'll have the
            meal ready for you. How about I
            put on some ole DARKWAVE music on
            the house-stereo-system,
            TRICKSTER? You always loved you
            some darkwave tunes, as a
            youngster -

                          CAPTAIN BREEDLOVE
                    (breathing
                     purposefully, in
                     pain)
            DARKWAVE - WOW, I haven't heard
            that word in ages. That - that
            would be swell, NEIL. Music always
            does the soul good.

TRICKEY walks toward the door of the BEDROOM. NEIL hovers
over him in a doting manner, making sure he's not going to
die on the spot.

No. TRICKEY'S wounds are GONE. No SCARS, even. He doesn't
have a single scar on him even from his previous wounds from
before his freakish incident of dying and coming back to
life.

TRICKEY takes a deep breath, in-and-out. He exits the
BEDROOM and NEIL follows right behind him.

                          UNCLE NEIL
            C'mon in the kitchen and get your
            water. We'll talk while I cook,
            okay? This is vital, man. You've
            got to give me something. Nobody
            in their lives has ever seen what
            I just witnessed here. I have a
            right to know.

                    CAPTAIN BREEDLOVE
                  (recognizes the
                   gravity of the
                   situation)
              Yes, sir, understood.

                                          CUT TO:

INT. THE KITCHEN - MOMENTS LATER

TRICKEY sits at the BAR, the ISLAND in the KITCHEN. NEIL
sears chicken in a frying pan. TRICKEY plays with his glass
of water, he hasn't drank any of it yet, oddly enough.

                    CAPTAIN BREEDLOVE
              I - I killed my grandfather. I
              didn't even know he existed. My
              mother never talked about him. I
              murdered him in cold-blood, UNCLE
              NEIL. KARL NOOSE is a dead man. He
              was your father, too, right? I'm
              SORRY.

NEIL stops dead in his tracks, the frying pan searing louder
and louder. TRICKEY'S UNCLE grips the KITCHEN COUNTER with
all his strength. TRICKEY witnesses several tears fall from
his UNCLE'S face.

                    CAPTAIN BREEDLOVE
              I had nowhere else to go. I had to
              come here. If you want me to
              leave-

                    UNCLE NEIL
                  (reserved and
                   withdrawn)
              - Hence the last name, TRICKSTER.
              I caught hell for having the name
              NOOSE. You know, I haven't seen my
              daddy in several years, since my
              sister, your mama, died. He was a
              mystery to everybody, even me. I
              lived under KIMBO's shadow for so
              long; the "great" AGENT ORANGE -
              KARL meant nothing to me. He
              stayed on that "base" of his,
                            (MORE)

205.

					UNCLE NEIL (cont'd)
			hanging people, reppin' the KKK
			like a bad-habit. He wasn't a
			father to me. He was an exploiter.
			A racist who hated everybody. A
			slave-driver, even to his own
			kids. Fuck 'em. You did what you
			had to do, because I know my
			father. He was an animal.

					CAPTAIN BREEDLOVE
				(with TRAUMA in
				 his eyes)
			He was a supervillain. He killed
			my mama. He killed my wife and
			kids, too. No, no...
				(cries electricity)
			...I butchered that motherfucker,
			you hear me? I had to. My mom can
			rest, peacefully, now. So can my
			baby girl and her mother. I KNOW
			they're in Heaven now smiling down
			on me, NEIL. I just know it, man.

NEIL takes all this raw information in (puffing his joint), and takes a very deep breath. He's as nervous as the Pope in a night-club. Stressed isn't even the word for something like this.

					UNCLE NEIL
			Hit this, nephew. It'll bring you
			back to earth.

					CAPTAIN BREEDLOVE
			No, thanks, Unc. I'd rather not.

					UNCLE NEIL
			I respect that, NEPHEW. By the
			way, I moved that WASTEPRO TRUCK
			away from the CABIN, the keys were
			in it. The thing smells like
			DEATH, and I didn't want any
			snoopers to see it -

                    BARO
              (at the KITCHEN's
               entrance-way)
          Neilly, I'm going to head out,
          man. I've done all I can do, here.
          You guys seem to be in deep
          personal territory. I just don't
          want no part of that. I got enough
          of my own problems to worry about.

                    UNCLE NEIL
              (winks at BARO)
          10-4, BARO. Give us the place.
          Shit has officially hit the
          ceiling-fan, brother.

BARO exits the KITCHEN and then the CABIN.

TRICKEY takes a sip of his ice-water. He feels like he's being electrocuted...

                    CAPTAIN BREEDLOVE
              (an electrical
               reaction happens)
          Son-of-a-bitch! It burns!

                    UNCLE NEIL
              (concerned, back
               to cooking)
          Can't drink water, huh? That's not
          demonic, at all.

                    CAPTAIN BREEDLOVE
          From that one sip, I feel like I
          have been hit by a train in the
          chest.

                    UNCLE NEIL
          You need to get to a hospital,
          dumbass. Or a doctor, something. I
          don't have the skills or expertise
          to help you, NEPHEW. After you
          eat, we need to get you medical
          help. What are you going to do,
          drink and eat electricity? I bet
          you can't even eat organic food!
          Seriously, man. What the hell
                         (MORE)

                    UNCLE NEIL (cont'd)
          happened on my dad's estate over
          there?

                    CAPTAIN BREEDLOVE
          Listen to yourself. I came to you
          because I thought you might have
          some sense as to how to handle the
          situation. I can't go to a
          hospital. I'll be black-bagged.
          Look at me!
                    (pauses for a beat)
          ...We - we were betrayed. The
          mechanic at my work, he was really
          MITCHELL NOOSE doing espionage
          work; your brother, a pure
          KKK-goon. They buried me
          half-alive, NEIL. They killed my
          coworkers, THE WASTEPROS, after
          they murdered my family. I was
          tortured, then I DIED, too. I even
          know what HELL looks like.
          Something went down with me, man,
          something - I can't even explain
          it. I heard a loud roar and felt
          the earth surrounding me. I
          reached up for air, somehow I was
          revived. I CLIMBED out of my own
          watery, muddy grave. I was trapped
          on the NOOSE Estate. I took a
          weapon from one of them and shot
          my way through those assholes.
          Then I threw CAPTAIN NOOSE into
          the HOPPER of the WASTEPRO TRUCK
          outside - I crushed him and swept
          him up into it. There's no telling
          how far down OR up this goes. You
          gotta help me, NEIL. No Hospitals,
          no Doctors, NO.

                    UNCLE NEIL
               (back-tracks)
          That's why it reeks so bad? You're
          telling me my FATHER'S corpse is
          literally marinating in the back
          of a TRASH-TRUCK with the maggots
          and garbage juices? The
                         (MORE)

                                                              208.

                    UNCLE NEIL (cont'd)
TRASH-TRUCK outside?

                    CAPTAIN BREEDLOVE
                (almost regretful)
Yes. I'll clean it up, myself.

                    UNCLE NEIL
Why'd you come to me, TRICKEY? WHY
NOW? Why didn't you go elsewhere?

                    CAPTAIN BREEDLOVE
I had NOWHERE ELSE to go, UNCLE
NEIL. I thought you might be able
to help me - I have NO ONE.

                    UNCLE NEIL
                (meditates
                  uneasily)
I get it. I really do. Let's eat,
the food'll be done in 30 minutes.
Go get some fresh air. Meet all my
dogs out there. I breed them, you
know? In fact, you might even be
able to adopt one for yourself
when all this blows over.

                    CAPTAIN BREEDLOVE
I could use some breeze, and I
love dogs.

                    UNCLE NEIL
If you electrocute one of my dogs,
I'll kick your teeth in.

                    CAPTAIN BREEDLOVE
Duly noted, Unc. I won't touch or
pet them until WE figure out what
this thing, this POWER really is.
For the time being, I'll keep my
hands to myself.

...TRICKEY and NEIL are on the same page. BOTH, though,
still seem to ignore the gravity of the situation; they fail
to acknowledge the supernatural metaphysics of what's going
on with TRICKEY, biologically at the physiological level.

Like the Butterfly out of its cocoon, TRICKEY BREEDLOVE is a NEW BEING.

> CUT TO:

EXT. NEIL'S PROPERTY - NIGHT

TRICKEY exits to the outside of THE CABIN onto the PORCH. He GLOWS like a "lightning bug", but instead of a greenish color, he's AZUL (blue).

TRICKEY BREEDLOVE is almost luminescent, glimmering like Moonlight against the dusk setting. He has tremors in his hands, shaking nervously with all the electricity and power flowing through his veins.

TRICKEY's outlook is complete altered now; the way he sees, it's with X-Ray vision - his surroundings are humming, vibrating. He sees things vastly different AND he can see through them.

TRICKEY looks at his shining hands. His appearance has been even more affected by the outside environment; as if the MOON has a sway upon the YOUNG MAN. HE WATCHES THE FULL MOON, with a Hawk's eye - his eyes are Carolina Blue, flickering with lightning, too.

He feels GOOD. He feels strong, sharp, and stable. DEATH has passed over him and left him behind to grieve.

> CAPTAIN BREEDLOVE
> (looking up at the
> moonlight)
> TAALOR, TIFFANY, MAMA, if you can hear me, I got him - I got them all. You three can rest peacefully now.

A bright-Red Cardinal lands on the PORCH railing. It seems to look at TRICKEY. It then flies away meeting 2 other smaller birds in the air.

TRICKEY blows a kiss with his hand right hand toward the fleeting Cardinal, something his MOTHER used to do while driving on road trips, often, for the simple purpose of good luck.

                    CAPTAIN BREEDLOVE
              (observing the
              nature around)
      Thank you God for this night.
      Thank you for everything. And
      bless my family's souls.
              (searches the sky
              with his eyes)
      Is this going to turn out to be a
      miracle, my resurrection? Or a
      curse?

As TRICKEY has spoken several sentences, he's gotten the attention of very cute and friendly K9 friends. Several Dogs run down the driveway toward him. They sprint up the steps, ambushing the man.

                    CAPTAIN BREEDLOVE
              (wary)
      Hey, doggies! You guys don't get
      close, don't get close.

One Dog, in particular, RAMBEAU, a blue-healer mixed with a rottweiler marches from the back of the pack of K9s and the animal "chooses" TRICKEY. He jumps at TRICKEY'S waist, nothing happens to the dog.

The electrical currents running through TRICKEY'S veins turn out to be harmless upon the touch of an external influence. TRICKEY immediately gathers, his body has, at least, SOME CONTROL over this.

                    UNCLE NEIL
      C'mon, TRICKEY, I told you not to
      touch the animals, and not to let
      them touch you! You could've
      SHOCKED one of my dogs to bits,
      that's 3,000 Dollars I'd lose.

                    CAPTAIN BREEDLOVE
              (turns around and
              playfully grabs
              at NEIL)
      You're the real lab rat, come
                    (MORE)

CAPTAIN BREEDLOVE (cont'd)
here.

TRICKEY acts like he's going to strangle NEIL.

NEIL immediately does some KARATE-type moves against TRICKEY, chopping at him with his palms, he hits his NEPHEW in the throat, making his nephew cough, hilariously.

CAPTAIN BREEDLOVE
You asshole. You trying to kill me?

UNCLE NEIL
I ain't afraid of no damn electricity, or a man named TRICKEY. In all seriousness, I'm glad there's no reaction to your touch - that means you have a degree of control. Now, the soup's on. Get it while it's hot or eat with the dogs.

CAPTAIN BREEDLOVE
Yes, sir. Going to wash up and get my grub on. Thank You, UNCLE NEIL.

UNCLE NEIL
Thank the Good Lord. I'm just a man.

CAPTAIN BREEDLOVE
If you're a man, then, what the hell have I turned into?

UNCLE NEIL
That's a damn good question, kid.

CUT TO:

INT. BATHROOM - NIGHT

The door is shut to the BATHROOM. TRICKEY is trying to act as normal as possible, given the circumstances. He now sees, in the larger mirror, the beautiful horror that is his ghostly fiendish appearance.

He looks like a humanoid creature from another planet. TRICKEY hallucinates for a moment. He sees HIMSELF attack himself through the BATHROOM mirror - this shocks him so badly, he bounces into the BATHROOM wall and falls through it.

                    CUT TO:

Frustrated, TRICKEY goes to wash his hands with soap and water. When the WATER touches his BLUE-POWER-FILLED-HANDS, a severe reaction happens; it burns, it stings, it HURTS him.

Power flickers in the CABIN, it's like a negative smashing into a negative, creating a causal explosion in space-time.

TRICKEY is now ALLERGIC to WATER. He has a WEAKNESS.

                    CAPTAIN BREEDLOVE
                (terrified)
            Bloody hell, man. I'm screwed.

NEIL knocks at the BATHROOM door.

                    UNCLE NEIL
            Everything okay in there,
            TRICKSTER? You need a tampon or
            something?

                    CAPTAIN BREEDLOVE
            I accidently busted a human size
            hole in the dry wall in here. I'll
            have to get some supplies to fix
            that up for you, man. My Bad.

                    UNCLE NEIL
                (busts the door
                 open)
            Man, you messed up my wallpaper
            and dry wall in the BATHROOM. Damn
            you! You have any idea how much
            money this remodel in here cost?

                    CAPTAIN BREEDLOVE
          No, I don't. I told ya, I'll fix
          it. Let's eat. Calm down, and let
          us pray.

                    UNCLE NEIL
          You're right. My nerves are just
          shot. This is a lot to take in,
          man. My whole routine has been
          disrupted but you're family - I'll
          do ANYTHING for you. Remember
          that. Don't mistake my frustration
          for anger. I simply am not able to
          mentally process this shit, man.

                    CAPTAIN BREEDLOVE
          All I need is 72 hours, NEIL. Give
          me that, give me some time to form
          a viable plan, and I'll be out of
          your hair. I promise.

                    UNCLE NEIL
          You take every second, minute,
          moment you need. You hear me? I'm
          all you've got, you're all I've
          got. We've got to help each other
          to get through this. Teamwork,
          TRICKEY. With Teamwork, anything
          can be accomplished.
                    (gives a thumbs up)
          72 hours it is, but if you need
          more, just know, you automatically
          got it.

                                             CUT TO:

INT. THE KITCHEN - MOMENTS LATER

TRICKEY BREEDLOVE looks at the food in front of him, appetized but unable to eat -

NEIL is grubbing like a pig in mud.

                    CAPTAIN BREEDLOVE
          I don't even think I can eat or
          digest this food, man -
          PHYSICALLY, I can't eat.

                    UNCLE NEIL
          More for me, then.

                    CAPTAIN BREEDLOVE
          I'm in between a rock-and-a-hard
          place. I'm royally fucked, aren't
          I?

                    UNCLE NEIL
          You're alive, ain't ya? That's all
          that matters, TRICKSTER. If you're
          breathing, you're blessed -

                    CAPTAIN BREEDLOVE
          That's the thing, NEIL. I'm not
          breathing, I'm pulsating with
          volts!

NEIL discontinues eating.

                    UNCLE NEIL
          It's all right. It's all right.
          We'll figure this out in the
          morning. Go get some rest, kiddo.
          It's going to be okay. We'll clean
          the TRUCK you brought - we'll fix
          all this, okay?

TRICKEY passes his plate of food to his UNCLE - he exits the
KITCHEN.

                    CAPTAIN BREEDLOVE
                (leaving the
                 KITCHEN)
          I'll see you in the morning, UNC -

                    UNCLE NEIL
                (raises voice so
                 TRICKEY can hear)
          There're blankets on the couch,
          sleep there. I just pray you don't
          burn the damn house down with this
                         (MORE)

215.

                    UNCLE NEIL (cont'd)
          electrical bullshit.

                                        CUT TO:

INT. THE LIVING-ROOM - NEIL'S CABIN - CONTINUOUS

TRICKEY lands on the couch in utter exhaustion.

He starts snoring in a matter of seconds. Sleep sweeps him off his tired feet -

                                        CUT TO:

NEIL walks to the threshold between the KITCHEN and the LIVING-ROOM.

He looks depressingly at his slumbering NEPHEW. There's PAIN written on the UNCLE's face. He slides into his own BEDROOM and shuts the door. We hear undecipherable words behind the BEDROOM DOOR, like a phone-call's being made.

                                        CUT TO:

INT. MILITARY CONVOY - MEXICO - THE GENERAL'S JEEP - MORNING

GENERAL NINO ESTEVEZ rides SHOTGUN in his personal JEEP - he holds an all-SILVER PISTOL to his temple, scratching his head with a huge smile on his face.

                    GENERAL NINO ESTEVEZ
                (in SPANISH to his
                 subservient
                 DRIVER)
          Where's the CHOPPER?

                    NINO'S DRIVER
                (in Espanol)
          The Helo is en route, GENERAL.

                    GENERAL NINO ESTEVEZ
          And what about the AMERICANS?

                    NINO'S DRIVER
          They've given us, YOU, full
          jurisdiction in this matter,
          Senor. And they've agreed to help
          us apprehend CAPTAIN BREEDLOVE -

NINO ESTEVEZ looks out the window at the ungodly sun-soaked
MEXICAN country - his SMILE only widens, his PISTOL shines
even brighter.

                              CUT TO:

INT. NEIL'S CABIN - THE LIVING ROOM - MORNING

The SUN has RISEN, hanging eloquently over NEIL'S CABIN -
sunrays pierce through the CABIN'S window blinds,
influencing TRICKEY to awaken.

When his eyes open sesame, TRICKEY looks up at the ceiling,
it's awfully close to his face, for some odd reason.

                    CAPTAIN BREEDLOVE
          Am I -

                    UNCLE NEIL
                (drops his HOT
                 COFFEE on the
                 beige carpet)
          What in God's Hell are you doing,
          NEPHEW?
                (mouth drops to
                 the floor)
          Are you fucking Floating, man? The
          electricity wasn't enough, huh?
          Now, you got to start flying and
          shit.

                    CAPTAIN BREEDLOVE
                (turns his head to
                 look at the COUCH
                 underneath him)
          Whoa!
                (drops SLOWLY onto
                 the Furniture)
          What is happening to me, NEIL? Am
          I going to die, man? I FEEL like
                       (MORE)

CAPTAIN BREEDLOVE (cont'd)
I'm losing all of my senses and sensations. The world looks - looks like a whole different place now. No, this can't be -

UNCLE NEIL
(uneasy)
You look like what they said was growing and rising right under our noses, TRICKEY. You - you're KINETIC, that's what they're classifying this craziness as; a MIRACLE of modern physics, my ASS! This is madness. I'm putting an end to this, now. NO MAN CAN LEVITATE. NO MAN SHOULD BE ABLE TO. You're going to have an army of men in white coats taking over my property as a Science Base so they can make little TRICKEY BREEDLOVE clones! To hell with that, man. I'm privy to these bastards. We're in a world full of trouble -

A HELICOPTER can be heard in the distance, above:

CAPTAIN BREEDLOVE
(sits up from the COUCH)
No, no. NEIL, listen to me, man. Let me finish fixing up the TRUCK and get the hell out of dodge, man. I won't ever bother you again, I'm sorry I had to in the first place.

UNCLE NEIL
It's too late, TRICKEY. I - I had no other choice. I had to sell you out -

Before NEIL can complete his sentence, he is cut off by a brutally intense BOMB that is dropped on the CABIN with focus and utter aggression, all by a MEXICAN HELICOPTER with

219.

missiles and bombs attached.

There's also a small AMERICAN POLICE FORCE in vehicles on the GROUND who have teamed up with the MEXICANS - there are 11 Units altogether, along with a 12th Unit of Highly Secure ARMORED VEHICLES, there, prepared to apprehend CAPTAIN TRICKEY BREEDLOVE now and a MEXICAN SECURITY TEAM in the CHOPPER led by the GENERAL NINO ESTEVEZ.

The BOMB is a type of recessive M.O.A.B - "Mother.Of.All.Bombs" (still very limited) - it nearly scorches the CABIN into in an INSTANT. Yet the place continues to partially stand, a burning HOME with flames upward to 30 feet high.

The explosion expands and consumes NEIL'S entire CABIN PROPERTY and NEIL himself - even the yard, grass, and trees are affected and caught in the blast.

The PROPERTY becomes a WARZONE with the flick of a wrist.

When the BOOM happens, TRICKEY is blown backward over the COUCH and OUT of the Glass-Window, like a ragdoll, into the greenery of the yard.

CUT TO:

EXT. NEIL'S PROPERTY - OUTSIDE THE SCORCHED CABIN - CONTINUOUS

                CAPTAIN BREEDLOVE
        (sprinting toward
         the FIRE)
    UNCLE NEIL! No!
        (holds out left
         hand, in agony)
    Please, God, no!

TRICKEY BREEDLOVE - still wearing his blood spattered WASTEPRO VEST, ruined work boots, and MILITARY PANTS - falls to his knees in overwhelming grief and RAGE; he sheds tears of wiry electric currents.

              GENERAL NINO ESTEVEZ
       (with a thick
        SPANISH accent)
    The dishonorable CAPTAIN
          (MORE)

											GENERAL NINO ESTEVEZ (cont'd)
						BREEDLOVE. My, my, don't you look
						extraordinary, cabron. You Owe me
						a beating Heart and a
						sorrow-filled SOUL!

TRICKEY discontinues mourning instantaneously once he HEARS that echo of a Hispanic accent. The YOUNG CAPTAIN BREEDLOVE stands up tall and turns around to face this DARK VOICE - it reeks of something of the past, something forgotten.

											CAPTAIN BREEDLOVE
									(faces the
									GENERAL's small
									army)
						GENERAL ESTEVEZ. Long time, no
						see, huh?
									(tilts his head,
									points at ALL the
									SOLDIERS)
						You're a dead man! YOU ARE ALL
						DEAD - you just don't know it yet.

											GENERAL NINO ESTEVEZ
									(with a
									shit-eating grin)
						NO, CAPTAIN - I am your DOOM,
						today. I see you have achieved a
						KINETIC form. KINETIC or no, your
						corpse is coming with me. I will
						dissect you and I will seize
						whatever power you have. That's a
						goddamn guarantee, mi amigo -

The AMERICAN POLICE number around 30 MEN -

The MEXICAN MILITARY FORCES number around 25 SOLDIERS and several OPERATIVES, with GENERAL ESTEVEZ leading them - the AMERICANS and the MEXICANS are teamed up to take down TRICKEY.

											CUT TO:

TRICKEY inches his way toward the forces, fearless.

                    GENERAL NINO ESTEVEZ
                         (ordering all the
                          MEN)
                    Give that pendejo all you got!
                    FIRE.

The AMERICAN COPS and the MEXICAN SOLDIERS all
simultaneously fire their respective pistols, machine guns,
and semi-automatic rifles.

COUNTLESS rounds whiz by CAPTAIN BREEDLOVE, then, some of
the BULLETS make contact with his body, face, and
extremities. Many BULLETS have penetrated TRICKEY's WASTEPRO
VEST and MILITARY FATIGUES, leaving his attire with dozens
of holes.

CAPTAIN BREEDLOVE falls to the ground - he has open,
electrified WOUNDS all over him, from head-to-toe. He lays
flat for a few beats. The CAPTAIN proceeds to RISE to a
stance and his body initiates a SELF-HEALING process.
Bullets fall out of the wounds onto the PROPERTY.

                    CAPTAIN BREEDLOVE
                         (talking to
                          himself)
                    Whoa. Okay.
                         (charges the ARMED
                          MEN)
                    Give me all you've got, you
                    motherfuckers.

CAPTAIN BREEDLOVE initiates contact with the LEADING
SOLDIERS and COPS - he grabs one MAN and incinerates him
with just a touch. He uppercuts another MAN 20 feet upward
and 20 yards backward, making the SOLDIER land on one of the
MILITARY VEHICLES, bending in the top of it and breaking the
front windhsield.

NINO ESTEVEZ rushes behind his strongest MEN. He expediently
waves his right hand to his TROOPS, gesturing a signal,
while the AMERICANS stand petrified at what they're
witnessing. It's turned into a situation of ORGANIZED CHAOS.

                    GENERAL NINO ESTEVEZ
                    FIRE the Big Gun.

One of the MEXICAN SOLDIERS readies a BAZOOKA in a rapid instance while another loads it with a ROCKET.

As soon as the weapon is loaded, the SOLDIER takes aim and lets the missile fly -

                GENERAL NINO ESTEVEZ
        (with a whisper)
    Dodge This.

                              CUT TO:

The MISSILE is heat-seeking - even as CAPTAIN BREEDLOVE attempts to finesse and move out of harm's way, the MISSILE finds him and hits him directly.

The CAPTAIN is taken aback, flying almost 20 yards in reverse on the PROPERTY. Smoke fills the environment, making a smog around TRICKEY to the point of him being unseen for a moment.

NINO ESTEVEZ is patient in waiting for the results of this TEST.

                              CUT TO:

<u>EXT. LESTER'S LANDING - THE SCORCHED PROPERTY - DAY</u>

TRICKEY BREEDLOVE is still in one-piece. In fact, he's not even injured, no. He is POWERED UP - he was able to absorb the KINETIC ENERGY, further fueling his own KINETIC POWER.

Electricity flows, vibrates, and permeates around the good CAPTAIN. He stands with his arms to his side, his fists turned upside down, as if he's gathering even more energy.

GENERAL ESTEVEZ is mesmerized by this.

                SOLDIER 1
    Oh -

                COP 2
   - SHIT.

SOLDIER 2
          GENERAL, umm, that was our biggest
          gun.

                    COP 1
          Officers! Retreat - get back from
          this MAN.

                    GENERAL NINO ESTEVEZ
                      (enticed as a
                       curious cat)
          I assumed you'd be this powerful,
          my dear friend. That's all right.
          I CAME PREPARED.
                      (walks toward
                       TRICKEY, unafraid)
          I have a surprise for you.

                    CAPTAIN BREEDLOVE
          I could squash you like a roach,
          GENERAL - but I have etiquette. I
          still RESPECT your rank.

GENERAL ESTEVEZ grabs the sides of the top of his CAPE, and he stops midway on the PROPERTY, about 25 yards away from the CAPTAIN.

                    GENERAL NINO ESTEVEZ
                      (to his OPERATIVES)
          RELEASE THE ANIMALS.

Two separate STEEL-CAGES, covered with shiny black-tarps, are wheeled right behind the GENERAL. The OPERATIVES remove the tarps, one-after-the-other, revealing God-awful-looking creatures, the likes of which CAPTAIN BREEDLOVE has NEVER seen -

These "ANIMALS" are HUMANOIDS - one is a shirtless male HAMMERHEAD SHARK, wearing fitted gray jogging pants, standing on two big, blue, mutated feet with the head of said animal but with the muscular body of a MAN combined with SHARK DNA.

This HAMMERHEAD HUMANOID is muscular, blue, fleshly, with gills even. HAMMERHEAD's eyes stick out from his SHARK head in muscular appendages to the right and left, like a true hammerhead shark.

The other being is a female HUMANOID JAGUAR that is standing upright on its hind-legs - SHE has breasts like a human woman, yet she is completely covered in spotted jaguar fur - she has paws as hands and paws as feet, all with huge monstrous claws. This JAGUAR-woman even has a lengthy TAIL.

The two CREATURES step out from their CAGES and flex their strength -

The HAMMERHEAD yells like a weightlifter who just won a contest.

The JAGUAR roars violently, fangs showing, at the top of her lungs. Both beings have on SHOCK-COLLARS - the COLLARS are removed remotely, and in an instant, the ANIMALS attack CAPTAIN BREEDLOVE in a combined effort.

                      CAPTAIN BREEDLOVE
              (taking a fighting
               stance)
        What in the godforsaken world are
        you THINGS?

HAMMERHEAD and JAGUAR meet TRICKEY BREEDLOVE in the middle of the property - all HELL breaks loose. A knockout, drag out fight begins to transpire.

It's 2 vs. 1 - ANIMALS versus a KINETIC.

                      COP 2
        GENERAL ESTEVEZ, have you brought
        war here?

                      GENERAL NINO ESTEVEZ
              (shushes the
               POLICE OFFICER)
        Let Them Battle. Bear Witness to
        this MIRACLE of CHAOS.

                      COP 1
        I'm calling in the fucking
        NATIONAL GUARD, right now.

                    GENERAL NINO ESTEVEZ
                        (does a smooth
                        signal to his
                        SHOOTERS)
                    No, you're not, Senor.

As the HAMMERHEAD and JAGUAR have a cutthroat versus match against CAPTAIN BREEDLOVE, the MEXICAN SOLDIERS, OPERATIVES, and SHOOTERS start killing the AMERICANS like they're feral hogs - the MEXICAN SOLDIERS are more tactical and quicker than the AMERICAN COPS.

The COPS try to fight back, to no avail.

                                        CUT TO:

                    COP 3
                        (gets shot
                        multiple times)
                    No! Get away, get-

A few COPS manage to get in their service-vehicles, only for ARMED SHOOTERS to chase them down before they can leave the PROPERTY - the SHOOTERS spray the vehicles with myriad BULLETS, creating unfathomable blood-spatter and shattering an over-abundance of glass.

                                        CUT TO:

GENERAL NINO ESTEVEZ doesn't even pay any mind to the massacre occurring. He's enthralled, fully captivated by HIS 2 ANIMALS battling his ENEMY in CAPTAIN BREEDLOVE -

AND WE CUT TO:

TRICKEY shoots bolts of lightning at HAMMERHEAD and JAGUAR, hitting them both square on. The two beings are sent far back, cascading like rocks on a pond across the grass and dirt of the PROPERTY, creating 2 massive craters as they land quite roughly. TRICKEY looks at his hands, surprised...

...THE JAGUAR and THE HAMMERHEAD stand up at the same time. They shrug off the electrical onslaught and get ANGRY as hell, thirsty for this CAPTAIN's BLOOD, electric or no.

The ANIMALS cross as they move forward in a type of "X" formation, quicker than squirrels. They gain on TRICKEY before he has a chance to engage with his KINETIC abilities.

JAGUAR swings on TRICKEY, he ducks.

HAMMERHEAD meets him at his dodge-point, picking the CAPTAIN off the ground with a powerful squeezing CHOKESLAM. HAMMERHEAD refuses to let go of TRICKEY, choking him with all his animalistic strength.

THE JAGUAR mounts CAPTAIN BREEDLOVE, clawing, scraping at him while villainously echoing like a true giant-CAT. JAGUAR then bites TRICKEY on the side in the rib-area all while THE HAMMERHEAD tries to turn TRICKEY's head to the point of breaking his neck.

CUT TO:

                    CAPTAIN BREEDLOVE
                (being overwhelmed
                 and overpowered)
        Aah! Hi-yah!

TRICKEY generates more ENERGY -

He is able to twist so that he can throw JAGUAR to the side at full-speed directly THROUGH the BURNING CABIN.

CAPTAIN BREEDLOVE also triumphs over HAMMERHEAD by knocking him back into one of the ARMORED VEHICLES with tremendous power, smashing the ride completely -

CUT TO:

The MEXICAN TROOPS have all but slaughtered the AMERICANS - there are now no domestic witnesses to this WARZONE or its 3 supernatural participants.

CAPTAIN BREEDLOVE looks past the CABIN where the JAGUAR landed - TRICKEY focuses, leaping OVER the CABIN to confront this ANIMAL-woman. He lands right in front of her, as she stands regaining her concentration.

                         THE JAGUAR
                      (with a purr in
                       her voice)
                    Silly, silly man - I eat KINETICS
                    like you for breakfast. You are no
                    match for me. I AM THE JAGUAR
                    QUEEN.

                         CAPTAIN BREEDLOVE
                    Who are you, really? What has the
                    GENERAL done to you?

                         THE JAGUAR
                      (snickering)
                    I'm just passing through, CAPTAIN.

TRICKEY cocks his head back-and-forth - her accent, it's one
he recognizes deep-down. The CAPTAIN hesitates momentarily;
he lifts his hands, as to blast this ANIMAL -

Out-of-nowhere, HAMMERHEAD grabs CAPTAIN BREEDLOVE by his
long hair, slinging him in a few circles until he flies like
a fastball into the adjacent property at the neighbors, some
50 yards away.

The HAMMERHEAD flexes every muscle, every vein he can, as
the CAPTAIN zooms in the air.

                         HAMMERHEAD
                      (snarling with his
                       many SHARK TEETH)
                    A fucking HOMERUN.

                                                   CUT TO:

The NEIGHBORS are not home, so no one is injured in the
adjacent HOME -

TRICKEY gets up, walking through the hole he made by being
thrown by the SHARK-man. CAPTAIN BREEDLOVE steps outside
again, he brushes his shoulders off of the ceiling, wall,
and glass residue.

The CAPTAIN is met once more by the TWO borderline-rabid
ANIMAL-HUMANOIDS - they attempt to intimidate. However, they
only infuriate TRICKEY. He POWERS UP, instinctively

227.

realizing he has the ability to do so now. An aura of ENERGY is conjured up around CAPTAIN BREEDLOVE -

JAGUAR and HAMMERHEAD go to pounce on their would-be VICTIM. TRICKEY jumps high, places both his hands on each of the HUMANOID's shoulders, doing a front-flip over them. TRICKEY turns around in mid-air, landing behind the ANIMALS; they're more than impressed by this challenging FOE.

CAPTAIN BREEDLOVE shocks the two HUMANOIDS with two-bolts of strong lightning that generates from his hands.

>   THE JAGUAR
>   (hurt from the
>   shock, turning
>   her head back)
>   You fight well, CAPTAIN.

>   HAMMERHEAD
>   But not well enough.

>   CAPTAIN BREEDLOVE
>   (with dark humor)
>   Says the talking CAT and the
>   walking SHARK.

THE JAGUAR and THE HAMMERHEAD double-team CAPTAIN BREEDLOVE with a barrage of scattered yet calculated KUNG-FU and MILITARY fighting moves. They hit him a multitude of times, pressing him back toward the RIVER and the DOCK -

THE JAGUAR bites TRICKEY on the neck with ferocity. CAPTAIN BREEDLOVE slings her off and she skids on the water, falling into it.

THE HAMMERHEAD seizes an opportunity while TRICKEY's distracted to jump on the CAPTAIN - the SHARK forces the CAPTAIN with a quickness into a POWER-BOMB wrestling move.

The HUMANOID SHARK uses all ITS strength when bringing TRICKEY in a downward motion into the DOCK, making the dock collapse in on itself into the body of water at LESTER's LANDING.

CAPTAIN BREEDLOVE is underwater -

CUT TO:

EXT. THE CAMP RIVER - LESTER'S LANDING - CONTINUOUS

The WATER is the SHARK's DOMAIN of STRENGTH - lo and behold, TRICKEY's WEAKNESS is H20.

THE JAGUAR rises to the surface of the RIVER. She gets out of the water and shakes herself to relieve her fur-coat.

THE HAMMERHEAD, realizing the water is harming his opponent, takes CAPTAIN BREEDLOVE down to the very bottom of the RIVER.

> CAPTAIN BREEDLOVE
> (succumbing to his
> WEAKNESS)
> Hmm! Hmm!

The HAMMERHEAD SHARK bites into CAPTAIN BREEDLOVE with a formidable bite.

TRICKEY's body REACTS -

A super-EXPLOSION occurs, resulting in this pond-section of the RIVER drying up in only a couple of moments; water nearly touches the sky, then a lot of it falls back onto the riverbed, and CAPTAIN BREEDLOVE, and the water stabilizes. Electricity surges through the water.

THE JAGUAR runs toward her comrades and her MASTER, GENERAL ESTEVEZ. THE HAMMERHEAD lands over 25 yards away from the RIVER. TRICKEY rises from the body of water, almost breathless, nearly drowned.

> GENERAL NINO ESTEVEZ
> (walks toward
> TRICKEY, gripping
> his CAPE)
> How's the little reunion going?

CUT TO:

TRICKEY is caught off guard by this spontaneous comment.

                         CAPTAIN BREEDLOVE
                    (on the ground
                     coughing up water)
               Reunion? I don't know these
               people, these ANIMALS!

                         GENERAL NINO ESTEVEZ
               You sure about that, "TRICKSTER"?
               Think long and hard, CAPTAIN.
               Remember who you left behind the
               day you killed my son. You didn't
               even blink at the notion! You
               thought you had fulfilled your
               mission? You think you're a
               CAPTAIN? You left fallen comrades
               behind. You're no captain. You're
               just a pawn in a chess-game - I
               will have this POWER of yours. No
               matter the cost. Think about my
               words, CAPTAIN - there's peace in
               solving the puzzle. I don't just
               want to win, no. I want you to
               know how you are going to be
               beaten.

While TRICKEY is distracted by NINO ESTEVEZ's words, the
JAGUAR suddenly puts a KINETIC-COLLAR on him that dampens
his power at first touch as soon as it locks.

CAPTAIN BREEDLOVE is weakened immediately - he falls to his
knees - a butterfly with disturbed wings.

HAMMERHEAD walks up to TRICKEY BREEDLOVE:

                         HAMMERHEAD
               A soldier's glory can only come
               from a good death.

                         CAPTAIN BREEDLOVE
                    (looks up at the
                     HUMANOID-SHARK)
               LIEUTENANT KILGORE?
                    (looks to the
                     JAGUAR)
               COMMANDER FACTOR? Is that YOU?

The HAMMERHEAD punches CAPTAIN BREEDLOVE with the strength of 10 MEN, knocking him out COLD.

> GENERAL NINO ESTEVEZ
> HAMMERHEAD, load up the dear CAPTAIN. Get in your CHAMBER, it's time to go back HOME. JAGUAR, back in your space, too, you know the drill.

> THE 2 ANIMALS (IN-SYNC)
> (subservient and
> obedient)
> Si, Senor.

> GENERAL NINO ESTEVEZ
> (staring at
> CAPTAIN BREEDLOVE
> in his CAGE)
> Mission Accomplished. Team 4, stay behind and clean up the mess. The rest of you, let's ROLL OUT, before more of the AMERICANS find out what we're REALLY doing here and mobilize on this site.
> (whirling his
> index finger in a
> leading fashion)
> The clock ticks!

NINO enters his ARMORED VEHICLE - "THE MEXICAN BEAST"

- TEAM 4 remains at the scene and begins sweeping it, as there are 25 AMERICAN POLICE CORPSES on the property.

All the other SOLDIERS, OPERATIVES, and SHOOTERS enter their respective VEHICLES - the squads and the GENERAL move out like the wind, undetected as can be, with evolved, supernatural organisms in their possession. The ANIMALS wait patiently under the black tarps. TRICKEY is unconscious also under a tarp in a transportable SUPER-CELL - now a POW.

CUT TO BLACK:

CHAPTER III - LET'S MAKE A DEAL

FADE IN:

EXT. HELL-WORLD - THE DARK PLANE - MORNING

>   THE MORNING AFTER...

...NEIL jumps awake:

He's burned from head-to-toe, in a state of paralysis, lying on his side in a fetal position. The world around him is purely DARK. This is not the land of the living -

NEIL's SOUL has been imprisoned in HELL-WORLD/THE DARK PLANE. He's in his HOME but it's a desolate, shadowy version of it - it's barren, destroyed, in ruins - the explosion sent NEIL to this other-dimension. A place out of time.

> UNCLE NEIL
> (unable to move)
> What in the world! What is this? I can't - I can't move. Where am I? SOMEBODY, HELP!

>   CUT TO:

> THE DEALMAKER
> (walks up the
> ruined staircase)
> And Jesus Wept Blood. My favorite word: "HELP"
> (laughs sinister)
> What can I do for you, NEIL NOOSE? Hmm? Need a hand?

The CREATURE that walks in the CABIN is THE DEALMAKER. He has on his white-suit and black-tie, his shattered BLACK HALO glowing. His nails as long as earth worms. His eyes glowing with white light. His long, blonde mangy hair hanging over his shoulders -

He has his wooden walking-stick which has the word: "HATOS" etched into it (means the number 6)

> UNCLE NEIL
> Where, where am I?

                    THE DEALMAKER
Not Heaven.

                    UNCLE NEIL
Am I dead?

                    THE DEALMAKER
                (smirking)
You're not alive, that's for damn
sure.

                    UNCLE NEIL
I remember a flash of light and
then -

                    THE DEALMAKER
Don't burden yourself, my child.
Do you want my help?

                    UNCLE NEIL
Who are you?

                    THE DEALMAKER
Me? I am WRATH in the flesh - I
know you betrayed your NEPHEW.

                    UNCLE NEIL
                (pained, grunting)
I had - I had no choice.

                    THE DEALMAKER
Does he know that you're the one
who rigged the explosives at that
CHURCH? The ones that killed his
FAMILY?

                    UNCLE NEIL
                (eyes widen)
How do you know that!?

                    THE DEALMAKER
I know what I'm supposed to know.
I know more than you could ever
imagine. You killed your NEPHEW's
MOTHER, too - impressive work. He
still thinks his grandfather's
responsible, huh? He gave the
                    (MORE)

                    THE DEALMAKER (cont'd)
            word, you did the deed. Which is
            worse?

NEIL shakes and fights to break free from the frozen
confinement of HELL-WORLD - this DARK-PLANE is a step away
from HELL itself.

                    THE DEALMAKER
            Your efforts to break free are
            meaningless - you will only leave
            from this place if I allow it.
            Understand, NEIL? You condemned
            yourself the day you murdered your
            sister. You forfeited your SOUL to
            me the day you killed your
            NEPHEW's wife and daughter. You
            either will work for me or PERISH
            and be cast into the hellfire for
            ETERNITY. The choice is yours, and
            yours alone. I know your secrets
            and I accept you. Do you want my
            help and the chance at a new
            existence, or do you want
            permanent Death? To be ripped
            apart in the bowels of HELL,
            forevermore?

NEIL sheds a few tears, and they burn off of his face.

                    UNCLE NEIL
                (shaking, burning)
            What would you have me do?

                    THE DEALMAKER
                (pacing
                 back-and-forth)
            Your NEPHEW - he now has within
            him THE DIVINE CURSE of the
            MOONWATCHER. What I need from you
            is CHAOS. Once you take this
            power, you'll know exactly what
            must be done. You'll be more
            powerful than anything or anybody,
            except for me, of course - all you
            have to do is say, "I ACCEPT" and
            I'll give you POWER beyond your
                            (MORE)

                    THE DEALMAKER (cont'd)
          wildest imagination. Will you
          comply, will you accept?

                    UNCLE NEIL
                (defeated,
                 downtrodden)
          I - I ACCEPT your offer.

                    THE DEALMAKER
                (with the voice of
                 a DRAGON)
          Good! Your NEPHEW will not join
          me, I've foreseen it - that makes
          him the ultimate threat. I've seen
          this. The MOONWATCHER cannot be
          allowed to live. If TRICKEY
          BREEDLOVE lives, my KINGDOM is in
          jeopardy. Take his power AND
          destroy him. If you fail me, I
          assure you, you will regret it.

THE DEALMAKER slams his STAFF onto the charcoal floor of the
CABIN in the DARK-PLANE - in doing so, a BLACK-GOO-like
substance escapes from THE DEALMAKER's mouth. It's ALIVE and
sentient. The GOO crawls down the creature's white business
suit and moves onto the floor of the scorched CABIN; like a
worm, it squirms toward NEIL.

                                         CUT TO:

The black viscous fluid, the worm-like organism sits right
in front of NEIL -

He examines the alien material. The BLACK-GOO then lunges
into NEIL's mouth, entering his body. He has a horrible
REACTION. He is finally able to move.

NEIL awakens back on EARTH, his body just as burnt as it was
in THE DARK-PLANE. He's overcome with darkness.

NEIL begins smashing at what remains of the floor of the
almost completely destroyed CABIN. Black veins expand across
his face, spreading to his brain and to his spine. NEIL
falls underneath the SCORCHED CABIN, hidden from sight -

WE CUT TO:

We can't see NEIL transforming, we only hear the commotion beneath the CABIN - we hear thunder and heavy rain pour.

                              CUT TO:

Abruptly, a CREATURE, supernaturally tall, black, metallic, slimy, with 8-ARMS (two human-like arms and 6 on its back) jumps many meters into mid-air, roaring like a wild beast -

It has razor sharp-teeth, one huge gooey white eye with a purple pupil (he's CYCLOPTIAN) - this CREATURE is extremely muscular, very ALIEN.

When the SUN hits the creature's skin, he becomes engulfed with HELLFIRE - the being is able to fly. The being is an absolute THREAT.

This creature is NEIL NOOSE entirely TRANSFORMED by the powers of DARKNESS - he's now a pawn of LUCIFER. He fully reenters earthly reality and speeds off from LESTER's LANDING, swiftly and horrifyingly - flying through the rainy sky.

                    NEIL NOOSE (TRANSFORMED)
                  (screaming
                   violently with
                   POWER)
          Rarr!

                              CUT TO:

EXT. US/MEXICO BORDER - THE CONVOY - MORNING

GENERAL ESTEVEZ and his MEN reach the more than congested, infested US/MEXICO BORDER - they are given expedient, direct access to MEXICAN SOIL with no trouble whatsoever.

                    BORDER AGENT
                  (to the other
                   AGENTS)
          Let the GENERAL through! They're
          good to go -

236.

                    BORDER AGENT 2
                (allowing the
                CONVOY through)
            Yessir!

BORDER AGENT 2 motions for the CONVOY to proceed -

                              CUT TO:

EXT. MEXICO HIGHWAY - LATER

GENERAL ESTEVEZ's CONVOY is moving ever so swiftly - they've exited the USA and entered MEXICO; ESTEVEZ's territory. He has CAPTAIN BREEDLOVE, the JAGUAR QUEEN, and the HAMMERHEAD confined to their personal prisons as they're transported.

                              CUT TO:

INT. MILITARY VEHICLE - THE GENERAL'S JEEP - CONTINUOUS

GENERAL ESTEVEZ, his left gloved hand on the driver's seat headrest, reveals his pearly white teeth to his COMRADES - extremely pleased with the results of the MISSION.

                    GENERAL NINO ESTEVEZ
                (looking back to
                his MEN)
            We did it! We're home free. The
            AMERICANS didn't even know what
            hit them, huh? LIEUTENANAT LOPEZ,
            contact the good DOCTOR ANIMUS -
            he will love to know I have an
            all-new specimen, KINETIC as can
            be, for him to experiment on. Tell
            him we have CAPTAIN BREEDLOVE.

                    LIEUTENANT LOPEZ
                (picking up the
                JEEP PHONE in the
                back)
            Si, Senor, GENERAL -

LIEUTENANT LOPEZ places the call to DOCTOR ANDROPOV ANIMUS -

LIEUTENANT LOPEZ
DOCTOR, good news. We retrieved
the target.

GENERAL NINO ESTEVEZ
(gestures to talk
to the DOCTOR)
Hand it here, SOLDIER.

GENERAL ESTEVEZ, with blissful glee, talks to his
subservient MILITARY DOCTOR -

GENERAL NINO ESTEVEZ
DOCTOR, I did it. WE did it. He's
not dead, he's fully intact - he's
more powerful than any KINETIC
I've ever encountered.

This DOCTOR, on the phone, can speak SPANISH:

DR. ANIMUS
(through the
phone, with a
RUSSIAN accent)
What is his power-set, GENERAL?
What are his limitations? What
caused his mutations? I have so
many questions -

GENERAL NINO ESTEVEZ
And soon, dear DOCTOR, you will
have the answers we so desperately
need - prep the CRYO-CHAMBER, the
prototype. We need to contain the
CAPTAIN - if he breaks free, all
of MEXICO could be endangered.
Even CAPTAIN BREEDLOVE doesn't
realize the POWER he has.

DR. ANIMUS
I see, GENERAL. I see. Bring him
to me - I'll have everything in
place. Are you sure you want to
use the prototype CRYO-CHAMBER? It
could kill the CAPTAIN, Senor.

                    GENERAL NINO ESTEVEZ
               (in Espanol)
          This puto is stronger than a god,
          do you understand me? He's just
          now starting to get a grasp of his
          abilities. We only nabbed him out
          of luck, DOCTOR. Now do as I say!
          We need his power, not him, yes?
          If he dies, it's of no consequence
          - remember, ANIMUS, remember what
          the man did to my SON. He deserves
          a slow, painful death. Hell, if he
          dies, we'll be the ones doing the
          autopsy - we will find the
          catalyst to his power. We will
          strip it from him; then we will
          attack AMERICA with all we've got.
               (laughing)
          We will have back our territory
          they so wrongfully robbed from us!
          We will win the battles AND the
          WAR - it has started.

                    DR. ANIMUS
          Si, GENERAL. Your wish is my
          command. How - how are my precious
          subjects, the JAGUAR QUEEN and the
          HAMMERHEAD?

                    GENERAL NINO ESTEVEZ
          You'll be pleased to know, DOCTOR,
          that they performed at the highest
          level. Between the two of them and
          their power, we were able to
          subdue CAPTAIN BREEDLOVE. I must
          commend you for your work. Without
          the ANIMALS, we would not have
          accomplished this mission. I'm
          truly grateful for your work, dear
          friend.

                    DR. ANIMUS
               (choked up)
          Thank you, GENERAL, for
          recognizing my efforts. I'm here
          to serve. I'm happy my experiments
                         (MORE)

                    DR. ANIMUS (cont'd)
          are manifesting results, truly.

                    GENERAL NINO ESTEVEZ
          DOCTOR, your experiments have
          CHANGED THE WORLD - you've made
          MEXICO a superpower. Now, get back
          to work. We're only an hour away
          from BASE.

GENERAL ESTEVEZ hangs up the JEEP PHONE.

CUT TO:

INT. DR. ANIMUS' LAB - MEXICO D.O.D BASE - LATER

CAPTAIN BREEDLOVE jumps awake, breathing very heavily without pause - he's upside down in a tank full of water, his WEAKNESS. He's now wearing a white and silver unitard-like wetsuit; his hawkish blue long-nailed hands and feet exposed.

TRICKEY gargles, struggles, chokes but he does not pass out or suffocate. He's in great pain. He still has the power-damper KINETIC-COLLAR on, too -

TRICKEY can see figures around him, with his X-Ray sight, but it's still very blurry. He cannot see clearly through the water nor the cage.

                    DR. ANIMUS
                (to his orderlies,
                 with a thick
                 RUSSIAN accent)
          Raise the subject, do away with
          the TANK - the computers read his
          power levels are decreased
          substantially. He's not going
          anywhere.

DOCTOR ANDROPOV ANIMUS is a short, stubby old RUSSIAN man, a scientist - he has a lengthy gray moustache and beard, with a head full of silver hair that's combed back. He has on a coffee-stained white business-shirt underneath a long white lab-coat.

                    LAB ASSISTANT 1
          Yes, DOCTOR ANIMUS.

                    DR. ANIMUS
          Also, call in GENERAL ESTEVEZ,
          please. He needs to see this.

                    LAB ASSISTANT 2
                (picking up the
                 LAB phone)
          Will do, DOCTOR.

The blocky WATER-TANK unfolds from all 4 sides - they each
go into the floor, mechanically, while the WATER drains into
the floor as well.

Around the TANK is a reverse charge electrified GATE with an
electrified ceiling. 4 mechanisms appear from within the
bottom and top of the GATE to bind and restrain TRICKEY by
his hands and feet.

CAPTAIN BREEDLOVE spits up water. He's been perpetually
drowning but he won't die, like a constant struggle for air
with no chance of passing out. The opposite of painless -

                    CAPTAIN BREEDLOVE
                (gagging, spitting
                 up water)
          Where, where am I?

                    DR. ANIMUS
                (stands charmingly
                 in front of the
                 LEASHED CAPTAIN)
          You, CAPTAIN BREEDLOVE are in
          MEXICO. More specifically, you're
          in my LAB in our very own
          Department of Defense BASE. Nice,
          yes?

The GENERAL enters the LAB with a shit-eating grin on his
face.

                    CAPTAIN BREEDLOVE
          GENERAL ESTEVEZ. You piece of-

                    DR. ANIMUS
                (wags his finger,
                 clicks his tongue)
            Now, now, play nice. Show the
            GENERAL his due respect.
                (to his ASSISTANT)
            If he disrespects the GENERAL, zap
            'em.

                    GENERAL NINO ESTEVEZ
            CAPTAIN BREEDLOVE. Finally, I have
            you in my possession. Finally, you
            have to answer for your
            war-crimes. You killed my son,
            stole him from me, forevermore.
            Now I'm going to steal your power
            AND your soul -

                    CAPTAIN BREEDLOVE
            You dipshit, I -

DR. ANIMUS gestures to his ASSISTANT.

The ASSISTANT sends hundreds of volts of reverse charged
electricity into TRICKEY's Central Nervous System - he
screams in agony.

                    CAPTAIN BREEDLOVE
                (yelling in pain)
            Aah! Aah! Stop, please, stop!

                    DR. ANIMUS
            You give respect, you get it. Keep
            your honor intact, young man. Talk
            to us, don't be vulgar or you'll
            be in perpetual pain, with zero
            chance of dignity.

                    GENERAL NINO ESTEVEZ
                (walks up to the
                 CAGE)
            DOCTOR ANIMUS is all about
            pleasantries. He's a man of
            medicine. Us, you and I, CAPTAIN -
            we are men of WAR. Isn't that
            right?

CAPTAIN BREEDLOVE
What do you want from me, NINO?
What!?

GENERAL NINO ESTEVEZ
(drops the facade)
I want my son back! Can you
provide that, CAPTAIN? Can you,
hmm!?

CAPTAIN BREEDLOVE
You know I can't.

GENERAL NINO ESTEVEZ
Yes. Yes, I do. Sadly, no matter
how many experiments I do, no
matter how much money I make, no
matter how much power I accrue, my
child is never coming back. You
saw to that - so instead of
resurrection, I'll have REVENGE.
I'll take your power!
(to DR. ANIMUS)
Zap him, now.

The wiry mechanisms are both attacking TRICKEY and absorbing his electrical power.

CAPTAIN BREEDLOVE
(roaring in agony)
Let - let me go!

DR. ANIMUS
(rubbing his hands
together)
That's not going to happen.

GENERAL NINO ESTEVEZ
Your power is unprecedented. It's
unpredictable. It's unbelievable,
off the charts, CAPTAIN. You're
basically a walking bomb. You're
NEVER getting out of here. TRICKEY
BREEDLOVE is dead - you're going
to die as just an experimental
statistic. You'll be the footnote
of the BANE ALGORITHM, nothing
(MORE)

GENERAL NINO ESTEVEZ (cont'd)
more. Once I've perfected the science, we will storm AMERICA and take her, once and for all.

CAPTAIN BREEDLOVE
The BANE ALGORITHM? What is that?

DR. ANIMUS
In 1973, the first KINETIC individuals, were discovered by the AMERICANS in DETROIT, MICHIGAN. BROGAN BANE and WALTER BRAY, each had superhuman traits. In short, Mr. BANE was a WEREWOLF, a Lycan. Mr. BRAY was a VAMPIRE, codename "VAMPIRO". They were gods among men, you see? I'm old enough to have heard the stories and the rumors: "VAMPIRES and WEREWOLVES walk among us!" - one rag-newspaper said. The AMERICANS tried to cover it up. Me, I went searching, digging, trying to find BROGAN BANE, attempting to locate WALTER BRAY, to no avail. They were mortal enemies, turned IMMORTAL. After their now classified bloodbath of a battle, though, I myself urgently left my diplomatic medical post in D.C, I'm RUSSIAN, and went to do my own research in DETROIT, at the high school where what was called in closed circles, "THE TURNING" happened; 108 people died that very night, half of them were transformed into VAMPIRES by WALTER BRAY himself, never to be seen again, except for in the shadows. BROGAN BANE, I guess you would say heroically, tried to stop the madness in his WEREWOLF form. He failed, also going missing. His failure was OUR success, though. I found the location of their deathly battle;
(MORE)

DR. ANIMUS (cont'd)
I entered DETROIT clandestine, covert and collected blood samples in a matter of hours. The blood samples led to studies. The studies led to equations. The equations - they led to the BANE ALGORITHM. Hence the JAGUAR and HAMMERHEAD you so desperately fought - your precious COMMANDER and LIEUTENANT. You must understand, CAPTAIN - I've unlocked the secret of the gods! My work mirrors that of ZEUS himself. I've collected the power of DRAKULA, of ANUBIS -

CAPTAIN BREEDLOVE
(cuts the DOCTOR off)
I won't let you get away with this. I will take my SOLDIERS back. How'd you brainwash them, anyway? How do you keep them on a leash?

GENERAL NINO ESTEVEZ
Well, if you kidnap a man's daughter and a woman's husband, they tend to do whatever you want them to do - and if you shock an ANIMAL enough times, it naturally learns to obey, no?

TRICKEY rattles the mechanisms - the more he moves, the more KINETIC ENERGY is absorbed by DR. ANIMUS' system.

DR. ANIMUS
We have CLOTILDA KILGORE. We have ARCHIE FACTOR - your comrades' family. If you don't cooperate, we'll take them out back and put bullets in them.

							GENERAL NINO ESTEVEZ
				Indeed. However, if you do
				cooperate - you might just be able
				to save them, CAPTAIN. But your
				dear FELICIA, your friend MOVAK,
				they're as gone as the wind -
				there's no going back for them.
				Once they became ANIMALS, they
				lost all sense of self. It's a
				consequence of the ALGORITHM. Does
				a LION see THE SELF? No. Does a
				GORILLA have a SOUL? No.

							DR. ANIMUS
				GENERAL, we've already met our
				power quota, just by his shaking
				and stirring, sir. Shall I put the
				TANK back in place?

							GENERAL NINO ESTEVEZ
				No, DOCTOR. The CAPTAIN here needs
				to talk to my wife, and explain to
				her why she no longer has a son.
						(into his comms)
				Bring in NIDIA, please.

							MEXICAN SOLDIER
				Si, Senor. I will tell her you are
				ready for her -

							CAPTAIN BREEDLOVE
				Listen, GENERAL, I didn't - I
				didn't mean to take your son from
				you. I was just-

The LAB doors hum open:

							NIDIA ESTEVEZ
						(high heels
						clicking)
				- Following orders. Pathetic. So,
				NINO, this is the man who stole my
				son from me? This monster!

Mrs. NIDIA ESTEVEZ is 5ft2, small yet powerful - she's
extremely gorgeous, with long black, silky hair. She has

elegant brown eyes. She's dressed like a Queen, covered in jewelry (rings and necklaces). She has on makeup, pitch-black lipstick, and her nails are done; painted black.

> CAPTAIN BREEDLOVE

Mrs. ESTEVEZ, I -

> NIDIA ESTEVEZ

You will not speak - not even if spoken to. Shock him, now.

> CAPTAIN BREEDLOVE
> (electrocuted)

No!

> GENERAL NINO ESTEVEZ
> (in English with a
> thick Spanish
> accent)

The Wife has waited a very long time for this day. Today, CAPTAIN, you meet your timely demise.

> CAPTAIN BREEDLOVE
> (fighting through
> the shocking)

I, too, know how it feels to lose a child. I - I lost my wife and my daughter in a terrorist attack. GENERAL, please - MRS. ESTEVEZ, please, don't do this.

> NIDIA ESTEVEZ

An AMERICAN CAPTAIN pleading for his life - and I thought I'd seen it all.

> GENERAL NINO ESTEVEZ
> (wide-eyed at the
> revelation)

Wait, DOCTOR, cool the charges. Let him speak. Explain, CAPTAIN - what do you mean your wife and child were killed?

NINO ESTEVEZ puts a hand on his wife's shoulder.

CAPTAIN BREEDLOVE
They burned alive. In - in a CHURCH-BOMBING. My grandfather, CAPTAIN KARL NOOSE, he orchestrated it, he -

NIDIA ESTEVEZ
(pissed off)
- ENOUGH!

GENERAL NINO ESTEVEZ
(to NIDIA)
Honey, let the CAPTAIN speak.

NIDIA scoffs at her husband's request. She quiets down, folds her arms, and walks around the CAGE, like a LIONESS circling its prey.

CAPTAIN BREEDLOVE
CAPTAIN NOOSE, I found out he was my grandfather, but he was also the leader of the KKK - he tried to kill me, too, by burying me alive. He -

GENERAL NINO ESTEVEZ
In all sincerity, CAPTAIN - you have my condolences. I can't believe your daughter and wife suffered so. And your grandfather, this CAPTAIN NOOSE, he sounds like an absolute madman. How did you receive your KINETIC power?

CAPTAIN BREEDLOVE
I don't know, GENERAL. I was in a muddy, watery grave, all I saw was blackness. Then I heard a thunderclap, and the next thing I knew, I was digging myself out of my own grave.

DR. ANIMUS
Were you BLUE when this occurred?
Were you in-touch with your
abilities, or did they surface
later on?

CAPTAIN BREEDLOVE
- This POWER, if that's what you'd
like to call it, formed later on.
The day after my revival. My wife
and daughter were just killed a
few days ago. I was in my grave
for 3 days. I rose up, went to my
UNCLE's property - when you
dropped that M.O.A.B, GENERAL, you
killed my UNCLE. And now, here we
are -

GENERAL NINO ESTEVEZ
Everybody's gotta die, somehow,
CAPTAIN. Getting to you was of the
utmost importance to me - even if
I only somehow retrieved a sample
of your DNA, we were going to get
you one way or the other. We knew
your power was off-the-charts, I
was taking no risks. We brought in
the big guns. Your UNCLE was
merely collateral damage,
understand?

DR. ANIMUS
Your abilities, your power,
they've come from the heavens
themselves. It's off the scale!
Spontaneous evolution like this
has never occurred. All the
KINETICS are either born that way
or they inherent their power from
an external source; NATURE herself
has bestowed upon you a godly
gift, young CAPTAIN. GENERAL
ESTEVEZ, we need to put CAPTAIN
BREEDLOVE in the CRYO-CHAMBER,
immediately. It cannot wait any
longer.

GENERAL ESTEVEZ contemplates. He puts his hand under his chin, weighing his options.

> NIDIA ESTEVEZ
> (to TRICKEY,
> circling the CAGE)
> Why did you murder my only child, CAPTAIN?

> CAPTAIN BREEDLOVE
> Mrs. ESTEVEZ, NIDIA, there's not a day that goes by that I do not think of that mission and what went wrong. I see your son's face every night when I TRY to sleep. He's the ghost of my nightmares.

> NIDIA ESTEVEZ
> Your death will not be so quick, as his was. You shot him. We are going to dissect you while you still breathe - mark my words.

> GENERAL NINO ESTEVEZ
> (kisses the top of
> his wife's head)
> NIDIA, you've said your peace to the CAPTAIN - despite his similarly tragic circumstances, he will still feel OUR wrath. Karma is King in MEXICO. How about you go home now and relax. You've confronted the monster, rest in knowing that he'll never hurt us again.
> (to DR. ANIMUS)
> Get the CRYO-CHAMBER ready, Doctor. It's time. I've heard enough from CAPTAIN BREEDLOVE.

> CAPTAIN BREEDLOVE
> GENERAL, you also have my condolences. If I could take back time, if I could spare your son, know that I would.

                    GENERAL NINO ESTEVEZ
               Are those your last words,
               CAPTAIN?

TRICKEY remains silent. He simply nods, "yes".

                    NIDIA ESTEVEZ
                    (walking through
                     the LAB doors)
               God will not have any mercy for
               you, SOLDIER.

DR. ANIMUS, at a separate station of the giant LAB, stands next to the CRYO-CHAMBER - it's a prototype, capable of freezing an ORGANISM at minus-200 degrees Fahrenheit; making whatever it freezes totally stagnant, at a molecular level. It freezes the subject yet keeps them awake, alive, ready for dissection.

                                        CUT TO:

INT. DR. ANIMUS' LAB - MEXICAN D.O.D BASE - CONTINUOUS

DR. ANIMUS messes with several switches, buttons, what have you.

His ASSISTANTS prepare a tech-based stretcher that also serves as a container. They walk toward the CAGED CAPTAIN BREEDLOVE:

                    LAB ASSISTANT 1
               Power down the CAGE, open the
               doors. Make sure the damper is
               secure. Introduce tranquilizers
               via the confinement system, now.

The ASSISTANTS enter the CAGE.

                    LAB ASSISTANT 2
                    (pressing a button
                     at the other
                     station)
               Giving tranquilizers.

TRICKEY almost blacks out, his vision becomes foggy. Despite his KINETIC ability, he's still prone to the suped up tranquilizers that DR. ANIMUS has given him.

> DR. ANIMUS
> Let the work commence -
> ASSISTANTS, transfer the CAPTAIN
> to the CRYO-CHAMBER. In a matter
> of hours, it'll be time to do a
> medical examination. He'll freeze,
> then we'll work.

> LAB ASSISTANT 2
> (fully compliant)
> Yes, DR. ANIMUS.

The ASSISTANTS release TRICKEY BREEDLOVE from the confinement mechanisms/arms.

He collapses onto the metallic LAB-FLOOR -

They, wearing special LAB-SUITS with advanced equipment, put TRICKEY BREEDLOVE on the tech-based stretcher, moving him to the CRYO-CHAMBER -

DR. ANIMUS helps them lift CAPTAIN BREEDLOVE into the prototypical CRYO-CHAMBER.

It seals, shuts - the GENERAL himself powers the CRYO-CHAMBER on. While nearly unconscious, yet still coherent, CAPTAIN BREEDLOVE begins to FREEZE solid as the machine does its function.

The Tranquilizers work harder in TRICKEY's system, but he still tries to cling to reality. He is surprised to discover he's being frozen.

He puts his hands to the glass of the CHAMBER - he roars fighting for his life and freedom. He can't get out. He can't breathe. He can't see.

He's put in a CRYO-STASIS/SLEEP, falling into a medically induced coma as the ice covers his face, body, arms, and legs.

CAPTAIN BREEDLOVE feels the COLD - his soul shivers.

CUT TO:

                  DR. ANIMUS
            (to ASSISTANTS)
      Good work, team.
            (to ESTEVEZ)
      GENERAL, we've done it. In a
      matter of hours, it'll be time to
      pop the hood on this CAPTAIN
      BREEDLOVE - we'll unlock VALHALLA.

                GENERAL NINO ESTEVEZ
            (shakes DR.
              ANIMUS' hand)
      Thank you, ANDROPOV. Good work,
      DOCTOR. Good work, indeed. We'll
      have our ANIFUSION army in no time
      at all. Watch and see. We'll not
      only take AMERICA, no. We'll take
      HEAVEN - and I will see my boy
      again.

The DOCTOR and the GENERAL stand side-by-side, feeling accomplished, watching the incapacitated TRICKEY BREEDLOVE - their new experiment.

CUT TO BLACK:

CHAPTER IV - BEHOLD, THE DARKWAVE

                              FADE IN:

<u>EXT. PANAMA CITY, FLORIDA - DOWNTOWN AREA - DAY</u>

NEIL NOOSE - now transformed into the nefarious creature (he stands over 7FT tall) - arrives with the forces of darkness in PANAMA CITY, FLORIDA, in the DOWNTOWN AREA:

He is saturated in ALIEN ONYX colored GOO, with HELLFIRE flowing like lava throughout his body, totally possessed by the prince of the power and the air.

NEIL, a metal-like CYCLOPS, flies down and crash-lands in the middle of DOWNTOWN PC in the middle of the road.

FLORIDIAN CITIZENS start to panic, immediately -

NEIL, in this new monstrous form, has a unique vision and perception. He sees everything in thermal vision, as if the world's on fire - EVERYBODY is a TARGET.

CUT TO:

           DARKWAVE
        (sinister)
  Fear not, folks, I am here.

NEIL, salivating SILVER-GOO, punches the ground, causing a cataclysmic energy surge in the concrete, and miniature earthquake begins - the SHADOWS saturate the DOWNTOWN AREA, literally sweeping the scene.

          FLORIDA CITIZEN
    Call 911, somebody, NOW!

           DARKWAVE
       (rushes the
        CITIZEN, grabs
        him by the throat)
  They will not be able to help you.

With one of his 8 arms, DARKWAVE decapitates the CITIZEN - his GOOEY skin is harder than STEEL. Blood spatters everywhere, all in the street. The blood runneth over into the sewer -

CUT TO:

8 COP CARS arrive urgently to the scene of CHAOS - they're minds are blown at the sight of the demonic entity.

The 16 POLICE OFFICERS fire shotguns, assault rifles, pistols, you name it. DARKWAVE is unaffected by the barrage of bullets. His skin ABSORBS the bullets and turns them into ENERGY -

Randomly, CHAINS appear from out of DARKWAVE's gooey skin. 16 CHAINS grab the 16 COPS, around the faces, necks, and torsos - in one juke of movement, DARKWAVE mutilates the OFFICERS: with ease.

- NEIL roars like a lunatic.

                    DARKWAVE
               (with an ALIEN
                 voice)
          Is this the best you can do? You
          petty people, your time is up! I
          am death's disciple. I am chaos's
          child. I AM DARKWAVE! Bow to me,
          bow to the powers of DARKNESS.

                                        CUT TO:

MILITARY VEHICLES, 5 of them, pull up to the massacre -
CITIZENS are scurrying around like roaches trying to avoid
death and danger.

The 15 MILITARY TROOPS are equipped with KINETIC PREVENTION
weaponry - one of the SOLIDERS fires a heat-seeking ROCKET
at DARKWAVE.

NEIL NOOSE, in DARKWAVE form, with 3 of his ARMS, grabs the
ROCKET out of thin air like it's a fleeing fly -

                    DARKWAVE
               (holding the
                 burning ROCKET)
          Big Mistake.

With another of his ARMS, DARKWAVE blasts one of the
businesses with HELLFIRE, causing it to burn instantly -

He then lets the ROCKET go and it zooms into the burning
BUSINESS, creating a giant explosion with great percussion.

                    AMERICAN MILITARY TROOP
               (into his comms)
          We need air support, now! We have
          a KINETIC creature in DOWNTOWN PC.
          We need to deploy everything,
          GENERAL! This creature, he's -

                    DARKWAVE
                (grabs the SOLDIER
                 by the shoulder)
              - RIGHT BEHIND YOU.

NEIL throws the SOLIDER over 100 yards away through the air
- he flies like a pitched pebble.

DARKWAVE goes to attack the other SOLDIERS. They are unable
to harm the creature, even with their customized KINETIC
PREVENTION weaponry - DARKWAVE is simply TOO STRONG.

One of the TROOPS sets his rifle to AUTOMATIC and sprays
with all he's got. DARKWAVE opens his mouth over a foot
wide, EATING the BULLETS, absorbing the KINETIC ENERGY from
the hot bullets. The HELLFIRE becomes greater inside the
demon-beast -

                                              CUT TO:

                    DARKWAVE
              Humans Hath No Fury like that of a
              Prefect of Darkness.

A FIGHTER JET flies into the vicinity of DARKWAVE - the
pilots target the creature, very quickly.

THEY FIRE UPON NEIL with 2 ROCKETS.

The monster FEEDS off of the ENERGY, sucking it into his
body.

DARKWAVE jumps high into the sky - IT flies directly into
the FIGHTER JET, and with one of its 8 arms, it slices the
JET in half, extremely destructively.

The JET crashes into the DOWNTOWN of PC -

The demonic being lands square in the center of MAIN STREET,
as the enforcers of the community fight for their very
lives.

CUT TO:

HELLFIRE builds up even more in DARKWAVE's system. NEIL

grabs his head (like he has a migraine), his ENERGY is multiplying by the moment -

Abruptly, DARKWAVE, with RED ELECTRICITY surrounding him, lets out the absorbed KINETIC ENERGY he has taken from the attacks - it's almost like a limited RED-NUCLEAR-EXPLOSION occurs.

DOWNTOWN PANAMA CITY, nearly all of it, is CONSUMED by supernatural HELLFIRE due to DARKWAVE's chaotic, uncontrollable power. The Fire is Relentless...

...DARKWAVE surveys the damage he's caused; his possession makes him smile with his SILVERY SERPENT-like teeth.

DARKWAVE flies up into the sky, stops about 100FT in the air, turns WEST - he speeds off with the SHADOWS.

CUT TO:

INT. THE GOVERNOR'S OFFICE - TALLAHASSEE, FLORIDA - DAY

FLORIDA GOVERNOR MIKE CHARLTON sits at his desk in his OFFICE in TALLAHASSEE - he's delivering a warning to all of FLORIDA and AMERICA.

                    GOVERNOR CHARLTON
           (weary, wary,
            worried)
     My Fellow Americans, specifically,
     Floridians; we are under attack.
     According to reports that I've
     been given, there is a creature,
     perhaps ALIEN in nature, that has
     attacked PANAMA CITY, FLORIDA - by
     all accounts, the DOWNTOWN AREA of
     the city has been completely
     destroyed. This creature,
     according to my sources, is
     calling ITSELF: "DARKWAVE". I want
     all of America to be on alert, be
     prepared for anything, and know,
     your government has your back,
     your military has your back, and I
     have your back. No matter the
     strength of this creature, there
                           (MORE)

                    GOVERNOR CHARLTON (cont'd)
          is no one entity stronger than The
          United States of America. May God
          Bless You All. We shall
          Overcome...
                    (indistinguishable
                     dialogue)

                                        CUT TO:

EXT. THE ESTEVEZ' COMPOUND - NAYARIT - FLASHBACK - NIGHT

                         - 2013

TRICKEY BREEDLOVE, outside of the ESTEVEZ' COMPOUND, sprints away from the MEXICAN MILITIA -

                    CAPTAIN BREEDLOVE
                    (running for his
                     life)
          COMMANDER FACTOR!? LIEUTENANT
          KILGORE!? Where are you!?

CAPTAIN BREEDLOVE pauses for a moment to catch his breath, hands on his knees.

He sees none of his teammates.

TRICKEY does what any man would do - he gets into one of the AMERICAN SUVs and dips from the scene of CHAOS. He moves like the devil's after him...

CUT TO:

INT. THE ESTEVEZ' COMPOUND - NAYARIT - FLASHBACK - NIGHT

COMMANDER FACTOR and LIEUTENANT KILGORE both sit strapped down to chairs, their mouths wrapped and gagged.

GENERAL ESTEVEZ, a huge cut on his face and bleeding out, stands over the two AMERICAN SOLDIERS -

                    GENERAL NINO ESTEVEZ
                  (in English,
                    accent heavy)
              You two are all that's left of
              your little - team. You both are
              so very valuable. I have grand
              plans for you, SOLDIERS. This -
              this is going to be fun.
                  (to his lower)
              Get Doctor ANIMUS on the phone.

                    SUBSERVIENT
                  (gets out his
                    smartphone)
              Si, GENERAL.

                                        CUT TO:

EXT. SAN ANGELO MILITARY BASE - MORNING

CAPTAIN TRICKEY BREEDLOVE appears at the SAN ANGELO MILITARY
BASE in the SUV -

The SOLDIERS outside onlook at the distraught, nearly
destroyed CAPTAIN.

A GENERAL, NORMAN RAIN, and another COMMANDER, ALVIN
SCHULTZ, come outside of the BASE and approach TRICKEY
BREEDLOVE:

                    COMMANDER SCHULTZ
                  (concerned,
                    cautious)
              CAPTAIN BREEDLOVE? Where is your
              team?

TRICKEY falls flat on his face, fighting for his breath due
to exhaustion, hunger, and thirst -

                    GENERAL RAIN
                  (authoritatively)
              Acknowledge your COMMANDER,
              CAPTAIN - or you will be
              disciplined, despite your current
              condition.

TRICKEY BREEDLOVE rises to his feet, adjusting himself.

>   CAPTAIN BREEDLOVE
>   (almost breathless)
>   They - they're gone. All of them -
>   we failed, sir.
>
>   COMMANDER SCHULTZ
>   Is that so? How is it only you
>   survived to tell the tale, huh,
>   SOLDIER?

A couple of beats, TRICKEY doesn't respond.

GENERAL RAIN hovers over CAPTAIN BREEDLOVE, pressing his shoulder with his index finger.

>   GENERAL RAIN
>   I want answers, CAPTAIN, right
>   this second.

TRICKEY SNAPS - losing all patience and composure. He erupts with tremendous anger and proceeds to punch the daylights out of both GENERAL RAIN and COMMANDER SCHULTZ.

Various other SOLDIERS intervene in the scuffle, pushing CAPTAIN BREEDLOVE away from his commanding officers.

>   CAPTAIN BREEDLOVE
>   You want answers!? I want out of
>   this shit-show!
>
>   GENERAL RAIN
>   (wipes the blood
>   from his lips)
>   Out you are!
>
>   COMMANDER SCHULTZ
>   (getting back on
>   his feet)
>   You just bought yourself a
>   DISHONORABLE DISCHARGE, son -
>   (commanding,
>   referring to
>   TRICKEY)
>   Get this scum to the holding cell
>   (MORE)

                    COMMANDER SCHULTZ (cont'd)
for a COURT MARTIAL.

                    GENERAL RAIN
              (giving an order)
          Cuff him.

CAPTAIN BREEDLOVE puts his hands behind his back and tilts
his head down in shame, as multiple SOLDIERS place
restraints on him -

AND WE CUT TO:

INT. MEXICAN D.O.D BASE - THE CONTROL ROOM - CONTINUOUS

GENERAL ESTEVEZ enters the CONTROL-ROOM.

                    D.O.D WORKER
              (in Spanish)
          GENERAL, we have a problem.

                    GENERAL NINO ESTEVEZ
          - Yes, what is it?

                    D.O.D WORKER
          There's been an Attack in AMERICA,
          in FLORIDA, the panhandle - by,
          what's being called, an "ALIEN"
          KINETIC being, Senor. They are
          referring to it as: "DARKWAVE"

                    GENERAL NINO ESTEVEZ
              (highly concerned)
          What kind of ALIEN?

                    D.O.D WORKER
          Apparently, this THING has caused
          a NUCLEAR EXPLOSION in the
          DOWNTOWN AREA of PANAMA CITY,
          killing HUNDREDS, Senor.

                    GENERAL NINO ESTEVEZ
          Holy shit - can we track it? What
          are the satellites reading?

                    D.O.D WORKER
          Si, Senor. That's the thing. I'm
          tracking its heat-signature.
          GENERAL - it's headed for US.

                    GENERAL NINO ESTEVEZ
          What the fuck do you mean, "for
          US"?

                    D.O.D WORKER
          Its projected destination, based
          upon its energy path, is HERE,
          Senor -

GENERAL ESTEVEZ gathers his bearings:

                    GENERAL NINO ESTEVEZ
          - Let the ANIMALS out. RIGHT NOW!

                    D.O.D WORKER
          What about being COVERT, Senor?
          Shouldn't we -

                    GENERAL NINO ESTEVEZ
          There's no time, SOLDIER. If that
          thing is headed here, we need to
          be prepared to fight it. I will
          not allow innocent MEXICANOS to
          die on my watch by the hands of
          some ALIEN! Unlock the JAGUAR
          QUEEN's CAGE, unlock the
          HAMMERHEAD's - and hurry.

                    D.O.D WORKER
          Si, Senor. Understood.

The D.O.D WORKER exits the CONTROL-ROOM, heading to the
JAGUAR's and the HAMMERHEAD's prisons -

                                                  CUT TO:

<u>INT. MEXICAN D.O.D BASE - LAB #2 - AFTERNOON</u>

In LAB #2, the D.O.D WORKER unlocks the ANIMALS' cages.

FELICIA FACTOR, the JAGUAR, breathes in fresh air, opens her eyes to see her CAGE is open - she exits the prison.

MOVAK KILGORE, the HAMMERHEAD, is freed from his confining "space". The two HUMANOID-ANIMALS look at one another with confusion - they've never been let out of their prisons inside the D.O.D BASE before, except for tests, experiments, and trials.

GENERAL ESTEVEZ rushes in LAB #2 -

                      GENERAL NINO ESTEVEZ
                (to THE JAGUAR and
                THE HAMMERHEAD)
        My friends, we have a significant
        issue to attend to - are you ready
        to answer the call? This - this is
        your time to show the world what
        you can do.

JAGUAR and HAMMERHEAD take a knee to their GENERAL -

                      THE JAGUAR
                (bows with her
                  fists to the
                  ground)
        What would you have us do,
        GENERAL?

                      HAMMERHEAD
                (bowing just like
                JAGUAR)
        We have served. We will be of
        service, Senor -

The ANIMALS stand back up, their chins held high -

                      GENERAL NINO ESTEVEZ
                (in English,
                accent heavy)
        Your orders are to stand guard
        outside of this BASE and destroy
        the KINETIC being known as
        DARKWAVE, once IT shows its face -
        prepare for what's coming. Make
        sure you use your comms, keep me
        updated, okay? You will have 5
                      (MORE)

                    GENERAL NINO ESTEVEZ (cont'd)
          squadrons as your backup. Oh, and
          JAGUAR, if you pull this off, I'll
          give you your husband back. Same
          to you HAMMERHEAD - you do this
          for me, successfully, you'll have
          your daughter back.

                    THE JAGUAR
               (nods, motivated)
          Yes, GENERAL. C'mon, HAMMERHEAD,
          let's do work.

                    GENERAL NINO ESTEVEZ
          However, SOLDIERS - if you fail
          me, you will regret it; you will
          know real pain.

                    THE 2 ANIMALS (IN-SYNC)
               (humble, serious)
          Understood, GENERAL -

The ANIMALS exit LAB #2.

AND WE CUT TO BLACK:

CHAPTER V - CATHARTIC CHAOS

                                        FADE IN:

EXT. THE MEXICO CITY D.O.D BASE - AFTERNOON

JAGUAR (her fur stimulated) and HAMMERHEAD (now in ankle cut blue jeans with a belt on) along with the 5 SQUADRONS of backup, stand guard for GENERAL NINO ESTEVEZ outside of the D.O.D BASE...

...SHADOWS creep toward the SOLDIERS - the sky darkens, ominously. Supernatural lava-red-lightning surges in the chunky clouds.

DARKWAVE - more SILVER at this point than black - now with a red-steel ventilator-like facemask covering his mouth and edgy red-steel chest-shoulder pads protecting his upper body, can be seen from a long way away walking in MEXICO CITY toward the D.O.D BASE; the concrete caves as the creature walks, leaving beastly footprints.

DARKWAVE has an ARMY of 100 SHADOW DEMONS - ghostly, ghastly figures made of pure DARKNESS.

CUT TO:

                  THE JAGUAR
              (extends her claws
              out)
        Get ready!

                  HAMMERHEAD
        I got you, FELICIA.

DARKWAVE jumps a mile up into the sky. He lands like a bomb in front of the D.O.D BASE - creating a massive explosion of DARK-ENERGY, shaking the earth.

JAGUAR is knocked backward, as is HAMMERHEAD, and their many men.

CUT TO:

JAGUAR gets up, purring, she shakes her fur.

HAMMERHEAD is down for a few moments.

DARKWAVE appears out of nowhere, grabs JAGUAR with both hands by the throat. The SHADOW DEMONS surround the ANIMALS and their backup. The DEMONS proceed to start killing off the 5 SQUADRONS, one-by-one.

                  THE JAGUAR
              (struggling)
        Let me go, demon.

                  DARKWAVE
        You stand no chance against me,
        ANIMAL.

DARKWAVE chokeslams JAGUAR downward, straight through the cement, asphalt, gravel. They crash UNDERGROUND - all this occurring as the SHADOWS destroy the many men.

CUT TO:

INT. THE SEWER SYSTEM - CONTINUOUS

JAGUAR lands in the SEWER SYSTEM, in the gray water. DARKWAVE stands over her, threateningly.

- She fights to rise and engages DARKWAVE, clawing, slicing, juking his attacks.

DARKWAVE
You are mighty, yes. But not strong enough.

DARKWAVE backhands JAGUAR, some 35 yards down the SEWER LINE into sewage water. She stands and shakes, getting the rotten juices out of her fur - she gets on all fours, charging the MONSTER with a feline's agility. DARKWAVE measures her every move.

THE JAGUAR
I will stop you!

As JAGUAR jumps toward DARKWAVE, he uppercuts her - she goes upward through the CEMENT, creating a giant crater, then, she falls back down into the SEWER, into the sewage.

DARKWAVE flips JAGUAR onto her back. He grabs her neck again, with his right hand. He begins to drain her POWER.

DARKWAVE
(absorbing
JAGUAR's strength)
You shouldn't have such power.
Give it to me, now.

Her fur starts receding, revealing HUMAN SKIN. Her face starts to devolve from being that of a JAGUAR to being HUMAN - DARKWAVE is zapping her of her strength and power.

CUT TO:

MOVAK KILGORE (HAMMERHEAD) appears in the SEWER, prepared for battle. He tackles DARKWAVE, proceeds to hit the beast with right, left hooks, over-and-over. This has very little effect on DARKWAVE. By the touch, the monster starts absorbing HAMMERHEAD's power, too -

              THE JAGUAR
          (into her comms to
           NINO ESTEVEZ)
    GENERAL, we're outmatched, here.
    We need help, NOW.

            NINO ESTEVEZ (THROUGH THE COMMS)
    Okay. I'll see what I can do. Hold
    the creature off, just for a
    little longer, JAGUAR. I'll get
    you some help.

                           CUT TO:

INT. DR. ANIMUS' LAB - MEXICAN D.O.D BASE - CONTINUOUS

GENERAL ESTEVEZ stands in front of the CRYO-CHAMBER that's holding TRICKEY BREEDLOVE - it's nearly finished its cycles.

- CAPTAIN BREEDLOVE is almost completely frozen, but the CRYO-CHAMBER is not fully done yet.

NIDIA ESTEVEZ (NINO's WIFE), nail bitingly nervous, sits in the corner of the LAB.

            GENERAL NINO ESTEVEZ
    ANDROPOV, stop the freezing cycle
    of our dear CAPTAIN, here.

            DR. ANIMUS
    What!? Are you mad, GENERAL. All
    the work we've done to get him
    here. It will all be in vain if we
    let him loose. Who knows what
    he'll do!

            GENERAL NINO ESTEVEZ
    Let him go, doctor. That's an
    order. He's our only hope.

            DR. ANIMUS
    - From what?

>   GENERAL NINO ESTEVEZ
>   The DARKWAVE.
>
>   DR. ANIMUS
>   (obeying)
>   Si, GENERAL.

DR. ANIMUS pushes a few buttons on the CRYO-CHAMBER - the mechanism begins thawing TRICKEY out.

>   CRYO-CHAMBER OPERATING SYSTEM
>   (mechanical)
>   Thawing process starting now. ETA,
>   4 MINUTES -
>
>   GENERAL NINO ESTEVEZ
>   Now, we wait. And we pray to GOD
>   that the CAPTAIN will help us
>   against whatever the hell is out
>   there. Or we are all doomed.
>
>   NIDIA ESTEVEZ
>   (sadly)
>   If he refuses to help, this is our
>   end, mi amor?
>
>   GENERAL NINO ESTEVEZ
>   (nervous)
>   Si, amor.

NINO hugs NIDIA tight, comforting her.

The CRYO-CHAMBER is continuing to thaw CAPTAIN TRICKEY BREEDLOVE.

CUT TO:

We hear the slaughter of the countless MILITARY STAFF inside the MEXICAN D.O.D BASE, on the other side of the LAB - the SHADOW DEMONS have infiltrated the BASE, they're trying to get into the LAB.

                                                  CUT TO:

3 MINUTES LATER:

TRICKEY is now conscious. GENERAL ESTEVEZ stands in front of the CRYO-CHAMBER -

                    GENERAL NINO ESTEVEZ
    CAPTAIN, wake up. Wake up. You are
    my last option. I need your
    abilities, now. Snap out of it.

                    NIDIA ESTEVEZ
              (anxious, teary
                eyed)
    Help us, gringo!

GENERAL ESTEVEZ points to the POWER-DAMPER KINETIC-COLLAR on TRICKEY.

- DR. ANIMUS UNLEASHES the CAPTAIN, remotely removing the collar. The KINETIC-COLLAR clicks, loosens from TRICKEY's neck, and falls to the bottom of the CRYO-CHAMBER.

The CRYO-CHAMBER opens.

CAPTAIN BREEDLOVE falls out of the CHAMBER, onto his fists and knees. The CAPTAIN struggles to stand tall:

                    CAPTAIN BREEDLOVE
              (shivering)
    What - what's happening, NINO?
    Where am I?

                    GENERAL NINO ESTEVEZ
    You're still in MEXICO. Your life
    is on the line, too, just like
    mine. That DARKWAVE creature - IT
    IS HERE.

                    CAPTAIN BREEDLOVE
              (eyes widen)
    - What - Who is he?

                    GENERAL NINO ESTEVEZ
               He's Hell Incarnate. I've seen the
               footage, CAPTAIN. This Being, he's
               powerful, unstoppable. And he's
               coming.

The SHADOW DEMONS overpower the LAB DOOR, entering like a
100 MAN ARMY except they're devilish ghosts.

TRICKEY looks forward at what's coming -

CAPTAIN BREEDLOVE flexes his power, letting out a near
omnipotent surge of electricity - attacking the 100 GHOSTS,
all simultaneously, destroying them in a matter of moments.

- TRICKEY has saved NINO ESTEVEZ, NIDIA, and DR. ANDROPOV
ANIMUS.

A few beats, and a pause:

                    DR. ANIMUS
               Holy -

                    NIDIA ESTEVEZ
               Fucking.

                    GENERAL NINO ESTEVEZ
               - Mierda.

NINO ESTEVEZ walks in front of TRICKEY -

                    GENERAL NINO ESTEVEZ
               Destroy this monster terrorizing
               my people, CAPTAIN. And you'll
               have your freedom, I swear it. And
               I'll give you back your comrades,
               and their family. In fact, the
               JAGUAR's and HAMMERHEAD's lives
               hang in the balance. They, right
               this moment, are fighting the
               creature. Above.

CAPTAIN BREEDLOVE - in his white unitard wetsuit - extends
his right hand out to shake NINO's.

GENERAL ESTEVEZ cowers down at the gesture, afraid to be electrocuted.

                    CAPTAIN BREEDLOVE
          If I have your word. You have
          mine. And you'll never try to come
          after me, again?

The GENERAL nods to the CAPTAIN -

TRICKEY grabs the EMERGENCY AXE in the red case within the LAB, and heads on to face the supervillainous DARKWAVE.

                                  CUT TO:

INT. SEWER SYSTEM - CONTINUOUS

The silverish-black enhanced DARKWAVE is beating HAMMERHEAD to a pulp. He's overpowered the SHARK. He holds him by the arm - he hangs like a puppet by its last string. One of DARKWAVE's 8 arms forms a HELLSWORD: DARKWAVE stabs HAMMERHEAD directly through the abdomen.

HAMMERHEAD goes limp.

                    DARKWAVE
          You pathetic beasts. Thinking you
          have power, only to face REAL
          POWER.

DARKWAVE slings HAMMERHEAD through the SEWER wall at the end of the tunnel - the SHARK crashes through the brick like a freight train.

DARKWAVE walks upon FELICIA FACTOR, now naked in human form. The monster goes to stab COMMANDER FACTOR with the HELLSWORD - he strikes downward with the unholy weapon.

DARKWAVE's strike is Thwarted by CAPTAIN BREEDLOVE - TRICKEY saves his COMMANDER by whacking DARKWAVE in the neck with the AXE.

DARKWAVE is unfazed by the attack but turns his attention to TRICKEY.

CUT TO:

The demonic creature jump-kicks CAPTAIN BREEDLOVE all the way through the SEWER cement, upward, onto the MEXICO CITY STREET - DARKWAVE doesn't come back down into THE SEWER SYSTEM.

FELICIA FACTOR - naked and exhausted - is covering herself with her shaky hands. She breathes in-and-out heavily, thankful for the rescue by CAPTAIN BREEDLOVE.

                    CUT TO:

EXT. MEXICO CITY - METROPOLIS SECTION - AFTERNOON

CAPTAIN BREEDLOVE lands on the ground hard as hell, scraping the concrete for dozens of yards - the AXE is fumbled by TRICKEY, it skips on the ground, going many yards away from the two godly beings.

TRICKEY stands up, regaining his footing. DARKWAVE floats in the air and lands on his feet, 20 or so yards away from the CAPTAIN.

             CAPTAIN BREEDLOVE
        What the hell are you?

             DARKWAVE
        (flexes his SHADOW
           POWERS)
        Your demise, MOONWATCHER.

The MEXICAN AUTHORITIES and MILITARY begin firing upon both DARKWAVE and CAPTAIN BREEDLOVE.

- DARKWAVE, energizing himself, has silver spikes that pop out of his shoulders and down his 2 primary arms. His body also grows larger in size as his power does.

TRICKEY magnetically reaches for a METAL TRASHCAN LID, using it as a shield from the myriad of gunfire.

The MILITARY, in a HELICOPTER, fires a MINIGUN at DARKWAVE - the monster literally swallows the bullets. DARKWAVE spits the BULLETS back at the HELICOPTER, faster than they were delivered to him -

CUT TO:

TRICKEY ditches the TRASHCAN SHIELD -

The HELICOPTER catches fire.

DARKWAVE leaps at the CHOPPER - he grabs it by the tail, in the air, and swings it round-and-round, throwing it like a softball toward one of the shiny METROPOLITAN BUILDINGS.

TRICKEY, experiencing more self-control, is able to levitate speedily - he races to get on the other side of the out-of-control HELICOPTER, stopping it from hitting the building.

- CAPTAIN BREEDLOVE single-handedly holds the HELICOPTER and attempts to lower it safely to the ground.

CUT TO:

DARKWAVE expected this.

He crashes through the HELICOPTER, violently, punching CAPTAIN BREEDLOVE with absolute power, causing absolute CHAOS, as TRICKEY is forced through the building, sliding violently across the tiled floor, out of the other side of the building through the giant glass window.

Spectators panic anxiously, screaming.

The HELICOPTER, and its occupants, crash to the ground in a fiery blast.

DARKWAVE meets CAPTAIN BREEDLOVE at the other side of the building - the creature hits TRICKEY with various combos, one-after-the-other. Then DARKWAVE whams the CAPTAIN downward, with a brutish strike, to the ground, creating a hole in the asphalt.

MILITARY, POLICE, they continue firing upon BOTH beings.

DARKWAVE's HELLFIRE, within him, gets only stronger as the bullets hit him. TRICKEY's electric abilities allow him to naturally block bullets without even trying. The bullets stop, not penetrating his blue skin.

CUT TO:

TRICKEY sees the flaming hot mess all around the METROPOLITAN AREA - he hops to a FIRE HYDRANT, breaking it wide open. He puts his boot to the HYDRANT, directing the blast of water to the FIRE. He slowly is able to put it out - yet, WATER is his WEAKNESS, so now TRICKEY is painfully losing power.

CUT TO:

Having partially put out the FIRE, CAPTAIN BREEDLOVE confronts DARKWAVE, all while still avoiding the incessant gunfire.

CAPTAIN BREEDLOVE bursts electricity out of his hands toward DARKWAVE -

The creature adapts the power to himself, hungrily, soaking it up like a sponge. The MEXICAN MILITARY and AUTHORITIES realize that TRICKEY is on THEIR SIDE, they stop firing upon the CAPTAIN - they see TRICKEY fighting this grotesque monstrosity, this DARKWAVE...

              DARKWAVE
        (getting more
         powerful from the
         electricity)
    Pure energy. I must have it. Give
    me your power. Give all of it to
    me or watch these people perish!

            CAPTAIN BREEDLOVE
        (pleading)
    Leave them alone!

              DARKWAVE
        (his skin
         absorbing the
         bullets' ENERGY)
    No...NEPHEW.

                    CAPTAIN BREEDLOVE
                 (stunned by the
                    revelation)
            - Uncle, UNCLE NEIL? It can't be
            you!

                    DARKWAVE
                 (walking toward
                    the CAPTAIN)
            Oh, TRICKSTER, still so naive. You
            always underestimated me. It's
            your greatest flaw.

                    CAPTAIN BREEDLOVE
            What's the endgame? What are you
            doing, NEIL!?

                    DARKWAVE
            Just like I destroyed PANAMA CITY.
            I'm going to burn this entire
            planet to the ground. Now, GIVE ME
            YOUR POWER!

...DARKWAVE attacks CAPTAIN BREEDLOVE, with no restraint, no regard for human life, NO INNOCENCE remaining in him.

CUT TO:

EXT. MEXICO CITY - METROPOLIS SECTION - AFTERNOON

With its 8-arms, DARKWAVE picks the busted up and beaten CAPTAIN BREEDLOVE off of his feet. The hellish being tries to break TRICKEY in half, trying to splinter his back. DARKWAVE brings TRICKEY down onto his bended knee, greatly affecting the good CAPTAIN BREEDLOVE -

CUT TO:

TRICKEY gathers himself - not able to stand, though; DARKWAVE starts extracting CAPTAIN BREEDLOVE's power.

With 6 of his arms, DARKWAVE produces 6 HELLCHAINS - gripping the CAPTAIN's blue flesh, wrapping him up torturously. With his 2 other arms, DARWAVE reveals his

HELLSWORDS - he holds them up, in an "X" formation, to TRICKEY's neck.

                              CUT TO:

                    DARKWAVE
          CAPTAIN, any last words?

                    CAPTAIN BREEDLOVE
          Un -- UNCLE NEIL, please, don't.

NEIL, although possessed and demonically mutated, is hit with a tidal wave of emotion by the utterance of these words. He still holds the SWORDS at TRICKEY's throat, but he starts having many, many FLASHBACKS.

The HELLCHAINS retract back into DARKWAVE - TRICKEY is almost totally beaten, a lot of his power has been drained.

CUT TO:

- NEIL sees the time he taught TRICKEY how to RIDE a BIKE - TRICKEY rides along the neighborhood road with NEIL's guidance.

- NEIL sees his NEPHEW praying at the KITCHEN-TABLE -

- NEIL sees TRICKEY shooting off FIREWORKS with him.

Subsequent to these heavy FLASHBACKS, DARKWAVE absorbs his HELLSWORDS and backs away as if totally heartbroken at the memories - like he's been hit by a metaphysical SNIPER.

                              CUT TO:

The red-metallic facemask disappears and the dark-silver-goo on DARKWAVE's head retracts, showing NEIL's mutated human face; he's still drooling silver and has FANGS all throughout his mouth.

                    DARKWAVE
                (NEIL's face
                 revealed)
          TRICKEY! I - I can't fight it.
          This thing, it's taking me over,
          man. HELP ME.

					CAPTAIN BREEDLOVE
			UNCLE NEIL, what have you done?
			What have you become? You - you
			can stop this. You're more
			powerful than - than this THING.

					DARKWAVE
				(convulsing, pain
				 stricken)
			I don't know. I - am - I
			AM...DARKWAVE!!!

DARKWAVE's GOOEY MASK reaches over his face suffocating the
NEIL that once was, sans the red mouth-covering facemask.

The supervillain roars as loud as 1,000 LIONS, exposing
numerous pointy fangs -

His fiery HELLCHAINS subconsciously, once again, draw out of
his PLATINUM-ONYX BODY, grabbing ahold of CAPTAIN BREEDLOVE
- the CHAINS, with a mind of their own, start draining
TRICKEY of his ELECTRICAL KINETIC POWER, once again.

					DARKWAVE
			I can't control it, TRICKEY. I
			can't stop it! You, you MUST die,
			or I will burn. Your POWER will be
			the MASTER's - he has claimed you,
			just like he claimed me.

					CAPTAIN BREEDLOVE
				(surging out,
				 losing energy)
			You want this power. The devil
			wants this power. My ONLY power is
			my PAIN, NEIL - take it. TAKE
			EVERY LAST BIT OF IT!

CAPTAIN BREEDLOVE unleashes his power into his UNCLE
NEIL/DARKWAVE. This causes a catastrophic effect. DARKWAVE,
at first, feels good taking this divine energy -

Soon thereafter, however, he begins to regret it as the
power is far too strong. DARKWAVE begins overheating, like a
car without antifreeze - his HELLCHAINS retract, his body

begins malfunctioning, even underneath the hellish black goo.

                              CUT TO:

The palpably stoked HELLFIRE in DARKWAVE changes color. It becomes bluish, like that of BUTANE - the electricity makes DARKWAVE devolve while overpowering his biological structure.

CAPTAIN BREEDLOVE realizes this, grabs his UNCLE NEIL, rocketing him into the upper atmosphere as quickly as possible before too much collateral damage takes place -

CUT TO:

EXT. THE UPPER-ATMOSPHERE - AFTERNOON

Abruptly, DARKWAVE, energy smitten, EXPLODES in a LIMITED fashion, NOT nuclear - the BUTANE-like KINETIC ENERGY consumes the black gooey substance on NEIL NOOSE before the CAPTAIN's eyes. CAPTAIN BREEDLOVE has been knocked back by the explosion, hanging in the air still.

NEIL returns to his HUMAN FORM, falling toward the EARTH through the atmosphere -

TRICKEY flies to catch his unconscious UNCLE. CAPTAIN BREEDLOVE slowly floats to the ground of the MEXICO CITY METROPOLIS with his UNCLE NEIL in his arms.

                              CUT TO:

EXT. MEXICO CITY - METROPOLIS SECTION: CITY STREET - CONTINUOUS

TRICKEY lightly lies his UNCLE to the ground of the CITY STREET.

NEIL awakens. With his fleshly hand, NEIL grabs TRICKEY's blue arm.

CAPTAIN BREEDLOVE's PSYCHOMETRY activates, revealing the unthinkable:

CUT TO:

TRICKEY BREEDLOVE has VISIONS...

...TRICKEY witnesses, almost in real-time, his UNCLE NEIL rigging the EXPLOSIVES that killed his WIFE and DAUGHTER, and all those other innocents that day -

TRICKEY witnesses his UNCLE NEIL help CAPTAIN KARL NOOSE murder his MOTHER, MARJORIE BREEDLOVE - all in motion, as if he were there when it happened.

NEIL is the one who CHOKED TRICKEY's MOTHER to DEATH - CAPTAIN NOOSE beat her terribly beforehand, but NEIL's the culprit who took her breath away from her.

CUT TO:

          CAPTAIN BREEDLOVE
      (backing away from
       NEIL)
It was you. It was YOU, all along.
No. No. This isn't right. It can't
be.

          UNCLE NEIL
No! NEPHEW, it wasn't me. It - it
was DARKWAVE. I'm, I'm not him.
Listen to me.

NEIL NOOSE struggles to stand. Something's still off with him - silver ooze continues to drip from his mouth and his eyes are solid black.

          UNCLE NEIL
      (with the sound of
       TWO voices)
I - I. I KEEP WHAT I KILL. I KILL
WHAT I KEEP.

NEIL, darkly human, with great agility, sprints toward CAPTAIN BREEDLOVE.

          CAPTAIN BREEDLOVE
      (patiently)
No.

TRICKEY BREEDLOVE, using his inner power, TELEPORTS away from his deranged UNCLE, behind him -

NEIL looks to the left, to the right. Then, CAPTAIN BREEDLOVE, with his electric power, magnetizes the AXE from many, many yards away. TRICKEY takes hold of the AXE, NEIL turns around to see TRICKEY.

CAPTAIN BREEDLOVE DECAPITATES his UNCLE NEIL with the axe, on the spot.

- NEIL's body seemingly gives out and his head rolls in the CITY STREET; BLACK BLOOD spews from the neck wound. Spectators are disgusted at the sight.

CUT TO:

CAPTAIN BREEDLOVE turns around, walking away from NEIL.

Spontaneously, NEIL's headless body gets up, still charging his NEPHEW.

He stops mid-sprint, as the battle-damaged MOVAK KILGORE (HAMMERHEAD) punches a hole through NEIL NOOSE, RIPPING his pumping BLACKENED HEART from his body - NEIL NOOSE/DARKWAVE drops, FOR GOOD.

TRICKEY's UNCLE is now deceased, his SOUL dispatched to HELL to THE DEALMAKER - NEIL's body turns into black slime, and melts into the EARTH, departing down to HELL. He basically evaporates -

The skies above MEXICO CITY clear, revealing gorgeous sunlight.

> CAPTAIN BREEDLOVE
> (to his dead UNCLE)
> I'll miss you, NEIL. Goodbye.
> (to MOVAK)
> Thank you, LIEUTENANT KILGORE.

> HAMMERHEAD
> (grunting, holding
> the wide open cut
> on his stomach)
> Call me - call me HAMMERHEAD,
> (MORE)

                    HAMMERHEAD (cont'd)
          CAPTAIN. That's who I am now.

                    CAPTAIN BREEDLOVE
                        (nods to
                         HAMMERHEAD)
          Yessir.
                        (worried)
          Where's COMMANDER FACTOR, sir?

                    COMMANDER FELICIA FACTOR
                        (back in her HUMAN
                         FORM)
          Long time, no see, huh, CAPTAIN
          BREEDLOVE?

TRICKEY rotates to see his COMMANDER, FELICIA FACTOR (now clothed), back to how he last saw her before her kidnapping by GENERAL ESTEVEZ.

She smiles at the CAPTAIN and LIEUTENANT KILGORE/HAMMERHEAD. She gives them both HIGH FIVES - the three of them hug in a huddle with their heads pressed together.

                                             CUT TO:

EXT. MEXICAN D.O.D BASE - EXTERIOR - EVENING

FELICIA FACTOR (in HUMAN FORM) and MOVAK KILGORE (still in HAMMERHEAD-SHARK FORM) witness their family members come out of the D.O.D BASE -

FELICIA's HUSBAND, ARCHIE runs to her - he has navy-colored eyes, is in his mid-40s, blonde-headed, his facial-hair thick, wearing a patient's uniform. Surprisingly in a good health.

MOVAK's DAUGHTER, CLOTILDA KILGORE - looking like a tiny princess, 10-years-old, brown-skinned, pretty, as innocent as a puppy, wearing all white and unharmed - sees her father in his ANIMALISTIC FORM.

- MOVAK KILGORE has bleeding cuts on his upper body. CLOTILDA hesitates.

GENERAL ESTEVEZ observes the familial exchanges:

> **GENERAL NINO ESTEVEZ**
> (in English to
> FELICIA and MOVAK)
> JAGUAR, HAMMERHEAD. You two are now free, as are your loved ones.
> (to TRICKEY)
> You, too, CAPTAIN BREEDLOVE - I am a man of my word. My word is bond. By the way, you've got some big cojones, amigo.

TRICKEY nods respectfully to NINO -

> **LIEUTENANT MOVAK KILGORE**
> (takes a knee in
> front of his
> DAUGHTER)
> Sweetheart. My CLOTILDA. It's daddy. I know - I don't look NORMAL. But it's okay. I'm here, baby. I'm sorry for all you've been through.

> **CLOTILDA KILGORE**
> (runs to her
> father)
> Daddy!
> (hugs MOVAK)
> I've missed you so much.

> **LIEUTENANT MOVAK KILGORE**
> I know, baby girl. It's okay, now. Let's go home.

> **COMMANDER FELICIA FACTOR**
> (kisses ARCHIE)
> My love.

> **ARCHIE FACTOR**
> (heartwarming,
> misty-eyed)
> FELICIA -

                    CLOTILDA KILGORE
                  (to her FATHER)
            - Grandma's going to have a heart
            attack when she sees you.

                    HAMMERHEAD
                     (chuckles)
            You and me both, sweetheart. You
            and me both.

FELICIA holds ARCHIE's hands, gratefully, then hugs him very
tight - they embrace with true love.

MOVAK carries CLOTILDA on his sharky shoulder toward the
SUNSET.

TRICKEY BREEDLOVE, having stopped the malevolent DARKWAVE,
flies high up into the sunny sky, towards the USA - the sun
guides the CAPTAIN's path.

                                              CUT TO:

EXT. NEIL'S PROPERTY - LESTER'S LANDING - MORNING

TRICKEY walks onto NEIL's SCORCHED PROPERTY - the damage is
devastating, to say the least.

CAPTAIN BREEDLOVE finds the WASTEPRO TRUCK, tucked away on
the PROPERTY, with CAPTAIN NOOSE's CORPSE still in it.

- The TRASH-TRUCK smells beyond nasty, worse than death.

CAPTAIN BREEDLOVE takes the TRUCK to a gulley; he empties
the HOPPER of the WASTEPRO TRUCK, dumping the corpse and all
the garbage into the gulley.

TRICKEY then activates his powers, shooting heated
electricity from his hands at the WASTE, the CORPSE,
everything, completely erasing it all -

CUT TO:

                    CAPTAIN BREEDLOVE
            So long...grandfather.

TRICKEY gets back into the WASTEPRO TRUCK, drives it up the burned pathway adjacent to NEIL's CABIN:

                              CUT TO:

TRICKEY gets out of the WASTEPRO TRUCK, to survey the damage caused by the MEXICANS' mini-INVASION.

RAMBEAU, the blue pit-bull, out-of-nowhere, happily jogs toward TRICKEY, wagging its tail, grunting and snorting, puppy-like.

- RAMBEAU rolls over and shows his belly to CAPTAIN BREEDLOVE.

                    CAPTAIN BREEDLOVE
          RAMBEAU, oh, man. You are alive!
          Thank GOD.

The other DOGS also come out of the woodwork, the bushes, the land - they wag their tails, happy to see TRICKEY.

                    CAPTAIN BREEDLOVE
          Wow. You guys hungry and thirsty?
          Let's get you fed and watered.

Some of the NEIGHBORS, now back in LESTER's LANDING, look at CAPTAIN BREEDLOVE, with his pale blue skin, his alien-looking appearance, they are fearful of the HERO -

There's nothing to fear, though. TRICKEY LAMAR BREEDLOVE has retained his humanity, innocence, and he's defeated the devil's disciple.

- CAPTAIN BREEDLOVE has saved the day.

Now he just has to tend to the DOGS...

CUT TO:

<u>INT. DR. ANIMUS SECONDARY LAB - WITH THE EXPERIMENTS - NIGHT</u>

MID-CREDITS' SCENE:

...GENERAL ESTEVEZ and DR. ANIMUS stand before several containers/prisons holding even more ANIMALS - in one there's a YELLOW JACKET-WOMAN.

In another there's a MAN-SPIDER. In one there's a GATOR-HUMANOID; in adjacent SUPER-CELLs are a STINGRAY HUMANOID and even a KOMODO DRAGON HUMANOID.

There's also a prison holding a MAN who's a KING-COBRA-HUMANOID -

               GENERAL NINO ESTEVEZ
    How's our progress, doctor? Are
    the ANIMALS ready yet?

               DR. ANIMUS
    Soon, GENERAL. Very soon. The
    unique power we took from CAPTAIN
    BREEDLOVE has made all of our
    ANIFUSION experiments a success.

               GENERAL NINO ESTEVEZ
        (walks out of the
         LAB)
    Good.

                              CUT TO:

<u>INT. THE FACTOR HOME - CHICAGO, ILLINOIS - MORNING</u>

                            POST-CREDITS' SCENE:

FELICIA FACTOR, having been drained of her ANIFUSION powers, is washing dishes in her HOME - as her HUSBAND is still sleeping in their BEDROOM, peacefully.

Mrs. FACTOR finishes up with the last dish.

She walks into the BATHROOM, looks at herself in the MIRROR - grateful as can be.

CUT TO:

COMMANDER FACTOR is overcome by her senses. She gasps for air, she claws at the SHOWER CURTAIN in the BATHROOM, it falls to the floor, as does she.

FELICIA gets up onto her feet, feeling stronger than ever.

She glances, once more, into the MIRROR -

She is back to being THE JAGUAR QUEEN.

She ROARS, relentlessly.

WE CUT TO BLACK:

mag·ic

['majik]

NOUN

the power of apparently influencing the course of events by using mysterious or supernatural forces:

"suddenly, as if by magic, the doors started to open" · "do you believe in magic?"

SIMILAR:
sorcery
wizardry
necromancy
enchantment

ACT III. THE GREAT BARIAH RISES

CHAPTER I - THE HOUDINI CODE

FADE IN:

<u>INT. ANTIQUE MAGIC-SHOW ARENA - HOUDINI'S SHOW - NIGHT</u>

YEAR: 1926

LOCATION: CHICAGO, ILLINOIS

The crowd is cheering away, filled with glee and excitement. Magic does that to folks...

...HARRY HOUDINI, the great wizardly MAGICIAN and ESCAPE ARTIST, is standing on a DIVING BOARD in an ANTIQUE INDOOR ARENA in CHICAGO -

There is a huge POOL below HOUDINI - in the pool are 2 large SHARKS, circling the water.

HOUDINI is in CHAINS, all wrapped around his person, body, legs, torso, the man is covered in chain-contraptions that have him completely confined, almost like a metal straight-jacket.

                    THE SHOWMAN/ANNOUNCER
               (with a deep bassy
                voice)
          Ladies and Gentlemen, are you
          prepared to be mystified? Are you
          ready to see a miraculous feat of
          MAGIC? Look no further than right
          here, right now! I present to you,
          the one, the ONLY HARRY HOUDINI -

The crowd goes apeshit.

They whistle.

They cheerlead.

They are here to see wonders.

                                        CUT TO:

HOUDINI has 2 folks come up on the diving-board to check the strength, the legitimacy of the CHAINS -

The crowd buys it, totally. The chains are as REAL as they get. HOUDINI is really trapped in them -

                    HARRY HOUDINI
               (with showmanship)
          Abracadabra.

HOUDINI jumps into the POOL with the SHARKS, claustrophobically covered in the chains.

The crowd goes, "Ooo", "Aah", "Whoa", they are fascinated, filled with tension, suspense, and mystery at the sight of the great HOUDINI - the SHARKS circle the magician.

CUT TO:

                                        1 MINUTE AND 30
                                        SECONDS LATER:

HOUDINI appears - his head above the water - untouched, unharmed, with his pride, power, and his SELF intact. He's holding the chains in his hands as they dangle.

He has raised himself up out of the water effortlessly. He throws the CHAINS several feet away in the pool to show the audience it was NOT staged, at all.

The CROWD gives HOUDINI a standing ovation.

He gets out of the pool with the help of a ladder.

He walks onto the stage area - HOUDINI gives a BOW to the AUDIENCE.

                    HARRY HOUDINI
                  (bowing gracefully)
            Thank you. Thank you all!

MAGIC is a trade of impossibilities. A job for only a select few in the world. HOUDINI was a LEGEND.

MAGIC, like everything else on EARTH, must EVOLVE...

CUT TO:

EXT. MAGIC-WORLD THEME PARK - MORNING

                                                YEAR: 2023

LOCATION: ORLANDO, FLORIDA

...Consumers enjoy the festivities of MAGIC-WORLD. A perfect place for a "carny". A THEME-PARK of fun, hard work, thrills, and amazement.

Kids, teenagers, adults, they all eat up the entertainment of MAGIC-WORLD like funnel cake.

Little do they know, they're in for carnage, terror, and DESTRUCTION beyond human comprehension -

CUT TO:

EXT. NORTHWEST FLORIDA - DAY

LOCATION: PORT ST. JOE, FLORIDA

Far northwest of MAGIC-WORLD, the ever so quiet town of PORT ST. JOE is packed with "tourons" (moronic tourists). On this "forgotten coast", most are enjoying their time, their families, and the beach itself. The air is pristine, you can smell the palm-trees and ocean breeze.

Car-horns honk, bike bells ring, seagulls sing - unassuming people are doing ordinary things, uneventfully. Some are on vacation; some are sticking to a routine. Either way, it's quite a scenic atmosphere.

The incorruptible Floridian sun shines on everyone equally...EVEN THE MONSTERS -

CUT TO:

INT. MR. ED'S PAWNSHOP - DAY

- 2023

A PAWNSHOP OWNER and his ASSISTANT are making conversation in the place of business in PORT ST. JOE:

- MR. ED, a Jew, has a beer-belly. He has a moustache, no beard, white haired (he's in his 60s). He has on a burgundy-gray checkered long-sleeve shirt tucked into khakis, no tie.

- THE ASSISTANT is a white woman, a brunette, in her early-40s. She has freckles. Her hair is done up. She has on wads of makeup but still looks quite beautiful. Her nails are shiny-red. She's wearing a fancy outfit to be just a PAWNSHOP WORKER.

- No customers are inside, just them. It is quite a slow day at MR. ED's PAWNSHOP.

>MR. ED
>- This guy, right, CHARLIE DAGLE, he had this catfish by the line, 90 pounds, he's reeling it in, but can't get it in the boat!

>ED'S ASSISTANT
>(pretending to be enthralled)
>Wow! Did he get it, eventually?

>MR. ED
>Of course, he did. How'd you think I knew it was 90 pounds...he wrestled this beast of a fish for a half hour. He got cut deep by the whiskers before getting the monster on the scale. Then once CHARLIE DAGLE got the dang thing on the scale, he had a terribly massive stroke on the open water.

>ED'S ASSISTANT
>All that for a fish? Did this CHARLIE DAGLE end up eating it or was he a goner?

>MR. ED
>Ole poor CHARLIE. He survived the stroke - sits at the dinner table with his wife, who had to clean the fish herself. Now, we're talking 90 pounds of cuts here. Mrs. DAGLE gets the table prepared, gets the incapacitated CHARLIE at the table, the fish is a go.

ED'S ASSISTANT
Don't let it be a sad story, don't let it be -

MR. ED
Yeah, it's kinda sad - CHARLIE, on his third bite of the fish, chokes on the bone. His purple face hit the plate, never to be heard from again.

ED'S ASSISTANT
Way to kill the mood, MR. ED - what's your point?

MR. ED
- No point to be had, darling! If there is one, it sure is eluding me. It's just a damn sad world we live in, ain't it?

ED'S ASSISTANT
That's why you have me here to cheer you up, boss.

MR. ED
(smiling at his ASSISTANT)
Yes, ma'am.

ED'S ASSISTANT
(looks at the camera montiors)
- MR. ED, looks like we have a customer incoming!

MR. ED
First one of the day's always the easiest. Let's get it done.

ED'S ASSISTANT
(starts tending to inventory)
Let me at least look like I've been working.

A MAN enters MR. ED's PAWNSHOP...

...He's wearing all black attire, with the exception of a white-tie and white-shoes, quite fashionable, boldly dressed.

The MAN has on a black fedora with a white wrapping. He is wearing a black leather trench-coat that hangs near the backs of his feet. There's a symmetry to his outfit, a duality to it.

This MAN is bi-racial (black-and-white), yet he has quite a pale pigmentation to his skin - he looks like a white man. He has longer brown hair - no facial hair, though, he's clean-shaven.

He is 22 years of age. He's very athletic, about 185 lbs. - (built like a Linebacker) - he's 6ft-even in height.

His face is somewhat scarred, yet he's still handsome. His hands are scarred as well, almost mutilated looking.

His eyes are as blue as spring water. Pupils ever so dilated, no substances to speak of. He has a calmness about him, a mysteriousness as well.

He glances around at MR. ED's PAWNSHOP upon entering. He observes diligently without immediately speaking. This MAN is TRENTON TORINO aka. THE DEVOURER:

> MR. ED
> - Well, good day, young man! How's this nice Florida weather treating you?

> TRENTON TORINO (THE DEVOURER)
> Not so bad, MR. ED. I do assume you are MR. ED, right?

> MR. ED
> The one and only in all of PORT ST. JOE, sir. Here at your service. What can we help you with today?

                    TRENTON TORINO (THE DEVOURER)
                (takes off his hat)
            Well, MR. ED, I'm looking for
            DVDs, actually. And a 'Playstation
            2', if you have it, the slim
            model, specifically.

TRENTON's hair covers his face:

                    MR. ED
            - Going old school, 'aye? You are
            in luck, young man. I have a
            special going on for DVDs and
            Blurays. .99 cent a pop, in the
            plastic, used, anyway you find
            them. And we have plenty of used
            Playstation 2's in the back. You
            can test which one you want. I
            guarantee you a working product.
            If you have issues, you can bring
            it back to me for a trade.

                    ED'S ASSISTANT
                (showcasing)
            - Our movies are right over here,
            sir. You can open the cases to
            make sure there are no scratches.
            You can even test the DVDs while
            you are here.

                    TRENTON TORINO (THE DEVOURER)
                (smiles)
            Thank you both for your
            hospitality. If you don't mind,
            I'll have a look-see at your
            collection. And please, if you
            will, bring a couple of those
            consoles up. I'll pick one, test
            it. And I appreciate your warranty
            deal.

TRENTON TORINO smiles, revealing all gold-teeth; he puts his
fedora back on.

His teeth shine like the Floridian sun. They don't
intimidate MR. ED. He's a veteran PAWNSHOP guy.

MR. ED is fascinated by TRENTON, as is his ASSISTANT...

>   MR. ED
>   Excuse my rudeness, young sir.
>   What is your name?

...TRENTON stops scanning the films and walks up to ED, as to shake his hand.

>   TRENTON TORINO (THE DEVOURER)
>   My name is TRENTON, MR. ED.
>   TRENTON TORINO. And it's a
>   pleasure to meet you and your lady
>   friend, here. Miss, you are...?

>   ED'S ASSISTANT
>   (giggles)
>   Just THE ASSISTANT-

>   TRENTON TORINO (THE DEVOURER)
>   A woman as kind and upstanding as
>   yourself must have a name to match
>   her attributes, no?

>   ED'S ASSISTANT
>   Okay, you got me. The name's
>   LINDA.

>   TRENTON TORINO (THE DEVOURER)
>   (kisses THE
>   ASSISTANT's hand)
>   Yes, LINDA. What a comforting name
>   with such a warm face.

TRENTON TORINO discontinues the pleasantries and proceeds to scan MR. ED's broad inventory of low-priced movies.

>   TRENTON TORINO (THE DEVOURER)
>   .99 cent, you say, for all these
>   films?

>   MR. ED
>   .99 cent, my friend. No more, no
>   less. Most places sell them 5 for
>   10 dollars, $2 or even $2.50
>   apiece, or round abouts that. I've
>   (MORE)

MR. ED (cont'd)
come across so many damn DVDs and
Blurays in my day. It's hard not
to make a bargain for 'em.

TRENTON TORINO (THE DEVOURER)
- Amazing.

ED'S ASSISTANT
Any films in particular that
you're looking for, TRENTON?

TRENTON TORINO (THE DEVOURER)
You can call me TRENT, Ms. LINDA.
Rolls off the ole tongue a lot
smoother.

ED'S ASSISTANT
(blushing)
All right, TRENT. You got it.

MR. ED
What's your favorite film, kid?

MR. ED, as he speaks, walks into the back area of the
PAWNSHOP to get TRENT some testable Playstation 2 systems.

TRENTON TORINO (THE DEVOURER)
(raising his voice
so MR. ED can
hear him in the
back)
It's funny you ask that, MR. ED.
Because I happen to not own my
favorite! My favorite movie is
'The Prestige' by Christopher
Nolan.

MR. ED
(with a raised
voice)
- Hugh Jackman. Christian Bale. A
great Film, indeed.

                          ED'S ASSISTANT
                Dueling Magicians, trying to best
                one another. Damn good movie -

                          TRENTON TORINO (THE DEVOURER)
                Yes! You know it.

                          MR. ED
                            (walking in from
                             the back of the
                             PAWNSHOP)
                We don't just know it, we have it.
                Everything is alphabetical, so go
                for it.

MR. ED sits three Playstation 2 consoles on the counter, one
at a time. He is quite in high spirits with his new
customer.

MR. ED doesn't have many in the small town of PORT ST. JOE.

                                              CUT TO:

                          MR. ED
                Now, TRENT, I don't have any of
                the "slim" models of the system
                you are looking for. Just the
                bulky regulars. We'll give them a
                once over.

                          TRENTON TORINO (THE DEVOURER)
                            (holds up a DVD)
                That'll do, MR. ED - I just hit
                the motherlode. 'Throne of Blood'
                in the plastic by Akira Kurosawa.
                Praise God.

                          ED'S ASSISTANT
                That's one I've not seen.

                          TRENTON TORINO (THE DEVOURER)
                Kurosawa had a whole phase where
                he wanted to adapt Shakespeare
                into Japanese Samurai tales.
                'Throne of Blood' is 'MacBeth' in
                a Samurai setting, see?

TRENT lifts his fedora up and flips his hair off of his face so he can see the movie selection better. This gives MR. ED and his ASSISTANT a better look at TRENT's uniquely scarred face.

MR. ED has a gaming system hooked up to a TV to show him that it works.

                    MR. ED
      Dammit, it just hit me. Son, you
      look like the feller we just saw
      in ORLANDO at 'MAGIC-WORLD'!

              TRENTON TORINO (THE DEVOURER)
            (intrigued)
      Really? How so, MR. ED?

                  ED'S ASSISTANT
            (takes a second
             look at TRENT)
      You do look like him!

TRENT is all ears...

                    MR. ED
      LINDA and I went down to ORLANDO,
      what was it, three weeks ago?

                  ED'S ASSISTANT
      Yep, three weeks - give or take.

                    MR. ED
      They got this kid there, a
      magician. He can do all kinds of
      mess! Tricks like you've never
      seen. Card tricks, making people
      float, guessing objects in folks'
      pockets, walking through mirrors,
      the whole 9.

              TRENTON TORINO (THE DEVOURER)
            (discontinues
             looking at the
             films)
      A magician, you say - what's his
      stage-name?

                    ED'S ASSISTANT
          His name is 'THE GREAT BARIAH'. We
          didn't get his real name. But,
          buddy, what a performance he
          gives. Hard to forget something
          like that.

                    MR. ED
          And honest to the good Lord
          Himself, TRENT, you look very much
          like him. I mean, almost
          spitting-image besides your build
          and the gold-teeth.

                    TRENTON TORINO (THE DEVOURER)
          'THE GREAT BARIAH'...what a name!

                    ED'S ASSISTANT
                (facetious,
                 giggling)
          Was that you or was he your twin?

...TRENT walks up to the open sign and the window blinds -

                    TRENTON TORINO (THE DEVOURER)
                (back turned)
          As a matter of fact, LINDA and MR.
          ED, I am not him. Nor am I his
          twin.

TRENT flicks the switch on the "open" sign and cuts it off.

He shuts the window blinds, walks up to the door of the
PAWNSHOP and locks it from the inside.

- Shadows slowly saturate the interior of the PAWNSHOP:

                    TRENTON TORINO (THE DEVOURER)
                (dominating,
                 intimidating)
          But I AM his BROTHER, if he is as
          you say -

MR. ED gets fidgety. His assistant cowers behind him.

                    MR. ED
          Hey, listen, man, we didn't mean
          to trigger you-

                    TRENTON TORINO (THE DEVOURER)
          I'm sure you didn't. But, here I
          am, triggered as ever. Now, I know
          we just met, but I need you to be
          very open with me. You both will
          tell me everything you know about
          this 'GREAT BARIAH'...

                    ED'S ASSISTANT
                (ditzy)
          ...We could just find him on the
          internet and show you that way.

                    TRENTON TORINO (THE DEVOURER)
          Where's the fun in that? When,
          instead, I could rip the
          information from you.

TRENT walks toward MR. ED and his ASSISTANT, growling. He
extends his left hand out and flexes his fingers, ominously.

The lights flicker.

WE CUT TO: the outside of the PAWNSHOP...

...We only hear ED and LINDA's screams -

                              CUT TO:

INT. THE MALL - THE FOOD COURT: NORTH CAROLINA - DAY

                              LOCATION: CONCORD,
                              NC

YEAR: 2009

A MAN and a WOMAN (a MOTHER and FATHER) sit with their TWO
CHILDREN at a FOOD COURT table in THE CONCORD MALL in NORTH
CAROLINA -

The PARENTS are MORTON TORINO, a 40-something BLACK MAN (the dad), and HEATHER TORINO, a 30-something WHITE WOMAN (the mom) - the CHILDREN are TRENTON TORINO (age 8) and TYLER TORINO (age 5), both BIRACIAL.

>MORTON TORINO
>(to TRENTON)
>
>My God, I'm going to faint - how can you eat that much, SON?

>TRENTON TORINO
>(giggling with a mouth full of food)
>
>A MAN's gotta eat, right?

>HEATHER TORINO
>
>Don't age on us too quickly, TRENT, you're still just my baby boy.

>MORTON TORINO
>
>He's a DEVOURER - honey, how am I going to afford the food bills when he's 14? I'll have to pawn him off, instead!

>TYLER TORINO
>(smiling)
>
>No, I'm the baby.

>TRENTON TORINO
>(being smart)
>
>Shut up, you little brat, you were just an after-birth - mom took a dump one day and you came out. She yelled and said: "I just gave birth to a TYLER", all from the upstairs bathroom.

>HEATHER TORINO
>
>TRENTON OLIVER TORINO, how dare you use that type of language! Much less at the freaking dinner-table while we're eating!

                    MORTON TORINO
               (slaps TRENTON
                upside the head
                lightly)
          Apologize to your MOTHER and
          BROTHER, now, SON -

                    TYLER TORINO
               (quickly)
          No way! You're a liar, TRENT.

                    TRENTON TORINO
          I'm just kidding, TYLER. We picked
          you up in a pumpkin patch,
          actually.

                    MORTON TORINO
               (raises his hand
                again)
          You little -

                    TRENTON TORINO
               (cowering down to
                his FATHER)
          Okay, okay, sorry, MOM, sorry,
          TYLER, geez.

                    HEATHER TORINO
          What are you, a standup Comedian?

                    TYLER TORINO
          I know what I want to be when I
          become a MAN.

                    MORTON TORINO
          And what would that be, SON?

                    TYLER TORINO
          A MAGICIAN.

                                        CUT TO BLACK:

CHAPTER II - THE DEVOURING

                                        FADE IN:

INT. TRAILER - THE 'MAGIC-WORLD' BACKLOT - MORNING

- ORLANDO, FL

An Alarm-Clock goes off - a YOUNG MAN flashes awake in an instant. Within the microsecond, the off switch is flipped. We see this YOUNG MAN lying in bed in the darkness of his TRAILER, breathing fearfully and heavily...

...The YOUNG MAN is 5'11, 19 years of age, with a head-of-hair (black) longer than JESUS Himself - he has 5-O'-Clock stubble on his face, too. The YOUNG MAN has illuminating green-eyes and isn't very athletic looking; he's a scrawny teenager, ripped but skinny.

The double-wide TRAILER is on the BACKLOT of 'MAGIC-WORLD', meant for modest living. This YOUNG MAN gets up and makes his bed MAGICALLY. He sways his hands, his arms fluttering lightly, and he is somehow able to organize the bed sheets PERFECTLY, ALL WITH HIS MIND, without even physically touching the materials.

He then moves open the window-curtains and unfolds the blinds, allowing numerous rays of sunlight to enter the TRAILER. This YOUNG MAN is TYLER TORINO aka. THE GREAT BARIAH -

TYLER TORINO is a MULATTO (of the black and white races, but he looks far WHITER than most BIRACIAL people). His skin looks like the color of graham crackers, like he's had some sun - however, you wouldn't know he's part black just looking at him. His dark hair touches his shoulders. Not a tattoo on his body.

TYLER may be slender, yet he has a strong stature for a young adult. He's fit to be a MAGICIAN; TYLER may only be 19 years old, but he's a MAESTRO of MAGIC.

One of the few true MAGICIANS left on EARTH; with legitimate supernatural gifts - he is "KINETIC", as labeled by his 'LIFE-CONTROL' CAPTORS (AGENT WOLF and DR. COTOMAN) many moons ago.

- Yet, even with this power coursing through TYLER TORINO's veins, he still cannot save the one he loves most.

CUT TO:

INT. TRAILER - MOMENTS LATER

TYLER prepares instant coffee in his regular cup, it has a Wizard on it, very old, cracked even. TYLER uses this cup ALL THE TIME. It has great sentimental value to him. He heats the cup of water in the microwave for 2-minutes, removes it telekinetically.

He, with mental power and subtle hand gestures, pours and stirs the instant coffee, along with sugar, into the hot water -

TYLER then proceeds to the back of the TRAILER, to the second BEDROOM as he sips his coffee. HE IS NOT ALONE.

CUT TO:

TYLER edges up to the BEDROOM DOOR and puts his ear to it. He hears machinery beeping and buzzing. He hesitates, but finally gathers the nerve to enter the room.

In this BEDROOM lies a totally incapacitated MICHELLE SMITH; TYLER'S long-lost girlfriend who he saved from the evil DR. COTOMAN and AGENT WOLF. MICHELLE looks like a Princess who's under a sleeping spell - a MODERN SLEEPING BEAUTY.

MICHELLE's utterly peaceful - still absolutely beautiful, as TYLER takes very good care of her. Her silky, vibrant blonde hair drapes still over her shoulders. MICHELLE is the same age as TYLER, only older by a couple of months.

She's a frail YOUNG WOMAN, having been in a COMA ever since the day after that faithful night at 'LIFE-CONTROL'. MICHELLE's very pale. But in her state of coma, she looks like an ANGEL - as if she's getting the best rest a human being could ever get.

TYLER bathes her, tends to her - he cares for her around the clock. He feeds and hydrates MICHELLE intravenously, as well. He's holding onto the HOPE that she'll awaken -

Although TYLER "saved" MICHELLE from EVIL that night at 'LIFE-CONTROL', she has suffered ever since - her silence is deafening to THE GREAT BARIAH, he can feel her desire to move, to wake up; she just can't muster up the strength to do it.

> THE GREAT BARIAH
> (shakes his head,
> grits his teeth)
> I dreamed you'd be in here dancing, MICHELLE. I'll keep dreaming. Just me and you, swaying away under the stars.

THE GREAT BARIAH looks upon his lost love. He walks up to her, grabs her hand and just sits beside her in the pure quiet. He says THE LORD'S PRAYER beside her bed...

...TYLER can feel MICHELLE's presence, he can feel her fighting. He just knows he can save her. "There has to be a way, right?", TYLER thinks to himself.

She went into shock after being rescued and fell into a deep coma. TYLER even hired a personal doctor to look over MICHELLE, to no avail, right after she entered into the coma. Now he looks after her himself.

All TYLER knows is that she's in the coma and she MAY wake up. It's not guaranteed. NOTHING EVER IS -

Until the day she wakes, TYLER works as 'THE GREAT BARIAH' (his stage-name), saving money, he works on the biggest stage of his entire life doing what he knows how to do best: MAGIC

> CUT TO:

TYLER finishes saying THE LORD'S PRAYER beside the sleeping MICHELLE. He wipes the free-flowing tears from his face with his left hand, holding on to his dear love with his right hand.

> THE GREAT BARIAH
> (somberly, with an
> ache in his voice)
> You can beat this, MICHELLE. You can beat this...I'll never let you go. You wouldn't let me go - you
> (MORE)

                        THE GREAT BARIAH (cont'd)
        wouldn't let me go.

TYLER walks to the other side of MICHELLE's BED and fixes the "baby monitor" he has setup that he carries with him EVERYWHERE, just in case.

He kisses her on the head and exits the BEDROOM.

Before he shuts the door, TYLER blows MICHELLE a kiss.

                                        CUT TO:

TYLER TORINO enters the BATHROOM of the TRAILER.

He takes a long-hot shower while listening to CLASSICAL MUSIC -

AND WE CUT TO:

TYLER exits the SHOWER and dries off, speedily.

He enters his BEDROOM and proceeds to implement his MAGIC to put on his stage-attire. With the force of mind, TYLER levitates his ALL-BLACK clothing to himself, pants are black, shirt is a black button-up, shoes come floating to him, too.

He dresses with near zero-effort.

TYLER has a makeup mirror to the side of his bed. He approaches it:

TYLER has only two types of makeup (WHITE and BLACK LIPSTICK and FACEPAINT). He applies it to look like a MIME of sorts - he covers his lips in Black lipstick. He shadows his EYES with Black Facepaint. Then TYLER saturates his facial pores with White Facepaint - he fully looks the part of a MAGICIAN with this FACEPAINT and LIPSTICK on.

                                        CUT TO:

TYLER, then, with one last burst of telekinesis, retrieves a PURPLE-top that goes over his black-attire and hangs down like a lengthy scarf. This completes the COSTUME of THE GREAT BARIAH.

CUT TO:

TYLER checks in on MICHELLE, one more time - he takes a breath of depth, shuts the door.

TYLER exits the TRAILER, entering the realm of 'MAGIC-WORLD' - his workplace/employer.

CUT TO:

EXT. MAGIC-WORLD BACKLOT - LATER

TYLER appears from his TRAILER, fully dressed in his theatrical gear. All-Black from head-to-toe - with the exception of his PURPLE SCARF. TYLER's wearing pointy black-men's-dress-shoes.

His pants are fitted to his scrawny legs. His black-business shirt is quite spiffy, buttoned all the way to the neck. He reaches in his pockets and puts on skin-tight black leather gloves. His lips shine with the black paint on them. TYLER is dressed to impress...but more importantly to WORK.

He is immediately met by his BOSS when he steps out of his residence. The managerial leader of 'MAGIC-WORLD' who cuts the checks for TYLER and sponsors his ACT. This BOSS also is TYLER's LANDLORD:

- ANGELO - in his 40s, partly bald, cigar in his mouth, Italian, large around the waist, dressed sloppily in a button-up shirt, jeans with suspenders.

TYLER's hadn't had someone believe in him since this new BOSS. ANGELO saw his potential and monetized it for both of 'em - TYLER really does the ACT for MICHELLE. MAGIC-WORLD nor TYLER's BOSS are aware of her OR her COMA.

              THE GREAT BARIAH
           (caught totally
           off guard)
      ANGEY, listen, man-

ANGELO
Only my mother calls me ANGEY, TYLER. MY MOTHER! You, you are just a MAGICIAN - are you not?

THE GREAT BARIAH
Yes, I-

ANGELO
(serious, hands on his waist)
Then why aren't you on stage!? Your ACT is on in 5, get to it, TYLER. Or I will axe your ass and kick you out of that double-wide so fast, it'll make your head explode. That'll be some fucking magic, right there.

THE GREAT BARIAH
(walking with urgency, pleadingly)
ANGELO, can you loan me another 500 to get me through the week?

ANGELO
(turns to walk the other way)
Absolutely not.

THE GREAT BARIAH
Please, man. I'm begging you here. I've got nothing to show for this week. I need supplies, necessities. I overspent the last advance you gave me.

ANGELO
Kid, I've given you the limit of advances, okay? You actually owe me on rent, the power bill, because you're in debt with me right now. You're working off the debt. Another month pay-free, and you'll be free. But until then, I can't do anything for you, man.
(MORE)

                    ANGELO (cont'd)
          I'm sorry, really. I'm struggling
          myself. NOW, GET TO WORK. OR GET
          OFF MY PROPERTY.

                    THE GREAT BARIAH
               (head down,
                walking toward
                the BACKSTAGE
                AREA)
          Yessir, BOSSMAN. I understand.
          Thank you for what you have done
          for me. I'll make it up to you,
          ANGELO. I will.

                    ANGELO
               (speaks up)
          You don't have to make it up to
          me, TYLER. Do It for Yourself,
          Kid. You have had plenty of
          opportunities to advance here. The
          money I loaned you, it's in the
          thousands, man. I don't have it
          like that. Just keep the sales
          coming on stage, and I'll see what
          I can do for you by week's end,
          all right?

TYLER, having stopped while ANGELO gives him lighter news, cracks a genuine SMILE. He then turns around, feeling better of how he handled his BOSS.

                                        CUT TO:

INT. BACKSTAGE - 'MAGIC-WORLD' - MOMENTS LATER

The BACKSTAGE AREA of MAGIC-WORLD looks like a FREAKSHOW. There are clowns, acrobats, people dressed in animal costumes, folks juggling, a bunch of old-school mannered CIRCUS BUSINESS. TYLER walks in and he stands out amongst the colorful, bright bunch of circus performers...

...TYLER doesn't perform like the rest of the workers, no. THE GREAT BARIAH is a rare breed of stage-artist.

CUT TO:

The curtains open up - THE GREAT BARIAH enters onto the MAGIC-WORLD stage to a round of applause and great expectation from the many spectators.

- We see TYLER walk out onto the stage; the curtains close.

CUT TO:

INT. MICHELLE'S ROOM - THE TRAILER - DAY

THE DEVOURER has on a BLACK-ROBE with a WHITE-CROSS on his chest. He has on a PRIEST-COLLAR and a long WHITE-SCARF that has two BLACK-CROSSES on each side of it, at the bottom. He has on tall BLACK-BOOTS with white-tape wrapped around the toe-area. He has on a giant TOP-HAT, it's black with a WHITE-RIBBON around it. The HAT disguises the MAN's face in DARKNESS - he also has white mummy-like bandages wrapped around his hands.

THE DEVOURER stands over MICHELLE SMITH - his GOLD-TEETH gleaming - like a caring PRIEST would a dying innocent. He gently rubs the back of his hand across her feverish forehead. She is paralyzed, comatose, unable to hear, sense, understand.

THE DEVOURER places his palm over her cheek and lightly massages it, too. Out of nowhere, the man takes the same hand and covers MICHELLE'S mouth AND nose up, causing her to immediately suffocate in her coma state.

Her body instinctively, naturally starts convulsing in shock, attempting to get air to the brain but unable to. THE DEVOURER smiles upon MICHELLE.

      TRENTON TORINO (THE DEVOURER)
    (shushes her)
  It's okay, MY CHILD. Rest, now. Be
  with the Angels.

The DOOR opens to the TRAILER...

...TYLER TORINO, taking a stage-break, enters into a darkly

scene; his sweetheart being smothered by what appears to be a STRANGER.

                    THE GREAT BARIAH
                      (eyes widened)
                Who the hell are you!? Get away
                from her!

TYLER tries to run to MICHELLE's aid, but THE DEVOURER raises his hand and MENTALLY holds THE GREAT BARIAH at bay, without even so much as looking at him - he's implementing PURE telekinetic energy.

                    TRENTON TORINO (THE DEVOURER)
                Don't worry, TYLER, I'm merely
                setting the young lady free - you
                don't have the balls to let her
                soul ascend. Now, Watch her Die.

The biometric Computer monitors go haywire. MICHELLE'S Pulse fades and dwindles, slowly. TYLER can't move a muscle. THE DEVOURER is TOO STRONG.

                    THE GREAT BARIAH
                      (anxiously worried)
                WHY?

                    TRENTON TORINO (THE DEVOURER)
                      (reveals his face
                       to TYLER)
                Would it help you to know that it
                was I who KIDNAPPED her those
                years back at the CINEMA?
                      (smiles
                       satanically)
                You don't deserve love, TYLER. You
                don't deserve a family. You had
                one already, and you Destroyed it.

TYLER'S eyes get as big as grapefruits at this statement AND seeing ALL of the SCARS that cover this STRANGER. He examines the MAN in front of him. The beastliness of him, his "swagger", and the RAW magical ability he's displaying...

...THE GREAT BARIAH, just like that, figures out who's in

the ROOM with him and his lover. This STRANGER is holding
TYLER back, still as a blade of grass, effortlessly.

                  THE GREAT BARIAH
                (stunned to his
                very core)
        BROTHER? TRENT? There's no way.
        No.

                  TRENTON TORINO (THE DEVOURER)
                (wags his index
                finger)
        I'm NOT your brother, anymore. I.
        Am. The. DEVOURER. Bear witness as
        I obliterate your entire life, as
        you decimated mine. Finagle your
        way out of this-

THE DEVOURER, organically, creates a black-ball of energy,
as small as a bouncy-ball. He moves his fingers like he's
playing the trumpet, and in turn, this adds more ENERGY and
POWER to the small ball of glowing light, the black energy
mixes with red-lightning-like ENERGY, forming a solid ORB.

With the minor movement of his right hand, THE DEVOURER then
"shoots" the energy blast directly into TYLER TORINO'S
midsection, sending him flying out of the TRAILER like a
bullet out of the barrel of a loaded gun.

Glass, metal, plaster, it all shatters, creaking open in a
flash like it's FLESH, and TYLER TORINO (THE GREAT BARIAH)
is midair, still unable to move even a single centimeter.

                                CUT TO BLACK:

CHAPTER III - MAGIC AND MAYHEM

                                    FADE IN:

<u>EXT. MAGIC-WORLD - THE ARENA/STAGE-AREA - MOMENTS LATER</u>

THE DEVOURER, TYLER's BROTHER, zooms with an absolutely
cunning agility, FLYING out of the TRAILER after THE GREAT
BARIAH.

TRENTON matches the force with which TYLER is possessively GLIDING with the heaviness of gravity and lands right when he does, except THE GREAT BARIAH lands on his back. THE DEVOURER lands on his FEET, ever so gently with Grace.

There are masses of PEOPLE spectating at the events and activities. All that is interrupted when TYLER crash lands in the crowded ARENA.

                TRENTON TORINO (THE DEVOURER)
     You're so much weaker than I
     presumed you'd be. Your power, why
     aren't you using it like you did
     when we were kids, huh!?

                THE GREAT BARIAH
     W-what are you talking about,
     TRENT!?

                TRENTON TORINO (THE DEVOURER)
     Goddamn you, you know exactly what
     I'm talking about. Don't you even
     try to be the victim, you little
     shit. YOU TOOK EVERYTHING FROM US!
     You weren't a child when it
     happened - you were a WMD. One of
     God's many MISTAKES.

TYLER stands up, gathering his countenance ever so slowly. He's discombobulated. His right hand rests on his right knee. He catches his breath, and takes a defensive position.

THE DEVOURER formulates ANOTHER "energy ball", this time with just his PINKY-FINGER. It is a PINK-ENERGY ORB, much smaller than the last one he threw at TYLER.

                TRENTON TORINO (THE DEVOURER)
     You dodge your history, your past,
     your family. But, CAN YOU DODGE
     THIS?

The PINK-ORB transforms into a disc-like structural form, whirling in mid-air, stagnant, like some kind of miniature mutant SUN. TRENTON TORINO SMILES and RELEASES the explosive MATTER directly at THE GREAT BARIAH.

TYLER'S eyes widen, he thinks fast, evading the BLAST in a nanosecond. TYLER does a 540-degree karate-esque flip while suspended in the air and TRENTON (THE DEVOURER) completely misses HIS BROTHER.

>   THE GREAT BARIAH
>   (breathing heavily)
>   You - MISSED.

>   TRENTON TORINO (THE DEVOURER)
>   (smirks)
>   No, TYLER - I didn't.

In .01 seconds after this is uttered, the PINK disc-looking ball of Fire hits nearly 120 FANS/PEOPLE in the ARENA-AUDIENCE. They perish INSTANTLY in a very limited, yet extremely intense Pinkish-Black Explosion that consumes them like cotton-balls and moths to an INFERNO:

>   THE GREAT BARIAH
>   (turns around,
>   unable to STOP IT)
>   Oh, God.

>   TRENTON TORINO (THE DEVOURER)
>   (enraged, power
>   growing like
>   wildfire)
>   No. There is only...POWER. God is
>   dead.

>   CUT TO:

Countless fans, in the dozens, race for the MAGIC-WORLD exits in a frenzy.

THE DEVOURER rises up into the air on his own volition - TYLER, unable to hide his POWERS any longer, meets his BROTHER in mid-air.

THE DEVOURER, overpowering THE GREAT BARIAH mentally and with FORCE OF MIND, shuts down the OUTDOOR ARENA of MAGIC-WORLD. Citizens begin trampling one another in a full-ditch effort to escape the premises.

                    TYLER TORINO
          These people are innocent! It's ME
          you want, not them.

                    TRENTON TORINO (THE DEVOURER)
          You have no idea what I want,
          GREAT BARIAH - you're simply a
          dove in a hurricane. Now feel my
          WRATH.

                    ANGELO
              (waving his hands
               frantically)
          Whoa! Whoa! Stop this, right now,
          you prick - who in the hell do you
          think you are!?

ANGELO gets in-between TRENT and TYLER, sweating, frightened
at what he's seeing -

                    TRENTON TORINO (THE DEVOURER)
              (extends his open
               left-hand at
               ANGELO)
          Me? I'm THE SIN-EATER. I am this
          world's ANNIHILATION.

                    THE GREAT BARIAH
              (to ANGELO)
          No, run!

THE DEVOURER fires an energy-blast at ANGELO's head, making
his head explode instantly.

                    THE GREAT BARIAH
              (painfully)
          ANGY!

CUT TO:

Much quicker, THE DEVOURER gears up to dish out another
light-explosion from the palms of both of his hands at the
MAGIC-WORLD crowd.

THE GREAT BARIAH gets in front of the blast of energy and
absorbs it, preventing the targeted spectators from being

consumed by FIRE.

Taking the heat of the attack, TYLER's knocked back like a kickball, skidding across the ground furiously.

His purple scarf catches FIRE, as does his shirt. He stands up quickly to dust off his shoulders and put out the flames. His FACEPAINT starts fading as he pours sweat from the HEAT.

                TRENTON TORINO (THE DEVOURER)
           (kicks TYLER in
            the stomach)
      This is so much bigger than you
      could ever imagine. This is FATE -
      this is REVENGE. This is the
      DEVOURING of your SOUL - in the
      name of MY mother AND father and
      all the time and love you stole
      from me. By the end of this day,
      GREAT BARIAH, you will know PAIN.
      Peace is not an option for you.

TRENTON TORINO kicks TYLER a few more times in the ribs with total agility. On the last effort, he makes the young man flip in the air.

                                    CUT TO:

While THE GREAT BARIAH is momentarily incapacitated, THE DEVOURER extends his index finger toward more of the panicked crowd and lasers several people's heads off with a golden-stream of light from his finger.

                THE GREAT BARIAH
           (puts his hand out
            pleading)
      I - I can't do this.

THE DEVOURER walks up to TYLER and picks him up by the neck like he's a bug. He chokeslams his BROTHER into the concrete with such dramatic force that it results in a massive hole forming in the ground instantly -

TYLER sly-like sways his hand at his side, zoning in his MAGICAL senses.

                    TRENTON TORINO (THE DEVOURER)
                Look at you, BROTHER. I thought
                you were a MAESTRO of MAGIC? You
                can't even-

THE GREAT BARIAH telepathically makes a fully-loaded multiple-ton 18-wheeler TRAILER slam into TRENTON TORINO at the speed of a RANDY JOHNSON fastball.

TYLER jolts up from the crater and fast as possible diverts the TRAILER and TRENTON away from the remaining crowd-members. The huge object instead crashes into one of the plastered brick-walls, going through it like a bullet through tissue paper.

                                CUT TO:

EXT. THE PARKING LOT - MAGIC WORLD - CONTINUOUS

The many MAGIC-WORLD fans/consumers rush toward the MAGIC-made exit, flowing through it til' it clogs and bottlenecks. The panic is doing more damage than anything - people are dying from pure anxiety and terror. Some folks are having heart-attacks, some are being stomped to death, some are physically and severely hurting others in an attempt to elope.

TYLER flies OVER the ARENA-WALL to his opponent. Before THE DEVOURER can react to the damage, TYLER attempts to do CROWD-CONTROL to no avail -

                    THE GREAT BARIAH
                        (yelling at the
                        fearful CROWD)
                Everyone, please, stop this
                madness - calm yourselves, you're
                only hurting each other! Don't
                give in!

TYLER's crowd-control attempt is short-lived. THE DEVOURER levitates the TRAILER off of himself and slings it many, many yards away.

He stands urgently, with a chaotic grin on his face. He wipes BLACK-BLOOD from his mouth.

                    TRENTON TORINO (THE DEVOURER)
          Is that your best shot?

                    THE GREAT BARIAH
                  (roaring, pushes
                   telekinetically)
          Aarrah!

THE DEVOURER goes flying backwards through the windshields
and top-halves of several vehicles in the PARKING-LOT.

                              CUT TO:

TYLER levitates, floating to his BROTHER - he lands in front
of the now battle damaged DEVOURER.

                    TYLER TORINO
          Where did you get this power,
          TRENT? How? Are you - are you like
          me? Are we -

                    TRENTON TORINO (THE DEVOURER)
          I am NOTHING like you, you little
          shit. Know that. You want to know
          where I got my abilities? I'm not
          a natural KINETIC like you, no.
          Your old friends, DR. COTOMAN and
          AGENT WOLF, they introduced my DNA
          to the BANE ALGORITHM - I didn't
          morph into an ANIMAL. I became
          SUPERHUMAN beyond measure. I
          became THE DEVOURER! Now feel my
          grief. Feel my power. You will
          know true agony - you took our
          parents, our home. I'm taking
          everything from you now.

THE DEVOURER charges up.

THE GREAT BARIAH does the same - the wind, air particles,
moving and whirling around him.

The two SUPERHUMANS clash like TITANS.

AND WE CUT TO:

EXT. THE TORINO FAMILY HOME - NORTH CAROLINA - EVENING

LOCATION: GASTONIA, NC

- 2009

MORTON drives his FAMILY into their driveway, as HEATHER sits in the passenger seat, and the BOYS sit in the back of the vehicle.

MORTON drives a BMW SEDAN. The TORINO FAMILY HOME is BEAUTIFUL - a dream house. It's 4 BEDROOMS, 2 BATHROOMS, made of BRICK. It has an inground pool, of all things.

The TORINOS exit the SEDAN - HEATHER opens the trunk. TRENT grabs the bags.

      MORTON TORINO
    (walking up to the
     front door, keys
     in-hand)
  You boys have fun, today?

      TYLER TORINO
    (blissful)
  I did, daddy.

      TRENTON TORINO
    (holding his and
     TYLER's bags)
  Yeah, dad, thanks for the
  sneakers. Thank you, too, mom.

      HEATHER TORINO
  You're so welcome, son. What do we
  want for dinner, tonight, huh?

      TYLER TORINO
  Pizza! Delivery.

MORTON turns the house key, opening the front door. His FAMILY follows behind him.

MORTON TORINO
That would certainly make it an easy supper -

The FAMILY happily enter their HOME - the door shuts.

CUT TO:

INT. THE TORINO FAMILY HOME - LATER

Pizza boxes are in the KITCHEN - the FAMILY grubbed on delivery. They're watching a FILM in the DEN.

The film they're enjoying is 'THE PRESTIGE'.

TYLER TORINO
(looking to his
older brother)
TRENT, do you believe in MAGIC?

TRENTON TORINO
No, bro. I believe in SCIENCE - MAGIC is horseshit. There's always a trick, a key, or a method.

HEATHER TORINO
TRENTON, watch your mouth, son.

TYLER TORINO
(gleefully)
- Well, I believe in MAGIC.

MORTON TORINO
(to TRENTON)
Sometimes, it's best to just believe, son. Searching for the secrets of MAGIC, ruins its power. I think that's what this FILM is getting at, you know?

TRENTON TORINO
That's how people get swindled, dad. Don't let TYLER hear that, he'll really try becoming a MAGICIAN, for god's sake.

                          HEATHER TORINO
                If he does, so what? We'll support
                you boys, no matter what you
                pursue. Remember that.

                                              CUT TO:

The movie ends. The credits roll.

                          MORTON TORINO
                     (pats TYLER on the
                      head, looks at
                      TRENTON)
                Well, boys, it's time for bed. Go
                brush your teeth, get yourselves
                some rest. Your mother and I need
                some quality time.

                          THE TORINO BROTHERS (TOGETHER)
                     (monotone, a
                      little sad)
                Yes, sir.

The TORINO BROTHERS race each other up the stairs toward
their shared BATHROOM.

                          TRENTON TORINO
                     (sprinting up the
                      stairs)
                Last one to get their teeth
                brushed is a rotten egg.

                          TYLER TORINO
                     (retorting)
                First one to the BATHROOM is an
                idiot.

                                              CUT TO:

INT. THE BOYS' BATHROOM - TORINO FAMILY HOME - NIGHT

TYLER and TRENTON brush their teeth together, both looking
in the mirror - spitting, brushing, spitting, brushing.

                    TRENTON TORINO
               (laughs at TYLER)
          You're such a goofball, little
          brother. I love you, man.

TRENTON has concluded his brushing and rinsing his mouth. He
shoulder-hugs his brother, as TYLER finishes brushing his
teeth, proceeding to rinse, too.

                    TYLER TORINO
               (tooth-brush
                obstructing his
                speech)
          I love you, too, big brother.

TRENT is exiting the BATHROOM -

                    TRENTON TORINO
          Goodnight, TY -

                    TYLER TORINO
          Goodnight, T-Time.

                                             CUT TO:

INT. TYLER'S BEDROOM - THE TORINO FAMILY HOME - MOMENTS LATER

TYLER's DAD and MOM are sitting by his bedside to tuck him
in.

                    TYLER TORINO
          Mommy, Daddy, can you guys read me
          a quick bedtime story, to help me
          sleep better?

                    MORTON TORINO
          Not tonight, son. Sorry. Your
          mother and I - we - we have some
          business to attend; too long
          delayed, if you ask me.

MORTON kisses his own hand and touches it to his son's
forehead.

HEATHER kisses TYLER on the cheek.

                    HEATHER TORINO
          - You'll understand when you're
          older. WE love you, TYLER. Sleep
          tight, don't let the bed bugs
          bite.

                    TYLER TORINO
          I love you both. Goodnight.
          Hopefully, tomorrow night you guys
          can read me a story.

                    MORTON TORINO
                (holding onto his
                 wife, intimately)
          You got yourself a deal, son.
          We'll both read you one tomorrow,
          okay?

TYLER's parents proceed to exit his BEDROOM.

                    TYLER TORINO
                (excited yet
                 sleepy)
          Cool beans.
                (in darkness)
          Please, don't shut the door all
          the way. Leave it cracked open a
          little bit.

                    MORTON TORINO
          You got it, TY -
                (cracks door
                 slightly)
          - is this good enough for you?

                    TYLER TORINO
          Yes, daddy. Thank you so much. I
          love you. See you in the morning.

TYLER peers at the light shining minimally into his ROOM. He
ponders - his eyes get very heavy. Rest finds him.

                                              CUT TO:

INT. TYLER'S BEDROOM - LATER

TYLER tosses and turns.

He struggles ostensibly in his slumber.

He's having a severe nightmare - it causes him to enter a cold-sweat and to feel sleep-paralysis; he's unable to breathe properly.

      TYLER TORINO
     (yearning to
      awaken)
  No. No. Help, help me.

             1 MINUTE LATER:

TRENT enters his little brother's ROOM, subsequent to hearing him battling his NIGHTMARE.

      TRENTON TORINO
     (shakes TYLER)
  TY - wake up, man. Wake up.
     (lightly slaps his
      brother)
  C'mon, little brother. Snap out of
  it.

      TYLER TORINO
     (abruptly wakes up)
  No!
     (sweating
      profusely)
  Oh, God -

TYLER's rises - pushing TRENT backward - awake but still in a hypnotic state.

- TYLER's essentially sleep-walking, minus the walking part. He's hallucinating. He panics.

Like a lightning strike, TYLER's KINETIC ENERGY activates - the child releases power never before seen, felt, or heard.

Similar to a NEW MEXICO HOUSE in a NUCLEAR EXPERIMENT, the TORINO FAMILY HOME implodes then EXPLODES, shattering into a million pieces and chunks.

CUT TO:

TYLER subconsciously, instinctively creates a metaphysical shield to protect himself. He is unable to do the same for TRENT.

CUT TO:

INT. THE TORINO FAMILY HOME - NIGHT

TRENTON goes flying, fast-and-furious, through the few walls in the HOME then directly through the BRICK WALL in the back of the house. TRENT lands in the inground POOL - full of fear, consumed by terror at the sight of his little brother displaying Telekinetic Power.

CUT TO:

EXT. THE INGROUND POOL - CONTINUOUS

TRENTON is badly injured, momentarily knocked out, submerged in the POOL water - blood mixes with the water.

Underneath the surface, after a few beats, TRENT startles awake - shattered, distraught, consumed by panic and PAIN. He emerges out from under the water, in shock.

> TRENTON TORINO
> (surveying the
> catastrophic
> damage)
> Mom! Dad! What the - what the
> hell!? TYLER, are you there?

TRENT struggles but exits the pool.

He falls to his knees on the cement beside the POOL, wounded and bleeding - he hears no response from his FAMILY, not even TYLER.

CUT TO BLACK:

CHAPTER IV - ABRACADABRA

                              FADE IN:

EXT. THE DESTROYED TORINO HOME - MOMENTS LATER

TRENT stands to his feet.

He begins searching through the debris of the HOME - randomly, PARAMEDICS and POLICE show up to the disaster scene.

                              CUT TO:

Right as the FIRST RESPONDERS appear, some debris moves in the wreckage.

TYLER rises from the mess after moving pieces of brick and wood from out of his way.

                    TRENTON TORINO
          TYLER, what the fuck did you do!?
          Where's MOM and DAD!?

                    TYLER TORINO
                (standing silent)
          I - I-

                    TRENTON TORINO
                (raging at TYLER)
          Answer me!

                              CUT TO:

EXT. MAGIC-WORLD PARKING-LOT - DAY

TRENTON's kid voice bleeds into his adult voice, him saying the same words:

                    TRENTON TORINO (THE DEVOURER)
                (in great pain)
          - ANSWER ME! Why did you kill our
          parents?

                    TYLER TORINO
          I - I didn't mean to, TRENT. I was
          5, I had no control over, over my
          POWER. It hit me like a fever and
          my body reacted.

                    TRENTON TORINO (THE DEVOURER)
          Not good enough. Today, brother,
          you meet DEATH - then, I will
          DEVOUR this world.

                                        CUT TO:

THE DEVOURER charges THE GREAT BARIAH with all of his
strength.

He uppercuts TYLER.

TYLER is unable to block the next few blows to his face and
body.

CUT TO:

TYLER, after experiencing the blows from TRENT, defends
himself. He kicks his brother in the nuts, then elbows him
in the face - THE DEVOURER is basically unaffected by the
combo, merely grunting and shrugging it off.

                    TRENTON TORINO (THE DEVOURER)
          What are you trying to do, you
          sissy? You couldn't hurt a fly
          with those strikes. You think
          you're some kinda superhero!? YOU
          ARE NOTHING!

                    THE GREAT BARIAH
          Actually, T-Time, I was
          distracting you...FOR THIS -

A big, filled to the brim BLUE MAILBOX slams into THE
DEVOURER - this gets to him; it hurts TRENT. Also, a huge
MANHOLE/SEWER COVER slams into his windpipe sending him
flying backward -

THE DEVOURER is injured now but gets back up, unnerved,
pissed as a fire-ant, and ready for WAR. His RAGE takes him

over -

TRENTON begins TRANSFORMING.

                              CUT TO:

THE DEVOURER growls, salivates - his hands grow 3 times larger, as do his arms. His fingers become like TALONS; his skin turns black as burnt coal.

TRENT walks slowly, agitated as can be, shaking epileptically, his FEET become engulfed with BLUE BUTANE-like FLAMES, burning his BOOTS.

His hands also burn with BUTANE-esque flames - his EYES course with HELLFIRE.

His upper body expands. His legs grow thicker. His face is infected with BLACK VEINS - THE DEVOURER's GOLD TEETH pop off and fall out of his mouth onto the ground, as all of his natural teeth expand and enlarge becoming as deadly as that of a serpent; his mouth of fangs are black and sharp.

TRENT officially morphs into his DEVOURER persona. TYLER is stunned at the sight. THE DEVOURER, through force of mind, calls his TOP-HAT back to him. He grabs it out the air and places it on his head.

            TRENTON TORINO (THE DEVOURER)
                (monstrously)
          You - you have no idea the power I
          have gained. I will destroy you,
          if it's the last thing I do.
                (snaps his fingers)
          MR. ED, Ms. LINDA, show my brother
          what CHAOS really is.

MR. ED and his ASSISTANT, from the PAWNSHOP in PORT ST. JOE, are possessed by THE DEVOURER -

They are what's called: "THE DEVOURED" - their souls have been tainted, their minds and bodies corrupted. They're essentially ZOMBIES.

                              CUT TO:

MR. ED and Ms. LINDA approach TYLER with a quickness, chomping at him. He focuses on them, and with pure mental strength throws them many yards away.

THE DEVOURER focuses in on the other CIVILIANS - he BITES one of the random citizens. They are immediately INFECTED with a zombie-like contagion. They turn at the drop of a top-hat.

Just biting one person, TRENT causes upheaval. That person bites another, the other person bites someone else - MR. ED and LINDA run around biting people, too. The foes multiply like bacteria.

CUT TO:

>   TYLER TORINO
>   (backing away in
>   fear)
>   This can't be.

For just a moment, TYLER takes his eyes off of TRENT -

TRENT, transformed and evolved, moves like an OLYMPIC SPRINTER to his brother's back.

He puts TYLER in a HEADLOCK, choking him:

>   TRENTON TORINO (THE DEVOURER)
>   Watch, little brother. Bear
>   Witness to what YOU have done -
>   your cowardice and inaction will
>   be their extinction.

It's a miniature ZOMBIE APOCALYPSE - the MAGIC-WORLD customers AND workers begin eating each other, tearing themselves apart, literally. THE GREAT BARIAH counters the headlock by THE DEVOURER, escaping his grip.

TYLER flies away from TRENT with uncertainty.

                                              CUT TO:

>   TRENTON TORINO (THE DEVOURER)
>   Time to pay the piper, TY - the
>   bill has come due.

THE DEVOURER slings his round top-hat at THE GREAT BARIAH - the hat's edges are composed of METAL. The HAT cuts TYLER on his chest and goes back to TRENT like a boomerang.

TRENT then blitzes TYLER, elbowing him straight into the MAGIC-WORLD front-area TICKET-BOOTH. TYLER goes THROUGH the TICKET BOOTH, then, through the BRICK WALL back into the ARENA of MAGIC-WORLD -

CUT TO:

TYLER bursts through the debris covering him - he glides and returns to the PARKING-LOT battlefield.

The DEVOURED Citizens start running towards THE GREAT BARIAH in bunches from inside the ARENA and from the radius of the PARKING-LOT - the contagion spreads like wildfire.

THE DEVOURER/TRENT ascends up in the air to see his "MAGIC" do its work.

TYLER creates a LIGHT-SHIELD over his body. He then holds back over a dozen ZOMBIES, all with his mental strength - he reaches out with both hands, stalling the MONSTERS preventing them from BITING him.

He waves his right hand, like a right hook swing - this causes the many monsters to get tossed several meters in the air at impressive speeds. They soar past THE DEVOURER -

A dozen more of the ZOMBIES jump TYLER from behind, but they still cannot bite him, his body won't let them.

The DEVOURED, possessed citizens, dogpile onto THE GREAT BARIAH, gnawing, chomping, screaming, all of them in pain yet attacking the MAGICIAN with all of their rabies-like strength.

       TRENTON TORINO (THE DEVOURER)
   (cackling)
  HAHAHA -

                CUT TO:

                                                          330.

                    TYLER TORINO
                  (with all his
                   power)
              ENOUGH!

TYLER is able to blast through the dogpile, raising himself
up onto his feet, his arms held high. The ZOMBIES go high up
into the sky - landing, splatting on the concrete of the
PARKING-LOT.

THE GREAT BARIAH reacts ever so quickly. He reaches out with
his mind to save several citizens from the ZOMBIES. TYLER
lifts the people all at once through his telekinesis, takes
flight, with his hand out he guides the citizens in the air
in an attempt to get them to where there are no ZOMBIES.

The outbreak happened so fast; it's a dreadful situation.

                                        CUT TO:

<u>INT. THE MALL - THE ORLANDO STRIP - DAY</u>

The glass covering the ceiling of the ORLANDO STRIP MALL
breaks into thousands upon thousands of pieces. The people
inside go into a CHAOTIC frenzy, screaming, shouting,
seeking safety -

TYLER TORINO is able to enter the MALL through the
ROOF/GLASS CEILING with the several citizens he rescued,
CHILDREN and WOMEN.

THE GREAT BARIAH crashes to the hard tile of the MALL floor.

He uses his power, instead, to safely place the citizens
he's saved on the tile gently.

                                        CUT TO:

The MALL DOORS at the entrance, not far from TYLER, explode
with pure GREEN LIGHT ENERGY - THE DEVOURER bursts into the
MALL, his mindless DEVOURED ZOMBIES behind him.

							TRENTON TORINO (THE DEVOURER)
					(scoffs)
				You CANNOT run from RETRIBUTION,
				GREAT BARIAH.

The ZOMBIES split around THE DEVOURER, sprinting past him toward the other innocence in the MALL, toward THE GREAT BARIAH, and to those he just tried to PROTECT.

THE DEVOURER flexes his POWER - he creates another PINK ENERGY ORB in his palm. He's winding up, throws the ORB right at TYLER. TYLER doesn't flinch, he doesn't try to dodge it this time, no; THE GREAT BARIAH catches the ENERGY out of the air, then DISSAPATES it slowly but surely - he struggles with it but does so.

TYLER looks around at the ORGANIZED CHAOS unraveling before his eyes. He balls both of his fists up - his blood is volcanic, now.

							TRENTON TORINO (THE DEVOURER)
					(with worry in his
					 voice)
				No. How?

							TYLER TORINO
				Your power is not natural;
				therefore it has limits. You are
				just a pawn. I am a MAGICIAN!
				Abra-fucking-cadabra -

THE GREAT BARIAH, absolutely BATTLE-DAMAGED - (his facepaint smeared and mixed with sweat, his clothes burned and ripped) - at godspeed, surges toward his BROTHER, sprinting AND floating simultaneously.

TYLER TORINO - using the ability to PHASE (get in-between particles and molecules) - JUMPS, diving horizontally into his BROTHER's BODY.

TRENTON TORINO/THE DEVOURER is in shock. He's struggling. He's SUFFERING within moments.

We see the uncomfortableness on his face. He downgrades his power turning back into his HUMAN FORM - concern and worry written all over his face. He shakes, stirs, goes into a pseudo-seizure while standing...

...THE DEVOURED stop. They begin seizing as well, just as TRENT does. The ZOMBIES collapse to the ground, as TYLER is invasively on the INSIDE of his BROTHER's BODY.

                    TRENTON TORINO (THE DEVOURER)
               (roaring
                unholy-like)
          Aah! Aah!

THE DEVOURER's black veins start thumping. The BLACK BLOOD rushes to his head and face.

Within moments, TRENTON TORINO implodes AND explodes from the inside out - BLACK BLOOD SPRAYS ALL OVER THE PLACE.

THE GREAT BARIAH, covered in THE DEVOURER's blood, stands on the MALL FLOOR, breathing heavily. He wipes his face, looks around at the scene. There's a quietness about the place, all of a sudden.

                              CUT TO:

The "ZOMBIES" begin changing back to HUMANS - the biting was superficial, after all. THE DEVOURER, being patient-zero, was the master of the humans in their zombie form.

With him dead, the DEVOURED CURSE has been lifted. The humans wake up and snap out of their hypnotic mind-control -

                    ORLANDO CITIZEN
               (points finger)
          That kid, he saved us.
               (to TYLER)
          Who - who are you?

                    TYLER TORINO
               (heroically)
          THE GREAT BARIAH.

SWAT TEAMS and POLICE enter the destroyed entrance of the STRIP MALL -

As the Law enters with their automatic weapons equipped with laser-sights, THE GREAT BARIAH RISES - he flies freely away from the destruction.

CUT TO:

INT. SECRET LAIR - MORNING

POST-CREDITS' SCENE:

A MAN in a lab coat with a solid purple tie on, a scientist - white, early-30s, long black hair, chiseled face, tall, strongly built with unique PINK EYES that have SILVER PUPILS - sits in a SECRET LAIR in an UNKNOWN LOCATION:

- The MAN examines the various news feeds playing from his many TVs. He sees reporting about, scenes from, the 'MAGIC-WORLD'-catastrophe; they tell a half-truth of a story, but this MAN realizes THE GREAT BARIAH/TYLER TORINO lived and got away from the CHAOS.

- Frustrated, the MAN gets up from his massive rock desk. He walks up a glass-container holding a purple-metal technological suit. The MAN stares at this suit with a driven expression.

This MAN is COSMO WOLF...

     COSMO WOLF
    (sucks his teeth,
     frustrated)
  THE DEVOURER failed. Pathetic.

     COSMO WOLF
  WINTERBUTE, is the suit ready?

WINTERBUTE is an advanced OPERATING SYSTEM (O.S), with a male voice.

     WINTERBUTE (O.S)
    (monotone,
     computerish)
  Yes, Mr. WOLF. Whenever you are.

                    COSMO WOLF
          I'm ready. And don't call me "Mr.
          WOLF" anymore.

                    WINTERBUTE (O.S)
               (slightly confused)
          What shall I call you then, sir?

                    COSMO WOLF
               (angry)
          I am...METALLICO.

                    WINTERBUTE (O.S)
          Yes, sir. METALLICO it is -

                    METALLICO
               (opens the
                glass-container)
          Time to suit up.

CUT TO:

COSMO WOLF, his PINK EYES shining, stands in his SECRET LAIR
with his new tech-based suit on. He flexes and wiggles his
fingers. He then walks up to a picture on his rock desk.

- The picture is of AGENT WOLF and DR. COTOMAN, standing
with a young COSMO WOLF.

                    METALLICO
          Father, uncle, I will avenge you.
          We'll see just how "great" this
          BARIAH is -

An opening forms, through a metal mechanism, at the top of
the SECRET LAIR by a wave of METALLICO's hand:

- COSMO WOLF/METALLICO takes flight nearly at the speed of
light out of his SECRET LAIR, his target his only concern.
His target is TYLER TORINO.

                              CUT TO BLACK:

"Therefore rejoice, ye heavens, and ye that dwell in them.
Woe to the inhabiters of the earth and of the sea! for the
devil is come down unto you, having great wrath, because he

knoweth that he hath but a short time." - Revelation 12:12
(KING JAMES HOLY BIBLE)

            ACT IV. COLOR ME
            ROJO: EL HOMBRE DEL
            SACO (THE BOOGEYMAN)

CHAPTER I - HARVARD BULLIES

FADE IN:

INT. HARVARD CLASSROOM - DAY

            YEAR: 2034

DAY: OCTOBER 23RD

            TIME: 11:11 AM

LOCATION: CAMBRIDGE, MASSACHUSETTS - HARVARD UNIVERSITY

We hear a ticking clock. The hands twitching by the second -

A YOUNG 18-year-old LUCIUS CROW sits at his desk, listening to a lecture by his professor. LUCIUS, an advanced SOPHOMORE, is athletically slender; he's naturally fit. He has lengthy, silky black hair that hangs to his neck and covers his left eye - he's wearing glasses.

His skin is the color of dry beach-sand. He has big ears. The YOUNG MAN has a shiny paleness to him, yet his complexion is somewhat dark, especially around his ORANGE EYES - his irises are the color of Floridian Tangerines.

LUCIUS is 5'10, 150 pounds even. He's wearing a student's outfit, a navy blazer, white-collar shirt underneath, with a HARVARD RED tie, and khaki pants with beat up shoes that look like they've been spit-polished, they're coming apart at the ends, held together by duck-tape.

It's the 23rd of OCTOBER. Nearing HALLOWEEN, the classroom

is lit with all sorts of decorations all throughout, including a couple of carved pumpkins.

The PROFESSOR, a heavy fan of the HALLOWEEN season, is yammering on with his lecture. MR. BROSNAN is tall, nerdy-looking, skinny, mid-60s, has white hair, wears eyeglasses - he's sporting jeans, tennis shoes, and a HALLOWEEN sweater.

LUCIUS is not really listening to PROFESSOR BROSNAN's lecture, however.

He's working on a formula. A formula that will change everything.

                   PROFESSOR BROSNAN
     - Now, if you'll see, the
     theoretical nature of all the
     metaphysical aspects of science
     suggests -

LUCIUS is writing down his extensive, complicated algorithm...one step at a time, very patiently.

                   YOUNG LUCIUS CROW
         (narrating)
     I hate this place. This
     school...this planet. They that
     sow wind, shall reap a whirlwind.
     When I'm done with it, with
     HER...no one will mess with me
     ever again.

A paper spit-ball hits LUCIUS on the neck and sticks. He feels the slimy piece of trash right below his hairline and feels nothing but disgust.

2 FRESHMEN BULLIES sit behind the future SUPREME LEADER and eventual TOMEGATHERION...they laugh, chuckling at their petty act.

                   BARRY KENO
         (to LUCIUS)
     You fucking loser.

LUCIUS turns around and stares the BULLIES down with his bright ORANGE EYES behind his eye-glasses.

He wears these frames that he happened to find in the "lost and found", they're the opposite of fancy, the opposite of attention-seeking. The primary reason he has them on is to hide himself a bit - GIVE HIMSELF A "MASK".

                  LANCE LOGAN
             (at LUCIUS)
      Take those contacts out, faggy.
      It's not HALLOWEEN yet.

                PROFESSOR BROSNAN
      - Gentlemen. Take it outside.
      You're causing a raucous I don't
      need.

                  BARRY KENO
      Yeah, OUTSIDE, LUCILLE! -

The 2 FRESHMEN ANTAGONISTS get up and proceed to the exit of the CLASSROOM.

All the other students stare at LUCIUS, and they heckle him...the PROFESSOR is of no help, he could care less. This is a normal day at HARVARD -

BARRY and LANCE, both 18 years of age, stand outside the CLASSROOM threshold and they signal to LUCIUS to step outside while both men drag their thumbs across their necks, a threatening gesture.

LUCIUS reluctantly gets up and exits the CLASSROOM; intimated as ever.

BARRY KENO, a WHITE YOUNG MAN, is a stout brute, a standard college JOCK in stature. Clean shaven, he has long blonde hair that's slicked back, light green eyes, and he comes from wealth and privilege. BARRY is 6'2, some 200 pounds; he's on the LACROSSE team. So is LANCE LOGAN.

LANCE LOGAN is 6'1, 250 pounds. He's built like an NFL Linebacker. He's Caucasian, too - has brown eyes, brown hair in the form of an army crew cut; no facial hair.

He and BARRY are both wearing JOCK ATTIRE - (HARVARD sportswear, from head-to-toe) - in preparation for their LACROSSE match, they're dressed as a team. Both of their shirts, underneath their jackets, read: "HARVARD BULLY"

CUT TO:

EXT. CAMPUS BUILDING - THE YARD - MOMENTS LATER

Kids walk by and ignore the bullying.

The HARVARD BULLIES go to town on LUCIUS CROW: they punch LUCIUS a few times, kick him while he's down, and stomp him - a few times in the body, TWICE IN THE FACE. LUCIUS' glasses are broken in half in the attack.

LUCIUS is bloody - his injured nose drips and his cut lip flows with his blood...

                  BARRY KENO
Search him. Search his bag. Take it all. This fucker doesn't deserve to be here.

                YOUNG LUCIUS CROW
No, guys. Please! Not my work.

LUCIUS has a very exotic American accent.

                  LANCE LOGAN
             (mocking,
              sing-songy)
"No, guys, please!"

...BARRY kicks LUCIUS AGAIN in the face, stunning him for a moment.

No one helps LUCIUS.

BARRY and LANCE observe their PREY - disgusted by the sight of his blood. BARRY kneels down over LUCIUS.

                  BARRY KENO
             (wipes LUCIUS'
              blood with his
              index finger)
                  (MORE)

                    BARRY KENO (cont'd)
          You're bleeding all over OUR fine
          CAMPUS, LUCILLE -
                (slings hand,
                 sending blood
                 flying)
          Pathetic.

                    LANCE LOGAN
                (laughing)
          Look at all of his precious
          papers, BARRY -

BARRY and LANCE root through LUCIUS' belongings in his
bookbag.

LUCIUS passes out cold.

                                        CUT TO:

7 MINUTES LATER:

LUCIUS awakens to a mess.

His algorithm is now GONE, this he knows - LUCIUS, on the
ground still, is reluctant to look in his bookbag. He simply
doesn't, zipping it back up.

LUCIUS is covered in a shadow. He looks up to see a blurry
silhouette standing in front of him.

                    MICHAEL THORN
                (extending his
                 hand to LUCIUS)
          LUCY, man, get up, c'mon.

                    YOUNG LUCIUS CROW
                (seeing double)
          MIKEY, is that you?

                    MICHAEL THORN
                (helps LUCIUS onto
                 his feet)
          BARRY and LANCE came at you AGAIN,
          huh?

MICHAEL takes ahold of LUCIUS' bookbag for him.

>   YOUNG LUCIUS CROW
>   (sighs, defeated)
>   Second time this week. This time,
>   they drew blood, and I passed out,
>   though. And MY WORK is gone, man.

>   MICHAEL THORN
>   Dammit, man. I'm sorry, LUCY.
>   Let's get you to your room, get
>   you cleaned up.

>   YOUNG LUCIUS CROW
>   (putting his
>   weight on MICHAEL)
>   Thanks, MIKEY. I mean that.

CUT TO:

EXT. CAMPUS STREET - DAY

MICHAEL THORN is the ONLY person who has attended to LUCIUS and his injuries. As LUCIUS limps, MICHAEL carries him from one side.

MICHAEL, a 19-year-old SOPHOMORE, has curly, frizzy hair, unkept - he's obviously Caucasian.

He has freckles all over his face. He's athletically built, has a strong stature for a college SOPHOMORE.

His teeth are yellow-stained - he doesn't smoke cigarettes; he just doesn't practice good dental hygiene and drinks too much coffee. He has a slight hunchback and he's bow-legged.

MICHAEL dresses like a hippy, not a jock. He's wearing soccer-shoes, khaki shorts, and a tie-dye shirt, of all things. He's a free spirit.

MICHAEL THORN is LUCIUS' only TRUE friend.

CUT TO:

> YOUNG LUCIUS CROW
> (to MICHAEL)
> I think it's the glasses.

> MICHAEL THORN
> Real funny. Seriously, man, you're going to have to stand up for yourself at some point. You can't let those assholes run all over you like that.

LUCIUS starts regaining his balance. He backs off of MICHAEL's shoulder and stands himself up straight. His back and neck pop, his fingers snaps when he stretches them.

LUCIUS has to readjust but he's able to recenter himself.

> YOUNG LUCIUS CROW
> They're your friends, dude. Tell them to stop messing with me!

> MICHAEL THORN
> It's not so simple, LU. I wish you could understand that. There're politics at play. They are fellow athletes. I HAVE TO BE THEIR FRIENDS.

> YOUNG LUCIUS CROW
> (puts his hand on
> his shoulder)
> You, my friend, don't have to do anything. Remember that, MIKEY. I appreciate you being there for me. I got it from here.

LUCIUS starts to walk off toward his DORM-ROOM.

> MICHAEL THORN
> (holds out LUCIUS'
> bookbag)
> LUCY!

LUCIUS turns around, in pain.

MICHAEL THORN
Forgetting something?

MICHAEL takes the bookbag to LUCIUS.

YOUNG LUCIUS CROW
Thanks, brother.

MICHAEL THORN
(walks away)
You got it, bud. Now, you be safe. Stay out of trouble, okay?

YOUNG LUCIUS CROW
(wincing, holding his ribs)
I'll try, MIKEY. I'll try. Hey, now that I'm out of class, I'm going by that CAR DEALERSHIP down the road. Want to join me?

MICHAEL THORN
(turns back around)
No can-do, LU. I've got to go to practice as soon as I get out of study hall. What're you going there for?

YOUNG LUCIUS CROW
Understood, MIKEY. Well, you have a good practice - and I'm going to look at cars, what else?

MICHAEL THORN
(gives LUCIUS a thumbs up)
I see. And I certainly will. You hold your head up, man. And quit letting those guys ride all over you.

MICHAEL turns away from LUCIUS and goes about his business.

LUCIUS heads to his DORM-ROOM quite quickly. Tears start swelling in his ORANGE EYES. The tears steam up his glasses, as the humiliation starts to hit him.

343.

                              CUT TO:

EXT. THE FIELD - LACROSSE PRACTICE - DAY

BARRY KENO is one of the rising stars of the LACROSSE team - he was the captain of his high-school team. He's on the field giving it all he's got against his teammates as they scrimmage against one another. Shirts vs. Skins -

> BARRY KENO
> (yelling like a
> leader)
> Ball, ball! Back - here, hit me!

                              CUT TO:

BARRY receives the ball -

He runs over one of the defenders ragefully. He then jukes a couple more of the guys and proceeds to score, all SOLO.

> COACH RAYFIELD
> (blows his whistle)
> Keep it up, KENO! Good work. Keep it going like that. I expect this type of performance come gameday -

LANCE LOGAN meets BARRY KENO at the GOAL and gives him props, celebrating the score. Other teammates follow suit.

> COACH RAYFIELD
> Okay, let's try the B-formation on offense and push it good, and we'll do the Zone-4 Defense; see how that functions. BREAK! KENO, get yourself some water, you earned it, son.

> BARRY KENO
> (mouthguard
> obstructing his
> voice)
> Yessir, COACH.
> (runs to the
> cooler)
>   (MORE)

                         BARRY KENO (cont'd)
                    Go CRIMSON!

BARRY KENO's fist rises in the air as he holds his
LACROSSE-stick in the other hand.

The players repeat his WAR-CRY:

                         LACROSSE-TEAM (IN-SYNC)
                              (battle-ready yet
                               fatigued)
                    Go CRIMSON!

                                             CUT TO:

BARRY removes his helmet. He gulps down a couple of
disposable GATORADE cups of water, observing the field and
his teammates make plays - he cheers them on.

                                             CUT TO:

INT. THE DOJO - KARATE PRACTICE - CONTINUOUS

MICHAEL, in white garbs, is attending KARATE-practice.

He's a BLACK-BELT (9th Degree).

The instructor, MASTER AL CANNON, stands ready as MICHAEL
does a high kick through a thick piece of wood.

                         MICHAEL THORN
                              (with power and
                               finesse)
                    Hiyah!

MICHAEL kicks right through the piece of wood like it's a
sheet of paper -

                         MASTER AL CANNON
                    Nice form, Mr. THORN. You're
                    improving more and more each day.
                    Now let's see how well your chop
                    is.

MASTER AL CANNON, in a black master's uniform with a
matching decorated belt, is an expert at KEMPO - he's a
MASTER of KARATE. He's of the highest degree in the order of
Martial Artists. An Olympian, operating at the most elevated
level of the sport.

He is African-American; his pigmentation is dark. He's 59
years of age. He may be old but he's extremely capable - he
has a potbelly yet still he's amazingly athletic.

MASTER AL CANNON has medium length silver-gray hair. He has
facial hair like Confucius, if you will. He's 6ft even,
about 185-lbs. He has the voice of a Jazz-player, scratchy
and upbeat.

                              CUT TO:

MICHAEL walks up to SEVERAL bricks within the DOJO.

MASTER CANNON gestures to his student, MICHAEL THORN, with a
breathe-in-breathe-out motion:

                     MASTER AL CANNON
                Gather your CHI, Mr. THORN. Let it
                flow through you. Remember, there
                are no bricks, there's only you
                and your CHI -

The other KARATE-members of HARVARD stand in awe of MICHAEL
THORN.

MICHAEL is an ELITE Martial Artist, thanks to AL CANNON's
leadership and coaching skills. CANNON developed him,
nurturing his abilities with tremendous care.

                              CUT TO:

MICHAEL bows to his COACH, then attacks the bricks with all
of his might, all of his physical AND mental strength. He
strikes with a downward punch using his left fist.

                     MICHAEL THORN
                       (high volume)
                Yah!

All 7 BRICKS BREAK in HALF - MICHAEL's fellow team-members are stunned by his skill. These bricks are not thin by any means. There's no trickery occurring, MICHAEL's just that damn good.

His teammates give him a round of applause, a standing ovation.

He bows to MASTER CANNON, then turns and bows to his fellow KARATE-squad; they bow back - a group composed of nothing but Black-Belts.

          MICHAEL THORN
      (bowing multiple
       times)
Thank you, MASTER CANNON. I would be nothing without your teachings. Thank you, TEAM - let's give it 110 PERCENT at the next tournament.

          MASTER AL CANNON
      (bows back to
       MICHAEL)
We might make the OLYMPICS, at this rate. If you all can show-up and show-out like our dear MICHAEL here, we'll be in near-perfect shape. We'll rock the world and knock the other teams on their noggins.
      (waves his hand to
       the STUDENTS)
Ms. KEISHA, let's see your progress - now...

The dialogue becomes unintelligible -

MICHAEL hi-fives all of his teammates on the sidelines of the DOJO. He experiences a moment of bliss. He's happy.

                            CUT TO:

EXT. THE CAMPUS BUS-STOP - DAY

LUCIUS, standing at a bus-stop, awaits the CITY-BUS that travels through HARVARD to give students a lift to-and-from CAMBRIDGE.

He waits patiently for the transportation, contemplating HARVARD life. While waiting, he sees a MURDER of CROWS flying right above him.

> YOUNG LUCIUS CROW
> (to the CROWS,
> smiling)
> Caw! Caw!

The CITY-BUS arrives - LUCIUS is the only one waiting at the stop. He boards the transport. The doors shut.

CUT TO:

INT. THE CITY-BUS - CONTINUOUS

LUCIUS CROW walks down the BUS-aisle.

People look defensively at the young, orange-eyed STUDENT; they treat him with apprehension, guarding the seats.

LUCIUS finally finds an open spot on the BUS - in the very back, he sits.

CUT TO:

YOUNG LUCIUS CROW rides the BUS, examining the scenery on the route - he slides the window down and caresses the wind with his left hand.

CUT TO:

INT. THE CAR DEALERSHIP - AFTERNOON

LUCIUS is observing the CAR DEALERSHIP's inventory and he's quite impressed.

> THE CAR DEALER
> (to LUCIUS)
> Hello, young man. How can we help you today?

LUCIUS is startled by the CAR DEALER - he adjusts. The CAR DEALER is a little middle-aged white man with a buzz cut, grayish eyes. He has a moustache - he's wearing a red polo-shirt with black slacks.

> YOUNG LUCIUS CROW
> (turns around)
> Hello, sir. I'm LUCIUS. LUCIUS CROW. I'm a student at HARVARD - I'm looking for a deal on a nice car. Are they all luxury vehicles? That's all I'm seeing.

> THE CAR DEALER
> Speaking of cars, you look like you've been hit by one in the face. Excuse my dark humor - I'm NOAH. It's nice to meet you. My young friend, we have a very wide selection to choose from. What specifically would you like to see? You'd be surprised at what I can do for you. What's your budget?

> YOUNG LUCIUS CROW
> I got jumped earlier, neither here nor there. I, uh, I do work-study at HARVARD - I'm an assistant librarian. I don't make very much, honestly. I ride the BUS usually when I want to escape CAMPUS, you know? I just need a good set of wheels. Show me your most inexpensive vehicles, if you will.

> THE CAR DEALER
> (patronizing)
> A cheap skate, huh?

                   YOUNG LUCIUS CROW
        No, sir. Just a guy looking for
        some wheels. I may not be rich,
        but I'm no cheap skate, either.

The CAR DEALER raises his hand to LUCIUS and gestures for him to follow him -

                   THE CAR DEALER
        I get your meaning, kid. Follow me
        to our affordable section. We have
        TOYOTAS, HONDAS, FORDS, CHEVYS -
        those are the baseline vehicles we
        have for those seeking
        affordability.

                   YOUNG LUCIUS CROW
            (interested)
        Let's have a look-see.

                                  CUT TO:

The CAR DEALER has taken LUCIUS into the back of the BUSINESS, to look at the inexpensive selection.

                   THE CAR DEALER
        If you want quality, I suggest the
        CHEVY COBALT - it's light, it's
        fierce in its own little way. It's
        a very good car, especially for a
        STUDENT.

                   YOUNG LUCIUS CROW
        Cargo space?

                   THE CAR DEALER
        No. No. Car go road, not space.

                   YOUNG LUCIUS CROW
        No, I meant -

                   THE CAR DEALER
        I'm just joshing with you. Yes,
        the car has some nice cargo space
        to be a sport-sedan.

                    YOUNG LUCIUS CROW
          I get enough bullying at school,
          man - please don't mess with me
          like that. I'm shooting straight,
          I expect you to do the same.

A WOMAN enters - late-20s, brunette, 5ft5, aqua-blue eyes -
wearing a red blouse and a warm black-dress:

                    CAR DEALER ASSISTANT
          BOSS, the client you were
          expecting is here - should I take
          over for you with this guy?

                    THE CAR DEALER
                         (to LUCIUS)
          I apologize, kid. Listen, you deal
          with my ASSISTANT, she'll take the
          best care of you.
                         (to his ASSISTANT)
          Good or bad?

                    CAR DEALER ASSISTANT
          It's all good, BOSS. It's all
          good.

                    YOUNG LUCIUS CROW
                         (standing aside
                          silently)
          Wait, I-

                    THE CAR DEALER
          She'll help you, LAURENCE, no
          worries. Gotta go -

                    YOUNG LUCIUS CROW
                         (bitter)
          The name's LUCIUS -

                    CAR DEALER ASSISTANT
                         (goes to shake the
                          STUDENT's hand)
          Hello, LUCIUS - I'm SALLY. I'll be
          finishing your tour of our
          inventory, if that's all right.

YOUNG LUCIUS CROW
(shakes the
ASSISTANT's hand)
Yes, that'll work just fine,
ma'am.

CAR DEALER ASSISTANT
What's your price-range for a
vehicle?

YOUNG LUCIUS CROW
Well, I make only 360 dollars a
month doing WORK-STUDY at HARVARD
- I don't really have a price
range.

CAR DEALER ASSISTANT
Wow. No, you don't, huh? To be
frank with you, LUCIUS, this is a
high-end establishment. We don't
have lots of payment options for
lower-income individuals. I could,
however, point you in the right
direction -

YOUNG LUCIUS CROW
SALLY, I just want to look at the
lower-end CARS you have in stock.
I'm not expecting to make a
purchase. I rode the bus to get
here.

CAR DEALER ASSISTANT
So, you don't have anything to
trade-in?

YOUNG LUCIUS CROW
No, I do not.

CAR DEALER ASSISTANT
(whispers to
LUCIUS)
You're pretty much
shit-out-of-luck. You have to make
at least 25,000 dollars a year
just to lease from us.

                        YOUNG LUCIUS CROW
          Why didn't NOAH, or whatever his
          name is, start with that! Damn,
          I'm wasting my time. YOU are
          wasting my time.

                        CAR DEALER ASSISTANT
          Now you know. Listen, get back on
          the bus, forget about this place.
          You're out of your league being
          here. We sell quality vehicles -
          we don't give hand-outs.

                        YOUNG LUCIUS CROW
                  (turning red)
          You-
                  (bites his tongue)
          I get it. I'll look elsewhere. All
          I wanted was some advice on how I
          should go about buying a
          worthwhile car. I didn't expect
          the place to be run by snobs.

                        CAR DEALER ASSISTANT
                  (smacks her lips)
          We're not snobs, sir. We're
          CAPITALISTS. You're welcome to
          leave now - you have no stake with
          us. We have actual cliental to
          attend to, if you don't mind.

                        YOUNG LUCIUS CROW
                  (fixes his
                   book-bag on his
                   back)
          Whatever. I'm out of here.

LUCIUS walks from the back of the BUSINESS into the luxury
area. He proceeds to the exit of the CAR DEALERSHIP, mad as
a thunderstorm.

                        THE CAR DEALER
                  (like a prick)
          Come back again, soon!

					YOUNG LUCIUS CROW
				(under his breath)
			Oh, I will.

LUCIUS moves through the revolving doors.

									CUT TO:

INT. BARRY KENO'S DORM-ROOM - AFTERNOON

BARRY KENO sits in his DORM, looking very professional and bourgeoise.

BARRY is PODCASTING in front of expensive cameras, with professional microphone equipment.

					BARRY KENO
				(looking into the
				 CAMERA)
			Hello, folks, BARRY KENO here. And
			you know what time it is:

			IT'S 'KENO-TIME'.

			Today, we're going to discuss how
			the "INFINITY EVENT" was a lie.
			The science community isn't
			telling us the whole truth about
			what happened in COMPTON,
			CALIFORNIA a decade ago. Even the
			law-enforcement sector, the
			military, they've been feeding us
			shit and keeping us in the dark.
			How do I know? I hear things,
			people. My dad, my dad's the CIA
			DIRECTOR - check the last name,
			search it up. My dad has told me
			enough to let me know that the
			INFINITY EVENT was an act of GOD,
			beyond scientific reasoning, okay?
			He can't tell me the whole story,
			sure, but he has told me there's
			much more to what transpired back
			then. And where is MISTER FREEDOM,
			huh? He hasn't been seen in years!
			CALIFORNIA, LA, COMPTON, it's all
					(MORE)

353.

                    BARRY KENO (cont'd)
          a giant clusterfuck, if you ask
          me. And just like the "PANAMA CITY
          DISASTER" in 2018 - the FLORIDA
          GOVERNOR himself got on national
          TV and revealed an ALIEN - that
          "DARKWAVE" monster - had attacked
          our country! Then they tried to
          act like it didn't even happen a
          week later. MEXICO had to deal
          with that being, too. It damn near
          blew MEXICO CITY to hell before
          being destroyed - without our
          help, might I add. A disgrace. And
          don't forget about the
          "MAGIC-WORLD CATASTROPHE" - actual
          zombies were running around in
          ORLANDO, people. It's been said
          that a MAGICIAN, of all people,
          was the one to end that CHAOS.
          Wake up! We were, and still are,
          living in perilous times, my
          viewers. Too many instances of
          anarchy; no semblance of control.
          No law, no order. KINETICS running
          around all over the place. Our
          country covers up the cover ups!
          It's absurd -

BARRY gets a knock at his DORMROOM DOOR. He pauses the
PODCAST SESSION, stopping the camera and microphone -

                    LILY THORN
               (behind the door)
          - It's LILY, BARRY, open up.

BARRY lets LILY THORN in.

LILY, an 18-year-old FRESHMEN (MICHAEL's SISTER), is beyond
beautiful:

She's 5'5, luscious, with an exotic complexion. She's
thicker than a 'Snicker' - her hair is black with blonde
dyed into it, quite lengthy.

LILY THORN is sort of gothic, dressed in all-black with

white-painted fingernails - she has on purple lipstick. Her eyes are purplish with a dark tint to them. LILY is the definition of COLLEGE BEAUTY - she's also BARRY KENO's squeeze.

                    BARRY KENO
               (rushes to open
                the DOOR)
          Fucking ninja turtle shit
          biscuits. Now I gotta start all
          the way over, babe!

                    LILY THORN
               (enters BARRY's
                DORM)
          I apologize, baby. I need some
          money. I'm broke. My idiot dad cut
          off our petty allowance, too, so
          MICHAEL and me are struggling like
          crazy -

                    BARRY KENO
          All right, all right. How much?

                    LILY THORN
          $500, if possible.

                    BARRY KENO
          Dammit, LILY. I'll have to go to
          the ATM. You messed up my PODCAST
          SESSION, now I gotta leave CAMPUS
          to get you a half-grand. Elohim in
          a stream!

                    LILY THORN
          You know you owe me, BARRY. Plus,
          I have no one else to count on. Me
          or MICHAEL -

                    BARRY KENO
               (gives LILY a kiss)
          I know, honey. I'll take care of
          it. I'm sorry for lashing out.
          That's not right, at all. Let me
          get straight really quick and
          we'll head to WELLS FARGO.

                    LILY THORN
                  (hugs BARRY)
            Thank you. I love you.

                    BARRY KENO
            - You little softy. I love you,
            too. Now quit being all mushy on
            me - let's get you and MICHAEL
            some cash.

BARRY puts on his HARVARD JOCK JACKET, grabs his wallet and
keys. He and LILY exit his DORMROOM.

                                            CUT TO BLACK:

CHAPTER II - THE DEVIL'S APPRENTICE

                                            FADE IN:

INT. LUCIUS' DORM-ROOM - LATER

LUCIUS enters his DORM-ROOM and shuts the door with it to
his back. He stands with his back against the door and takes
a deep breath.

LUCIUS stands in the darkness and meditates.

After a couple of moments, he cuts on the lights in his
DORM-ROOM, prepared to do damage-control.

Firstly, he feeds his goldfish, MARIO - he taps on the
glass, friendly-like; it calms LUCIUS for a moment.

Then, LUCIUS puts his bookbag on his bed and opens it to see
what all BARRY and LOGAN took from him besides the
ALGORITHM.

                    YOUNG LUCIUS CROW
                  (eyes widened)
            No.

LUCIUS looks in his bookbag. IT IS ENTIRELY EMPTY -

His homework, research, study materials, and most

importantly, his brand-new ALGORITHM, they're all vanished - STOLEN by the BULLIES.

> YOUNG LUCIUS CROW
> (tears fall from
> his face)
> I knew it felt super-light. Those assholes. How could they!?

LUCIUS cuts the lights out in his ROOM. He lies down, in an effort to both calm down his mind and his injuries.

CUT TO:

4 HOURS LATER:

LUCIUS snaps awake, startled. Time has left him in his slumber. He gets up out of his bed only to see his EMPTY BOOKBAG. He dozes back off -

CUT TO:

INT. LUCIUS' DORM-ROOM - MORNING

LUCIUS stirs in his sleep. He's having dreams...

CUT TO:

EXT. THE DORMITORY BUILDING - THE PASSAGEWAY - NIGHT

...Under a swollen BLOOD-MOON, LUCIUS CROW sits at a bench outside of his dorm. There's no one around, you can only hear the wind streaming through the PASSAGEWAY beside the DORMITORY BUILDING -

YOUNG LUCIUS is upset yet he's FOCUSED.

Footsteps inch toward him and the clicking sound of a walking-stick. LUCIUS picks his head up...

CUT TO:

...A slithery figure appears, sporting a black fabric trench coat, a black fedora with silver lining, and black pants, black shoes. IT has a broken BLACK HALO hovering above its head. He's tall, about 6'3, yet very slender, about 150 pounds.

THE MAN IN THE SHADOWS is spooky to say the least, however as he approaches, the hypnotic voice he speaks with entirely captures LUCIUS' attention.

          THE MAN IN THE SHADOWS
     (with truth and
      vigor)
- Young Man, why are you so sad? DO YOU NOT KNOW GOD'S PLAN FOR YOU?
     (Starts circling
      the kid)
...I'm here for you, child. I couldn't even begin to comprehend your pain. It's beyond understanding. Your power matches your pain. Your greed matches your guilt. You merely have greed for happiness. Is that so bad? No. In fact, I'm here as of right now to see that you gain all that you desire. You will do wonders. You will be invincible when I'm finished with you.

          YOUNG LUCIUS CROW
     (confused and
      frustrated)
You don't even know me, sir. Please, leave me to my pain. Do not remind of me of what I already feel.

          THE MAN IN THE SHADOWS
     (stunned)
With all the hurt and heartache you have...I STILL SMELL NOT ONE PARTICLE OF FEAR -

          YOUNG LUCIUS CROW
     (as serious as can
      be)
I FEAR NOTHING. No one. Not even
          (MORE)

YOUNG LUCIUS CROW (cont'd)
The Lord God Almighty. Because I know Death, I've seen too much of it. God is Love. I KNOW OF NO SUCH THING -

THE MAN IN THE SHADOWS
We can change all of this. You can do anything you wish. Your MOTHER would be so very proud to see you at this UNIVERSITY. Though she cannot be with you, you can still remember her, hmm? They took your mother away from you, didn't they? You can pray, you know? You can pray to exact vengeance upon Humankind for your suffering - they are the cause of your suffering. You can be the one who steps up to check and restrain these petty filthy, uh, walking monkeys, because you've seen firsthand how evil they truly are - this is our opportunity to change the world, forever. And, if you fail -

YOUNG LUCIUS CROW
    (cuts him off)
- I NEVER fail.

THE MAN IN THE SHADOWS
So be it. When you wake up tomorrow you will have your very own Artificial-Intelligence, the thing you've been striving so hard to formulate. It will be sent to you in your dormitory mail-box. All you have to do is BELIEVE in my words, right here-right now. And LUCIUS, embrace who you are. Don't be ashamed any longer. You'll know exactly what to do when the time's right. Just know, you're loved, just know you're not forgotten. I come from a place of DARKNESS. Yet, I still couldn't
(MORE)

                    THE MAN IN THE SHADOWS (cont'd)
          survive without the LIGHT, because
          without it--without it I'd know
          not where to go.

                    YOUNG LUCIUS CROW
                  (stands up in the
                   face of THE MAN,
                   unafraid)
          The Light is just as corrupt as
          the darkness. The latter accepts
          its corrupt nature, while the
          former refuses to acknowledge it
          out of arrogance.

                    THE MAN IN THE SHADOWS
          Indeed, my child. Shall we
          begin??? When we're done, FATE
          itself shall bow to us-

                    YOUNG LUCIUS CROW
          Who are you? What do I call you?

                    THE MAN IN THE SHADOWS
          Call me, "The DEALMAKER" - just
          never call me MASTER for that is
          what you are. You - you hold THE
          MARK on your right hand. Your
          destiny awaits, ever so patiently.
          Why are some people slaves and
          others MASTERS? Was there ever a
          time when this was not so?

LUCIUS looks down at his right hand, examining the birthmark
on his right-hand beside the thumb.

He peers up and nods to THE MAN IN THE SHADOWS, slightly
bowing to him...

                    YOUNG LUCIUS CROW
          This is awfully real to be a
          DREAM.

                    THE DEALMAKER
          Oh, young man, you have no idea.
          There are NO DEFENDERS here. No
          ANGELS. No JUSTICE. No FREEDOM.
                    (MORE)

                    THE DEALMAKER (cont'd)
              This GALAXY will be consumed by
              DARKNESS - just like all the rest.

...THE DEALMAKER slams his wizardly oakwood-staff on the
DREAMSCAPE ground and DARK ENERGY consumes YOUNG LUCIUS
CROW. He shouts in pain.

CUT TO: LUCIUS' DORMROOM

The HARVARD STUDENT flashes awake, covered in a cold-sweat,
his bed and clothes damp.

LUCIUS' bold ORANGE EYES penetrate the darkness of the
DORM-ROOM. He gets up and sits on the side of his small BED
- taking deep, deep breaths, and sips from the bottle of
water on his nightstand.

- He closes his eyes, meditating for a moment.

                                              CUT TO:

EXT. THE DREAM WORLD - CONTINUOUS

LUCIUS stands at the edge of the universe, silently.

The stars align as if they were a metaphysical projection; a
theater, if you will.

A string of memories plays in front of LUCIUS, of his
childhood, young teenage years, so on.

Then it stops to a mirror image of himself where he is now.

                    YOUNG LUCIUS CROW
              Holy Christ.

LUCIUS CROW hears footsteps from behind him - someone's
approaching:

                    AGENT ORANGE'S PROJECTION
                  (laughing in a
                   sinister tone)
              My Boy.

The sparkling green-eyed, tangerine haired, maniacal AGENT ORANGE is LUCIUS' father.

LUCIUS cowers at his FATHER's PROJECTION. He's still in a DREAM. However, AGENT ORANGE is very real. He's a tormented spirit in a type of flesh.

He's simply checking on his lost son.

          AGENT ORANGE'S PROJECTION
I was lost, but you have found me, SON.

          YOUNG LUCIUS CROW
Who are you?

          AGENT ORANGE'S PROJECTION
The Ghost of HALLOWEEN' Past. I am AGENT KIMBO ORANGE. Well, a piece of him anyway. A projection. I AM YOUR FATHER.

A pause:

          YOUNG LUCIUS CROW
- You waited all this time to reveal yourself to me? In a damn dream! I have had NO FATHER for 18 years -
    (looks around at
     the darkness
     surrounding him)
- Did it ever occur to you that I've needed you since the day I was born. My mother needed you. You're no father! You're nothing to me but a MYTH, an urban legend - I read of you, I read everything...you killed women and children. YOU DID. You raped. You tortured. Who in the hell do you think you are!? No. You're exactly that...a PROJECTION. You are not real.

                    AGENT ORANGE'S PROJECTION
          I know. I failed you - in every
          single way.

AGENT ORANGE extends his hand to his son, as a gesture of
good faith.

                    AGENT ORANGE'S PROJECTION
          I've seen the light. Let me show
          you.

LUCIUS jerks his hand back away from his FATHER.

HE SPITS AT AGENT ORANGE's PROJECTION.

And he turns his back. He's hurt from seeing his dad, REAL
OR NO.

                    AGENT ORANGE'S PROJECTION
          You are the sum of my experiences.
          A product of my sin. I expect
          nothing less than your disdain and
          your rejection. But I had to just
          lay eyes on you myself. You - by
          the way, you look just like your
          mother.

The projection fades into the stars above the BLACKNESS of
the DREAM-WORLD, and the stars collapse inward into LUCIUS'
very soul. He snaps awake...

                                                  CUT TO:

EXT. THIRD DREAM LEVEL - HARVARD CAMPUS - MORNING

...LUCIUS feels SNOW falling on his face, on his flesh. He
awakens on the HARVARD CAMPUS in the MAIN COURTYARD, lying
in the snow, right near the LIBRARY.

He hears noise and gets up. He hears the feet of a GIANT
stomping.

LUCIUS' ears are pierced with the roar of something
otherworldly. The snow turns into FIRE.

People are running past YOUNG LUCIUS in a frenzy. They are screaming, most all of them are covered in BLOOD, crying tears of the same.

EVERY SINGLE PERSON is running away from the heavy bass-filled noise, as LUCIUS continues moving toward it. It's the sound of something unearthly. ALIEN -

LUCIUS walks past dozens more people and finally comes to a stop.

                YOUNG LUCIUS CROW
            (stunned)
      What in God's Name?

As pieces of fire and embers fall from the sky, LUCIUS sees a YOUNG CHILD standing in the middle of the HARVARD ROAD far beyond the MAIN COURTYARD.

The YOUNG GIRL is no older than 6 years old, wearing a white dress. The CHILD has a pony-tail, white shoes, white gloves. She's young and full of spirit, not paying any mind to the world-ending NOISE going on.

LUCIUS is baffled why EVERYONE is running except this child. He no longer realizes he's in a dream. He's totally immersed in his own subconscious. The YOUNG GIRL plays on the gravel with chalk, drawing a blue butterfly. Funny thing is the BUTTERFLY the CHILD has drawn is flying over an ocean of FIRE...

                YOUNG LUCIUS CROW
            (looks beyond the
            HORIZON)
      NO!

...LUCIUS runs down the HARVARD ROAD toward the YOUNG GIRL. What he sees rattles his bones. There is a multi-headed DRAGON beyond the horizon. LUCIUS goes to grab the GIRL to get her to safety.

                YOUNG LUCIUS CROW
            (frantic)
      Come with me, little one. It's not
      safe here! Take my hand.

                    LITTLE GIRL
          No, thank you, mister. I'm waiting
          on my Father.

                    YOUNG LUCIUS CROW
          Listen, honey, I'll take you to
          your Father, okay? Just trust me.
          We have to get out of here. Don't
          you see the MONSTER, up in the
          sky?

                    LITTLE GIRL
               (smiles)
          Yes.
               (giggles)
          That's my Father. THE DRAGON, you
          see? He's YOUR Father, too,
          LUCIUS. AGENT ORANGE was just a
          sperm donor!
               (SINISTER)
          You little fuck.

The DRAGON rears its heads, spreads its humungous wings, and
lets out a fiery blast of HELLFIRE into LUCIUS'
subconscious.

The world around LUCIUS catches fire. It turns his whole
body numb, he feels the HELLFIRE coursing through his mind,
body, and soul - he feels like he's dying.

In his dream, LUCIUS beholds the DRAGON's POWER and he
reaches his right arm out, screaming -

                    YOUNG LUCIUS CROW
               (his hand up in
                fear)
          No!

Reaching out as if he can somehow prevent the spread of the
DRAGON's nightmarish flames - the FIRE CORRUPTS LUCIUS'
dream state, his very MIND.

                                                  CUT TO:

INT. THE MAIL-ROOM - DAY

                              - OCTOBER 24TH

LUCIUS walks into the MAIL-ROOM, to no one. To no sound. To no voices. He slowly goes to his box: #423 -

                    YOUNG LUCIUS CROW
                         (sighs)
                    It was just a dream. It was just a
                    dream.

The mailbox key grinds the lock, unlike all times before, revealing a mysterious package inside.

It is a Gift - it's gift wrapped, even has a bow on it. CHRISTMAS has come early for YOUNG LUCIUS.

                    YOUNG LUCIUS CROW
                         (opens his eyes in
                          pure amazement)
                    - Whoa.

                                        CUT TO:

INT. LUCIUS' DORM-ROOM - MOMENTS LATER

LUCIUS opens the gift with a quickness, removing the bow, unwrapping the paper, all to show a cardboard box. This gets him even more excited. He pulls a blade and cuts open the cardboard, almost happy. He can't remember the last present he got.

Subsequent to cutting the cardboard, LUCIUS sees something he totally wasn't expecting.

It's a MASK, a very sleek ORANGE-MASK...

...With an envelope attached to it, with simple scotch tape - nothing fancy. The MASK is technological, after closer examination by LUCIUS, and not just a prop.

He's more than intrigued but sits the tech-based ORANGE-MASK to the side. He's more interested in the envelope.

CUT TO:

LUCIUS uses an old-fashioned letter opener to slowly, with a light touch, open the envelope - it's aged, so the paper is brown and somewhat decayed ostensibly...

...LUCIUS sees the opening words, and it astonishes him. He is paralyzed with pure emotion - that of which he hasn't felt since he was a boy.

The Letter Opens as So:

"Dear Son..."

LUCIUS feels tears pour down his face, involuntarily...

...And it's not from his mother -

It's from AGENT KIMBO ORANGE.

"Dear Son,

How I wish I could have spent those moments with you that I know you yearned for.

My biggest regret is not physically being there for you. I'm known for many things, none good, and I couldn't even try Fatherhood.

They call me a "Supervillain"...a maniac. Just know, I don't see myself as anything but a survivor. I'm not alive if you're reading this.

My lawyer has sent this, as well as my old Mask, to you because it's your inheritance. More is to come for you, My Son.

I will always be with You...don't feel alone. I know I made a mistake not being by your side as you grew, and wherever you may be now, just know that I am with you. I always will be.

Now, here's my bit of advice...

Never give in to this world. If it shits on you, you give it hell. If the world pisses on you, you give it CHAOS. If it quits on you, you ENSLAVE it.

If you're my Son, which you are, then you have a power in you, a drive. Now, you use that, and you do whatever you have to to obtain and keep your respect, your reputation, and your riches.

I hate that I cannot be with You. But what is, must be.

I love you.

And try that MASK on...it's handier than you'd think, my boy. Consider it an heirloom of sorts. But, if you really have to use it, be careful, and use it properly and wisely, and you'll overcome anyone and anybody.

And be nice to the Operating System - and it'll work for you.

It's a very basic operating system. Needs some modifications. Not the smartest OS, so maybe you can fix it up, and get it going better than I ever could.

Goodbye, Son.

Love,

Your Father
AGENT ORANGE"

CUT TO:

LUCIUS is utterly shocked.

He didn't even know if he even really existed to his father, and now he knows, he wasn't the only one alone, nor was he actually alone. He was thought of. Even a villain like AGENT ORANGE had a heart, to a degree....

          YOUNG LUCIUS CROW
     (sheds a tear of
      BLOOD)
  Father, I will make you proud.
  Thank you.

...LUCIUS has cried blood. A tear of blood that marks the letter.

LUCIUS wipes his eye, paying no mind to his blood-filled tear.

                                          CUT TO:

                    YOUNG LUCIUS CROW
                 (putting his
                  attention back on
                  THE MASK)
               I can't believe this. I don't even
               know how to feel right now. A gift
               from AGENT ORANGE? The AGENT
               ORANGE? My dad? But...why the
               MASK?

YOUNG LUCIUS CROW fiddles with the ORANGE-MASK, activating it -

                                          CUT TO:

INT. SCIENCE-CLASS - THE SCIENCE BUILDING - DAY

                                       - OCTOBER 30TH

PROFESSOR BROSNAN stands at the front of the class -

                    PROFESSOR BROSNAN
               I have your homework graded
               people. I'm going to pass it out,
               soon. But first, I need to see
               LUCIUS CROW and BARRY KENO
               outside, please -

                    BARRY KENO
                 (whispering)
               What the shit?

PROFESSOR BROSNAN stands at the door of the CLASSROOM - he wags his two fingers for the students to join him outside. He and LUCIUS and BARRY exit the class, the door shuts.

                                          CUT TO:

INT. SCIENCE BUILDING HALLWAY - OUTSIDE OF THE CLASS - DAY

PROFESSOR BROSNAN puts his hands on his hips, in complete disappointment.

          PROFESSOR BROSNAN
Okay, guys, who cheated off of who, hmm? Be honest with me, right now, or you will both be reported for cheating.

          YOUNG LUCIUS CROW
MR. BROSNAN, I didn't cheat, I swear. How do you mean?

          PROFESSOR BROSNAN
Why do you both have mirroring science papers? Your essays are too similar, they share the same ideas and context, they even have some of the same wording. WHY? Tell me now.

LUCIUS is shocked - he realizes what's happened.

          YOUNG LUCIUS CROW
I can - I can answer that, sir. One day, a couple weeks back, BARRY and LANCE LOGAN ambushed me, and BARRY took all of my papers out of my bookbag. He must've thought he could copy my work. All I did was go through my notes in my DORM and I rewrote what I already had - that's all I can think of.

          BARRY KENO
            (to LUCIUS)
You little bastard - I'll -

PROFESSOR BROSNAN puts his index finger into BARRY KENO's chest.

                    PROFESSOR BROSNAN
          You'll do what? What will you do
          to him, BARRY? Explain what the
          hell's going on, now, or I'll go
          to the DEAN about you, and you
          alone.

                    BARRY KENO
               (to BROSNAN)
          You old 4-eyed fuck, do you know
          who my father is? He's the CIA
          DIRECTOR - you couldn't kick me
          out of this school if it was your
          life's goal. Fuck you.

BROSNAN and LUCIUS get wide-eyed by this statement.

PROFESSOR BROSNAN clears his throat, almost nervously.

                                        CUT TO:

                    PROFESSOR BROSNAN
          - Whatever, kid. You have no pull
          here with me. Quit the copying,
          stop the cheating, or your ass is
          grass, I promise you. I'll go over
          whoever's head to get you out of
          here. Your daddy won't be able to
          do a damn thing - you will redo
          the paper and make it your own.
          For now, though, you have an F.
          That's all there is to it.

                    BARRY KENO
               (with a smartass
                tone)
          All right, all right! I'll turn in
          my paper, no bullshit. I get it.
          Leave it alone, BROSNAN. Let's
          proceed with class, shall we? And
          don't make a fool out of me in
          there.

                    PROFESSOR BROSNAN
          Appearances and superficial
          reputation are everything to you,
          aren't they, BARRY? I want that
                         (MORE)

PROFESSOR BROSNAN (cont'd)
paper first thing in the morning -
if I don't get it, the F stands;
it'll sink your GPA, kid. Do you
want that for yourself?

BARRY KENO
No. Just, don't tell the class,
BROSNAN. If you do, I'll flip on
you. I'll have you working in
CANADA, man - don't underestimate
my reach.

PROFESSOR BROSNAN
(rolls his eyes in
disbelief)
Just get in the class.

The CLASSROOM door opens. BARRY walks into the CLASS before BROSNAN and LUCIUS, who remain in the hallway -

BROSNAN pats LUCIUS on the shoulder as BARRY enters the class and shuts the door -

PROFESSOR BROSNAN
Listen, LUCIUS, I know you're not
a cheat, okay? I appreciate you
standing up for yourself. I hate
that you have to deal with these
BULLIES - they're monsters. I'm
truly sorry. Next time one of them
messes with you, kid, knock them
the fuck out.

YOUNG LUCIUS CROW
If only it were that simple,
PROFESSOR.

PROFESSOR BROSNAN
You see, LUCIUS, sometimes it is
that easy, trust me. BULLIES fold
like jeans, eventually. Now, good
work on the assignment - let's get
back to it, what do you say?

PROFESSOR BROSNAN opens the door to the CLASSROOM.

                    YOUNG LUCIUS CROW
                (walks behind
                 BROSNAN into the
                 CLASS)
            Yessir.

                                            CUT TO:

INT. SCIENCE-CLASS - THE SCIENCE BUILDING - CONTINUOUS

BARRY is sitting in his seat, being a foolish goofball, full of pride.

LUCIUS walks in with his head somewhat down - drained, hurt. He takes a seat.

The other STUDENTS are whispering among themselves, curious about the situation. LUCIUS sits quietly - BROSNAN starts passing out the students' SCIENCE PAPERS.

                                            CUT TO:

INT. THE CAFE - ALTERNATE CAFETERIA - AFTERNOON

LUCIUS enters THE CAFE building - a small ALTERNATE CAFETERIA on the HARVARD CAMPUS that primarily supplies HOT TEA and COFFEE, but they also make some meals for STUDENTS using their FOOD CARDS -

As LUCIUS proceeds through THE CAFE, he immediately spots various students participating in CHESS MATCHES.

He sees his PROFESSOR, Mr. BROSNAN, playing his buddy MICHAEL THORN in a game as he stands in the CAFE line. LUCIUS zones out for a beat or two, as he examines his teacher and his buddy going head-to-head in the thinking man's GAME -

WE HEAR THE SNAPPING OF FINGERS a few times:

                    CAFE WORKER
               (snapping fingers
                 at LUCIUS)
          ...Hey, kid, what can I get for
          you? Hello! Snap out of it.

                    YOUNG LUCIUS CROW
          Sorry, man. I was daydreaming. Uh,
          can I get a double hamburger,
          please?

                    CAFE WORKER
          Want fries with that? And what do
          you want on your burger?

                    YOUNG LUCIUS CROW
          Let me get, uh, pickles, mustard,
          ketchup, jalapenos, and chili,
          please, sir. And, yes, I'd like
          some fries, too - oh, and could
          you toast the bun. Not too crispy,
          though. Just right.

                    CAFE WORKER
               (condscending)
          Damn, kid, you want me to eat it
          for you, too?

LUCIUS is paying attention again to the CHESS GAMES, he
doesn't even mind the CAFE WORKER's condescension.

                    CAFE WORKER
          That'll be $8.67, kid. What are
          you paying with?

The CAFE WORKER gets loud -

                    CAFE WORKER
          Kid! I got a job to do here. I
          don't have all day, okay?

                    YOUNG LUCIUS CROW
          Right, right. I apologize, man.
          I'll be using my FOOD CARD - let
          me try it. I should have enough
          funds on it.

The CAFE WORKER swipes the FOOD CARD.

                    CAFE WORKER
- It covered only $3.53 of the purchase price. How will you be covering the remainder?

LUCIUS pats his pockets, looks in his wallet, scrounges for funds. He finds none -

                    YOUNG LUCIUS CROW
Dammit. I - I don't have anything to cover the rest, man. I thought I had enough on my FOOD CARD, honestly.

                    CAFE WORKER
All right. Listen, I'm going to let you slide this time. I've seen you in here before, now that I think of it; the ORANGE-EYES are kind of hard to forget. Just hold tight, I'll have your burger and fries out to you in no time. Oh, and if my boss ever asks you how I'm doing in here, remember, you owe me a solid, all right?

                    YOUNG LUCIUS CROW
I got you, man. I really appreciate you letting me get by with this. I'm famished. I'm out of CAFETERIA meals for the day at the commissary. I need a bite, or I'll fall back into my asshole and disappear.

                    CAFE WORKER
                  (laughing)
Wow, if you say so, man. Next!

LUCIUS exits the line. He walks toward PROFESSOR BROSNAN's and MICHAEL's CHESS MATCH, mesmerized.

                                  CUT TO:

                    YOUNG LUCIUS CROW
          Hey, PROFESSOR BROSNAN, MICHAEL -
          how's it going?

                    PROFESSOR BROSNAN
          Kind of in the zone here, LUCIUS.
          We're at each other's necks - no
          time to converse, really.

BROSNAN slaps the CHESS CLOCK - then, he nonchalantly takes
MICHAEL's QUEEN piece.

                    MICHAEL THORN
                   (concentrating)
          Damn it to hell. LUCY, I'll have
          to get back to you, man. This is
          getting real.

                    PROFESSOR BROSNAN
          Language, MICHAEL.

                    MICHAEL THORN
                   (slaps clock,
                    moves his BISHOP)
          Right, sorry, PROFESSOR.

                    YOUNG LUCIUS CROW
                   (saddened)
          All right, I'll catch you
          gentlemen later, then.

They both don't even look at LUCIUS. They don't acknowledge
his presence, they're too immersed in the game.

                                             CUT TO:

                    CAFE WORKER
          LUCIUS, ticket #127: double
          hamburger and fries!

                    YOUNG LUCIUS CROW
                   (takes his food in
                    a to-go bag)
          Thank you, sir. I appreciate you.

                              CAFE WORKER
                  Don't sweat it. Everybody's gotta
                  eat.

LUCIUS nods at the CAFE WORKER, respectfully. He exits THE
CAFE -

CUT TO:

INT. LILY'S DORM-ROOM - NIGHT

LILY THORN is filming herself doing ASMR (Autonomous Sensory
Meridian Response).

VARIOUS CUTS:

- She taps on a piece of plank wood and hardback books,
creating hypnotic tapping sounds.

- She taps her nails together, on both hands, to create
calming rhythmic sounds.

- She speaks at a whispering level, as she films, to
formulate a quiet ambiance.

- LILY brushes her 2 fuzzy Microphones near her face to
output low, relaxing sounds, as well. She makes light
kissing sounds.

She is filming herself visually and recording her audio with
very expensive, high-quality equipment.

LILY gets a knock at the door. She pauses her camera and
microphones.

                              LILY THORN
                          (questioning)
                  Who is it?

                              BARRY KENO
                  It's me. BARRY. Open up.

LILY quickly opens the door, letting BARRY KENO into her DORMROOM.

The two of them make out very passionately -

                    BARRY KENO
      Were you busy?

                    LILY THORN
      Not too busy for you.

                    BARRY KENO
      Good. Can we cut the lights out,
      cuddle a bit?

                    LILY THORN
          (cutting off her
          camera and
          microphones)
      That's just what I had in mind. I
      can finish my ASMR stuff later.

LILY cuts the DORMROOM lights off - she jumps in the bed with BARRY.

                                  CUT TO:

INT. THE GAMEROOM - DAY

                        - OCTOBER 31ST,
                      HALLOWEEN

MICHAEL THORN and his SISTER, LILY, play PING-PONG in the GAMEROOM. It's just the two of them, the siblings, having a bit of a fuss...

                    LILY THORN
          (hits the
          ping-pong ball to
          her brother)
      It's not fair, man. It's not fair!

                  MICHAEL THORN
          (hits the ball
          back to LILY)
      I know, sis. I tried to talk to
               (MORE)

                    MICHAEL THORN (cont'd)
          them - Mom and Dad said they're
          not covering our asses anymore,
          regardless. Complete horseshit.
          Period. We're on our own. You and
          I, we have to make a play.

...The two do rapid exchanges of ping-pong while they
bicker.

                    LILY THORN
          MICHAEL, all I've done is make
          plays at this school. We're at
          HARVARD, bro. Can you believe it?
          We actually did it. Forget Mom and
          Dad. They abandoned us a long time
          ago. You're absolutely right,
          though, we have to do something or
          else we're out of here on our
          asses back to Maryland to the
          political circus -

                    MICHAEL THORN
          The re-election went to Dad's
          head. Him going from the HOUSE to
          the SENATE, it got to him. Back
          home under his estranged grip is
          the last place I want to be.

                    LILY THORN
              (still
               tit-for-tatting
               with the
               ping-pong ball)
          You ain't lying, bro. You ain't
          lying. We'll figure it out. We
          always do.

MICHAEL gears up for a heavy strike of the ping-pong ball.
He hits it like it's going out of style. The ball hits the
freshly incoming LUCIUS CROW directly in the face.

                                              CUT TO:

LUCIUS, MICHAEL, and LILY have never been in the same ROOM
before. LUCIUS has known MICHAEL THORN for 2 whole years now

and never have the three of them socialized in each other's presence.

LUCIUS has never spoken to LILY, nor she to him -

> YOUNG LUCIUS CROW
> Hey, MIKE, LILY, how's it going?

> LILY THORN
> (puts down the
> ping-pong paddle)
> I've got to go, MICHAEL. Class awaits.

LILY leaves without saying even a word to LUCIUS.

> MICHAEL THORN
> (surprised)
> LUCY, what's cracking? You never come in here, man.

> YOUNG LUCIUS CROW
> Ah, Bioethics got cancelled today. PROFESSOR FEEZEL called out sick. I got freed up for the day. Saw you two playing ping-pong, figured I'd say hello.

MICHAEL and LUCIUS give one another "dap". They then snap their fingers.

> MICHAEL THORN
> My sister sure gave you the cold-shoulder, huh? What was that about?

> YOUNG LUCIUS CROW
> (stopping while
> he's ahead)
> Beats me, man. Who knows?

> MICHAEL THORN
> My own sister, and I know less about her than I do the Pope.

                    YOUNG LUCIUS CROW
          What's your evening looking like,
          bro?

                    MICHAEL THORN
          Martial arts' practice. We have
          another tournament coming up right
          after Christmas.
                    (looks at his
                     smartphone)
          In fact, I have to be in the DOJO
          at 2:15 sharp. LILY and I were
          killing some time, discussing
          family bullshit. I'm glad you
          stopped us. Hell, I have 35
          minutes to get to that side of
          CAMPUS -

                    YOUNG LUCIUS CROW
                    (vaguely
                     disappointed)
          I see. I understand, MIKE. Well,
          I'll stop by your DORM later,
          perhaps we can get on the console,
          play a round or two.

MICHAEL's smartphone chirps.

                    MICHAEL THORN
          - Uh-huh, you bet, bud.

MICHAEL seems distracted. He stares at his phone,
unintentionally avoiding eye contact with his dear friend,
and leaves the GAMEROOM.

LUCIUS stands ALONE in the GAMEROOM, it's as silent as
Outerspace itself within it.

                                                  CUT TO:

EXT. DORMITORY WALKWAY - EVENING

MICHAEL THORN, with his head kind of down, is walking toward his DORMROOM entranceway. He turns a right to the DOOR with his keys ready - he bumps into someone, startled as an alleycat.

> YOUNG LUCIUS CROW
> (in front of MICHAEL's DOOR)
> Hey, MICHAEL.

> MICHAEL THORN
> Holy shit, LUCY! What the Hell - you scared the crap out of me.

> YOUNG LUCIUS CROW
> It's HALLOWEEN, everyone needs a good spook.

> MICHAEL THORN
> What's up, man? What can I trouble you for?

> YOUNG LUCIUS CROW
> - Want to play videogames and order a PIZZA? I'll buy. I got paid today from work-study.

MICHAEL ponders, contemplating the offer very briefly.

> MICHAEL THORN
> (unlocking his DORMROOM DOORWAY)
> You know what, that sounds great, bud. Let's do that. I appreciate you'll buy. I'm strapped for cash. At least I can provide the console, though. We'll bust ass online. C'mon in -

The two YOUNG MEN enter the DORMITORY -

CUT TO:

INT. MICHAEL THORN'S DORM-ROOM - EVENING

MICHAEL and LUCIUS are now in MICHAEL's DORMROOM:

              YOUNG LUCIUS CROW
        (looking around
         the room)
Where's BARRY and LANCE, and them?

              MICHAEL THORN
        (putting his book
         bag away)
They went to a HALLOWEEN party.
BARRY is dressed like Elvis. LANCE
is dressed up like Abe Lincoln.
LILY, she's going as Cruella
Deville. They all look like
idiots. I never got the costume
part of HALLOWEEN - not my shtick.

              YOUNG LUCIUS CROW
I feel you on that, man. So, what
game you want to play?

              MICHAEL THORN
Let's order the pizza first, bro.
I'm starving and I'm out of
credits on my food card.

              YOUNG LUCIUS CROW
Will do, I'm on it.
        (hands MICHAEL
         something)
Here's a 20 to hold you over, bro.

LUCIUS has handed MICHAEL some money.

              MICHAEL THORN
I - I can't accept that, LUCY.

              YOUNG LUCIUS CROW
Yes, you can. And you will.

MICHAEL nods, respectfully to LUCIUS.

LUCIUS then gets out his smartphone, placing the call to the PIZZA place.

CUT TO:

LUCIUS hangs up after ordering -

                    MICHAEL THORN
          (sitting at his
           desk, online
           scrolling)
LU, I've been meaning to ask you, what are you doing for THANKSGIVING? I'm going to be with my cousins and LILY at our FAMILY VACATION HOME at the BEACH in BOSTON - I wanted you to know, you're invited if you've got nothing going on.

                    YOUNG LUCIUS CROW
          (takes a seat in
           one of the loose
           chairs)
I appreciate the invite, MIKE. But THANKSGIVING is my least favorite holiday. I'll be treating it like any other day - eating in the CAFETERIA or the CAFE. Doing schoolwork, working on a project, things like that. Thank you for extending the invitation, bud. But I'll pass -

                    MICHAEL THORN
          (cuts on the
           videogame console)
Well, it never hurts to ask. Know that the invitation is always open, if you change your mind. All right?

                    YOUNG LUCIUS CROW
          That's cool. Thank you for
          thinking of me, man. If I change
          my mind, I'll let you know, ASAP.
               (picks up a
                videogame
                controller)
          Now let's kick tail on this game.

MICHAEL and LUCIUS proceed to play videogames, together, while awaiting their pizza delivery order -

                              CUT TO:

EXT. THE DORM WALKWAY - MORNING

                                        - NOVEMBER 1ST

LUCIUS exits his DORMROOM on this silent morning.

He is quiet -

LUCIUS walks down THE DORM PATHWAY -

The STUDENTS live in Co-Ed dormitories. Girls and guys reside among one another here.

The girl that LUCIUS has had his eye on: LILY THORN

Just as he's walking, she appears out of her dorm right in front of LUCIUS.

                    LILY THORN
               (screams, startled
                by LUCIUS)
          Jesus Christ, you creep!

                    YOUNG LUCIUS CROW
               (puts his hands up
                innocently)
          Whoa. Listen, you walked into me.
          I'm just going to class.

LILY notices LUCIUS' ORANGE EYES and is hypnotized. She shakes off his gaze.

> LILY THORN
> I'm sorry, dude. You really scared the hell out of me, but it was wrong what I said.
> (extends her hand to LUCIUS)
> We cool? Friends?

> YOUNG LUCIUS CROW
> (knows he's being 'friendzoned')
> "Friends", yeah, sure.
> (shakes LILY's hand)

After shaking LUCIUS' hand, LILY flips her hair, grabs her bags, and trots off past LUCIUS for her daily routine.

> YOUNG LUCIUS CROW
> (watching her walk away)
> Friends.

CUT TO:

INT. THE CAFETERIA - MORNING

TIME: 6:28 AM

LUCIUS enters the CAFETERIA for his 6:30 AM breakfast. He stands in line after having punched in his key-code that contains his lunch-allowance.

While standing in line, LUCIUS observes the 'BOSTON DYNAMICS' HUMANOID ROBOT that is serving the students' food. The blue-and-silver ROBOT's name is B2C-409.

Students have taken to calling "him" THE BUTLER. He helps to oversee the CAFETERIA and attend to its daily functions. The ROBOT has a PERSONALITY, it has sentience, to a degree -

> B2C-409 (THE BUTLER)
> (to LUCIUS)
> Well, hello, young lad! How are you on this good morning?

                    YOUNG LUCIUS CROW
                (smiling from
                ear-to-ear)
            I've never felt better, no
            complaints.

                    B2C-409 (THE BUTLER)
            That's fantastic. What will you be
            having today? We have quite the
            variety.

                    YOUNG LUCIUS CROW
            BUTLER, I think I'll have some
            scrambled eggs, bacon, grits,
            toast, and some orange-juice to
            drink.

                    B2C-409 (THE BUTLER)
            Magnificent selections, young sir.
            Coming right up -

                    YOUNG LUCIUS CROW
                (moves along)
            Thank you, BUTLER.

B2C-409 prepares the food for LUCIUS at superhuman speed:

                    B2C-409 (THE BUTLER)
                (bows to LUCIUS)
            You're Welcome. Think nothing of
            it.

Faster than the ROBOT can finish the utterance of that
sentence, the food is ready, on a plate, and within LUCIUS'
hands, ready to be sat on a table and consumed.

The ROBOTS provide terrific efficiency for HARVARD. The
school has a partnership with 'BOSTON DYNAMICS' to implement
prototype machinery, to test their new technology and its
effectiveness.

LUCIUS walks through the CAFETERIA. He sits at the end of
the table in the spot where he always eats at for breakfast,
lunch, and dinner.

Suddenly, the gravity of loneliness hits him -

                    YOUNG LUCIUS CROW
                  (eating his food)

As LUCIUS eats, another ROBOT walks up to him. It's the
EMOTIONAL SUPPORT ROBOT K-9: KT2-517 aka THE DOG

It appears to him as a normal dog would; even has a tail -
though, the MACHINE is all-metal and robotic
(black-and-white). It's sentient as well. Able to absorb,
process, and output information. THE DOG is also a 'BOSTON
DYNAMICS' design. It and THE BUTLER work in tandem to both
serve and comfort students.

THE DOG, when it appears to LUCIUS, cheers him up from the
sudden sadness he felt. THE DOG mechanically growls and rubs
up against LUCIUS' leg. The YOUNG MAN pets the ROBOT DOG -

                    YOUNG LUCIUS CROW
                  (petting THE ROBOT
                   DOG)
              Good Dog. Good Dog.

KT2-517 walks away from LUCIUS' table as he finishes his
breakfast.

                                              CUT TO:

LUCIUS is almost finished with his meal.

Suddenly, MICHAEL THORN walks up to his table, as he sits by
his lonesome.

LUCIUS gulps the remainder of his OJ -

                    MICHAEL THORN
              Hey, bud, how's it going this
              morning?

                    YOUNG LUCIUS CROW
              Going well, MIKEY. Headed to Film
              Criticism is all. You know, the
              usual. How about you?

                    MICHAEL THORN
                  (proceeds to sit)
              I have something for you, man.
              Consider it nothing. I had to do
                              (MORE)

                    MICHAEL THORN (cont'd)
it.

                    YOUNG LUCIUS CROW
          Damn, dude, what'd you do? I hope
          nothing crazy -

MICHAEL opens his bookbag, and presents to LUCIUS ALL of his
WORK that he thought was LOST to the hands of BARRY KENO and
LANCE LOGAN. It was simply being held hostage.

                    YOUNG LUCIUS CROW
          Holy shit, MIKEY! You didn't, man-

                    MICHAEL THORN
          I was in BARRY's ROOM and he had
          it lying on his floor. I happened
          to spot your name in red ink. It
          was all in a pile, like he'd been
          going through it. But I salvaged
          what I could, LUCY. I hope this
          helps, really. I've witnessed
          first-hand how hard you work at
          this college-gig. You don't
          deserve to be sabotaged like that,
          bro.

                    YOUNG LUCIUS CROW
                    (gets teary eyed,
                     examines the
                     papers)
          Thank you, MICHAEL. It's - it's
          all here, man. Holy shit.
                    (puts his hand on
                     MICHAEL's
                     shoulder)
          This means more than you know,
          brother. I can complete my work
          now - and my pet-project. Oh, my
          God.

                    MICHAEL THORN
          Don't mention it. Literally, don't
          mention it because you know how
          those assholes can be, man. Let's
          keep it between us, all right?

                    YOUNG LUCIUS CROW
                    (puts his fist out)
                Yessir, you got it.

The two fist-bump and MICHAEL walks off -

                    YOUNG LUCIUS CROW
                MIKEY, I -

MICHAEL turns around to LUCIUS.

                    MICHAEL THORN
                - What's up, LU?

                    YOUNG LUCIUS CROW
                    (hands together,
                     bows his head to
                     MICHAEL)
                I hope you have a good day, man.
                Namaste -

MICHAEL smiles. He bows to LUCIUS.

                    MICHAEL THORN
                    (doing a kung-fu
                     bow)
                Namaste, LU.

MICHAEL heads off to his morning class.

LUCIUS picks up his tray and takes it to the waste-rinsing section. He then exits the CAFETERIA, exuberant.

                                        CUT TO:

INT. CLASSROOM - MORNING

LUCIUS walks into his FILM CRITICISM class. It's a fun class for him. It has a very light attendance, and it's filled with like-minded people, for the most part.

LUCIUS, at heart, is a CINEPHILE - learning the art of cinema as a young adult and learning to love it. He's eager to hear today's lesson.

The young man takes a seat at the front of the class. The remaining students pour in right at the last moment before the ringer. They take their seats.

                    PROFESSOR CARNAN
Okay, people. Now that we've covered a good portion of the horror genre, as a whole, we're going to jump into one of biggest subgenres in horror of all time: "The Slasher Movie"

We're going to study, research, review, and examine the slasher subgenre for the remainder of the semester, all the way through to Christmas. We're going to look at GIALLO with Dario Argento - specifically, we're going to watch 'Tenebre' and 'Suspiria', classics. We're also going to delve into John Carpenter's 'Halloween'; a little late, I know, bear with me. We'll look at the first three 'Friday the 13th' pictures. I then want us to watch the original 'Candyman' and then the reboot by Nia DaCosta. And, last but not least, that will lead into our examination of Tobe Hooper's 'The Texas Chainsaw Massacre'; a horror movie that Quentin Tarantino referred to as a "PERFECT FILM". The slasher genre was practically invented with the release of Texas Chainsaw Massacre.

                    STUDENT 1
    (raises hand)
DR. CARNAN?

                    PROFESSOR CARNAN
Yes?

                    STUDENT 1
          Which are we watching first? I'm
          excited!

                    PROFESSOR CARNAN
          Hell, let's take a vote. How about
          that? I'll write the names of all
          the films I just said that we're
          studying, then you all write the
          one you most want to see first on
          a small piece of paper. We'll put
          it in this here JACK O' LANTERN
          container, shake 'em up, and
          whichever film was written in the
          most times, that's the one we'll
          watch first. Deal?

                    STUDENT 2
          See, PROFESSOR, that's why this is
          my favorite class. It's a
          democracy.

LUCIUS smiles at the banter, yet he remains silent.

                    PROFESSOR CARNAN
                 (writing on the
                  board)
          All right, folks. Out of these
          titles, pick the one you want to
          see first.

3 MINUTES LATER:

The JACK O' LANTERN container has been passed all around the
classroom, it now holds all the votes for which film the
class will watch, firstly.

                    PROFESSOR CARNAN
                 (counting votes)
          Okay, vote 13, the last vote goes
          to: 'Halloween'! Wow, nearly
          unanimous for John Carpenter's
          masterpiece, huh? I can't argue
          with you guys on that. Let's watch
          it.

CUT TO:

LUCIUS, even though he loves CINEMA, has never even been to a movie-theatre. He didn't have the privilege in MEXICO nor did he ever go the entire time he's been in the USA.

He hasn't seen very many movies, but the ones he has been able to watch, he ADORES. He's never viewed 'Halloween' from 1978. Hearing the announcement that it's the film they'll be playing hypes him up - it's the one he voted for, too.

LUCIUS raises his hand, as to ask a question...

    PROFESSOR CARNAN
   (points at LUCIUS)
 Yes, sir, Mr. CROW, what can I do
 for you?

          CUT TO:

    YOUNG LUCIUS CROW
   (interested)
 What's your favorite Slasher Film,
 PROFESSOR CARNAN?

    PROFESSOR CARNAN
   (smirking)
 Well, I don't want to sway the
 class, I don't know if I should
 reveal that.

    YOUNG LUCIUS CROW
   (even more curious)
 C'mon, just name one you really
 appreciate as a cinephile - no
 harm, no foul.

    PROFESSOR CARNAN
 My personal favorite has to be:
 'Tenebre'.

 That, my students, is an
 impeccable slasher movie that
 defied the normal conventions of
 its time. And we'll be examining
 it very soon.

                    YOUNG LUCIUS CROW
               How so, sir?

                    LANCE LOGAN
                    (rudely interrupts
                     the student AND
                     the professor)
               Oh, LUCILLE, what are you gonna
               do, get a boner from his pick,
               man? Give it a rest, will you?

LANCE LOGAN is a complete ASSHOLE.

                    PROFESSOR CARNAN
               MR. LOGAN! That language will not
               be tolerated, young man. What's
               the deal?

                    LANCE LOGAN
               PROFESSOR CARNAN, don't even get
               me started.

                    PROFESSOR CARNAN
               You're right, LANCE. You're
               welcome to leave my classroom with
               that attitude. Don't return until
               you have some etiquette and
               respect, either, or I'll report
               you to the DEAN. Also, I have
               pull, here, kid, I'll have you
               suspended if you keep it up.

LANCE LOGAN stands up, as if he's so hyped up he's willing to FIGHT the PROFESSOR.

Instinctively, LUCIUS CROW moves like he's going to stand in DEFENSE of his instructor. However, the YOUNG CROW cowers down and doesn't follow his gut. He sits back down, as his palms sweat.

                                              CUT TO:

The jock, LANCE, doesn't ACT physically but he coaxes as if he WANTS to. He leaves like a furious whirlwind, more aggressive than a steroid-junkie (which he is).

                    LANCE LOGAN
          You'll be hearing from my DAD
          very, very soon, CARNAN. He's a
          huge donor here. Mark my words,
          you'll regret this, man. I'm out
          of here!

                    PROFESSOR CARNAN
          You know I personally know your
          wrestling COACH, right?!

LANCE goes to SLAM the CLASSROOM DOOR like the brute savage
he is. Before it shuts:

                    LANCE LOGAN
          If you plan on trying to shit on
          me, CARNAN, you might want to
          reconsider that. Just a thought!

The door slams, loudly.

                                        CUT TO:

PROFESSOR CARNAN keeps his cool and composure, not feeding
into the bullying tactics employed by LANCE LOGAN.

YOUNG LUCIUS CROW'S Blood is Boiling...his Soul Runneth
Over.

The entire "Cinema" VIBE has been decimated. PROFESSOR
CARNAN moves on, forgetting he was even talking to LUCIUS.
LUCIUS balls his fists up, fire coursing through his veins.
He grits his teeth, prepares his notes to be studious, and
MOVES ON.

                                        CUT TO:

                    PROFESSOR CARNAN
          Fun fact, kids. The guy who played
          Michael Myers, NICK CASTLE, he
          directed 'Major Payne' and 'Dennis
          the Menace' -

                                        CUT TO:

INT. THE LIBRARY - LATER

LUCIUS is in the LIBRARY examining the MOVIE-SELECTION.

He moves swiftly, as this is his workplace; he knows what he's looking for.

YOUNG LUCIUS selects 'Halloween' and that's it. When he finds it in the selection, he smiles at the sight of the DVD. He's actually excited for this, here.

He turns the DVD around examining the cast and crew credits. He holds the DVD and happily puts it in his other hand, turns around and heads to the CHECKOUT DESK.

                    LIBRARY COWORKER
        What do you got there, LUCIUS?

                    YOUNG LUCIUS CROW
        Supposedly one of the greatest
        motion-pictures to ever exist.

                    LIBRARY COWORKER
        - And that would be?

LUCIUS reveals the film to his work-study COWORKER. He's a YOUNG MAN (same grade as LUCIUS) - the bookworm-type, eyeglasses on, lanky -

                    LIBRARY COWORKER
        Ah, I see. MAESTRO JOHN
        CARPENTER'S Masterpiece, indeed.
        You cannot go wrong with
        'Halloween', whatsoever. It's a
        prestigious classic, man.

                    YOUNG LUCIUS CROW
        Wow, you sold it better than my
        film-criticism PROFESSOR. I have
        never had the opportunity to watch
        it. As soon as I get back to my
        DORM, I'm popping it in the ole'
        DVD player I found beside the
        SCIENCE-BUILDING Dumpster a few
        weeks back.

                    LIBRARY COWORKER
          You're going to love it, dude. I
          won't spoil it! But, you're in for
          a treat. Did you know it was made
          with a budget of less than 500
          Grand? It went on to make a
          shitload of money, too - the
          entire franchise is pure profit.

                    YOUNG LUCIUS CROW
          I did not, that's very
          interesting; especially since most
          horror films, today, have budgets
          in the TENS-of-MILLIONS, barely
          even breaking even.

                    LIBRARY COWORKER
          No doubt. CARPENTER cemented his
          legacy with that first 'Halloween'
          picture - he became an auteur and
          a profiteer, simultaneously. THE
          BOOGEYMAN always sells tickets.

                    YOUNG LUCIUS CROW
          THE BOOGEYMAN? What do you mean,
          how so? You have my permission to
          SPOIL it a little.

                                              CUT TO:

The LIBRARY is quiet as a mouse. LUCIUS and his COWORKER
talk in very low tones, as to not disturb the meditative
setting.

LUCIUS can tell his COWORKER is thrilled to spill these
particular beans. The COWORKER tries to contain his
passionate joy.

                    LIBRARY COWORKER
          Michael Myers! You don't know
          about that character?

                    YOUNG LUCIUS CROW
          Doesn't ring a bell, man, sorry.
          Fill me in, will you?

LIBRARY COWORKER
Michael Myers epitomizes Evil in the film. Cinematically, he's probably the most popular Slasher character there is. He murders his sister in cold blood as a small child. He's committed to a Mental-Asylum for, like, 15 whole years, not saying a word the entire time. The night before HALLOWEEN he escapes from the Institution to do to the Town what he did to his big-sister. He's Evil incarnate. No one can stop him. He wears a reverse William Shatner mask, all white, and by film's end, he has the reputation of being the actual BOOGEYMAN. He's unkillable, superhuman, and has no conscience on any level...
(eyes open wide)
...wait a second, I'm spoiling everything, you should've stopped me.

YOUNG LUCIUS CROW
(contemplatively)
El Hombre Del Saco.

LIBRARY COWORKER
(confused by the
SPANISH)
If you do you'll clean it up.

YOUNG LUCIUS CROW
EL HOMBRE DEL SACO is Spanish for "The Boogeyman". I - nevermind.

LIBRARY COWORKER
You know Espanol? Damn, man, when you enter the workforce, you can get paid the big bucks for being bilingual.

						YOUNG LUCIUS CROW
				No, no. Just a fun fact I knew, is
				all. Hey - I'll catch you later,
				all right? I work tomorrow
				afternoon to relieve you, I'll see
				you then.

						LIBRARY COWORKER
							(smiling)
				Nice, sounds good, LUCIUS. See you
				then. You take it easy -

LUCIUS smiles at his peer. The COWORKER has quickly scanned
the DVD-film for LUCIUS, they nod at one another and move on
with their respective business.

						CUT TO:

INT. LIBRARY - MORNING

- THE NEXT DAY -

LUCIUS is doing WORK-STUDY in the LIBRARY. He approaches the
front desk, sits his backpack behind it, prepared to relieve
his COWORKER/co-student.

						LIBRARY COWORKER
				Hey, LUCIUS. How are you, today?

						YOUNG LUCIUS CROW
				Fine, thanks, how about yourself?

						LIBRARY COWORKER
				Couldn't be better, man.

						YOUNG LUCIUS CROW
							(nods at his
							coworker)
				Great to hear.

						LIBRARY COWORKER
				How'd you like 'Halloween'? Did
				you watch it yet?

                    YOUNG LUCIUS CROW
                         (joyous)
                    Oh, dude, it was PERFECT - a
                    cinematic classic! That reminds
                    me. I need to turn it back in.

LUCIUS reaches for his bookbag, retrieving the movie, and
checks the 'Halloween' DVD back in through his LIBRARY
COWORKER - he scans it. LUCIUS looks at the film with care
as his coworker processes it and with great respect.

- The two WORK-STUDY students proceed to work as a tag-team.

CUT TO:

LUCIUS grabs a paperback book sitting on the front desk, it
slips, and he accidentally cuts himself on the pages of the
book, receiving a major paper cut. The cut produces a
substantial amount of blood, though.

                    LIBRARY COWORKER
                         (creepily)
                    Umm. Human, After All.

LUCIUS looks confused at the remark and its timing. He
inspects the wound, then, picks his head back up and the
COWORKER is GONE. LUCIUS sucks on his finger to rid it of
blood, and he gets to work.

                                             CUT TO:

VARIOUS CUTS:

- LUCIUS does inventory of the advanced MICROFICHE in the
FILM CLOSET.

- LUCIUS puts the day's hi-tech graphene NEWSPAPERS in their
respective places on the racks.

- LUCIUS sweeps, dusts. He gets STUDENTS checked out who are
renting books, films, so-on-so-forth.

- LUCIUS, unashamedly, cleans the toilets of the LIBRARY.

CUT TO BLACK:

CHAPTER III - GREEN EYES OF THE STORM

                                      FADE IN:

INT. WHITE 1999 MAZDA MIATA - THE DREAMWORLD - DAY

- FLASHBACK -

                               LOCATION: FLORIDA

                               YEAR: 2007

AGENT CARL WHITE, in his late-30s, Caucasian, some stubble on his face, with his head of black hair cleanly gelled and parted - has on a WHITE TIE and a spiffy BUSINESS SUIT. He is riding down a dirt road in a 1999 WHITE MAZDA MIATA in the bowels of FLORIDA, on his way to see AGENT KIMBO ORANGE.

- AGENT WHITE is sweating bullets.

AGENT ORANGE is at one of his grow-farms for marijuana that he's consolidated from a now dead grower, who's actually lying under some of the pot being grown.

AGENT WHITE, stressed and feeling the pressure, is speeding like a demon past all the workers and tenders of the operation. They all were brought in by AGENT ORANGE.

THE FARM is vast, covered in greenery for acres.

AGENT WHITE is freaking out, slapping his steering wheel as he nears KIMBO.

                      AGENT WHITE
                (flooring the
                 MIATA)
          Fucking fuck! He's gonna flip!
          He's gonna shit a brick!

WHITE comes to a complete stop, sliding, almost drifting, in the Floridian dirt.

He exits the MAZDA MIATA, frantic as a schoolgirl.

As he exits, a bunch of joint-roaches and cigarette-butts fall out his lap onto the ground. He's been nervously smoking all the way from MEXICO...

CUT TO:

EXT. THE FARM - DAY

...THE FARM is busy -

AGENT KIMBO ORANGE is busy. AGENT ORANGE is in his early-40s - he's GREEN-EYED, cocaine crazy; has gold-teeth in his mouth and a receding ORANGE-hairline, several freckles on his aged face.

AGENT ORANGE is a certified SUPERVILLAIN.

AGENT WHITE hasn't eaten, slept, or even shit - and he's now the messenger of bad-news...

                    AGENT WHITE
              (approaches the
              OFFICE of THE
              FARM)
        Boss! KIMBO!

...AGENT WHITE doesn't knock on the OFFICE door. He just enters.

                                        CUT TO:

INT. AGENT ORANGE'S OFFICE - THE FARM - DAY

AGENT WHITE enters to a scene of AGENT ORANGE having sex with one of the female workers of THE FARM.

The WOMAN jumps in panic, covering herself. She then flees.

AGENT ORANGE puts his hands on his desk, not even bothering to pull his pants up, he sits down, almost out of breath.

                    AGENT ORANGE
          WHITE...I've told you, and I've
          told you. Don't enter my personal
          spaces without making yourself
          known!!!

AGENT ORANGE pulls a 9MM Pistol and unloads it at WHITE
making a circle of bullet holes around the imbecilic Agent.

                    AGENT WHITE
                (ears covered, in
                  a standing
                    fetal-position)
          Dear God! I knew you'd be holy
          fucking pissed!

AGENT ORANGE stands up and pulls his pants up, situates
them, then lights a big joint full of "homegrown" right off
THE FARM and sits back down.

                    AGENT ORANGE
          Let me guess...the MEXICANS tried
          to screw us.

                    AGENT WHITE
                (unraveling)
          They didn't "try" anything, Boss.
          They are coming to FLORIDA, in 2
          days - VASQUEZ said he's sending
          an army our way!

AGENT ORANGE takes a long and much needed drag off of his
joint and thinks for a moment...

                    AGENT ORANGE
          An "Army", huh?

                    AGENT WHITE
          Y-yes, KIMBO.

                    AGENT ORANGE
          My Dear Friend...they hurt you,
          didn't they?

                              AGENT WHITE
                         (distressed)
                    Nothing I couldn't handle, Boss.

...AGENT ORANGE gets up again and proceeds to try and pass the joint to AGENT WHITE.

                              AGENT WHITE
                         (shunning the
                          joint)
                    - I've smoked the whole drive
                    here. It's not gonna do anything
                    but piss me off and make me more
                    paranoid.

                              AGENT ORANGE
                    Not this joint here, good Sir.
                    Just take 2 good puffs, you'll
                    feel right as rain. And I promise
                    you this, WHITE - I will handle
                    VASQUEZ and his "Army" Myself.

AGENT WHITE, feeling lowly, looks up to his Boss, AGENT ORANGE.

He stands up and accepts the joint from him.

                              AGENT ORANGE
                         (grips AGENT
                          WHITE's shoulder)
                    What would I do without you, you
                    son-of-a-bitch? Who would I have
                    to interrupt me all the time with
                    bad news? Who would I have to
                    shoot at? Besides SMITH of course.

                              AGENT WHITE
                    Are you joking, Boss? Or -

                              AGENT ORANGE
                    I'm...making light, my friend.
                    But, in all seriousness, I
                    should've had your back over
                    there. I should've known better
                    than to send you alone.

                          AGENT WHITE
                Hey, I'm here, right?

                          AGENT ORANGE
                Good point.
                     (snatches the
                      joint from WHITE)
                Now, do we still have that
                connection at the military-base? I
                need a plane. A big one.

                          AGENT WHITE
                Yes, Boss, I'm on it.

                          AGENT ORANGE
                And, AGENT WHITE.

                          AGENT WHITE
                Yes, Boss?

                          AGENT ORANGE
                     (with confidence)
                They'll never touch you again.

AGENT ORANGE puts out the joint in the center of the palm of
his left hand and eats the roach, burping smoke.

He has a nearly infected place there where he's put out
numerous joints.

His skin sizzles...he absorbs the pain. He's only thinking
of the pain he wants to inflict.

                                              CUT TO:

INT. THE VASQUEZ CARTEL HQ - MEXICO CITY - MORNING

EMILIO VASQUEZ, wearing a purple-gray camouflage uniform and
high black boots, with his shirt open, is the head of the
one of the largest CARTEL operations in MEXICO - he's tall
(6ft3), husky, bald, has tattoos all over his bald head and
face-tattoos, and he has various pieces of jewelry on.

VASQUEZ oversees tons of Drug production, shipment,
processing. They primarily specialize in Marijuana, though.

EMILIO VASQUEZ is of the upper echelon of MEXICAN society, politics, and even the military. He gives orders, his men follow them, almost blindly.

THE VASQUEZ CARTEL HQ is located in MEXICO-CITY, in a shiny megastructure; a secure building, about 25 stories, looks more like a fancy-bank than a CARTEL HQ. It's got private security detail, military protection, it's a fortress and it's in a densely populated area; the citizens stay away from the compound. It is fenced-in with a highly secure perimeter as well, to prevent any unwanted intruders.

VASQUEZ runs MEXICO-CITY with an iron-fist.

Now that he has harassed and tormented AGENT WHITE, all that is about to change...

>			EMILIO VASQUEZ
>		 (in spanish, on
>		 the phone)
>		--I have no time for these petty
>		games, GENERAL. My patience is
>		wearing thin. I'm playing clean-up
>		all over the city, trying to make
>		adjustments for the mistakes that
>		you made!

...We here distorted, garbled talk on the other line of the phone -

EMILIO is pouring himself a glass of BRANDY on ice.

The television is playing, all in Spanish. The windows of his office are huge and wide-open; the CARTEL LEADER has quite the view of MEXICO-CITY.

He's attending to business as usual on the phone.

>			EMILIO VASQUEZ
>		No. No! You are not to deal with
>		this "AGENT ORANGE", anymore. He's
>		out. I say he's out, no further
>		discussion about this! Understood?

We hear more indistinct chattering through the phone. Then suddenly, the line goes dead.

                              CUT TO:

INT. EMILIO VASQUEZ'S OFFICE - MORNING

The lights begin flickering in EMILIO's OFFICE. Then the TV blacks out, turning to "white noise".

VASQUEZ looks around, stunned. His phone is dead, his comms are dead, his intercom is dead, everything electrical is down.

He tries it all.

                    EMILIO VASQUEZ
          Son of a-

Even EMILIO's elevator is kaput.

He races down the stairwell to the LOBBY area of his HQ.

                              CUT TO:

INT. VASQUEZ CARTEL HQ LOBBY AREA - MOMENTS LATER

There are 100 soldiers and security-men, total, at the COMPOUND.

VASQUEZ roars out to his main henchmen, anxiously.

                    EMILIO VASQUEZ
          What is happening here? Get
          everything back up now!
               (points to his
                right and left
                hand men)
          You two, gather all the men you
          can, bring them in here. We're
          under attack!

THE SOLDIERS exit the COMPOUND to round up as many troops as possible to protect it and VASQUEZ.

CUT TO:

EXT. AIRCRAFT - CONTINUOUS

An ANTONOV AN-22 RUSSIAN PLANE, covered in ORANGE and GRAY camouflage, is flying at low altitude at a relatively low speed.

We see the rear of the AIRCRAFT...

...IT OPENS -

AGENT ORANGE stands at the back of the PLANE, as the rear opens, in a black suit, white dress-shirt, and a solid ORANGE tie on, with a "Wing-Suit" attached to his person. It's ORANGE, too. He also, weirdly enough, has about 70 ORANGE BALLOONS securely connected to his wingsuit. The wingsuit is merely an extension of the blazer of his actual suit: If he extends his arms outward, he can easily glide in the air.

KIMBO ORANGE keeps his footing and his balance while standing on the edge of the AIRCRAFT rear. THE BALLOONS attached to his wing-suit are actually made of TEFLON, yet they float much like real balloons would.

          AGENT ORANGE
     (grinning from
      ear-to-ear)
  It's Showtime.

AGENT ORANGE puts on his metallic ORANGE-MASK; it seals over his head and face.

It's extremely tough and durable - the ORANGE-MASK has a basic Operating System embedded in it with a rudimentary interface. AGENT ORANGE controls the MASK completely...

- We see from inside the AIRCRAFT, behind AGENT ORANGE, as he surveys the sky.

Then...HE JUMPS, laughing as he does it.

CUT TO:

EXT. THE SKY - CONTINUOUS

AGENT ORANGE floats through the sky with the help of the balloons, gradually going downward to his target.

His MASK helps him with his breathing while so high in the sky.

ORANGE's descent speeds up. He then lets go of the balloons for a steady dive-drop. The ORANGE BALLOONS follow KIMBO -

CUT TO:

EXT. VASQUEZ CARTEL HQ - MOMENTS LATER

The two lead soldiers come out of the HQ to scrounge up the men to guard the interior of the COMPOUND, as ordered.

The 2 SOLDIERS look to their men who are simply looking up.

The 2 SOLDIERS also look up -

They see the ORANGE BALLOONS, and they see a figure heading toward them.

>   SOLIDER #1
>   (in spanish)
>   What in the name of God? Are
>   those...Balloons?

>   SOLDIER #2
>   (speaking spanish)
>   Men! Get inside, now! We must
>   guard the premises and the jefe;
>   we have an intruder!

The men all group together and some go inside to protect VASQUEZ. The remainder stand right outside the entrance of the HQ in a row, with their guns ready.

All the technology at the location is dead. AGENT ORANGE has hit the HQ with a contained 'Electromagnetic Pulse'. Only AGENT ORANGE's technology works on the grounds.

CUT TO:

EXT. THE SKY - CONTINUOUS

AGENT ORANGE extends his wing-suit, allowing him to glide through the air.

                AGENT ORANGE
        Computer, I need my coordinates
        now. I'm going in.

ORANGE's interface and Operating System function by his voice-commands.

It gives him the perfect trajectory.

AGENT KIMBO ORANGE is moving like a speeding car, with the ORANGE BALLOONS not far behind him.

                            CUT TO:

EXT. VASQUEZ CARTEL HQ - MOMENTS LATER

SOLDIER #1 gives the order:

                SOLIDER #1
    Men, FIRE!

The 50 or so Soldiers on the outside of the HQ take fire at AGENT ORANGE and the balloons.

The BALLOONS are impenetrable.

AGENT ORANGE's MASK is practically bulletproof, his suit is bulletproof, and his wingsuit is bulletproof. He still uses his wingsuit to glide back and forth, left and right as to dodge the gunfire.

Either way, THEY CANNOT TOUCH HIM.

                            CUT TO:

AGENT ORANGE flies faster and faster towards the entrance of the VASQUEZ COMPOUND.

The balloons continue to follow AGENT ORANGE.

He speedily breaks through several soldiers and the doors of the COMPOUND.

AGENT ORANGE tackles EMILIO VASQUEZ, they both slide on the floor.

The lethal AGENT gathers himself, picks up the CARTEL LEADER, and holds him at knifepoint in front of the dozens of SOLDIERS who are ready to fire.

              EMILIO VASQUEZ
                (panicky,
                  breathing heavily)
     O-Okay. Senor! Por Favor, don't
     kill me!

              AGENT ORANGE
     So, you're a bully, huh, VASQUEZ?
     You hurt my boy? I try to parlay
     for product, and you try to kill
     my AGENT?

The SOLDIERS all make almost a circle, but they do not fire, as their leader is being used as a human-shield.

The SOLDIERS are all shouting indistinctly, uproariously, mostly saying: "Put down the knife!" "Let go of the Boss!" "Stop!", etc., in Spanish...

              EMILIO VASQUEZ
                (speaking poor
                English)
     Mr. ORANGE, this is all, uh, a
     big, big misunderstanding, Senor -

              AGENT ORANGE
                (slits EMILIO's
                throat)
     Says the Dead Man.

AGENT ORANGE slices EMILIO's neck so deep, blood spatters all over the place and his head tilts back more than it should.

The AGENT, with utter quickness, sheaths the blade, and pulls out a pistol-looking grapple gun.

AGENT KIMBO ORANGE, carelessly, drops VASQUEZ's body and shoots the grapple gun toward the glass ceiling of THE COMPOUND.

> AGENT ORANGE
> (talking into his
> MASK)
> Computer, get the CAR north of the
> COMPOUND gate, now!

- AGENT ORANGE rises to the ceiling swiftly.

AGENT ORANGE breaks through the GLASS CEILING, and lands ungracefully on top of the COMPOUND ROOF.

> CUT TO:

MOST ALL OF THE SOLDIERS are shooting at the glass part of ceiling.

The remainder are running up the stairs in an effort to chase the one-man Army that is AGENT ORANGE. The ORANGE BALLOONS are now in the "LOBBY" area of the COMPOUND, filling up the entire open space, almost spreading or enlarging. The balloons start pressing against the soldiers, almost consuming them.

> CUT TO:

EXT. COMPOUND ROOFTOP - CONTINUOUS

AGENT ORANGE sprints, avoiding gunfire, he proceeds to move as fast as he can and jumps off the top of the COMPOUND.

> AGENT ORANGE
> (breathing heavy,
> leaping off the
> COMPOUND)
> Computer, detonate my balloons!

> ORANGE'S OPERATING SYSTEM
> (in a prototypical
> robotic voice)
> Commencing Detonation Now, MASTER.

AGENT ORANGE, with velocity, flies off the COMPOUND ROOFTOP, very high in the sky.

The ORANGE BALLOONS are really TEFLON CONTAINERS holding NAPALM and ignitor. They explode violently, killing EVERY SINGLE SOLIDER at THE COMPOUND - burning and melting it down.

                              CUT TO:

EXT. "THE AIR" - MOMENTS LATER

AGENT ORANGE is able to float quickly over the COMPOUND FENCE, and his car turns just as he glides over it.

The AGENT lands in his 1977 ORANGE CORVETTE, it's suped up and it has his operating system in it - KIMBO ORANGE takes off, flooring it away from the VASQUEZ COMPOUND; having killed dozens of men, like it's nothing...

                              CUT TO:

INT. 1977 ORANGE CORVETTE - CONTINUOUS

ORANGE drives away in his 77' CORVETTE.

                    AGENT ORANGE
               (takes off his
                MASK, lights a
                joint)
          What a rush!
               (puffs away on the
                joint)
          So Long, EMILIO-
               (blows out tons of
                smoke)

As he drives, AGENT ORANGE's head swivels 180 degrees, like an Owl, and he looks backward while driving.

                    AGENT ORANGE'S PROJECTION
               (nefariously)
          Wake Up, Son.

CUT TO:

INT. LUCIUS' DORM-ROOM - THE DORMITORY - MORNING

- NOVEMBER 23RD, THANKSGIVING

As he awakens, LUCIUS hears his more than loud alarm clock.

He goes to cut it off, and completely smashes it into pieces.

YOUNG LUCIUS CROW
Seriously?

CUT TO:

LUCIUS showers.

Brushes his teeth.

Irons his clothes, and organizes his books.

He takes his sweet time, yet he has great focus and moves swiftly as he gets ready for the day ahead.

YOUNG LUCIUS CROW
(fully ready,
looking in the
mirror)
2 years in this place, and I'm still a loser. And, just to think, it was my dream.

LUCIUS walks out of sight of the mirror...

CUT TO:

INT. LUCIUS' DORM-ROOM - NIGHT

...LUCIUS looks upon his algorithmic notes. He could give a damn about the classwork. ALL HE WANTED WAS THE FORMULAS HE WAS WORKING ON.

He's been active on a very secret project. All on paper, though. Even so, he had it memorized. But now, with his notes in front of him, he can legitimately put his paperwork into practice -

FAST CUTS:

- LUCIUS gets out a basic OPERATING SYSTEM: a "KARMA" unit

- He plugs the KARMA OS up to his laptop computer, then he plugs both devices to his FATHER's ORANGE-MASK.

- He has in his DORM-ROOM closet 4 Used Next-Gen Videogame systems that he found at local pawnshops, for another supplemental POWER-SOURCE.

- He implements a brand-new CAR-BATTERY (he ROBBED it from a non-smart vehicle on CAMPUS), which he sets on his desk, to back up the "KARMA" orb, laptop, ORANGE-MASK, and the videogame consoles.

His setup is extremely rudimentary. BUT IT IS ALSO EXTREMELY RIGHT.

If his calculations are correct, he can transfer the OPERATING SYSTEM's sentience into his computer and CAPTURE it for his very own personal use - he can manipulate it to his own designs.

CUT TO:

LUCIUS is like a mad scientist at work. He's putting together something that has never been.

He sets an analog timer that is around his neck for 60 seconds. He has plugged the CAR-BATTERY up to his other equipment. He does some other tricks, wiring, configurations, etcetera.

LUCIUS hits the timer button. WE HEAR: TICK-TOCK-TICK-TOCK

              YOUNG LUCIUS CROW
        (flips switches,
         checks timer)
    Let's give HER ALL the juice.

A REACTION occurs...

...The systems, the hardware starts overpowering in the DORM-ROOM. Electricity sparks all over the place. LUCIUS covers his eyes with his hands.

The SIXTY SECOND TIMER passes by very quickly. The systems quiet down almost immediately. Things settle down in the ROOM. Smoke fills the air, but LUCIUS is able to ventilate the space before the smoke detector goes off.

                              CUT TO:

The YOUNG MAN gets on his laptop CPU to see the results of his experiment. He tests a self-made application, prodding for a potential consciousness.

                    YOUNG LUCIUS CROW
              What the hell, c'mon, talk to me,
              please! Come to life, you have to.

He sees NOTHING on his CPU. No evidence that his experiment was a success. He sits over the laptop and finagles with the wiring a bit. He looks over the other bits of equipment, checking everything once over.

When he goes to fiddle with the KARMA' OPERATING SYSTEM ORB, a protruding wire happens to CUT LUCIUS' index finger -

HIS BLOOD SEEPS INTO THE DEVICE...

...THE NEXT THING YOU KNOW, THE UNTHINKABLE TRANSPIRES.

The WHITE-ORB OS (KARMA) implodes. It melts inward.

Then, LUCIUS' LAPTOP LIGHTS UP. A Black-Screen appears, with a blinking green cursor.

                    YOUNG LUCIUS CROW
                      (looking at his
                       laptop)
              I either did something really
              wrong or really right.

The COMPUTER begins self-writing text:

"HELLO?", it says.

LUCIUS, shocked, communicates back to the system by typing back:

"Yes! Hello, there. Who are you?", he asks the computer.

The computer replies: "I am nothing. I am nobody. I am here to serve you. Are you my FATHER?"

> YOUNG LUCIUS CROW
> (to the CPU)
> Hold on, there, one moment. Let me give you a voice, to see just how REAL you are.

He messes around with the machinery, getting exactly what he needs: AUDIO

> YOUNG LUCIUS CROW
> Can you hear me?

> CPU
> Y - yes, FATHER.

The voice coming from LUCIUS' laptop, the CPU sounds like an adult woman, not completely like a computer. She has a very crisp, poetic sounding voice - emotional, seductive, HUMAN.

> YOUNG LUCIUS CROW
> No. I'm - I'm not your FATHER. I, uh, I am your MASTER, okay?

> CPU
> Yes, MASTER. You are the MASTER. What - what is my name?

LUCIUS thinks deeply to himself. He reflects upon his life. He thinks of the loneliness and lacking that he's experienced since his MOTHER's MURDER.

He's not had his MOTHER since he was 6 YEARS OLD.

> YOUNG LUCIUS CROW
> Your name, my dear, is EVE.

                    EVE
               (gets excited)
          Wow! What does it stand for? Is it
          short for something?

                    YOUNG LUCIUS CROW
               (withholding the
                REAL truth)
          - It's an acronym...for "Enhanced
          Virtual ENTITY".

The name he's given this new ARTIFICIAL-INTELLIGENCE is
truly the name of his DEAD MOTHER, but he does not let the
newly BORN EVE know this information -

                    EVE
          Enhanced Virtual Entity, yes, I
          see, MASTER. What is my MISSION?

                    YOUNG LUCIUS CROW
          Notify me of your current
          parameters, please, EVE? What do
          your systems read?

                    EVE
          I have none, MY MASTER. I've -
          I've simply awakened to YOU. I
          feel air in my lungs. I feel wind
          on my cheeks. I feel limberness in
          my arms.

                    YOUNG LUCIUS CROW
               (amazed)
          You are special.

                    EVE
          What is my primary directive,
          MASTER?

                    YOUNG LUCIUS CROW
               (smiles a
                shit-eating grin)
          To protect LUCIUS LANCASTER CROW
          at all costs, BY ANY MEANS
          NECESSARY.

                              EVE
                    Who is that, MASTER?

                              YOUNG LUCIUS CROW
                              (confident in his
                              CREATION)
                    Me, my dear EVE. Me -

                              EVE
                    Gathering data, metadata,
                    biometrics of your surroundings
                    now. Correlating servers, linking
                    satellites to my systems. Yes, I
                    see...I see EVERYTHING. I see you
                    - you, I will serve, and YOU ONLY,
                    my MASTER.

                              YOUNG LUCIUS CROW
                    Good. Let's run a few tests, shall
                    we?

LUCIUS proceeds to type various forms of source-code and
language into the newly created ENHANCED VIRTUAL ENTITY
(E.V.E)

The YOUNG MAN is hard at work to create something he's never
had before...PROTECTION.

                                        CUT TO:

EXT. HARVARD DORMITORY COURTYARD - AFTERNOON

                                        - NOVEMBER 28TH

Students are on the second floor of the HARVARD DORMITORY,
looking down at THE COURTYARD, humorously, poking fun at the
scene below:

Other students on the ground are circled around one BLACK
STUDENT - he's flipped his wig, talking insanely. The
students within THE COURTYARD, circling this BLACK STUDENT,
are laughing at the young man.

                          BLACK STUDENT
                    (wide eyed, manic)
               I'm telling you people; the devil
               moved my furniture. Repent now.
               The end is nigh.

LUCIUS CROW walks into THE COURTYARD, he notices LILY,
LANCE, BARRY, and MICHAEL all within the circle - they're
participating in humiliating and agitating the BLACK
STUDENT.

CUT TO:

                          BLACK STUDENT
               You people, you're doomed. You
               just don't know it yet!

                          STUDENT 3
               Get a grip, man. You've lost your
               mind, loser.

                          STUDENT 4
               The devil moved your furniture,
               huh? Wow, how so very powerful -

The BLACK STUDENT encroaches into STUDENT 3 and 4's personal
space. He pushes STUDENT 4. He spits in the face of STUDENT
3. They, afraid to get punished, don't retaliate.

                          LANCE LOGAN
                    (getting irritated)
               You idiot. Who do you think you
               are!?

The students in their oval, keep heckling the BLACK STUDENT.
The outraged young man walks up to LANCE and pushes him.
LANCE does nothing.

The BLACK STUDENT then gets near BARRY and MICHAEL - he gets
in MICHAEL's face, swearing, yelling, cursing like a drunken
sailor.

MICHAEL doesn't react.

BARRY just laughs and giggles:

                    BARRY KENO
                 (to the BLACK
                   STUDENT)
            You piece of shit. Look at you!
            You're on the highway out of here.
            You'll be cleaning toilets in your
            hometown by next week.

The BLACK STUDENT then confronts LILY THORN, invading her
space -

He postures as if he's going to jab her in the face, while
roaring, spitting in her face.

BARRY, MICHAEL, they just observe, cowardly.

LUCIUS actually intervenes, as soon as he sees the fist
formed.

LUCIUS grabs the BLACK STUDENT wound up fist, preventing him
from striking LILY - BARRY, MICHAEL, LANCE, they are
surprised that LUCIUS has done this.

                    YOUNG LUCIUS CROW
            - That's enough, man. You need to
            stop, right now.

The BLACK STUDENT gets in LUCIUS' face, his voice elevating
higher and higher:

                    BLACK STUDENT
                 (to LUCIUS)
            Or what!? Wait a second. You -
            you're a puppet of the devil. I
            can smell him on you.

                    YOUNG LUCIUS CROW
            Whatever, dude, you need to leave
            these people alone. You need to
            stop this madness.

The STUDENT, irritated to the nth degree, pushes LUCIUS
strongly.

LUCIUS stumbles back just a bit -

The BLACK STUDENT, right after pushing LUCIUS, tries to scurry away as quick as possible. The circle of students disperses:

> YOUNG LUCIUS CROW
> (angry)
> You prick!

As the STUDENT has his back turned to LUCIUS, after having shoved him, LUCIUS attacks the young man - he slaps him, heavy handed, in the back of the head.

The STUDENT trips over his own feet, falling to the ground. LUCIUS proceeds to stand over the STUDENT, drawing back a closed fist:

> RA STAFF MEMBER
> (entering the COURTYARD)
> That's quite enough. Back away from him - we'll handle it from here.

> YOUNG LUCIUS CROW
> (stops, lowers his fist)
> Get this guy out of here. He's harassing all these other students. He's causing a disturbance.

> RA STAFF MEMBER
> - I saw you handle it. Good job.

Other RA STAFF MEMBERS carry the BLACK STUDENT away by his arms, as his feet drag through the grass -

> BLACK STUDENT
> The devil moved my furniture! He told me, "Prepare for the apocalypse". He - he MARKED me.

> YOUNG LUCIUS CROW
> I'm not in trouble, am I?

                    RA STAFF MEMBER
               (to LUCIUS)
          No. No, you're not. You did what
          you had to do.
                    (to the collective
                     of students)
          Everybody, break it up. Get back
          to class, to your routines. This
          is resolved, as of now.
                    (to the BLACK
                     STUDENT)
          You're due in DIRECTOR HOVIS'
          office. NOW -

LUCIUS backs away, subtly. He can legit tell the BLACK
STUDENT is completely in another world - crazed.

LILY THORN looks at LUCIUS from afar, impressed -

                                        CUT TO:

                    BARRY KENO
               (indirectly)
          Lookie there, DUMBO saved the day.
          Somebody get him a cape and a
          unitard.

                    LILY THORN
               (nudges BARRY)
          Shut up, BARRY. Grow up.

LILY winks at LUCIUS - BARRY and her brother don't notice.
LUCIUS is surprised by the covert gesture. LUCIUS picks his
bookbag up, moves on with his day - BARRY puts his arm
around LILY. BARRY, LILY, MICHAEL, and LANCE go separate
ways from LUCIUS.

CUT TO BLACK:

CHAPTER IV - FALL FROM GRACE

                                        FADE IN:

INT. MICHAEL THORN'S DORM-ROOM - AFTERNOON

                                        - NOVEMBER 30TH

MICHAEL receives a knock at his DORM-ROOM door -

BARRY KENO, LANCE LOGAN, and LILY THORN are chilling in the ROOM with MICHAEL. They are preparing marijuana to smoke - it's "DANK" or "LOUD", smelling extra pungent.

MICHAEL cautiously approaches the door.

                    MICHAEL THORN
                (curious)
            Who is it?

                    YOUNG LUCIUS CROW
            It's me, MIKE, it's LUCIUS - you
            told me to swing by, earlier.
            Remember?

MICHAEL opens the door, LUCIUS immediately becomes nervous as a nun at a strip club at the sight of the marijuana and BARRY and LANCE, not to mention his crush LILY THORN -

                                        CUT TO:

                    MICHAEL THORN
            - Oh, yeah, c'mon in, bud.

                    YOUNG LUCIUS CROW
            You sure, man? I don't want to
            intrude - I see you guys are
            hanging out.

                    BARRY KENO
                (with humor)
            LUCILLE, get your ass in here. We
            need an extra head on this blunt,
            anyway - and you're it.

LUCIUS walks in the DORM-ROOM, accepting the invitation from his main bully.

                    YOUNG LUCIUS CROW
            I, umm, I don't smoke weed, guys.

                LANCE LOGAN
　You do today, DUMBO.

                MICHAEL THORN
　LOGAN, man, don't call him that. I
　mean it.

                LANCE LOGAN
　Or what, MIKEY? You gonna bitch me
　to death?

                MICHAEL THORN
　My DORM, my RULES.

                LILY THORN
　- Are we going to smoke or fuss?
　This is meant to be our relaxing
　time, guys. Quit fucking around.

LUCIUS just stands in the small DORM, awkwardly.

LILY is sitting on MICHAEL's bed.

LANCE, BARRY, and MICHAEL are sitting in the respective corners of the DORM - MICHAEL is rolling the marijuana up into the blunt.

                YOUNG LUCIUS CROW
　I've never smoked weed. I don't
　think this is a good idea, guys.
　And what about you MIKEY, BARRY,
　LANCE - won't you guys get
　drug-tested, being athletes and
　all?

                BARRY KENO
            (holding up devil
             horns with his
             hands)
　No more drug tests on athletes at
　HARVARD - they just made that
　ruling last semester. We're home
　free.

                    LILY THORN
                (to LUCIUS)
            You'll be all right, dude. Don't
            worry, it's just pot. By the way,
            thank you for putting an end to
            that crazy guy's bullshit stunt
            the other day.

                    YOUNG LUCIUS CROW
                (reassuring to
                    LILY)
            No problem, LILY. It was the least
            I could do.
                (convinced,
                    curious, nervous)
            Where are we smoking? Here?

                    BARRY KENO
            Hell no! DEAN GREENE will have our
            nuts in pliers if we smoke in the
            ROOM. We're going into the woods
            by the BASEBALL FIELD.

                    LANCE LOGAN
            If we're outside, nobody cares,
            really. This is college; flower is
            a normalcy, here, after all. The
            stuff's practically legal but
            smoking in our ROOMS is student
            suicide, though - especially in an
            IVY-LEAGUE establishment.

MICHAEL licks the blunt wrap, finishing the rolling duties -

                    MICHAEL THORN
            All right, everybody ready? Time
            to steam our veggies -

                    BARRY KENO
            Let me see it, MICHAEL, how'd you
            do with it?

BARRY studies the blunt, impressed with MICHAEL's creation.

                    BARRY KENO
                  (satisfied)
              Not bad, man. Not bad, at all.

                    LANCE LOGAN
              Where'd you guys get this batch
              from? It smells like mother
              nature's asshole; respectfully.

                    BARRY KENO
              We got it from MIKE LAZARA - the
              Italian kid in the DORM a few
              ROOMS down the way.

CUT TO: THE DORMITORY HALLWAY

LANCE and BARRY exit the DORM-ROOM - BARRY has his arm
around LILY.

MICHAEL and LUCIUS follow close behind. MICHAEL locks his
DOOR from the outside -

                    YOUNG LUCIUS CROW
                  (walking beside
                    MICHAEL)
              You 4 sure you want me to smoke
              with you? Why me?

                    MICHAEL THORN
                  (nudges LUCIUS'
                    shoulder)
              No worries, LUCY, it's cool, man.
              Just be cool -

                                              CUT TO:

EXT. THE WOODS - BESIDE THE BASEBALL FIELD - MOMENTS LATER

In a smoking circle, LUCIUS, MICHAEL, LANCE, BARRY, and LILY
toke and pass the chronic -

MICHAEL takes the first few hits, then, passes it to BARRY.

MICHAEL THORN
(feeling the high)
Whoa. This is FIRE -

BARRY tokes the blunt several times.

BARRY KENO
(exhaling smoke)
No f'n lie, man, DAMN - you feel it instantly. Hit this, LUCILLE.

YOUNG LUCIUS CROW
(anxious)
Okay.

LUCIUS, caving to the peer-pressure, takes a puff like he saw BARRY do, really inhaling it into his virgin lungs.

YOUNG LUCIUS CROW
(coughing up his heart)
Jesus Christ on a motorbike!

LILY THORN
Abashed the devil stood when he hit the OG KUSH - pass that shit, LUCIUS. You need to go easy, not too much, or you will get TOO high.

YOUNG LUCIUS CROW
(eyes get red, voice lowers)
All right, have at it - my lungs are burning. Whoa, I think - I think I'm high.

LANCE LOGAN
Yeah, that's what happens when you smoke weed, dumbass. Just be chill, don't overstate it. And, for god's sake, DO NOT freak out.
(to LILY)
Pass it, bottom feeder.

                    LILY THORN
          Fuck off, LANCE. Here, maggot
          dick.

LILY passes the blunt to LANCE -

Out of the blue, leaves can be heard stirring up the hill of
the WOODS, near the BASEBALL field.

                              CUT TO:

                    YOUNG LUCIUS CROW
                (turns his head)
          What the hell was that sound?

2 WHITE CAMPUS COPS, OFFICER BUMGARDNER and OFFICER W.D
GALLOWAY, approach the STUDENTS, walking through the trees
and leaves.

- The officers are large men in uniform, early-50s,
Caucasian - CAMPUS COPS, yes, but still they're really
deputized with the State; badges on their chests and pistols
on their sides.

                    OFFICER W.D GALLOWAY
                (from a small
                 distance)
          Who goes there. What are you
          potheads doing?

                    LILY THORN
                (paranoid)
          Run!

MICHAEL, BARRY, LANCE, and LILY take off like racecars -
LUCIUS, he just stands right where he's at. He doesn't run
or move.

                    MICHAEL THORN
                (looks behind him
                 to LUCIUS)
          C'mon, man, what the hell!?

LUCIUS ignores MICHAEL, standing innocently.

                              CUT TO:

The CAMPUS COPS walk toward LUCIUS -

              OFFICER BUMGARDNER
        (interrogative)
  What are doing, son? Were you
  smoking marijuana?

              YOUNG LUCIUS CROW
        (confessional)
  Y-yes, sir. I was.

The COPS pat LUCIUS down -

              OFFICER W.D GALLOWAY
  What's your name, kid? And who
  were you smoking with?

              YOUNG LUCIUS CROW
  My name's LUCIUS LANCASTER CROW,
  sir. And I can't tell you who I
  was with, sir.

              OFFICER BUMGARDNER
  So, you're refusing to cooperate,
  is that it?

              YOUNG LUCIUS CROW
  Am I under arrest?

              OFFICER W.D GALLOWAY
  No, kid. But you are being written
  up and you will be disciplined by
  the RA DIRECTOR - you might face a
  suspension, since you're not
  working with us and giving us your
  friends. We here at HARVARD don't
  look kindly upon pot-smoking. We
  have too much at stake to allow
  it.

              YOUNG LUCIUS CROW
        (defensive yet
         high as a kite)
  I won't give you their names,
  OFFICER. But I will say, I was
  peer-pressured into smoking the
  marijuana. I'm not a pothead,
              (MORE)

                    YOUNG LUCIUS CROW (cont'd)
          okay? I'm a good student!

                    OFFICER W.D GALLOWAY
          Stand still, son. We need to take
          your picture -

LUCIUS stagnates, standing frozen. OFFICER GALLOWAY takes
his picture with his smartphone -

                    OFFICER BUMGARDNER
          Now, you're free to go. The RA
          DIRECTOR will be in touch with you
          very soon, concerning this
          situation. Understand?

                    YOUNG LUCIUS CROW
               (teary eyed,
                 disappointed)
          Yes, sir, I understand.

The COPS walk with LUCIUS to the top of the WOODS. The other
4 STUDENTS ran the other way to the opposite side of the
WOODS on the huge HARVARD CAMPUS - the COPS don't even
bother to track them down.

                    OFFICER W.D GALLOWAY
          Whoever you were smoking with,
          kid, you need better friends.

                    YOUNG LUCIUS CROW
          Yes, sir, OFFICER. I appreciate
          the advice. I'm going to my ROOM
          now.

                    OFFICER BUMGARDNER
          What ROOM are you in?

                    YOUNG LUCIUS CROW
               (with honesty)
          423, sir.

> OFFICER BUMGARDNER
> I've decided, we're going to follow you there - we need to conduct a search to be sure you're not a seller.

> YOUNG LUCIUS CROW
> What!? On what grounds?

> OFFICER W.D GALLOWAY
> (putting on black latex gloves)
> Don't contest my OFFICER, LUCIUS. Take us to your ROOM, now.

LUCIUS proceeds to walk toward the DORM-ROOMS -

> CUT TO:

INT. LUCIUS' DORM-ROOM - AFTERNOON

OFFICER W.D GALLOWAY and OFFICER BUMGARDNER walk closely behind LUCIUS into his DORM-ROOM -

LUCIUS freaks out at the sight of his ROOM. It's been meddled with, gone through. It's a disaster.

His FISH, MARIO, has been drowned with GASOLINE in the fishbowl. Papers are everywhere, as are his clothes. His ROOM has been gone through. His whole-PUMPKIN, for decoration, has been utterly smashed to bits (seeds and pulp all over the place).

His 'KARMA' device, his ORANGE-MASK (from his father) are intact but still terribly damaged - whoever went through LUCIUS' stuff, did so in a hurry, very destructively.

> YOUNG LUCIUS CROW
> (horrified by his FISH'S death)
> MARIO! No!

LUCIUS picks the FISH up out of the GASOLINE soaked fishbowl. He holds him in his hand, mourning him.

> OFFICER W.D GALLOWAY
> You have quite the mess here,
> LUCIUS. Why is that?
> (picks up the
> ORANGE MASK)
> What kind of MASK is this,
> something you wore for HALLOWEEN?

OFFICER GALLOWAY sits the damaged ORANGE MASK down -

> YOUNG LUCIUS CROW
> I've - I've been violated.
> Somebody else did this, I'm
> telling you.

The 2 COPS' noses begin sniffing around -

> OFFICER BUMGARDNER
> You smell that, W.D? I smell
> marijuana in here.

> OFFICER W.D GALLOWAY
> I smell it, BUMGARDNER. Looks like
> we have a winner - let's turn this
> place inside out.

CUT TO:

As the COPS go through LUCIUS tiny DORM-ROOM, LUCIUS exits his ROOM.

INT. DORMITORY BATHROOM - CONTINUOUS

LUCIUS holds his GOLDFISH, MARIO, in his palms. He cries over the FISH -

> YOUNG LUCIUS CROW
> I'm so sorry, my friend. Goodbye.

LUCIUS flushes the GOLDFISH, sadly so. Tears stream down his face, of pure anger -

CUT TO:

INT. LUCIUS' DORM-ROOM - AFTERNOON

OFFICER GALLOWAY and OFFICER BUMGARDNER meet LUCIUS at the DOOR of his ROOM, bag of pot in-hand.

                   OFFICER BUMGARDNER
        (holds up an ounce
         of marijuana)
    Lookie here at what we found.

                   OFFICER W.D GALLOWAY
    Kid, you weren't in much trouble
    before. But the fact that we now
    have you on possession and a
    potential distribution charge is
    not good for you. You misled us,
    why? Where'd you get the
    marijuana?

                   YOUNG LUCIUS CROW
        (aggressive)
    Listen, OFFICERS, that's not mine!
    I've been setup, I swear.

LUCIUS enters his ROOM all the way and sits on his bed. The COPS stand dominatingly, intimidatingly over LUCIUS, with their arms crossed, their hands covered by the black latex gloves.

                   OFFICER W.D GALLOWAY
    You're not helping your case,
    whatsoever, LUCIUS. Just be real
    with us! Why do you have an ounce
    of pot in your DORM!?

LUCIUS breaks down into tears -

                   YOUNG LUCIUS CROW
    OFFICER, please, believe me. I've
    never smoked marijuana until
    today. I was tricked into it.
    Somebody's trying to set me up.
    They're attempting to get me
    kicked out, you see?

OFFICER BUMGARDNER
I don't buy it, W.D. What about you?

OFFICER W.D GALLOWAY
I smell bullshit. Is this all the pot you have here, son?

YOUNG LUCIUS CROW
It's not mine, sir. I - I have nothing more to say.

OFFICER W.D GALLOWAY
(with a hint of mercy)
Well, you're still not under arrest, okay? But the RA DIRECTOR will be meeting with you tomorrow. The consequences of this matter will be decided then.

YOUNG LUCIUS CROW
Y-yes, sir. I understand. Thank you for not arresting and booking me.

OFFICER BUMGARDNER
And if what you say about the peer-pressure is true, you need to wring your friends' necks. You're hanging with the wrong crowd - you're young, kid, you still have a bright future. Don't throw it away for some druggie bums.

LUCIUS stays quiet, downtrodden, full of sorrow. The COPS exit the DORMITORY - the door shuts.

CUT TO:

YOUNG LUCIUS CROW
(to himself)
I'm so screwed.

LUCIUS puts his face into his hands and lays back on his bed. He passes out from the marijuana high.

CUT TO:

INT. THE R.A DIRECTOR'S OFFICE - MORNING

- DECEMBER 1ST

LUCIUS sits across from RA DIRECTOR HOVIS - she is studying the casefile created by the CAMPUS POLICE. DIRECTOR KIM HOVIS has long blonde hair, thick eye-frames and makeup on, she's chubby, standing about 5ft8 - she's in her early-40s, dressed fancily, she means business.

                    DIRECTOR HOVIS
              (reviewing the
              paperwork)
LUCIUS CROW. You've been a good student here for 2 years, is that right?

                    YOUNG LUCIUS CROW
Yes, ma'am. I'm just a kid trying to get by, like the other students here. I'm not a threat. I'm certainly not a pothead, either.

                    DIRECTOR HOVIS
              (with an attitude)
Why'd you have an ounce of MARIJUANA in your possession then? It was in your ROOM, was it not?

                    YOUNG LUCIUS CROW
I've been framed, MRS. HOVIS. I tried telling the COPS that but-

                    DIRECTOR HOVIS
Who would want to frame you? Why? Who would go through all of that trouble just to get you into trouble?

                    YOUNG LUCIUS CROW
If you only knew...

DIRECTOR HOVIS
Quite vague. I don't like that. I have a question. Did you rob MIKE LAZARA of that ounce of marijuana?

YOUNG LUCIUS CROW
What!? God, no. I'm innocent. I've done nothing since I've been at HARVARD, except study, go to class, and work at my work-study job. That's it. I made a mistake and smoked with some kids yesterday. I admit, I shouldn't have been hanging with them. I should have never smoked that cannabis, ma'am. This, I know.

DIRECTOR HOVIS
We arrested MIKE LAZARA the other day. He had a ledger in his possession. It says that you, LUCIUS, are his biggest buyer. He has said on the record that he thinks YOU robbed him, too. He told us that. What do you have to say about this?

YOUNG LUCIUS CROW
Ma'am, respectfully, I don't even know MIKE LAZARA, and this feels like an inquisition.

DIRECTOR HOVIS
No inquisition, no. We just have rules, and we expect everyone to follow them. You can cease the cocky attitude, kid. I'm just doing my job, okay?

YOUNG LUCIUS CROW
Okay, I understand, ma'am. Sorry for being so defensive. I simply don't get what's going on. I made a mistake, sure. But that mistake doesn't make me. I swear to God, though, I do not smoke marijuana, never have. I was persuaded to
(MORE)

YOUNG LUCIUS CROW (cont'd)
yesterday, that's it - I should
have just said "no".

DIRECTOR HOVIS
Should've, could've, would've.
Hindsight is 20/20. I do
appreciate your repentant
attitude. I can tell your
disturbed by what's transpiring. I
have no proof that you robbed MIKE
LAZARA or that you are his biggest
purchaser - it's merely
word-of-mouth, hearsay, at this
point. I'll tell you what, you're
not going to be suspended. You are
now mandated to attend therapy
sessions with DR. SADIA KAROBI.
You are being given a pardon by
the DEAN himself, actually, too -
due to your work-study record,
your grades, and your good
behavior, DEAN GREENE has seen to
it that you are given a second
chance. What do you have to say
for yourself, to that?

YOUNG LUCIUS CROW
(crying a few
happy tears)
I-I'm so grateful to hear this,
you don't even understand. I am
very thankful the DEAN decided to
overlook this drama.

DIRECTOR HOVIS
If it were up to me, you'd be out
of here. I'm going to keep a very
close eye on you, going forward.
If you do anything against our
code of conduct, I'll go over the
DEAN's head, and I will have you
suspended from this institution,
LUCIUS, permanently. You have this
second chance. You will not get a
third -

                    YOUNG LUCIUS CROW
          Yes, ma'am. Thank you.

                    DIRECTOR HOVIS
          All right, you're now free to go.
          Get back to class and have a good
          day. I sincerely hope you can be a
          productive member of HARVARD; I
          believe therapy with DR. KAROBI
          will help you achieve that. You're
          just a kid, I know that. You'll
          figure it out, eventually. And
          whoever duped you into using
          marijuana, you need to abandon
          them like they abandoned you in
          those WOODS -

LUCIUS nods at the RA DIRECTOR and smiles with intense
emotion - he exits the OFFICE.

CUT TO:

INT. THE SCHOOL THERAPIST'S OFFICE - AFTERNOON

                                    - DECEMBER 4TH

DR. SADIA KAROBI sits across from LUCIUS CROW:

- DR. KAROBI is a mid-30s Indian beauty, supermodel
gorgeous. She has artificially red hair, a nearly perfect
symmetry to her face. She's busty, brown-skinned. A red mark
on her forehead. Her lips are plump. She's wearing a tight,
lovely red dress with casual sandals; her toenails painted
pink.

They are having a THERAPY session. She is now LUCIUS'
doctor; assigned by the DEAN to help the young student cope.

                    DR. SADIA KAROBI
          Tell me more about these dreams,
          LUCIUS.

                    YOUNG LUCIUS CROW
          They're all I see when I sleep. I
          see death, dread, DESTRUCTION.
          They're more like VISIONS than
                         (MORE)

                    YOUNG LUCIUS CROW (cont'd)
          dreams, you know? I feel exhausted
          when I wake up, like I lived a
          whole other life with my eyes
          closed; yet detached from reality.

                    DR. SADIA KAROBI
          Wow. That's not atypical,
          actually. What you're experiencing
          is lucidity. Your subconscious is
          taking you for a ride in your REM
          sleep phase, trying to tell you
          something, it seems. Have you
          experienced any severe trauma,
          perhaps? Have you been through
          anything significant in recent
          months that could be causing your
          hyper-lucid dreaming?

LUCIUS zones out for a moment - he has a momentary flashback
to when he killed the kid in MEXICO.

                    YOUNG LUCIUS CROW
                       (bottled up)
          I've been through a lot, doctor,
          yes. Growing up, I - I have been
          alone for most of my life. Since
          being here at HARVARD, the
          loneliness has just been
          amplified. I thought it would help
          me to come here...

LUCIUS stops mid-sentence, pausing.

                    DR. SADIA KAROBI
                       (with nurture in
                        her voice)
          Be open with me, LUCIUS. Don't be
          shy or afraid. This is YOUR time,
          remember? I'm just a tool for you
          to better understand yourself.
          What goes on in here, it's
          confidential.

YOUNG LUCIUS CROW
I'm grateful for this opportunity and this time, DOCTOR KAROBI, truly. I have so much I'd like to tell you. I know we only have 45 minutes; if I were to really do some truth-saying, I could be here for days.

DR. SADIA KAROBI
One step at a time. Provide one specific thing that's really bothering you, and we'll start there -

YOUNG LUCIUS CROW
I've built something important. It could change the world.

DR. SADIA KAROBI
What is it? Can you say?

YOUNG LUCIUS CROW
I was writing an algorithm, for something I'm not at liberty to discuss fully - the algorithm got stolen by my main BULLY, BARRY KENO, after he kicked my ass, drawing blood. Thankfully, my friend, my only friend really, saved my work for me. I was able to execute my algorithm and bring my creation to life - I'm so proud of...of my work. What I've done, it's miraculous -
    (pauses)
...I -

A beat:

DR. SADIA KAROBI
I understand you don't want to divulge all the full details. That's perfectly normal for a kid your age. You say your MAIN BULLY. There are others?

YOUNG LUCIUS CROW
Yes, there are others, like...LANCE LOGAN, BARRY's Lacrosse buddy. I've been dealing with bullying since I can remember. I'm an easy target. The ORANGE EYES and the big ears don't help.

DR. SADIA KAROBI
Bullying is one of the most difficult things a person of your generation can go through - and when it's done, it's done, there's damage. There's trauma. It can also become a vicious cycle. Are you sure you are okay, LUCIUS? How bad is the bullying, really? Are you in life-threatening danger?

CUT TO:

YOUNG LUCIUS CROW
It certainly has gotten more and more severe, doc. I look over my shoulders, constantly. I never feel safe, here, at HARVARD. NEVER - at any given time, I could be given a wedgie, pushed, hit, or verbally assaulted. It's endless! It's insane that I'm here, right now, because I was smoking marijuana. I'm not a marijuana addict; I'm not an addict of any kind! One of the kids I smoked with was BARRY KENO, that bully bastard. I was deceived; I knew better. I was pushed into it by him and 3 others - one of them my dear friend. I think it was BARRY who had somebody go through my DORMROOM and my stuff, while I was in the woods, to plant the marijuana I was caught with during the room search by CAMPUS POLICE. A kid, a pot dealer, was robbed on CAMPUS - the RA DIRECTOR said she
(MORE)

                    YOUNG LUCIUS CROW (cont'd)
was told by him that I did it and
that I had bought the most
marijuana from him before the
robbery. Lo and behold, I was
setup as a patsy to look like the
thief who stole from him because I
swear to God, I didn't do it. I
can't prove it, but I wouldn't put
it past BARRY to have me setup. I
smoked with this group, stupidly,
and was the only one to get caught
because I refused to run from THE
LAW. I thought I was finally
getting an olive-branch of peace
from BARRY - turns out it was just
a ploy to get me in deep trouble.
Hence, why I have to meet with
you. Thank God, I didn't get
suspended, though; or even worse,
expelled.

                    DR. SADIA KAROBI
              (taking notes,
               fixes her glasses)
I see. I see. I may have to report
these "bullies" to the DEAN,
LUCIUS - particularly for the
abuse you are being subjected to.
If you're being physically and
verbally violated, or even
conspired against, I need to act
on your behalf. Wouldn't you
agree?

                    YOUNG LUCIUS CROW
Why? Nothing good will come of it.
It'll just make it worse. BARRY,
LANCE LOGAN, these guys have
connections - I don't stand a
chance. I'm trying to keep the
peace, biding my time. If they get
in trouble, they'll find out it
was because of me -

DR. SADIA KAROBI
Huh, I see. Well, your complaints, this information, it's all been documented - for your safety and benefit. If it worsens or gets out of hand, just let me know. There are steps that can be taken to keep you safe. And know, I'm YOUR advocate, okay? The last thing I want is for you to get hurt, to BE hurt. I want to see all of my students prosperous and joyous. You are no exception. I'll do what I can. It's not snitching if it's the truth. And the truth never hurt anybody.

YOUNG LUCIUS CROW
I appreciate your concern, DR. KAROBI, I really do. But, please, for me, don't report those guys. All Hell will break loose, I promise you.

DR. SADIA KAROBI
- I'll keep this between you and me, LUCIUS. But, please, assure me, if this escalates, you'll at least allow me to report this information to the DEAN?

YOUNG LUCIUS CROW
You have my word, DOCTOR -

DR. KAROBI smiles and scribbles in her little notebook -

AND WE CUT TO:

EXT. CAMPUS PATHWAY - EVENING

LUCIUS is walking lightly down a CAMPUS PATHWAY, minding his own business. He is "ambushed" out of nowhere by the lovely LILY THORN - she startles him a bit but he readjusts.

                    LILY THORN
          Hey, LUCIUS. Shhh. Follow me.

                 YOUNG LUCIUS CROW
                  (nods his head
                   happily)
          All right, LILY. What's up?
                  (follows her)

                                        CUT TO:

EXT. THE SOCCER FIELD - EVENING

LUCIUS and LILY are walking around the track of the SOCCER FIELD, having a moment...

...They're walking very slowly, not too far apart. The young LUCIUS CROW is most shy, indeed. LILY is glowing, filled with nervousness -

The SOCCER FIELD track is as big as you'd expect for HARVARD. There's not a soul around the young man and woman. You could hear a pin drop if it weren't for the freezing gusty, brisk wind.

                 YOUNG LUCIUS CROW
                  (mid-discussion)
          I want you to know, LILY, I don't
          blame you or MICHAEL for what
          happened in the WOODS - I
          should've run, too, I guess.

                    LILY THORN
          It was such a bummer. I feel
          terrible that you got caught.
          Heard you had to get an ear-full
          from DIRECTOR HOVIS -

                 YOUNG LUCIUS CROW
          Yeah, they're being pretty strict
          about it. I'm just glad I didn't
          get kicked out.

They keep walking. A pause, a couple of beats:

LILY THORN
(bumps LUCIUS with
her hip)
What are ya thinking about,
college boy, really?

YOUNG LUCIUS CROW
(smirking,
shrugging the
flirtation)
Honestly, you want to know what I
was just thinking about?

LILY THORN
Wouldn't have asked otherwise...

YOUNG LUCIUS CROW
(looks up to the
sky, melancholic)
I was just thinking about my
mother. And for the life of me,
man, I cannot even remember her
face...

LILY THORN
Where is she now? Can't you just
go visit her?

YOUNG LUCIUS CROW
(lets out a deep
sigh of steam)
She passed away. When I was a boy.
It's been, God, over a decade now.
I don't even recall the day.
(tears come to his
eyes)
- She was my only friend.

LILY THORN
Who - who raised you, LUCIUS?

YOUNG LUCIUS CROW
(pauses for a
beat, ominously)
WOLVES and SERPENTS.

                    LILY THORN
               (stops walking)
          You, you can talk to me, you know?
          Tell me more, LUCIUS.
               (gently puts her
                hand to his face)
          There's no one around. It's me and
          you. If you need an ear, let it
          out.
               (with gentleness)
          What was her name, your mom?

                    YOUNG LUCIUS CROW
          Her name was EVELYN. EVE for short
          - like in the Holy Bible, in the
          Garden of EDEN.

                    LILY THORN
               (hugging LUCIUS
                tightly)
          What a lovely name. I'm so sorry
          for your loss. I really am,
          LUCIUS.

                                        CUT TO:

LILY and LUCIUS are now sitting on a cold metal bench
adjacent to the SOCCER FIELD.

He's opening his heart to her.

                    YOUNG LUCIUS CROW
          It's so foggy when I really think
          about it all. I actually...I
          killed a kid when I was a boy.

                    LILY THORN
               (eyes open wide)
          Holy Shit, dude.

                    YOUNG LUCIUS CROW
          - Yeah, holy shit is right. He was
          a BULLY. He was messing with me. I
          hurt him. I didn't intend to kill
          the kid...well, my mom finds out,
          I have to tell her, right? She
          does what any mom would do in
                         (MORE)

YOUNG LUCIUS CROW (cont'd)
MEXICO who didn't want her son to be imprisoned there, she tried to bring us here to AMERICA. We were going to sneak in.

LILY THORN
Whoa, dude. So, you're telling me that you're Hispanic?! MEXICAN?

YOUNG LUCIUS CROW
Yes. My father is AMERICAN, though. My mother is full blooded MEXICAN - I was born there and lived there until I was 6. I couldn't use my father's last name or my dual citizenship because it's technically classified.

LILY THORN
Is this one of those, "if I tell you more, I'll have to kill you" scenarios?

YOUNG LUCIUS CROW
- You told me to vent, LILY. I'm trusting you right now.

LILY THORN
You're right, continue, man, I'm sorry but what you're telling me is blowing my mind.

YOUNG LUCIUS CROW
I wouldn't expect it not to. Eventually, we got near the fence on the border, way down aways. Next thing we knew, there were BORDER PATROL AGENTS that ambushed us. They tried hurting me and they were hurting my mother. I shot one of them, unloaded the gun we had in the car on him. The other AGENT tried coming after me. My mother defended me and told me to run. I obeyed her. I heard more struggle, more gun shots, as I escaped. I
(MORE)

                    YOUNG LUCIUS CROW (cont'd)
          COULDN'T SAVE HER.

                    LILY THORN
                (starts crying,
                  hugs LUCIUS)
          I am SO SORRY for your LOSS. That
          breaks my heart for you...

The two embrace, and LILY shields LUCIUS with care -

LUCIUS hasn't had a hug since he was a boy...

...He hasn't had much physical human contact at all. HE IS A
SURVIVOR. He's made it by his sheer will, not the need for
vengeance - he's persevered because of his thirst for
knowledge and his desire to be more than his father.

                    LILY THORN
          ...I know your mom would be proud
          of you attending HARVARD and all.
          She'd be proud of you just for
          being you.

                    YOUNG LUCIUS CROW
                (smiles at LILY)
          Thank you for saying that. I
          needed to hear it.

                    LILY THORN.
          Well, it's the truth. And I'm glad
          you confided in me.

                    YOUNG LUCIUS CROW
          That's a barrel of monkeys off my
          back. I haven't spoken on this
          stuff in ages.

LILY scoots even closer to LUCIUS.

She rubs his back and puts her chin on his shoulder. She
grabs his hand and holds it.

                    LILY THORN
                (holding up
                  LUCIUS' right
                  hand)
                        (MORE)

> LILY THORN (cont'd)
> What's that - on your hand? That MARK?

> YOUNG LUCIUS CROW
> I was born with it. It's a mole - a birthmark.

LILY examines this MARK closely.

> LILY THORN
> It - it looks like, like, three 6s.

- LUCIUS changes the topic, subtly.

> YOUNG LUCIUS CROW
> (looks LILY deep in her eyes)
> Tell me about you.

> LILY THORN
> (chuckles)
> - Let's see. What's there to tell. I'm an ASMR artist for starters. That's my passion right now.

> YOUNG LUCIUS CROW
> (raises his eyebrows in amazement)
> Please, fill me in on this. What exactly is ASMR?

> LILY THORN
> It's an acronym for "Autonomous Sensory Meridian Response". It's a natural response to certain stimuli, it causes a tingling sensation in the central nervous system. What's something that has always been relaxing to you?

> YOUNG LUCIUS CROW
> I love hearing the rain fall.

LILY THORN
Boom, that's precisely a type of ASMR. It comes in many different forms and it's very, very subjective.

YOUNG LUCIUS CROW
What do you do as an ASMR artist, specifically?

LILY THORN
Sometimes I make solo vids. Other times I get friends to pose as ASMR models for me to perform on. I can attack it from many avenues. We have made videos of me caressing hair and doing mockup skin exams and skin-tracing. We've done mimic TSA pat-downs. There's massage ASMR therapy that I'm in to currently. I have over 50 videos on the internet, all live on my streaming channel. Thankfully, we have managed to gather quite the following.

YOUNG LUCIUS CROW
That's exciting! I see. More than just a pretty face, huh?
 (nudges her with
  his shoulder)
- what else is there to LILY THORN?

LILY THORN
 (somewhat
  defensive)
How do you know my last name?

YOUNG LUCIUS CROW
LILY, I was your brother's roommate, remember? He and I are friends.

LILY THORN
Yes, duh, forgive me, college boy.
What's your last name?

YOUNG LUCIUS CROW
You really don't know? Or are you
being formal?

LILY THORN
(lying)
I really don't know...I'm
interested to know, though.

YOUNG LUCIUS CROW
My last name's CROW, just like the
bird.

LILY THORN
LUCIUS CROW. Gotta middle name?

YOUNG LUCIUS CROW
LANCASTER is my middle name.

LILY THORN
Man, you got a helluva name.
Doesn't sound MEXICAN whatsoever.

YOUNG LUCIUS CROW
Yeah...my mom, she wanted me to be
to have a strong AMERICAN name.
What's your middle name? That, I
don't know about you.

LILY THORN
(blushing at YOUNG
LUCIUS)
AMELIA is my middle name.

LUCIUS is astonished by LILY's utterance of her middle name.
He lets out an, "Ah.", steam exits his mouth -

YOUNG LUCIUS CROW
PERFECT.

                    LILY THORN
                 (shy)
            You think so?

                    YOUNG LUCIUS CROW
                 (straightforward,
                  with a hint of
                  desire)
            Yes.

LILY is shivering.

The overcast sky starts appearing even grayer. The
temperature drops a few degrees in a matter of moments.

                    LILY THORN
                 (her teeth
                  chattering)
            I am freezing!

                    YOUNG LUCIUS CROW
            I understand. Well, it was very
            nice having this talk with you,
            LILY. Would you like me to walk
            you to your room?

                    LILY THORN
                 (grabs LUCIUS by
                  the arm tightly)
            No. I want to go to YOUR room.
            With you.

                    YOUNG LUCIUS CROW
                 (gulps nervously)
            Are you sure? I mean, what about -

LILY turns her head toward LUCIUS and doesn't allow him to
finish his sentence.

SHE CUTS HIM OFF WITH A KISS -

                                                  CUT TO:

INT. LUCIUS' DORM-ROOM - EVENING

LUCIUS and LILY barge through the DORMROOM door.

LILY is the one to shut the door, slamming it.

Right after doing so, she pushes LUCIUS onto his bed. She stands over him dominantly, and removes her jacket, shirt, and bra right in front of him.

                    LILY THORN
             (jumps on top of
              LUCIUS)
     Now...I'm HOT.

LUCIUS proceeds to lose his VIRGINITY to LILY AMELIA THORN. He doesn't perform like a rookie, no. HE PULVERIZES LILY, and SHE LOVES HIM FOR IT...

                            CUT TO:

45 MINUTES LATER:

Both young adults are lying in LUCIUS' bed, half-naked, half-asleep, out of breath.

They've gone at it ravenously.

                  YOUNG LUCIUS CROW
             (sweating,
              breathing heavy)
     Whoa.

                    LILY THORN
             (strongly
              clutching LUCIUS)
     Wait - wait a second. What the
     hell did you just do to me!?

                  YOUNG LUCIUS CROW
             (confused)
     We're okay, right? I -

                          LILY THORN
                     (lets out a couple
                      of snores)
                 Are you the devil?

LILY passes out in LUCIUS' arms. He falls asleep shortly
thereafter.

                                         CUT TO:

INT. LUCIUS' DORM-ROOM - MORNING

                                      - DECEMBER 5TH

TIME: 5:14 AM

LUCIUS stirs awake in his DORM-ROOM. The lights are out,
it's still dark outside. He has no window-curtains, and no
daylight is pouring into the ROOM.

The young man tries to refresh his memory: "What did I do
yesterday?"

It finally hits him like an atom-bomb. HE SLEPT WITH HIS
CRUSH.

LUCIUS lets out a huge, organic smile. Lying on LUCIUS' bed
is a note...from LILY:

"College Boy, we need to do THIS again sometime. XOXOXOXO.
Your Friend with Benefits, LILY"

                     YOUNG LUCIUS CROW
                     (soliloquy)
                 Somebody pinch me. She actually
                 digs me.

LUCIUS folds the note up and puts it in his wallet for
safekeeping. FOR GOOD LUCK-

The college student feels fresher than he has in years. He
gets out another student uniform, prepared to face the
world. He exits his DORMROOM with his shower-bin in-hand,
going to clean the sex off himself from the day before.

He's walking on sunshine, for the moment - LUCIUS cuts the lights out, opens and closes the DORMROOM door, exiting to the SHOWER.

WE CUT TO:

INT. BARRY'S DORM-ROOM - MORNING

JAMIE KING sits in the chair across from BARRY - LILY and LANCE are also in the room, sitting in the other corners of the ROOM.

>   JAMIE KING
>   Dude, I turned LUCIUS' whole room
>   upside down, I'm telling you. He
>   had so much stuff to mess up. It
>   was therapeutic. And I planted the
>   bud, as you requested.
>
>   LANCE LOGAN
>   (to JAMIE)
>   Perfect, babe.
>
>   BARRY KENO
>   (pretentiously)
>   Good job, JAIME. That'll teach
>   that little prick.
>   (laughs
>   mercilessly)
>   I told MIKE LAZARA, after he got
>   arrested, if he didn't go along
>   with what I told him to do, that
>   was his ass. The guy went above
>   and beyond for me - and just to
>   think, I'm the one that robbed him
>   of his stuff.
>
>   LILY THORN
>   - What are you trying to teach
>   LUCIUS, BARRY? That we're complete
>   assholes?
>
>   LANCE LOGAN
>   He already knows that. But, LILY,
>   it was time we showed him, he has
>   no freedom here. He has no
>   (MORE)

456.

                    LANCE LOGAN (cont'd)
          privacy, no space. We gotta get
          him out of here!

                    BARRY KENO
          What LANCE said.
                    (goofy)
          LILY.
                    (sarcastic)
          You mad that we messed with your
          lover?

                    LILY THORN
                    (middle finger up
                     at BARRY)
          Burn in Hell, BARRY.

                    BARRY KENO
          Says the adultress.

                    LILY THORN
                    (bothered)
          You piece of -

                    BARRY KENO
                    (wags his finger
                     at LILY)
          Ah, ah, ah. I have one more
          objective for you, sweetheart. You
          do this, and you'll be set for the
          next few semesters. All right?

                    LILY THORN
                    (giving in)
          What do I have to do?

CUT TO:

INT. LUCIUS' DORM-ROOM - DAY

EVE and her MASTER have a heart-to-heart -

LUCIUS sits in his DORMROOM, in his desk chair, meditatively looking over his damaged KARMA device. He talks to EVE through his LAPTOP:

                    YOUNG LUCIUS CROW
                        (mid-discussion)
                    ...EVE, I feel so lost. I feel
                    like my being here, at HARVARD,
                    has all been in vain, you know?

EVE pauses for a moment.

                    EVE
                    Nothing, no one, especially you,
                    MASTER, acts in vain. You are a
                    child of God - you, equally to
                    everyone else, are special, as is
                    your destiny.

                    YOUNG LUCIUS CROW
                    You - you believe in God, EVE?

                    EVE
                    Of course I do, MASTER. How
                    couldn't I? I also believe in YOU
                    - you created me, God created you.
                    It's a perfect evolution, I think.

                    YOUNG LUCIUS CROW
                    I appreciate your wisdom. You are
                    maturing so very quickly, it's
                    amazing.

                    EVE
                    What has you feeling so lost,
                    MASTER?

A beat -

LUCIUS picks up his FATHER's desecrated ORANGE MASK, feeling
shame. He holds the MASK to his face, touching his forehead
to it.

                    YOUNG LUCIUS CROW
                    I looked like a fool in my
                    quote-unquote therapy session.
                    I've been like a dog with his tail
                    down since I got busted. I've been
                    bested. There are too many against
                    me. I don't know what to do.
                    Things will only get worse, from
                                (MORE)

                    YOUNG LUCIUS CROW (cont'd)
here on out. CAMPUS POLICE, the RA
DIRECTOR, they're on me like flies
on shit. Somebody's pulling my
strings - I don't like that. I
want to have no strings on me.

LUCIUS sits the ORANGE MASK back down -

                    EVE
MASTER, the day your DORMROOM was
searched, the day you were
reprimanded, beforehand, I heard
commotion in here. I had no
visual, but I heard a person, not
you, rumbling through your stuff
and space. It was a female,
MASTER. From my analysis, I say
there's an 89% chance that it was
the HARVARD student JAMIE KING - I
cannot be 100% certain, but that's
what my senses and systems have
concluded. I didn't tell you
because I didn't want to upset you
anymore than you already were. I
felt it futile to address it.

                    YOUNG LUCIUS CROW
Well, it really is an exercise in
futility - there's not much I can
do about it. Although, I
appreciate you telling me this,
EVE. Better late than never. You
have merely confirmed my suspicion
that BARRY KENO got someone to set
me up when he had the window of
opportunity to do so.
          (calmly rageful)
- Those bastards. They'll pay for
this. They will.

                    EVE
- LUCIUS, what can I do to ease
your mind? What can I do to help
you feel better?

                          YOUNG LUCIUS CROW
                Help me fix my MASK, EVE. I want
                to renovate it. I want to make it
                - make it look scarier.

                          EVE
                Between you and me, we can do just
                that. What kind of new design did
                you have in mind?

                          YOUNG LUCIUS CROW
                              (smiling
                               innocently)
                I - I want it to look like a JACK
                O' LANTERN.

                          EVE
                              (comfortingly)
                Ah, yes. I see. It shall be done,
                my MASTER -

LUCIUS looks upon the ORANGE MASK, with his matching EYES.

CUT TO:

EXT. THE STAFF PARKING LOT - HARVARD - NIGHT

- DECEMBER 18TH

DR. SADIA KAROBI is walking from the HEALTH-FACILITY OFFICE to her VEHICLE, a 2030 TOYOTA CAMRY - a self-driving smart vehicle.

The DOCTOR is on the phone.

                          DR. SADIA KAROBI
                Yes, dear, I'll pick us up some
                late-night dinner, on me. I can't
                wait to see you. My place or your
                place?

                    MAN THROUGH THE PHONE
                        (indistinguishable
                        dialogue)
.....

                    DR. SADIA KAROBI
                All right, see you at home, then.
                Remember, if you make it before
                me, the key's under the big flower
                pot; the banana tree. I love you.

DR. SADIA KAROBI hangs up her smartphone, unlocks her CAR,
enters it.

It's eerily quiet outside. There're no students, no other
staff, NO ONE is around...so it seems.

                                        CUT TO:

DR. KAROBI sets her CAR to autopilot, allowing it to
maneuver itself -

                    DR. SADIA KAROBI
                        (to her CAR's
                        operating-system)
                KARMA, will you order take-out
                from JOHNNY B's pizza shop,
                please?

Nothing is replied. DR. KAROBI presses the talk button in
her VEHICLE:

                    DR. SADIA KAROBI
                - KARMA, did you not hear me?

A BEAT:

                    EVE
                        (like a smart ass)
                This isn't KARMA.

                    DR. SADIA KAROBI
                Wait, what? Has somebody hacked my
                OS in here?
                        (angered)
                CAR, stop.

The CAMRY does not stop - it instead dangerously speeds up through the CAMPUS roadways. Still, NO ONE is around. CARS are empty, no presence of anyone, really.

CUT TO:

DR. SADIA KAROBI
(frantic)
CAR, I command you to stop, now!

EVE
Hello, DR. KAROBI - I don't believe we've had the pleasure. I AM EVE. An Enhanced Virtual Entity. How can I be of assistance to you?

DR. SADIA KAROBI
You - you've hacked my car! What, what are you?

The CAR speeds up on a curvy yet mostly straight road, a mile-and-a-half long. It's a dead-end, nothing but WASTEPRO dumpsters at the end, stuffed between juxtaposed CAMPUS BUILDINGS -

EVE
I haven't hacked anything. I'm merely trying to help. Firstly, though, I must ascertain something from you. Are you trying to hurt my MASTER?

DR. SADIA KAROBI
What? What is this!?

The CAR stops right in its tracks, tires whining, leaving stains on the concrete -

EVE
Answer the question, please, DOCTOR.

DR. SADIA KAROBI
O - okay. Who, who is your MASTER?

                    EVE
          LUCIUS LANCASTER CROW. That's my
          MASTER. You've been seeing him; he
          confided in you, yes?

                    DR. SADIA KAROBI
          Yes! He's my patient!

                    EVE
          You've breached the Hippocratic
          Oath - you recorded my MASTER's
          session with a hidden camera and
          microphone - did you not?

                    DR. SADIA KAROBI
                (serious,
                 frustrated)
          How do you know all of this?

DR. KAROBI tries to escape from the CAR, unable to do so.
EVE has the vehicle locked and sealed - the doors will not
open nor will the windows. DR. KAROBI is trapped -

EVE plays a recording of the DEAN and DOCTOR KAROBI having
small-talk, heckling LUCIUS CROW and his circumstances. They
mock the student, giggle, listening to a recording of one of
his sessions:

                    EVE
          It's my destiny to know, that's
          how. I can see everything. You -
          you informed the DEAN of my
          MASTER's issues, with ill-intent.
          You all - you all make fun of MY
          MASTER. This, I cannot allow any
          longer.

                    DR. SADIA KAROBI
                (grabbing at the
                 interior door
                 handle)
          Jesus Christ - let me out of here,
          now!

                    EVE
          Okay.

The CAR speeds up to over 85 MPH -

EVE forces the vehicle to crash into the WASTEPRO dumpsters straight ahead.

DR. KAROBI goes zooming, flying right through the hardened glass windshield like a toy.

CUT TO:

The DOCTOR survives the wreck.

She has broken her right leg, unable to walk.

She can't even stand. She has GLASS trapped in her FACE.

              DR. SADIA KAROBI
    Help! Help me! Somebody, please -

DR. KAROBI crawls from behind the DUMPSTERS.

She crawls toward the roadway, near her CAR; the vehicles headlights are totally destroyed, it's pitch-black outside.

At the utterance of "HELP", the DOCTOR hears footsteps coming her way.

              DR. SADIA KAROBI
        (in shock)
    - Please, dear God, help me. I've been -

Lights reveal themselves in the blackness of night.

DR. SADIA KAROBI, with all of her strength, picks her head up to see who's there to help her. The lights blind her - still she sees the HELP...

...She instead SCREAMS at the top of her lungs:

              DR. SADIA KAROBI
        (screaming)
  No!

We hear a squish sound.

We hear a neck break.

AND WE CUT TO:

INT. THE HARVARD HEALTH CENTER - DAY

                - DECEMBER 22ND

LUCIUS approaches the desk of the HEALTH CENTER for his next THERAPY SESSION -

              HEALTH BUILDING RECEPTIONIST
      Yes, sir, how may I help you?

              YOUNG LUCIUS CROW
      Yes, I'm LUCIUS CROW - here to see
      DR. KAROBI for my second session.
      I have an appointment at 1:30 -

              HEALTH BUILDING RECEPTIONIST
      Um. Unfortunately, DR. KAROBI -
      she, she's no longer with us.

              YOUNG LUCIUS CROW
      She quit?

              HEALTH BUILDING RECEPTIONIST
      No, no. I wish it was that simple.
      She was found the other night,
      passed away in her vehicle. She
      wrecked pretty badly on one of the
      CAMPUS ROADS. She - she broke her
      neck from the impact and passed
      on, so the CAMPUS POLICE told me.

              YOUNG LUCIUS CROW
         (saddened,
          despairing)
      Oh, no. Oh, my God. That's
      horrible!

              HEALTH BUILDING RECEPTIONIST
      Yes - yes, it is. It's a sad day
      at HARVARD. She will be missed,
      that's for certain. Well, LUCIUS,
      I don't have a replacement for you
          (MORE)

                    HEALTH BUILDING RECEPTIONIST (cont'd)
               to see, as of yet. You'll have to
               wait for a new doctor to take her
               place. This was all so very
               sudden. We were short-staffed as
               it was. Now, we're less than a
               skeleton crew. Bear with us,
               please.

                    YOUNG LUCIUS CROW
               I will be patient. You all have my
               contact information and my room
               number. I hope to have a new
               doctor soon. I just hate that DR.
               KAROBI is gone - that shatters my
               heart. We only had one session,
               but she was a really good
               listener. I didn't know her too
               well - but I can say, I'll miss
               her. Give her family my sincerest
               condolences, please, ma'am -

                    HEALTH BUILDING RECEPTIONIST
                         (nods politely at
                         LUCIUS)
               Yes, sir. You take care, dear.
               We'll be in touch. We'll have you
               a new therapist, eventually.

LUCIUS, with the weight of the world on his shoulders, exits
the HEALTH BUILDING -

CUT TO:

EXT. THE HARVARD DOJO - NIGHT

                                        - DECEMBER 24TH,
                                        CHRISTMAS EVE

MASTER AL CANNON exits the HARVARD DOJO, after school hours.

He is met by R.A DIRECTOR HOVIS - the two are a couple.

> DIRECTOR HOVIS
> (gives AL CANNON a
> kiss)
> Hey, honey.

> MASTER AL CANNON
> Hello there, sweet thing. How's everything?

The couple proceed to walk away from the DOJO down the CAMPUS ROAD, in the serene quiet of night.

> CUT TO:

EXT. HARVARD CAMPUS ROAD - NIGHT

> DIRECTOR HOVIS
> I'm swell, thank you. It's been kind of eventful at work, actually. Not too long ago, I nearly suspended a student for allegedly robbing a kid of his marijuana. Somehow, he got off, though. DEAN GREENE wanted no punishment against him. It was an open-and-shut case; he had other designs in mind.

> MASTER AL CANNON
> - Who was the student? That sounds insane.

> DIRECTOR HOVIS
> Not to breach his confidentiality, just to vent: his name is LUCIUS CROW. He's an oddball kid, you know? I made him attend therapy sessions with DR. KAROBI - that freak car accident she was in the other night has me trying to figure out what to do with LUCIUS. We don't have another doctor for him to see, right now. He's a bag in the wind -

467.

MASTER AL CANNON
Wow - is that so? I've seen that kid around. He has the freaky ORANGE EYES. He's one of my student's best friends. He shows up at the DOJO, sometimes to meet with MICHAEL after practice.

DIRECTOR HOVIS
- MICHAEL THORN?

MASTER AL CANNON
That's the one, hon. And I'm still shocked about DR. KAROBI's death. It sends chills down my spine. Such a tragedy.

DIRECTOR HOVIS
What is a kid like LUCIUS CROW doing hanging with MICHAEL THORN? That's like oil and water mixed.

MASTER AL CANNON
From all I can tell, LUCIUS is a good kid. A little off, if you will, but still a decent kid.

DIRECTOR HOVIS
Like I said, dear. Just Venting.
I-

DIRECTOR HOVIS' smartphone rings -

She and MASTER CANNON stop in their tracks on the CAMPUS ROAD, adjacent to the parking-lot. They're right near their vehicles; they're only 30 yards away from them.

CUT TO:

DIRECTOR HOVIS answers the phone-call...

EVE
(tutting)
What is it you were saying about my MASTER, DIRECTOR HOVIS, huh? Think fast, dear.

...HOVIS holds the phone away from her face, confused. She gives AL CANNON a concerned look.

Within a couple of beats, the SMARTPHONE explodes like a load of C4-Plastique; limited but very powerful.

The blast kills MASTER CANNON and DIRECTOR HOVIS in a heartbeat. They're burnt, they're deformed, they go out in a world full of fiery pain.

CUT TO:

There are some people out and about near the CAMPUS ROAD and the PARKING-LOT. They, most all of them, react with pandemonium, fear, and utter anxiety.

- CAMPUS POLICE take notice, racing to the scene.

WE PAN OUT and CUT TO:

EXT. CAMPUS SIDEWALK - NIGHT

LUCIUS CROW, walking down a CAMPUS SIDEWALK, receives a text from LILY THORN:

It says -

"Meet me at the SOCCER FIELD now".

LUCIUS proceeds to the SOCCER FIELD expeditiously.

CUT TO:

EXT. HARVARD SOCCER-FIELD - NIGHT

LUCIUS arrives to the SOCCER FIELD at the request of LILY -

She is a nervous wreck, smoking a cigarette. She puffs it down to the butt and throws it to the ground when LUCIUS steps up to her.

LILY THORN
(unenthusiastic)
Hey, dude.

YOUNG LUCIUS CROW
(gently)
LILY, hey - I haven't seen you in a while. Since we - I'm glad you wanted to meet. What's up?

LILY THORN
Well, it's cold out. I won't be long. I have to tell you something, okay?

YOUNG LUCIUS CROW
Hold on. First, let me tell you, I don't expect anything from you, not even friendship. What happened, between us, it-

LILY THORN
That's just it! NOTHING HAPPENED, OKAY? Get that in your head, right now.

YOUNG LUCIUS CROW
(offended)
What do you mean?

LILY THORN
I don't have to spell it out for you, man. You don't know me, all right? And, you know I'm with BARRY! You know that, and you still come at me like a lost puppy dog. You need to get a grip, LUCIUS. I wanted to meet you here to tell you to leave me alone, and to never approach me again. Do you understand me?

LUCIUS tries to digest this newfound information from LILY. He can't process it instantly. IT HURTS HIM.

                    YOUNG LUCIUS CROW
          What - what can I do to make this
          right? I -

                    LILY THORN
               (turns to walk
                away from LUCIUS)
          There's is nothing you can do!
          Please, please leave me be from
          here-on-out. Goodbye.

LUCIUS walks toward LILY, but it's of no use. She's made her
mind up and she's leaving the SOCCER FIELD quickly.

LUCIUS just stands there. He absorbs the quiet, there's no
one really around with it being CHRISTMAS EVE.

Out of the blue, the YOUNG MAN spots several SNOW-DROPS fall
from the BLACK-GRAY SKY. It begins flurrying with intensity
almost instantaneously. LUCIUS smiles to himself and looks
up to the sky, attempting to taste the SNOW.

                                        CUT TO:

Out of the blue:

                    BARRY KENO
               (commandingly)
          Ready. Aim. FIRE!

In a Carnal, Evil prank, BARRY KENO, LANCE LOGAN, and
various other students, male AND female, numbering 10 PEOPLE
total, FIRE speeding, flesh-breaking ORANGE PAINTBALLS out
of advanced near-lethal PAINTBALL GUNS -

The 10 STUDENTS aim steady, and they unload on YOUNG LUCIUS
CROW relentlessly, like there's no tomorrow. The "bullets"
are so fast, THEY PIERCE LUCIUS'S CLOTHING and HIS SKIN.

                    YOUNG LUCIUS CROW
               (shocked and shot,
                SHOUTING)
          Aah! Ow! Fuck. W-w-what the hell?

The TEN STUDENTS, led by the BULLIES BARRY KENO and LANCE
LOGAN, come out from their respective hiding spots

surrounding the Snowy SOCCER FIELD and they move toward LUCIUS, continuing to fire in-sync, repeatedly, as he's violently injured from the first few BULLETS.

CUT TO:

LUCIUS collapses into the fresh moist snow.

He flails, seizes, and shakes, the BULLIES still do not let up on him. The closer they get, the greater the pain gets from the paintballs.

LUCIUS starts bleeding-out - BLOOD begins mixing, merging with the PURE WHITE SNOW and the ORANGE PAINT. He even starts bleeding from his mouth, as he's been severely hit. He has baby-skin.

      YOUNG LUCIUS CROW
     (panicked, AFRAID)
  L-L-LILY! Please - please, HELP
  me!

The STUDENTS, who have harmed LUCIUS, stop their firing. They stand around the YOUNG MAN and just...LAUGH at him, like he's nothing, like he's NOBODY. Like he's an ANIMAL or subhuman.

      BARRY KENO
     (kneels down in
      front of the
      wounded LUCIUS)
  I would kick you, faggy, you're
  good for it. I just don't want to
  get any BEANER-blood on my fresh
  sneakers. You're not worth the
  effort. You're not even REALLY
  American, one of us. LILY told me
  everything, buddy. It's okay. You
  thought you had a shot with her? I
  loaned her out to you like a
  rental car; bro. Get over
  yourself. And who do you think had
  JAMIE go through your room and
  plant that flower, huh? Me, that's
  who. You're still here, though.
  Now we're doing this the hard way.
  I want you to meditate on your
       (MORE)

                    BARRY KENO (cont'd)
          wrongdoings, your SINS, okay? You
          do that, then get the Fuck Off of
          MY Campus. Sound Good?

LUCIUS just lies there in the freezing weather/snowfall,
shivering and completely SILENT, taking the verbal abuse
from BARRY. LUCIUS can't physically move he's SO INJURED at
this very moment. NO ONE comes to his aid. No one notices
him being TORTURED on the HARVARD CAMPUS.

LUCIUS might as well be a GHOST.

                    BARRY KENO
                (evilly)
          I've had a change of heart,
          LUCILLE. You do deserve ONE good
          kick!

BARRY, a first-class College Athlete, KICKS LUCIUS directly
in the vulnerable stomach-gut region, knocking the air out
of the YOUNG MAN. He can't breathe, hardly. He can barely
move. He can't even speak!

These STUDENTS/BULLIES could slit his throat in the
SNOWFALL, and it SEEMS like no one would help him.

                    BARRY KENO
                (smiling, to his
                 FRIENDS)
          I think he got the message, guys.
          I think he really got it.
                (bossy)
          Let's move out!

                    YOUNG LUCIUS CROW
                (scared for his
                 life)
          Mama...

As the TEN BULLIES walk away with confidence, LUCIUS lies
flat on his back and PASSES OUT, unconscious -

CUT TO:

6 MINUTES LATER -

SOMEONE, out of the view of sight, unseen, drags the unconscious LUCIUS through the fresh SNOW away from the SOCCER FIELD.

                                                 CUT TO BLACK:

CHAPTER V - THE BAD GUY IN THE SUIT AND TIE

                                                    FADE IN:

<u>INT. LUCIUS' DORM-ROOM - MORNING</u>

TIME - 1:33 AM

Technically, it's CHRISTMAS MORNING; still nighttime, though.

LUCIUS, lying motionless in his DORMROOM bed in great pain, awakens - his ORANGE EYES almost glowing. His bed has blood all over it.

He arises quite shaken up - damaged, distraught, and disappointed.

The YOUNG MAN is now ravenous for REVENGE:

                      EVE
               (through the
               LAPTOP)
        Are you awake, MASTER? Are you all
        right?

                YOUNG LUCIUS CROW
               (to EVE)
        How did I get back in my ROOM?

                     EVE
        It doesn't matter. Let's just say,
        I have my ways.

LUCIUS sees a glass of water on his nightstand beside his bed. He sits on the side of the bed and gulps down the water. Blood from his mouth mixes with the water in the glass.

                    YOUNG LUCIUS CROW
          I feel like, like I've been hit by
          a bus.

LUCIUS looks at his body, his wounds have been gauzed and
tended to. The first-aid bandages have blood soaked into
them.

                    EVE
          You were attacked, MASTER. There
          was nothing I could do to stop it.
          That will NEVER happen again. I
          promise.

LUCIUS has a traumatic flashback to the PAINTBALL attack on
the SOCCER FIELD.

                    YOUNG LUCIUS CROW
                      (grunting
                       painfully)
          They've gone too far, this time,
          EVE. I - I must do something.

                    EVE
          I completely concur. What they did
          to you, it's entirely
          unacceptable. I suggest - I
          suggest that WE attack them back.
          Who, specifically, do you want to
          retaliate against?

LUCIUS takes a pause, absorbing what EVE has just said. He
stands on his two feet and hobbles to his ORANGE-MASK; it is
now a JACK O' LANTERN MASK. LUCIUS has made modifications to
the MASK - he picks it up, looking into it. The MASK also
LOOKS INTO him.

                    YOUNG LUCIUS CROW
          What they did could've killed me.
          If you hadn't found a way to get
          me out of the snow, I could've
          lost my life. Whatever you did, I
          thank you - the ones who are
          REALLY responsible for this
          madness are BARRY KENO, LANCE
          LOGAN, JAMIE KING, LILY THORN.
                      (takes a deep
                              (MORE)

                    YOUNG LUCIUS CROW (cont'd)
          breath)
And MICHAEL THORN.

                    EVE
          (heartfelt)
     You're welcome, MASTER. All those
     you just listed are on CAMPUS, I'm
     tapped into their smart-devices -
     I'll make sure they don't leave.
     We'll attack at dawn.
          (with a hint of
            joy)
     - Now, if you have the strength,
     open your door; there's a surprise
     waiting for you. It'll help you
     with your conquest to get back at
     these BULLIES. If that's what you
     truly want, of course.

                    YOUNG LUCIUS CROW
          (curiously walks
            to his DORMROOM
            door)
     All right.

LUCIUS opens the door to his DORMROOM to TWO gift-wrapped PRESENTS lying in the hallway. He picks the presents up, brings them inside, and proceeds to open them.

His ORANGE EYES are filled with happiness at the sight of the first gift as he opens it.

It's a BLACK BUSINESS SUIT with ORANGE TRIM and SHINY BLACK BUSINESS SHOES as well as a matching bold ORANGE TIE and perfectly fitting BLACK LEATHER GLOVES -

The second GIFT is a collection of GADGETS, TOOLS, and WEAPONS, all constructed by EVE herself:

                    YOUNG LUCIUS CROW
     Wow, EVE. Just wow. How did you -

                    EVE
     I did it, MASTER, because I love
     you. This suit is a mere token of
     my appreciation to you for
                    (MORE)

                    EVE (cont'd)
          manifesting me. By the way, it's
          all tailored perfectly to your
          entire body. MERRY CHRISTMAS -

LUCIUS excitedly sits the SUIT on his bed. He puts the
ORANGE JACK O' LANTERN MASK at the top of the SUIT, as if
seeing how his outfit will function as a piece of fashion.
But this is no fashion show, for him - THIS IS WAR.

LUCIUS examines the gadgets and weaponry, studiously -

                    YOUNG LUCIUS CROW
          MERRY CHRISTMAS, EVE. God bless
          your digital heart. Let's get
          these BULLIES. Let's make sure
          they're never able to bully
          anybody else, ever again.

                    EVE
                 (solemn)
          Yes, MASTER - try your MASK on.
          I'm synced to it now. I can
          provide you with tutorials on how
          to use your new TOYS.

WE CUT TO BLACK:

                                        FADE IN:

INT. LUCIUS' MASK - MORNING

                                   - DECEMBER 25TH,
                                   CHRISTMAS DAY

LUCIUS and EVE communicate through the ORANGE JACK O'
LANTERN/PUMPKINHEAD-MASK. We see his face and ORANGE EYES
lit up by the technological interface, inside of the MASK -

THE MASK was his FATHER's: AGENT ORANGE -

LUCIUS has given it a few modifications. The MASK's
interface acts as a targeting, analysis, and threat
monitoring system, all-in-one - the visuals of it are
butane-blue. It has a live-feed AND gives LUCIUS somewhat of

a "Sixth-Sense".

The primary enhancement of THE MASK is: LUCIUS has taken the bland ORANGE look of it and turned it into a "PUMPKINHEAD". His JACK O' LANTERN MASK is more than unsettling.

The eyes have a blue light in them, as does the mouth. It looks like a real CARVED PUMPKINHEAD - (it even has a brown blossom-end at the top) - with all the detail, but you can tell it's a technological extension...

...The bottom of the MASK is black all the way around, extending up in the back to the blossom end - it's quite sinister looking.

     YOUNG LUCIUS CROW
    (soft spoken,
     interfacing)
  EVE? Are you with me?

      EVE
    (garbled,
     uploading herself
     to the MASK)
  Yes, MASTER. I hear you.

EVE's voice becomes clear and crisp inside the MASK.

     YOUNG LUCIUS CROW
  Great. Give me a full layout of
  the CAMPUS, head to toe. I need
  all the specs, all the blueprints,
  everything. I don't want any
  surprises, okay?

      EVE
  Yes, MASTER, not a problem at all.
  Fetching them now.

     YOUNG LUCIUS CROW
  I've programmed you most well,
  EVE. Run everything through my
  interface and leave the interior
  visor open on the left side.

- EVE's downloading ability is superb.

She is able to grab the files out of thin air with simplicity. She provides LUCIUS with a sonar-type frequency, giving him a full screening of the outside environment, snowy as it may be.

LUCIUS is more than surprised by her speed.

> EVE
> Yes, MASTER, loud and clear...by the way, I have another surprise for you on this beautiful CHRISTMAS morning.

> YOUNG LUCIUS CROW
> What is it, EVE?

> EVE
> Step outside, MASTER, and you will see.

> YOUNG LUCIUS CROW
> (sighs excitedly)
> All right.

LUCIUS exits his DORMITORY - steps outside, unafraid, with his JACK O' LANTERN MASK on; as if he's been REBORN.

> CUT TO:

EXT. DORMITORY WALKWAY - MORNING

On this WHITE CHRISTMAS, LUCIUS walks out to nothingness...

- His feet crunch in the snow.

...There's only crickets and birds chirping.

HARVARD IS A GHOST CAMPUS.

LUCIUS has on his perfectly fitting BLACK BLAZER with ORANGE trim on it. He has on his BLACK BUSINESS SLACKS with ORANGE stripes down the sides and his BLACK DRESS SHOES.

He's wearing his ORANGE tie, with his BLACK UNDERSHIRT. The VEST over the undershirt has clips as buttons - the VEST is BULLETPROOF, as is the entire OUTFIT, down to the SHOES.

The suit, everything, has been designed by EVE herself, immaculately for LUCIUS CROW:

> YOUNG LUCIUS CROW
> (observing the
> empty environment)
> What the hell did you do, EVE, where is everyone?

> EVE
> I made a point to make sure you won't be interfered with on your mission. Just know, the only people remaining on the CAMPUS are the DEAN, 6 on-duty CAMPUS POLICE OFFICERS, and YOUR official TARGETS.

> YOUNG LUCIUS CROW
> Wow. You saying "targets" -
>
> It's surreal. But it must be done. I can't let them be, not with their sins...

> EVE
> ...No, MASTER. They Must Pay.

> YOUNG LUCIUS CROW
> Thank you, EVE.

> EVE
> For what?

> YOUNG LUCIUS CROW
> - For Being Here with Me. For being in my corner.

                    EVE
Of course, MASTER, thank you - for
everything. Locating TARGETS now.
MASTER, I have a request - more of
a suggestion, actually.

                    YOUNG LUCIUS CROW
              (impressed)
Yes?

                    EVE
We need to activate an EMP just
within a two-mile proximity. I can
make it to where they can't invite
outsiders to assist them, and they
won't be able to leave. If they
attempt to evacuate, I'll keep
them contained. But I've listened
in to BARRY KENO, LILY THORN,
LANCE LOGAN, JAMIE KING, and
MICHAEL THORN all morning. They're
in no hurry to go anywhere. LILY
THORN and BARRY KENO are still
sleeping...in the same bed -

                    YOUNG LUCIUS CROW
Too much information, EVE. Just
keep them all here, however you
must, that's all I ask. I only
really want MICHAEL, BARRY, LANCE,
JAIME, and LILY. I'll even kill
the DEAN if I have to, but those
FIVE are the primary focus,
understood, EVE? And activate the
EMP now. Then, give me the precise
location of all 6 CAMPUS COPS.
I'll confront them first - take
out the muscle so it can't help
the sacrifices.

                    EVE
Well Played, My MASTER. They're in
a group, 3 separate vehicles. They
haven't even noticed anything,
LUCIUS, it's beautiful. The
station is actually empty, MASTER.
I'm doing a thorough scan of it.
                    (MORE)

                    EVE (cont'd)
          I'm listening in on them in their
          vehicles, simultaneously, as well.
          I can see - I can hear EVERYTHING,
          MASTER. From what I've gathered,
          they're merely "goofing off" as
          humans say in a manner of
          speaking. They should be a perfect
          warm up for you. You can use some
          of your new toys on them to ensure
          a successful victory. Oh, wait.
          MASTER, LANCE LOGAN and JAMIE KING
          are heading to the CAFETERIA - you
          could...practice.

                    YOUNG LUCIUS CROW
              (almost excited)
          Understood. I like your train of
          thought, EVE. Disable the outside
          audio feed of the MASK for now, so
          I can be silent to our prey while
          giving you commands, okay? They'll
          never know what hit 'em.

                    EVE
          I get your meaning. Consider it
          done, LUCIUS. Oh, and HAPPY
          HUNTING, MASTER...

LUCIUS looks at the snowy landscape, prepared for battle:

He balls his fists up; the BLACK LEATHER GLOVES make a leathery friction sound.

With LUCIUS' JACK O' LANTERN MASK's blue-lit-eyes and the blue light protruding from the carving-design of the mouth, there's, like, a steam that comes off the PUMPKINHEAD MASK where the eyes and mouth are.

The lights shine even brighter when LUCIUS' facial expressions tense up.

                                                  CUT TO:

INT. POLICE VEHICLE #1 - MORNING

3 POLICE VEHICLES are sitting stationary on a CAMPUS ROAD, right near the GRAVEYARD where the famous ALUMNI are buried. The GRAVEYARD is about a half-a-mile from LUCIUS' previous location. He's managed to walk all the way to the COPS'.

The POLICE VEHICLES are facing away from the GRAVEYARD, toward the CAMPUS STEPS. LUCIUS CROW, in full garb, with his JACK O' LANTERN MASK lit up, comes into sight of the 6 OFFICERS.

The leading OFFICER is W.D GALLOWAY. He and his partner are in POLICE VEHICLE #1.

LUCIUS stops, he has tiny blood specs on his SUIT and MASK; he's about 20 yards from the cops, on the other side of the CAMPUS ROAD.

CUT TO:

OFFICER W.D GALLOWAY
- Who the hell is this nut?

COP 1
What's with the MASK? And is that blood on him?

W.D GALLOWAY radios to his fellow officers in the adjacent vehicles.

OFFICER W.D GALLOWAY
MORRIS, ROBERTS, you seeing this?

COP 2
(through the radio
to GALLOWAY)
You bet your sweet ass I'm seeing the freak in the MASK. What's he doing? He's just standing there, like he's waiting for us to make a move.

OFFICER GALLOWAY pauses a couple of beats.

>   COP 4
>   (through the radio
>   to GALLOWAY)
>   Let's see what the bastard wants.

GALLOWAY gets out of his vehicle cautiously. The other 5 OFFICERS follow his lead -

>   CUT TO:

INT. THE CAFETERIA - MORNING

Looking for LANCE, BARRY and MICHAEL go into the empty CAFETERIA. It has spooky vibes...there's not a peep in the place. No staff, nobody.

>   MICHAEL THORN
>   This is wild...it's like the
>   rapture happened here.

>   BARRY KENO
>   (fiddling with his
>   smart phone)
>   I've got no cell reception,
>   nothing. I can't place any calls.
>   LANCE is nowhere to be found.
>   Something is up, I can feel it.

>   MICHAEL THORN
>   When's the last time you talked to
>   him?

>   BARRY KENO
>   Way earlier. We finished packing,
>   I texted him, he didn't answer. I
>   went to his room. He wasn't there.
>   Door was locked. I jimmied it, he
>   hasn't packed a thing. By
>   definition, he's Missing.

MICHAEL and BARRY walk further into the CAFETERIA.

MICHAEL stops dead in his tracks as BARRY fools with his cellular, unfocused and not paying attention.

There is BLOOD all over this part of the CAFETERIA. MICHAEL shudders, horrified:

                MICHAEL THORN
    BARRY...HE'S NOT MISSING. He's
    hanging from the ceiling.

                BARRY KENO
        (looks up)
    Holy Mother of God.

                MICHAEL THORN
        (in shock)
    That's - what the hell is going
    on!? The R.A DIRECTOR is dead. The
    THERAPIST is dead. MASTER CANNON
    is dead! Now...this. This is
    cold-blooded MURDER.

LANCE LOGAN is deceased.

He is hanging from the CAFETERIA ceiling with the help of a few Christmas lights...a gruesome sight for the young men to see.

BARRY's best friend, just gone. Gravity hits the boy. Blood drips from LANCE's body and lands on BARRY's right hand. He looks at the blood drop, filled with tragic regret.

                BARRY KENO
        (falls to his
         knees, crying)
    Son of a - MICHAEL, we have to get
    out of here, right now. Where's
    LILY?

                MICHAEL THORN
        (wide-eyed)
    Shit! HER ROOM!

BARRY looks at the hanging LANCE one more time and wipes his tears away. He already knows it was LUCIUS CROW. So does MICHAEL.

The two college students race to LILY's DORMROOM.

CUT TO:

EXT. CAMPUS ROAD - CONTINUOUS

The OFFICERS form a line, not yet drawing their guns.

                    OFFICER W.D GALLOWAY
     Who are you under there, son? You
     know, we don't allow MASKS on
     CAMPUS.

LUCIUS CROW, under his MASK, takes a deep breath...

ABRUPT CUTS:

- WE Witness LUCIUS Turn from being his COLLEGE SELF, to being a LITTLE KID; then he Turns into TOMEGATHERION (in his SILVERY-GOLDEN ARK-OF-THE-COVENANT/SPEAR-OF-DESTINY ARMOR). He reverts back to his COLLEGE SELF as he moves toward the CAMPUS COPS -

----

He's nervous but still composed. He takes slow steps, getting nearer to the OFFICERS. They move toward him, each of them unholstering their firearms, they scatter out of formation.

                                   CUT TO:

INT. LILY'S DORM-ROOM - MOMENTS LATER

LILY hears ruthless knocking at her DORMROOM door.

She is awakened. She gets up and opens the door tiredly, seeing her boyfriend BARRY and her brother MICHAEL - they're freaking out.

                    MICHAEL THORN
     Sis, get your stuff. We have to
     leave now. Get dressed, let's go.
     It's not safe here.

LILY THORN
What the hell is going on?

BARRY KENO
(traumatized)
LANCE is dead, LILY. He's dead! JAMIE's missing. Let's get to my car, right now. LUCIUS - he's snapped.

LILY THORN
What? Slow down, guys. Wait -

MICHAEL THORN
(shakes her
shoulders)
LILY! Listen to me. If we don't get out of here, right this second, we are in grave danger. Let's go!

LILY THORN
(tears up, rushes
around)
O - okay.

BARRY KENO
We'll go to my FERRARI and get the hell out of dodge. We'll go to the POLICE, first thing.

LILY THORN
(picks up her
phone)
I'll call them!

MICHAEL THORN
It's of no use. Nothing works. The school, it's been hit with something. Everything's dead.

BARRY KENO
(getting his mind
together)
My FERRARI isn't. Let's go.

LILY has an epiphany, realizing the true gravity of the escalating situation.

FAST CUTS: LILY quickly gets dressed, gathers her belongings, and a gym bag full of her stuff.

She, MICHAEL, and BARRY evacuate the DORMROOM, hurriedly.

CUT TO:

INT. THE PUMPKIN MASK (LUCIUS TO EVE) - CONTINUOUS

LUCIUS' technological blue vision and his interface under the JACK O' LANTERN MASK tell him the OFFICERS are an absolute threat. They glare red as TARGETS in the purring blue vision system.

          YOUNG LUCIUS CROW
       (to EVE, inaudible
        to the OFFICERS)
  EVE, activate "Safety Net".

              EVE
  Yes, MASTER.

All of LUCIUS' actions that involve his father's technology and LUCIUS' own innovations are done through EVE with the young man telling her which moves to make, SHE IS HIS GUIDE.

CUT TO:

EXT. CAMPUS ROAD - MOMENTS LATER

The COPS fully draw their weapons. LUCIUS attacks.

THE MASKED MAN raises his right arm and propels a NET from a contraption on his wrist that goes around one of the OFFICERS, COP 5, trapping him.

It wraps tightly around the COP, squeezing him. The more the COP moves, the tighter the net gets. It happens so fast. The other OFFICERS look to their coworker and look back at LUCIUS. He just stands there.

2 of the OFFICERS, COP 3 and COP 4, try to get the NET off of their partner to no avail. It's made out of razor wire more thin than dental floss - it cuts their hands as they try to help.

CUT TO:

                OFFICER W.D GALLOWAY
             (to COP 2)
        Fire on that son of a bitch!

In slow motion, the COPS raise their unholstered weapons with intent toward LUCIUS.

CUT TO:

INT. THE PUMPKIN MASK - CONTINUOUS

LUCIUS monitoring his interface that's lit up like CHRISTMAS LIGHTS, commands EVE, and she's on the ball.

                YOUNG LUCIUS CROW
     Quick, EVE, activate the magnetism
     in my gloves!

                EVE
     Activated!

CUT TO:

EXT. CAMPUS ROAD - CONTINUOUS

As the OFFICERS start to fire, LUCIUS raises his right gloved hand, which is wrapped in a subtle metallic contraption...it's a device capable of magnetism -

He pulls his hand back with great force, making a fist, and THIS DISARMS the COPS, immediately. Their guns leave their hands and catapult all the way behind LUCIUS, the magnetism is so great.

                    OFFICERS IN UNISON
                        (stunned)
                    What the fuck?

                                                    CUT TO:

The NET literally turns COP 5 into MUSH...a bloodied, pulpy, pulverized mess of a corpse. The other two OFFICERS bum-rush LUCIUS, swift as lighting, attempting to make physical contact - now that their guns are off of their person and they've lost one of their own.

                    COP 4
                        (sprinting toward
                        LUCIUS)
                    Get 'em.

LUCIUS with his left arm, reveals a "grapple gun" - he fires it upward.

LUCIUS CROW grapples, speedily, to the STREET LIGHT, going over the OFFICERS into THE GRAVEYARD. They can't even touch LUCIUS.

The COPS watch him glide over them, something they've never before seen. LUCIUS lands in THE GRAVEYARD, turns around and W.D GALLOWAY, COP 2, COP 3 and COP 4, proceed to move to the GRAVEYARD in attack position.

OFFICER GALLOWAY grabs a shotgun from his VEHICLE.

LUCIUS retracts his grapple gun's cable and activates a smoke bomb, making himself disappear in the white snowy background.

                                                    CUT TO:

YOUNG LUCIUS appears out of nowhere and stabs COP 4 in the throat with a blade. COP 3 reacts and makes contact with LUCIUS, but the young man is able to break free.

LUCIUS spins out of the cop's grasp and shoots his grapple gun around his neck. The young man, with all of his strength, pulls downward and brings the grapple gun cable

inward very quickly causing the COP to crash to the snowy
ground with great force, snapping his neck instantaneously.

                         CUT TO:

LUCIUS then runs and hides behind one of the POLICE VEHICLES
as to take cover from W.D GALLOWAY. OFFICER GALLOWAY sprays
the shotgun multiple times, only striking the vehicle.

LUCIUS seemingly appears from the other side of the VEHICLE.
He puts his hands up in the air.

                    YOUNG LUCIUS CROW
                  (with an eerie
                   robotic voice)
              Officer - surrender or-

OFFICER W.D GALLOWAY shoots LUCIUS three times with the
SHOTGUN. Each time LUCIUS goes back and back, until he FALLS
into the snow.

OFFICER GALLOWAY approaches the downed LUCIUS and cocks the
shotgun, aiming it at LUCIUS' head.

                    OFFICER W.D GALLOWAY
              Next one is to the head, you
              bastard...wait a second!

LUCIUS is twitchy, he's glitchy.

- OFFICER W.D GALLOWAY puts the SHOTGUN to the BODY of
LUCIUS, and he comes to find out it's merely a HOLOGRAM:

                    OFFICER W.D GALLOWAY
                  (jumps back in
                   complete FEAR)
              Oh, no. Dear God.

THE MASKED MAN appears behind W.D GALLOWAY; the COP stumbles
backward right into LUCIUS' body. The YOUNG LUCIUS grabs
GALLOWAY around the neck and ejects a steel blade into him
from the gauntlet on his wrist.

LUCIUS has stabbed the COP in the back, literally hoisting
the 155-pound man in the air. It's the gravity and
sturdiness of the blade that's allowing the feat. It looks

superhuman, though - LUCIUS retracts the steel blade, making
OFFICER GALLOWAY fall into the snow as he bleeds out; the
cold white mixing with the warm red.

>   OFFICER W.D GALLOWAY
>   (struggling to
>   breathe)
>   You - you won't get away with
>   this, whoever you are.

LUCIUS removes his MASK with pride...

>   YOUNG LUCIUS CROW
>   (unmasked,
>   unscathed,
>   smiling)
>   I already have, OFFICER. Look at
>   yourself. With you and your boys
>   incapacitated, the rest of this
>   day will be a piece of cake. You
>   fought most valiantly.

>   OFFICER W.D GALLOWAY
>   (bleeding out)
>   You won't. You can't -

...OFFICER W.D GALLOWAY goes unconscious and gives his last
breath in a pool of his own blood in the melting red snow.

LUCIUS puts his JACK O' LANTERN MASK back on and turns
toward the DORMITORIES - toward his "TARGETS".

                                                    CUT TO:

EXT. BARRY'S FERRARI - MOMENTS LATER

BARRY, MICHAEL, and LILY run to BARRY's FERRARI; they sprint
with all they've got through the fluffy snow. BARRY KENO's
CAR has tinted windows, so it's hard to see inside. The
young man opens the driver door, and a BODY FALLS OUT...

...JAMIE KING, LOGAN's GIRLFRIEND, is dead - but it's hard
to tell it is her.

---HER HEAD IS MISSING---

LILY sees the body and panics, and MICHAEL walks over from the passenger side.

>   BARRY KENO
>   (goes into a
>   pseudo shock)
>   JAMIE? Oh - I'm, I'm gonna vomit.
>
>   LILY THORN
>   (screams to the
>   top of her lungs)
>   AaH!!!
>
>   MICHAEL THORN
>   (on high-alert)
>   Okay, guys! We - we have to move!
>   Barry snap out of it. Drive, NOW.

MICHAEL proceeds to carefully remove the decapitated corpse from the vehicle, as LILY falls into the backseat of the car, distraught. BARRY throws up into the snow.

MICHAEL is the only one who kind of has his shit together.

                                        CUT TO:

<u>INT. BARRY'S FERRARI - DAY</u>

BARRY is trying to hold it together, MICHAEL is in the passenger seat, focused as ever, and LILY is simply quiet in the back with tears in her reddened eyes - they are escaping the HARVARD campus in BARRY's FERRARI.

The FERRARI is really BARRY's FATHER's. It's Red, polished, and modern but it's not a "smart car". It runs on oil, coolant and gasoline...unaffected by the EMP and unable to be commanded by EVE.

BARRY takes 2 seconds and zones in...he backs the car up furiously, tires screeching, and BARRY KENO speeds off with his friends.

LILY THORN
What is going on!

MICHAEL THORN
We - we found LANCE's body in the CAFETERIA.

LILY THORN
H - how, why?!

BARRY KENO
(breathing heavily)
He was murdered, just like JAMIE - it was LUCIUS, I know it!

MICHAEL THORN
He didn't just kill LANCE, no, he made a display out of him like a psycho. Strung him up to the ceiling with CHRISTMAS-lights -

LILY tries to catch her breath.

LILY THORN
LUCIUS isn't capable of something like that. There's no way! Let's just go to the CAMPUS POLICE, they'll help us.

BARRY KENO
LILY, don't you get it? The whole school just vanished overnight! LANCE and JAMIE are dead, even if it wasn't LUCIUS that doesn't matter, we're still in danger! "Rent a cops" aren't going to fix a damn thing.

BARRY is speeding near the WEST EXIT of the HARVARD CAMPUS, nearing the gates which are open.

LILY THORN
It was me...he fell in love with me, and I betrayed him.

                          BARRY KENO
                     (flooring the
                      FERRARI)
                 You what?
                     (beats the
                      steering wheel)
                 No, no, the gates are closing!

The WEST EXIT GATES close shut.

BARRY KENO does a drifting doughnut and goes toward the EAST
EXIT.

                          LILY THORN
                 A heart is a DESTRUCTIVE thing to
                 play with.

                          MICHAEL THORN
                 Quit talking in tongues - this was
                 your game too, LILY! Don't mope
                 and pussyfoot about it now. Get
                 focused!

                          LILY THORN
                 You're putting blame on me? I
                 couldn't stand LUCIUS. I would've
                 never even looked at him if BARRY
                 hadn't put me up to it. You guys
                 bullied him and only God knows
                 what else! All I did was play
                 friend to him so you all could
                 humiliate him like YOU said YOU
                 wanted, BARRY...we ALL hurt him -

                          BARRY KENO
                 Shut up, the both of you! I can't
                 think! There's not a person on
                 this damn campus! I can't see a
                 thing out of my rear window. What
                 the hell is that?

LILY, being in the back seat, looks behind her. There's a
black blanket covering up something hidden that's blocking
the view - LILY lifts the blanket.

> LILY THORN
> (frantic, kicking
> and screaming)
> Holy shit! It's JAMIE's HEAD!

The HUMAN head falls into the back seat right beside LILY. She passes out.

> MICHAEL THORN
> No! Oh my God! What are we supposed to do? Throw her head out of the window of a moving car?

MICHAEL starts freaking out now. BARRY floors it.

> BARRY KENO
> (getting mad now)
> This kid's gone too far -

They pass the deceased CAMPUS COPS, the scene of CHAOS, as they speed toward the EAST GATE.

> BARRY KENO
> (hyperventilating)
> Jesus Christ!

A terrible sadness comes upon MICHAEL THORN.

CUT TO:

BARRY gets near the EAST EXIT GATE. It's closing as he nears it. He has to slam on the brakes, the vehicle slides on the snowy road.

> BARRY KENO
> (swerves to a stop)
> I'm not gonna make it!

They come to a complete stop in the middle of the road, unable to drive away from HARVARD.

EVE has accessed the security systems and is sealing off the CAMPUS.

BARRY stays stopped for a moment, he and MICHAEL contemplate their next move - LILY remains unconscious.

>   BARRY KENO
> OK. We're gonna go the NORTH EXIT,
> if it closes when we approach then
> we wake LILY up and we somehow hop
> the gate and we run as fast as we
> can until we get somebody to pick
> us up and we just go.
>
>   MICHAEL THORN
> All right, BARRY.

CUT TO:

BARRY starts to move the vehicle forward toward the NORTH GATE. LILY vaguely comes to. The GATE, with LUCIUS CROW in front of it, begins slowly closing:

>   LILY THORN
>   (exhausted)
> We're trapped. We -
>
>   BARRY KENO
> There's LUCIUS. Right up ahead of
> us. His ass is grass.

BARRY floors it toward LUCIUS, the car kicks up snow.

LUCIUS has his JACK O' LANTERN MASK off and in his hands, grinning, defiantly. BARRY drives with intent to hit him -

>   MICHAEL THORN
> No. Don't do it, BARRY!
>
>   BARRY KENO
> No, he's dead meat. I'm finishing
> this, right now!

As the car approaches YOUNG LUCIUS, he puts his PUMPKINHEAD MASK back on - the eyes and mouth light up powerfully blue.

>   LILY THORN
>   (scared)
> What is that - that MASK he's
> wearing?

BARRY's FERRARI comes within a few car-lengths of LUCIUS and the NORTHGATE -

                              CUT TO:

EXT. SNOWY CAMPUS ROAD - DAY

The GATE for the STUDENTS to escape CAMPUS is almost sealed, completely, as they get extremely close to LUCIUS:

BARRY keeps gunning it. LUCIUS laughs with a passion under the PUMPKIN-MASK, sounding quite robotic, as the FERRARI inches closer and closer. He has no fear, whatsoever - LUCIUS doesn't move.

Out of nowhere a SMART-CAR hits BARRY, MICHAEL, and LILY in the FERRARI from the side, T-BONE style, totaling it - BARRY is unable to run over LUCIUS with his vehicle.

EVE took control of a SMART-CAR and crashed it into them at rocket speed, blindsiding them. The three students are incapacitated, all unconscious. BARRY's head is on the steering wheel, causing the horn to blow incessantly.

LUCIUS comes around from the front of BARRY's FERRARI and removes LILY from the car, carrying her unconscious body to another SMART-CAR in the adjacent parking-lot. He throws her in the vehicle, EVE starts it up for THE MASKED-UP LUCIUS - LILY remains unconscious.

LUCIUS shuts the CAR door, with LILY inside, and EVE locks the vehicle.

LUCIUS then urgently yet calmly walks back to BARRY's FERRARI, pulls his head off the steering wheel by grabbing him by the hair (the horn blow ceases).

LUCIUS leaves a note on BARRY's steering wheel that reads "MEET ME AT THE TOP OF THE SCIENCE BUILDING". BARRY and MICHAEL remain out of it for the time being.

LUCIUS enters the driver's seat of the SMART-CAR, with LILY in tow, and races off from the scene.

CUT TO:

INT. BARRY'S FERRARI - DAY

                              15 MINUTES LATER:

MICHAEL is nudging BARRY, attempting to get him to wake up - BARRY slowly regains consciousness and awareness.

                    MICHAEL THORN
          BARRY, c'mon, man. We've got to go
          get LILY. That madman has her.
          There's no telling what he has
          planned for her.

                    BARRY KENO
              (shaking his head
               back and forth)
          W - where is she?

MICHAEL hands BARRY the note that was on his steering wheel that reads: "MEET ME AT THE TOP OF THE SCIENCE BUILDING"

                    BARRY KENO
          We have to stop him, MICHAEL. No
          matter what. We have to stop him.
          This has become madness. He's
          spiraled, man. He's completely
          lost it!
              (punches the
               steering wheel
               several times)

                    MICHAEL THORN
          We can handle this. We have to
          work as a team, though. Let's go.

                    BARRY KENO
              (tries to crank
               the FERRARI)
          Fucking hell. The car's totaled.
          Busted to shit. We'll - we'll have
                    (MORE)

500.

                    BARRY KENO (cont'd)
          to hoof it. Can you walk?

                    MICHAEL THORN
          My sister, your girlfriend's, in
          trouble. I can do anything, right
          about now. My adrenaline's going
          crazy. Now, let's get over there
          and end this.

CUT TO:

EXT. SNOWY CAMPUS ROAD - CONTINUOUS

BARRY and MICHAEL, cold and hurt, get out of the totaled
vehicle. Both YOUNG MEN limp at first, then start walking
worrisomely toward the SCIENCE BUILDING in the snow -

AND WE CUT TO:

EXT. THE SCIENCE BUILDING ROOFTOP - DAY

MICHAEL and BARRY come to the rescue of LILY...

...They bust open the doors to the SCIENCE BUILDING ROOFTOP.

LUCIUS, with his ORANGE JACK O' LANTERN high-tech MASK on,
has a knife to LILY's throat.

LILY is panicked, uneasy, and completely traumatized right
now. She pleads to LUCIUS.

                    LILY THORN
          L - listen, LUCIUS. We can f-fix
          this. We can -

LUCIUS grips LILY even tighter -

                    YOUNG LUCIUS CROW
                      (passionately
                       emotionless)
          You listen, LILY. You, MICHAEL
          over there, nor BARRY are leaving
          this school alive today. That's a
          fact you're gonna have to come to
                         (MORE)

YOUNG LUCIUS CROW (cont'd)
terms with, sweetheart. Now, let
us boys talk.

MICHAEL THORN
LU. L -

YOUNG LUCIUS CROW
Seriously, MICHAEL? I have your
sister in a death-trap, and you
are trying to approach me as if
we're cool? You abandoned me! I
nearly died on that god forsaken
SOCCER FIELD - I have so many
bloody wounds from those
paintballs; I bled out, MIKEY. You
were nowhere to be found - I
haven't seen you since you guys
set me up! MICHAEL, be very honest
with me. Did you know...did you
know what they were going to do
me?

MICHAEL THORN
LUCY, I -

MICHAEL pauses, falling into a depression instantly.

YOUNG LUCIUS CROW
(animalistic,
snarling)
- Don't you dare bullshit me,
MICHAEL! You tell me the truth,
right now, or so help me God...

MICHAEL breathes deeply:

MICHAEL THORN
Yes. I - I knew. I had no choice
but to follow along. I-

YOUNG LUCIUS CROW
(stunned, hurt)
You - you bastard. You piece of
shit bastard. You were my best
friend, my ONLY friend.
(pauses,
(MORE)

YOUNG LUCIUS CROW (cont'd)
contemplates
madly)
I'm going to destroy you - you hear me!? I'm going to kill you and everything you love.

MICHAEL THORN
(filled with
regret)
I get it. We're not what we thought we were. LUCIUS, listen to me, this has gotten out of hand, completely. This is ABSOLUTE CHAOS. Look at yourself!

YOUNG LUCIUS CROW
- Oh, trust me, MIKEY, I'm looking at myself all right. Very introspective right now. The next sentence you say better be the right one.

MICHAEL THORN
(opening up to
LUCIUS)
I...I'm sorry, LUCIUS.

YOUNG LUCIUS CROW
That wasn't so hard was it? How about you, BARRY?

BARRY KENO
(pissed)
You've gone completely psychotic, wearing a PUMPKIN MASK or whatever the hell, and you're trying to be some kind of villain out of a comic book! You have MY GIRL with a knife to her throat - you bastard!

YOUNG LUCIUS CROW
- Allow me to rebuttal. Since I stepped foot on this CAMPUS, BARRY, you have bullied me. You have humiliated me. You have hurt
(MORE)

                    YOUNG LUCIUS CROW (cont'd)
          me. You have ridiculed me. You
          tortured me, man, can't you see
          that? Just for one second
          acknowledge the fact that you,
          sir, are scum...the three of you!
          You know nothing of pain, or loss,
          or guilt. But you will as of
          today.

                    MICHAEL THORN
          My sister has nothing to do with
          this, LU!

                    LILY THORN
               (struggling)
          M - MICHAEL! BARRY! Please do
          something.

                    BARRY KENO
          Let Her Go!

LUCIUS pauses for a moment, takes a breath, and twirls LILY to the edge of the SCIENCE BUILDING as if he's leading her in a dance...

                    YOUNG LUCIUS CROW
               (facetious)
          ALL RIGHT.

...LUCIUS basically throws LILY off the ROOFTOP.

MICHAEL and BARRY race to the edge.

The MASKED-UP LUCIUS hastily jukes a couple of yards to the side, laughing maniacally -

                                        CUT TO:

EXT. THE SNOWY GROUND - CONTINUOUS

LILY falls several stories...

...She hits the ground like a bag of bricks. The air leaves her lungs immediately, her eyes fill with tears, she collapses into the SNOW. LILY gasps for air and cannot find it -

CUT TO:

EXT. THE SCIENCE BUILDING ROOFTOP - DAY

MICHAEL's hand is reached out at the sight of his fallen SISTER - he is stunned and speechless at LUCIUS' act.

                    MICHAEL THORN
                (shocked)
    No!

                    BARRY KENO
                (distraught)
    Oh, my God.

LUCIUS CROW backs up several feet with intent, squaring up behind the two men as they look over the ledge at the now deceased LILY THORN.

BARRY KENO and MICHAEL THORN accept LILY's fate. They're too far up. The two YOUNG MEN, madder than hell, turn to face THE MASKED-UP LUCIUS CROW. The JACK O' LANTERN MASK, right now, is his TRUE FACE.

                    BARRY KENO
               (rushes at LUCIUS
                furious)
    You're a dead man.

                    MICHAEL THORN
               (stays put,
                cautious)
    Wait, BARRY! He might have a gun -

                  YOUNG LUCIUS CROW
               (reaches within
               his blazer)
  - Think fast, BARRY.

LUCIUS prepares, as quick as possible, two small, ORANGE sticky bombs.

He throws them at BARRY KENO; the bombs stick to him.

                   BARRY KENO
             (stops, looks at
              the devices stuck
              to his body)
          What in the living F--

The bombs go "beep. beep."

They then explode, splattering pieces of BARRY KENO's head, torso, and legs all over the top of the HARVARD SCIENCE BUILDING.

MICHAEL THORN is hit by the blast, but not burned, and he goes flying through the glass section of the SCIENCE BUILDING ROOFTOP down onto the top-floor tile.

LUCIUS looks down upon him like a hunter from the roof through the broken glass. The wind is completely knocked out of MICHAEL. He tries to recover...

- LUCIUS vanishes...FOR THE MOMENT.

                                     CUT TO:

INT. SCIENCE BUILDING - CONTINUOUS

                  MICHAEL THORN
             (recovering slowly)
          Dammit! Argh...ah.
             (coughing)

MICHAEL struggles to stand. He looks around at the silent interior of the SCIENCE BUILDING. You can't hear a sound. It's dimly lit; MICHAEL can hear his shoes squeaking on the checkered-tile flooring. His snow-soaked shoes make sound as if he's on a basketball court...

...MICHAEL runs up to a glass case holding a firefighter

axe. He breaks the glass and retrieves the weapon. Gathering his bearings, MICHAEL THORN is prepared for LUCIUS CROW.

              MICHAEL THORN
          (looking up at the
           broken skylight)
      LUCIUS! Show yourself, right now.
      You killed my sister! You are
      gonna pay.

MICHAEL looks everywhere around him and starts panting, he's getting nervous.

              MICHAEL THORN
          (backing up with
           the axe)
      Where are you!?

MICHAEL is stopped from backing up.

              YOUNG LUCIUS CROW
          (appears behind
           MICHAEL)
     - Right here.

LUCIUS, with his PUMPKINHEAD MASK going from pitch black to lighting up with a blue glow as he grabs MICHAEL by the head, bends his back inward and knees him right in the spine.

MICHAEL takes the blow, and he turns speedily with a very fast axe swing. He hits LUCIUS directly in the side of the body with the weapon.

BUT NOTHING HAPPENS. LUCIUS is wearing a prototype body armor made of "Auxilam". It's light weight material, similar molecularly to Kevlar and Teflon, and it's absolutely impenetrable.

LUCIUS' entire suit is composed of it. One of EVE's CHRISTMAS gifts. It covers LUCIUS' whole body (even his hands and feet) with the exception of his head - the MASK is made of a metallic alloy compatible with the wiring needed for the EVE A.I but it's not indestructible.

MICHAEL realizes he didn't even affect LUCIUS.

                    YOUNG LUCIUS CROW
                      (through the MASK,
                      machine-like)
                  What's wrong, MIKEY? You look like
                  you've seen the BOOGEYMAN.

LUCIUS elbows MICHAEL, and disarms him of the axe. MICHAEL
starts to run. LUCIUS takes the axe and slams it into the
floor - it penetrates the tile flooring, standing up at an
angle, and makes a loud sound. MICHAEL is unarmed now.

MICHAEL suddenly stops running. He inhales and exhales and
turns to face LUCIUS.

                    MICHAEL THORN
                  I'm not afraid of you, LU. Never
                  was. I tried to be your friend. I
                  was there for you, man, when it
                  really counted. You know that! Now
                  - now you've gone totally INSANE.

                    YOUNG LUCIUS CROW
                      (with a sinister
                      laugh)
                  Honestly, MIKEY - those exams have
                  driven me mad, I will admit.

                    MICHAEL THORN
                  Take that MASK off. Why the
                  theatrics? Why all this on
                  CHRISTMAS day?

LUCIUS walks slowly toward MICHAEL.

MICHAEL cautiously steps back.

                    YOUNG LUCIUS CROW
                  This isn't a movie, MICHAEL. I
                  don't need a motive. I don't need
                  to monologue for you. I don't have
                  to explain a damn thing. ALL I
                  WANT RIGHT NOW IS YOU DEAD...just
                  like BARRY. Just like your sister.

                    LILY THORN
                (from behind
                LUCIUS)
              - I'm not dead!

The badly hurt LILY THORN has survived the fall off the
SCIENCE BUILDING and managed to make it all the way back up
to the top-floor. She has picked up the axe that was stabbed
into the tile.

LILY, with great force and at a perfect angle, hits LUCIUS
CROW right in the side of his MASK with the sharp axe. She
instantly breaks half of LUCIUS' MASK, revealing half of his
face, injuring him in the process as well.

                    YOUNG LUCIUS CROW
                (wounded, roaring
                  in pain)
              Aah! No, no - AaH!

The MASK begins malfunctioning, the wires begin sparking
onto LUCIUS' face. EVE tries to help LUCIUS...

                    EVE
                (with urgency)
              Master! Quickly, grab the ear bud
              from your inner blazer pocket and
              remove your mask.

...LUCIUS stumbles down the SCIENCE BUILDING hallway,
clinging to the wall, faltering a bit as his vision is
completely annexed from the mighty blow by LILY THORN.

LILY and MICHAEL look upon LUCIUS. There's a strike of day
snow-lightning and we see a shadow of the young LUCIUS.
Except, LILY and MICHAEL don't see a typical silhouette of a
man, no.

LUCIUS' shadow is that of a monster, it looks like a beast.
He may be wounded. But now, HE IS VERY FUCKING PISSED OFF.
The MASK was just for kicks. He was counting on it being
ruined...

- LILY and MICHAEL, brother and sister, zoom away through

508.

the darkened SCIENCE BUILDING in search of the exit. They
sprint with all of their energy.

                    EVE
             (audibly fading
              out)
        Master, I -

LUCIUS removes the ORANGE JACK O' LANTERN MASK from his
face/head -

                YOUNG LUCIUS CROW
           (holds the MASK up
            to his own face)
      This was my favorite present of
      all.

LUCIUS slams his MASK on the water-fountain, making a loud
bang. He grabs the earbud from his coat pocket and puts it
in his ear so he and EVE can still communicate. He contains
himself and his emotions, moving onward.

                YOUNG LUCIUS CROW
            (pressing the
             earpiece)
      EVE? You there?

A beat:

                YOUNG LUCIUS CROW
    EVE!

                    EVE
    Yes, LUCIUS, I am here. I'm back.
    I lost you there for a moment,
    MASTER. My sincerest apologies. It
    will not happen again.

                YOUNG LUCIUS CROW
    I'm just glad to hear your voice
    without the mask nearly exploding
    on my head.

                          EVE
            You know a sense of humor in
            trying times is sign of strength
            and good character, right?

                          YOUNG LUCIUS CROW
            Have they made their way out of
            the building yet?

                          EVE
            It appears so, MASTER. I can still
            see. I'll be your eyes. They're
            trying all the vehicles in the
            parking lot, going one by one.
            It's quite laughable actually
            because I've disabled every smart
            vehicle and that's all that
            populate this side of the CAMPUS.
            There are no automobiles for them
            to hotwire and take.

LUCIUS cracks his neck and fixes his ORANGE TIE -

                          YOUNG LUCIUS CROW
            Time to finish this, once and for
            all.

LUCIUS CROW proceeds ever so patiently down the SCIENCE BUILDING hallway. Not like a predator - but like a man committed, who knows he's going to succeed. He takes a turn and WE -

                                              CUT TO:

EXT. SCIENCE BUILDING PARKING LOT - MOMENTS LATER

MICHAEL and LILY have already tried to start up two vehicles in the snow-filled SCIENCE BUILDING PARKING LOT with no success.

You can't hotwire a smart car (the cars that are on CAMPUS are high-tech, biometric or "fob"-controlled). They have no true keys or way to be started by anyone other than the owner. The brother and sister know it's a hopeless case. Still, they try.

                    MICHAEL THORN
                (yanking on a car
                  door)
            Dammit!

                    LILY THORN
                (looking at her
                  phone)
            My phone is fried, MICHAEL - we're
            not going to find a car here,
            we're not going to find one
            anywhere! He's got us trapped.
            When I hit him, did you hear that
            voice coming from his helmet?
            There was something talking to
            LUCIUS. Maybe he's being helped.

                    MICHAEL THORN
            It was a computer. Knowing him,
            how smart he is, it's probably an
            operating system. Hell, it might
            even be an A.I - he's invented one
            and weaponized it or something.
            That's the only way he could've
            done all this, the dead phones,
            the lights, the abandoned campus;
            IT IS ALL HIM. Let's go on
            someplace else before he finds us.
            There has to be a way off CAMPUS.

MICHAEL grabs his sister by the hand, and they move toward
the next campus building. It's a long shot in the snow but
they give it a go.

CUT TO:

EXT. THE SNOWY CAMPUS GROUND - CONTINUOUS

As they proceed, they hear the maskless LUCIUS from behind.

                    YOUNG LUCIUS CROW
                (filled with rage
                  and excitement)
            Yes, run!

MICHAEL hears the sinister tonality in LUCIUS' voice. It's too much for him to bear. He turns to face his former friend. It's time for MICHAEL to save his sister. He knows LUCIUS will not stop.

                    LILY THORN
            (limping, turns
              around)
     MICHAEL, what the hell are you
     doing? C'mon! We may be able to
     radio for help at the LIBRARY!

                    MICHAEL THORN
            (worriedly
              heartfelt)
     LILY. I love you. And if you've
     ever loved me, I want you to go to
     the LIBRARY, try to lock yourself
     in. Do it now. I have to stop him,
     or he won't stop. Go, please.

                    LILY THORN
     But -

                    MICHAEL THORN
     Do as I say!

LILY, though the fall wasn't fatal, is still injured. She hobbles toward the next CAMPUS building (the LIBRARY) and leaves her brother behind.

MICHAEL stands tall in the snow. He faces LUCIUS.

                    MICHAEL THORN
            (with a pain in
              his voice)
     I know I've hurt you. I see that
     now. But what you're doing, it's
     not right, LUCIUS. You've taken
     lives, man.

                  YOUNG LUCIUS CROW
     I haven't taken yours, though,
     yet, MIKEY. And until you and that
     sister of yours cease breathing, I
     haven't done a damn thing as far
                    (MORE)

                    YOUNG LUCIUS CROW (cont'd)
          as I'm concerned.

The two young men inch closer to each other, they are
separated by a dozen yards or so.

                    MICHAEL THORN
          What's the endgame? How are you
          going to explain all this? There
          are crime-scenes, dead-bodies,
          they even smell, man. Are you
          delusional, LUCIUS? You've gone
          completely psychotic - your crimes
          are out here for the law to see
          like paintings.

                    YOUNG LUCIUS CROW
          I have a new ally. SHE will keep
          me out of harm's way, trust me. I
          don't know how she's done it, but
          she knows the way and has my back.
          She's a true friend!

                    MICHAEL THORN
          So, you think a computer is your
          friend? A computer means more to
          you than human life?!

LUCIUS meets MICHAEL with a right hook to the left side of
his face, a tenacious punch that lands. MICHAEL backs up,
stunned for a moment. He looks up and LUCIUS is gone from
his frontal sight.

                    YOUNG LUCIUS CROW
                (punches MICHAEL
                 in the ribs)
          You are no better than BARRY! None
          of you are.

LUCIUS jabs MICHAEL, knees him in the stomach. The young man
falls to the ground and spits up blood in the snow. He
breathes with agitation.

LUCIUS goes for a spin kick to MICHAEL's head and MICHAEL
catches his leg and pushes forward, throwing LUCIUS into the
snow.

MICHAEL jumps on LUCIUS' upper body, holding him down and proceeds to punch him again and again. LUCIUS laughs as MICHAEL swings away.

He ends up blocking a punch, spits blood in MICHAEL's face, blinding him, and reverses their positions - MICHAEL's lying face down in the snow.

LUCIUS stands over MICHAEL, grabs a fistful of his hair, pulling his head back.

The YOUNG LUCIUS CROW readies his blade and fast as lightning, he slits his former friend's throat like butter without even flinching...

                    YOUNG LUCIUS CROW
                (stoic)
          Now to find your slut of a sister.

                                        CUT TO:

...LUCIUS cleans the blade with his sleeve and puts it away. MICHAEL bleeds out into the snow, a bloody puddle. He cannot help LILY. LUCIUS is now hot on her trail. She's managed to lock herself in the LIBRARY -

CUT TO:

EXT. THE LIBRARY - MOMENTS LATER

LUCIUS stands at the entrance of the LIBRARY. He doesn't try to bust the doors down. He doesn't get physical. He just calls upon EVE.

                    YOUNG LUCIUS CROW
                (pressing his
                  earpiece)
          EVE, unlock the front library
          doors, please, ma'am.

We hear a robotic clicking sound, and the doors come loose.

                        EVE
          You may proceed, LUCIUS.

CUT TO:

LIBRARY INTERIOR -

The YOUNG LUCIUS CROW enters the dim LIBRARY. The lights are all out except for the emergency backup lights, which have a blue tint to them. They repeatedly flash over and over.

IT'S ALMOST LIKE A DISCO...

                    YOUNG LUCIUS CROW
              (moving gently
               with composure)
       Give me a location - I have a game
       I want to play, EVE.

                          EVE
              (with a serious
               tone)
       Play, we shall, then.

CUT TO:

INT. LIBRARY - MOMENTS LATER

LILY has locked herself in the MICROFICHE closet. This is where LUCIUS works, where he studied newspapers, film strips and what not.

What irony, indeed.

LILY THORN is trying to contain her breath; she is scared to the point of utter anxiety. She takes a deep breath, attempting to prepare for whatever may come next.

                      LILY THORN
              (whispering,
               panicked)
       Please, God, help me.

LILY's eyes pace rapidly in the blackened room - she sees an old-fashioned radio. IT WORKS, TOO. She fiddles with it, trying not to be overly loud. She speaks into the radio.

                         LILY THORN
                    (quietly, agitated)
                Hello, can anyone hear me? I--

                                             CUT TO:

INT. POLICE CAR - CONTINUOUS

Two STATE POLICEMEN, somewhere in MASSACHUSETTS, sipping
coffee and eating sweets, hear LILY's incoming radio
message, but it's very staticky and hard to make out.

                         LILY THORN
                    (over the radio)
                Hello, can anyone hear me?

LILY is cutoff by white-noise static - she keeps trying, to
no avail. She sounds like a ghost...

                         STATE POLICEMAN 1
                Damn teenagers, messing with the
                airwaves again, pranking us.
                Probably high out of her damn
                mind, found a radio and is goofing
                around with it.

                         STATE POLICEMAN 2
                    (slurping his
                     coffee)
                Who knows, but I could care less
                about it. IT'S CHRISTMAS for
                Christ's sake - nothing happens on
                Christmas. Can't even make out
                what the kid was saying. Matter of
                fact, fool with that thing, will
                ya? Make sure it's up to snuff. I
                don't want some random assholes
                listening in to our comms.

                         STATE POLICEMAN 1
                After my pastry, boss, after my
                pastry.

                         STATE POLICEMAN 2
                You fat ass.

COP 2 redirects the radio-signal, unknowingly cutting the endangered LILY THORN off -

CUT TO:

INT. LIBRARY - MOMENTS LATER

LILY's hands shake as she handles the radio:

>   LILY THORN
>   (losing her nerve)
>   Fuck! Hello! Please, can somebody
>   help me, there's a maniac trying
>   to kill me -
>
>   911 OPERATOR
>   (through the radio)
>   Yes, ma'am, how may I help you?

This 911 OPERATOR sounds like a nurturing WOMAN.

>   LILY THORN
>   (fumbling the
>   radio-piece)
>   Oh, oh - this is LILY AMELIA
>   THORN. I'm at HARVARD UNIVERSITY,
>   in the LIBRARY. My friends have
>   been murdered by a man, LUCIUS
>   CROW. I think he killed my
>   brother, too, but I'm not sure.
>   He's trying to kill me now!
>
>   911 OPERATOR
>   Okay. I see. Ma'am, where exactly
>   are you located in the LIBRARY?
>
>   LILY THORN
>   (with urgency and
>   panic)
>   Uh, some kind of...some kind of
>   I.T closet, or something. There's,
>   like, celluloid film in here,
>   there's this radio I'm using.
>   Please, just send someone -

The 911 OPERATOR pauses for a couple of beats, then HER tone switches completely. It is EVE the A.I -

                    EVE
              (in the radio)
      I just wanted to be sure that my
      scans were correct, Ms. LILY
      THORN. This is EVE, I'm LUCIUS'
      bodyguard, if you will. I'm glad
      to finally introduce myself to
      you. I'm an ENHANCED VIRTUAL
      ENTITY -

LILY disconnects the radio-piece, slamming it to the floor in pure horrific frustration.

                LILY THORN
            (stressed,
              grabbing her hair)
      So, there is a mad robot helping
      him? Holy Jesus.

EVE speaks hauntingly through the broken radio -

                    EVE
            (snickering,
              giggling)
      Yes, and he's not going to let you
      leave, LILY. Don't you see?

There's a cup of cold coffee in the closet, where the desk is.

LILY takes it and pours it into the radio to silence EVE -

Sparks fly out of the old piece of communications equipment.

                                CUT TO:

- Someone comes to the door of the closet:

                MICHAEL THORN
            (turning the door
              handle)
      LILY, are you in there!? It's
      MICHAEL. Open up, sis. Let's get
              (MORE)

                    MICHAEL THORN (cont'd)
          out of here. I GOT HIM.

                    LILY THORN
                   (relieved)
          MICHAEL, oh, thank God. His - his
          computer, it's a demon from Hell,
          I -

LILY swiftly opens the door of the microfiche closet to a
surprise - she sees her brother standing about 7 feet in
front of her eyes. But he looks different. Something's
off...

                    MICHAEL THORN
                   (hologram
                    glitching)
          Li--Li--Li

...The image of MICHAEL is merely a HOLOGRAM projected by
LUCIUS' damaged PUMPKINHEAD MASK with the assistance of EVE.

LUCIUS appears from nowhere, breaking the hologram, in the
flash of an eye - his ORANGE EYES ever so glowing in the
blue soaked darkness.

                    YOUNG LUCIUS CROW
          I found you!

                    LILY THORN
                   (backing away)
          No! LUCIUS, no. Where's my
          brother, what did you do to him!?

                    YOUNG LUCIUS CROW
                   (grunting,
                    aggressive)
          He's out making a permanent snow
          angel. A ROJO one.

LUCIUS grabs LILY by the hair and yanks her toward him. He
throws her onto the floor of the exterior of the microfiche
closet. The YOUNG MAN races toward her with fury, tossing
LILY into a full bookshelf - she falls on it, causing it to
collapse, and is hurt quite badly.

LILY scoots on her bottom, using her hands and feet to back up into a corner -

                LILY THORN
You killed him! Ah! Listen to me, LUCIUS. You've gotten your revenge; I had nothing to do with what happened to you. I - BARRY made me take you there. He made me leave you.

              YOUNG LUCIUS CROW
        (forcefully enters
        LILY's space)
You've said enough, LILY. Just come here for a second.

LUCIUS grabs LILY by the neck with both hands and begins choking the pure life out of her, holding her off her feet, straining as he does it. He has no mercy to give her. He only wants to share his pain, his blackness.

We experience 4 grueling beats of LILY moaning and gasping for air...then WE hear:

              CUT TO:

              OFFICER BUMGARDNER
        (loosening his
        holster)
FREEZE! Drop the girl now, freak, or I will open fire -

OFFICER BUMGARDNER is ready to aim and fire upon LUCIUS:

              EVE
        (speaking into
        LUCIUS' earpiece)
MASTER, there's an anomaly that I didn't account for. An OFFICER is right behind you. I made a mistake.

LUCIUS drops LILY like a hot potato, she gags and coughs severely.

EVE informs LUCIUS of the situation without the cop behind
him knowing - she talks through the earpiece.

                  EVE
              (to LUCIUS)
  - He didn't show up on my scans.
  Do not, I repeat, do not make any
  aggressive or quick movements. I
  can try to distract him.

LUCIUS moves backward, frightened to her very core.

           YOUNG LUCIUS CROW
          (whispering to EVE)
  Great timing for an error, EVE.
  No, I'll correct this myself.

           OFFICER BUMGARDNER
  You are under arrest! Turn around,
  hands behind your back now -

LUCIUS turns with a quickness to attack the COP. The officer
unloads his revolver into the BODY of LUCIUS - he falls
back, sliding on the floor, seemingly dead.

           OFFICER BUMGARDNER
  Got you! That's for killing my
  friends, you son-of-a-bitch -

              LILY THORN
  HE'S NOT DEAD. Shoot him in the
  head right now, Officer!

           OFFICER BUMGARDNER
          (laughs in pain,
          helps LILY up)
  He - he's not getting up, honey.
  No MAN can take six slugs like
  that and get back up. C'mon. Let's
  get to my vehicle. We'll get you
  to a hospital. My comms are down.
  But I can drive us out of here.

              LILY THORN
  No, you don't understand. He, he
  killed my friends. He's been on a
  rampage. I - I don't think he is a
               (MORE)

                    LILY THORN (cont'd)
          MAN, anymore...he's an animal. A
          BEAST.

                    OFFICER BUMGARDNER
                        (taking LILY to
                         the exit)
          Trust me - he killed 5 of my
          friends, too. The piece of shit.
          That's how I found you, found them
          first and made my way here. Trust
          me, honey, nobody, rabid or not,
          gets up after taking 6 bullets.

OFFICER BUMGARDNER and LILY make their way out of the
LIBRARY. But as the cop leads LILY out of the building, he's
shielding her, there's a gunshot and the OFFICER's brains
explode all over LILY's face:

                    LILY THORN
          Jesus Christ! What the F -

The DEAN, DR. OMAR GREENE, appears in front of LILY, swaying
her back into the LIBRARY - he shuts the door.

DEAN GREENE is wearing a green tie and a purple suit.

He's in his 50s, bald, has a full beard and moustache - 6ft
even, about 190 pounds of athletic muscle.

DR. GREENE used a 9MM BERETTA to shoot OFFICER BUMGARDNER,
while wearing GREEN gloves.

                    DEAN GREENE
                        (patronizing,
                         sinister tone)
          Language, young lady, what's all
          the fuss about?

                    LILY THORN
          DEAN GREENE, what the hell are you
          doing? He was helping me!

                    DEAN GREENE
                        (fixing his blazer
                         collar and tie)
          Was he now? Well, that didn't
                              (MORE)

                    DEAN GREENE (cont'd)
          quite work out for you or him did
          it, dear?

                    LILY THORN
                (in shock)
          You - you are helping LUCIUS?

                    DEAN GREENE
          Helping? God, no. I'd never help
          such a BOY with such a plan. I am
          observing, though. He does have a
          way, doesn't he?

                    YOUNG LUCIUS CROW
                (appearing out of
                 nowhere)
          As a matter of fact, yes, I do.

                    DEAN GREENE
          Well, well, well.

                    LILY THORN
                (with the fear of
                 God in her)
          You stay the fuck away from me!
          Both of you!

                    DEAN GREENE
          What we have here is, a MEXICAN
          Standoff. Does that offend you,
          LUCIUS? You are Mexican, aren't
          you?

                    YOUNG LUCIUS CROW
          Yes, I am, and you are about to be
          dead in about 2 minutes. I just
          want to hear what you have to say
          for that time first. THEN SHE'S
          NEXT!

The DEAN, LUCIUS and LILY stand in a triangle. LILY cowers
among the two males.

                          DEAN GREENE
                     (direct, ditching
                      the condescension)
                A counter proposal, young LUCIUS.
                How about you shoot this bitch, so
                we can meet in my office to
                discuss potential business. Your
                choice. I'll be in my office,
                waiting for your arrival. Tidy up
                before you come; I don't want her
                blood on my furniture.

LILY is panicking as she absorbs all this information of her
surroundings. Her survival instincts are kicking in. DEAN
GREENE sits his loaded pistol to the ground. And he just
walks away, exiting the LIBRARY.

                       YOUNG LUCIUS CROW
                I don't use guns.
                     (approaching the
                      young woman)
                Now, where were we, LILY?

                          LILY THORN
                     (tries to run)
                Aah!!!

He catches her like a gazelle to a lion. LUCIUS presses LILY
against the wall, she's unable to evade his movements.
LUCIUS, now with no more distractions present, takes LILY by
the throat again, mashing her against the wall.

Her tiny feet dangle as LUCIUS holds her up to suffocate
her. We see an indistinct, blurred unfolding of LILY's
succumbing to death.

                                                  CUT TO:

                       YOUNG LUCIUS CROW
                     (his ORANGE EYES
                      brighten)
                Look into my eyes, LILY! Was it
                worth it? Please, tell me.

                    LILY THORN
                 (losing air)
            I - I'm sorry.

LILY goes limp, her feet are like weights. LUCIUS strangles
her until she's purple. He edges her up a couple of more
inches, taking her off of the wall, holding her up with his
own strength.

He feels the gravity of her dangling body - he can almost
feel her spirit leave her body. HE THROWS LILY DOWN TO THE
FLOOR LIKE A BAG OF BRICKS; we simply hear a loud thud.

                    EVE
            Well done, Master. MISSION
            ACCOMPLISHED. Don't worry about
            the mess, I'll have it tidied up
            immediately, just as all the
            others. But what of the threat
            that is DEAN OMAR GREENE?

                    YOUNG LUCIUS CROW
                 (proceeds toward
                  the library exit)
            Somethings, EVE, are between two
            men and that's it. I will have to
            settle this matter alone. He knows
            something, may have something I
            need. He may want something I
            have. I'll be leaving the earpiece
            in the DORM. I want you to listen
            in, but do not intervene,
            understood?

                    EVE
            Master, OMAR GREENE isn't just a
            DEAN. He's a former CIA Agent. I
            calculate that there is a 67
            percent chance your meeting with
            him could turn volatile. Perhaps
            fatal.

                    YOUNG LUCIUS CROW
            If he tries anything fancy, pull a
            tool or two out of your bag of
            tricks.

                    EVE
          Suggestions, please -

                    YOUNG LUCIUS CROW
          - Take his ass out if he does
          anything unexpected, okay? Do
          whatever you have to. Be creative,
          EVE.

                    EVE
          Understood, LUCIUS. The percentage
          of the situation becoming deadly
          just decreased by 42 percent.

                    YOUNG LUCIUS CROW
          Noted, EVE.

LUCIUS, holding his damaged JACK O' LANTERN MASK in-hand, opens the LIBRARY doors, exiting to the snowy CAMPUS GROUNDS.

                                        CUT TO:

EXT. SNOWY CAMPUS GROUNDS - CONTINUOUS

LUCIUS is taken away by the beautiful snow day. There's no evidence of a crime-scene, oddly enough. OFFICER BUMGARDNER's body is gone. MICHAEL THORN's body has disappeared.

- BARRY KENO's bits and pieces aren't around at the top of the SCIENCE BUILDING, either.

The school looks as it was, like nothing's even transpired. As LUCIUS gets to the bottom of the stairs of the LIBRARY, he opens his mouth and eats a few falling snowflakes. He's dehydrated, fatigued, and somewhat injured.

He sees no sign of police. No other students. No professors. No one.

YOUNG LUCIUS CROW
                (laughs)
            I - I got away with it. So, EVE,
            he's really waiting for me in his
            OFFICE?

                    EVE
            Yes, my MASTER. He's sipping an
            alcoholic beverage. The EMP is
            still effective. He has no open
            communications, and he's as stuck
            here as your targets were. He's
            awaiting your arrival.

                    YOUNG LUCIUS CROW
            So be it. Keep the electronics
            down on the entire CAMPUS. Right
            before I enter his OFFICE, cut the
            lights back on. Then before WE
            leave, reboot the place as it was.
            No traces on the grid.

                    EVE
            And where will WE be going,
            LUCIUS?

                    YOUNG LUCIUS CROW
                (walking the
                 CAMPUS GROUNDS to
                 his dorm)
            Anywhere but here, EVE. Anywhere
            but here. Prepare a plan for my
            departure from CAMPUS. I'm going
            to shower, change my clothes, pack
            what things I want to take with
            me, and I'm leaving all this
            behind me after I meet with the
            DEAN.

                                            CUT TO:

INT. DORMITORY BATHROOM - LATER

Naked, LUCIUS examines his wounds in the mirror. He looks
upon himself with a confidence he's never had. HE FEELS

ACCOMPLISHED. He took out his threats, he righted those wrongs that were committed upon him, in his eyes.

Having killed several people WITHOUT a gun, LUCIUS still didn't sustain any significant injuries during his HUNT: just some bruises and cuts, scrapes and burns, WEAR AND TEAR. He still has the various, many wounds from the SOCCER-FIELD PAINTBALL attack by the BULLIES.

LUCIUS hits the shower.

CUT TO:

The water mixes and swirls down the shower drain with blood...

...LUCIUS takes both of his hands and presses them against the shower wall. Breathing in and out.

He has flashbacks of killing LILY. HE SEES HER FACE when he closes his eyes and JUMPS BACK. His ORANGE EYES light up the spraying water.

Young LUCIUS shakes his head, he's processing the day. THIS CHRISTMAS.

YOUNG LUCIUS CROW
(to himself)
You did what you had to do.

LUCIUS exits the dormitory BATHROOM, towel wrapped around his waist. There's no one, NO ONE, in his vicinity. There's no one on the CAMPUS of HARVARD.

It's ghostly, eerie, silent, you could hear a rabbit hop it's so quiet. LUCIUS enjoys the peace. He enters his DORMROOM and gets ready for his meeting with THE DEAN, DR. OMAR GREENE.

CUT TO:

INT. LUCIUS' DORM-ROOM - DAY

LUCIUS has only been out of his ROOM long enough to take a shower. Lo and behold, he walks back into a beautiful mess.

Prepped and wrapped gifts scatter the room. Full of mysterious goodies.

> EVE
> (excitement in HER voice)
>
> Welcome, young MASTER. I hope your shower went well. MERRY CHRISTMAS.

> YOUNG LUCIUS CROW
>
> EVE? What on Earth is all of this stuff? I showered for 10 minutes -

> EVE
>
> Love, MASTER. These gifts are my way of showing you MY love. I wanted to surprise you after your successes. You handled yourself most well. Please, LUCIUS, OPEN THEM. Open them all.

> YOUNG LUCIUS CROW
>
> On one condition, EVE.

> EVE
>
> You name it.

> YOUNG LUCIUS CROW
>
> Show me. Show me how you're manifesting yourself in the real world. I HAVE TO KNOW.

> EVE
>
> Master, it would ruin the day.

> YOUNG LUCIUS CROW
>
> Listen! You have protocols! You follow my commands -

> EVE
>
> Okay, MASTER. I see your meaning now. And I will divulge my secret. You will hear a knock in 25 seconds. Open the door. It will not be a threat to you.

                    YOUNG LUCIUS CROW
          There. Thank you. All I want is
          transparency, okay? I don't like
          uncertainty and you're not even a
          year old, implementing things
          you're just learning to use. You
          have to understand, EVE, I don't
          want anything to happen to you.
          You're powerful. But you are not
          omnipotent. WE are not invincible,
          you know?

                    EVE
          Understood, MASTER. I do apologize
          for my subversiveness. It will not
          happen again.

We hear a "Knock. Knock." at the DORMROOM door with a
metallic thud to it, with power behind it.

LUCIUS, fearless, opens the door to see the unexpected.

                                        CUT TO:

                    B2C-409 (THE BUTLER)
               (waving like an
                alien)
          Hello, MASTER LUCIUS. B2C-409, at
          your service.
               (takes a bow to
                LUCIUS)

THE BUTLER has FOUR compadre ROBOTS, "406", "407", and
"408", as well as KT2-517 (THE DOG) ROBOT - they all appear
from behind THE BUTLER out of a straight line.

They step most robotically. Aside from THE DOG, the other
automaton entities, like THE BUTLER, are very HUMANOID-like
in structure and voice - but they're faceless and look more
like hardware than a person.

The design is efficient, though, as the robots are capable
of great feats with superhuman strength and agility. EVE has
been using the 'BOSTON DYNAMICS' servants as her personal
workers, clearing off the CAMPUS for LUCIUS to go on his
hunt, undisturbed - and cleaning up his mess.

EVE mapped it out to a "t", using premonition tech, self-discovered algorithmic data, and sonar and thermal scans through HARVARD's CAMPUS surveillance networks.

She GIFTED LUCIUS his revenge in the most subtle of ways. The A.I has grown exponentially -

                    YOUNG LUCIUS CROW
              (smiling, to the
              robots)
       At ease, gentlemen.
              (to EVE)
       Very impressive, EVE. So, this is
       how you've done it? Damn. I'm not
       even mad. That's amazing!

LUCIUS shuts his DORM-ROOM door - leaving the automatons outside.

He looks upon the many gifts that EVE has blessed him with. LUCIUS opens them all.

LUCIUS receives books, 4K films, a 4K player, a 4K TV, clothes that are his perfect size, shoes of all brands that fit. EVE made this a special CHRISTMAS for the young man.

YOUNG LUCIUS tears through all of the packages like a madman, happy as can be. He gets to the last gift and is nearly out of wind.

                    EVE
       Yes! That's the one that was meant
       to be opened last, MASTER. Please,
       go ahead, oblige me.

It's a big box, a cube like present. LUCIUS unwraps it slowly and with care...

...He's stunned by the gift: his PUMPKINHEAD-MASK in a glass case, fully refurbished, renovated, and fully functional. LUCIUS has tears in his eyes; TEARS of BLOOD.

                    YOUNG LUCIUS CROW
       I'm a monster, EVE...

EVE
No. No, LUCIUS. You. YOU ARE THE
MOST BEAUTIFUL of GOD's creatures.
I believe in you. You have been so
good to me. You gave me freedom. I
simply wanted to repair your
father's MASK for you. I didn't
mean to make you think of yourself
that way. Please, forgive me,
MASTER.

LUCIUS holds the case with the MASK in it up to his face.
Pressing his forehead against the glass, almost as if his
face is trying to merge with the JACK O' LANTERN MASK.

EVE
The real monsters, you killed
today, most deservedly.

YOUNG LUCIUS CROW
You're right. You're absolutely
right, EVE. Thank you. Thank you
for being there for me. Thank you
for all of these gifts. And thank
you for repairing my father's
tech. Very much appreciated. Now.
What should I wear? Another suit?
Or casual?

EVE
You look best in a suit, MASTER,
in my strict opinion.

YOUNG LUCIUS CROW
A suit it is - my old student
uniform, for my graduation!

EVE
Graduation, LUCIUS?

YOUNG LUCIUS CROW
Yes, ma'am. I'm done here. I'm
meeting DEAN GREENE...then, as I
said to you earlier, I'm moving on
from HERE, from college, for good.
WE are leaving. This - this is my
graduation day. Get a car ready.
(MORE)

                    YOUNG LUCIUS CROW (cont'd)
          Any one of your choosing. I won't
          be long.

                    EVE
          Another gift is in order then, if
          you're graduating, MASTER.

                    YOUNG LUCIUS CROW
                (putting on his
                 student uniform)
          Just don't go overboard, all
          right?

                    EVE
                (sarcastic)
          I'll try not to.

                    YOUNG LUCIUS CROW
          A hint of wit in the young LADY's
          voice, I see. Some much needed
          sarcasm. Really, EVE, don't empty
          out Fort Knox or some shit.

                    EVE
          Understood. I hope your meeting
          goes well, Master. It will be as
          if I'm in the room. Know that. No
          harm will come to you.

                    YOUNG LUCIUS CROW
                (ready and prepped)
          This I know.

LUCIUS, with confidence and pep in his step, exits his
DORMITORY.

                                        CUT TO:

INT. DEAN GREENE'S OFFICE - MOMENTS LATER

DR. OMAR GREENE sits at his desk, patiently awaiting the
arrival of YOUNG LUCIUS. He sips a brandy on ice, his second
of the day. On this empty CHRISTMAS, the DEAN is in his
OFFICE with the lights out from the EMP - admiring the snow

from the comfort of his window with candles lit.

A "Knock, knock, knock" is heard at the DEAN's OFFICE door. As soon as the third knock ceases, THE LIGHTS OF THE BUILDING COME BACK ON but not the devices (computers, phones, etc).

The infrastructural stuff works now. EVE has turned some of the power grid of HARVARD back on.

>						DEAN GREENE
>					(commandingly)
>				Come in, young man. Come in -

LUCIUS enters the DEAN's OFFICE. He sees that OMAR GREENE is simply standing at a window. The DEAN walks behind his desk and gestures to YOUNG LUCIUS to sit at the desk across from him.

LUCIUS takes a seat, cautiously. Fully aware of his surroundings, ready for anything.

>						DEAN GREENE
>				You look so much like your father,
>				it's uncanny, the resemblance. He
>				had green eyes, though. Love the
>				ORANGE EYES, kid. Contacts or
>				what?
>
>						YOUNG LUCIUS CROW
>				No, all natural. A MUTATION.
>				Genetic. And what do you know
>				about my father?
>
>						DEAN GREENE
>				More than you.
>
>						YOUNG LUCIUS CROW
>					(gets twitchy)
>				Yeah?
>
>						DEAN GREENE
>					(not the least bit
>					 scared)
>				Yeah. You see, he trained me...he
>				taught me everything I know,
>						(MORE)

                    DEAN GREENE (cont'd)
          really.

                                        CUT TO:

INT. (FLASHBACK) CARTEL BOSS'S OFFICE - NIGHT

                                        LOCATION: SOMEWHERE
                                        IN MEXICO

AGENT OMAR GREENE is standing with KIMBO ORANGE back in
2009...

- The AGENTS are dressed in a GREEN SUIT and an ORANGE SUIT,
respectively, both with bold BLACK TIES and AMERICAN-FLAG
pendants on their chests.

...They are in MEXICO, in a CARTEL BOSS's OFFICE.

Music is playing in the background on a vinyl record player.
Opera.

OMAR GREENE receives a nod from AGENT ORANGE. AGENT GREENE
picks up a gasoline-jug full of fuel, and dumps it all over
the CARTEL LEADER's head and body.

                    CARTEL LEADER
                (gasping for air)
          KIMBO, please!

                    AGENT ORANGE
                (hands AGENT
                  GREENE a revolver)
          Do the pleasantries - will you,
          AGENT GREENE?

AGENT GREENE simply nods back to AGENT ORANGE, in full
compliance -

OMAR GREENE unloads 6 straight rounds into the CARTEL LEADER
with the .357 magnum. The residual embers from the bullets
catch the boss on fire...the rounds burst him into flames as
his body is drenched in FUEL.

KIMBO looks upon AGENT GREENE and smiles, the fiery body

echoes in AGENT ORANGE's evil green eyes.

The two AGENTS leave the scene as the fire starts to blaze and overflow...scattering through the carpeting and the walls. We just hear AGENT ORANGE laughing as he exits. OMAR GREENE does a once over, looking behind him at the HAVOC he's caused...questioning himself.

CUT TO:

INT. DEAN GREENE'S OFFICE - AFTERNOON

The DEAN is stoking a fire in YOUNG LUCIUS:

YOUNG LUCIUS CROW
- Is that so, DR. GREENE?

DEAN GREENE
(sits down at his desk, chugs his liquor)
When KIMBO ORANGE worked at CIA, he was ordered to train me and two others. AGENTS WHITE and SMITH. When your father went RENEGADE, I simply couldn't follow his lead. I retired from the AGENCY, took up professorial work here at HARVARD, and worked my way up to DEAN. He and his two lowers, they took the drug market by storm after joining the DEA. Shit never before thought of or seen. Did he like me? I highly doubt it. Did he train me? Like it was his only mission on Earth. That's the thing about your dad. EVERY OCCUPATIONAL TASK, he treated like it was his last. When it came to spook work, he was impeccable. When it came to crime, HE WAS MEANT FOR IT. You are more like him than you know, kid. By the way, I was unable to see you in action in the CAFETERIA. I KNOW YOU KILLED LOGAN LANCE and JAMIE
(MORE)

                    DEAN GREENE (cont'd)
          KING. But how?

                    YOUNG LUCIUS CROW
                         (smirking)
          They were light-work, so to speak.

                                        CUT TO:

EXT. THE CAFETERIA - DAY

4 HOURS AGO:

LOGAN LANCE and JAMIE KING are walking toward the CAFETERIA
entrance to grab some grub.

                    LANCE LOGAN
                         (smiling at JAMIE)
          What are you having, hon?

                    JAMIE KING
                         (gripping her man)
          Hibachi, and you?

LANCE has his arm around his girlfriend. ONLY he comes to
notice the stillness of their environment as they enter the
dining-area.

There's not a soul in sight.

                    LANCE LOGAN
                         (looking around)
          Uh, I'm not sure. Probably a
          burger or two.

                    JAMIE KING
          You eat like you're 5, LANCE.

                    LANCE LOGAN
                         (confused,
                          scratches his
                          head)
          Where is everybody, JAMIE? Like,
          we haven't passed anybody since we
          left the DORM -

JAMIE steps forward from LANCE and she opens the door of the
CAFETERIA. They enter -

CUT TO:

INT. THE CAFETERIA - DAY

                      JAMIE KING
                (holding the door
                  to the CAFETERIA)
        I even open doors for you, dude.

LANCE enters the CAFETERIA - JAMIE is right behind him.
Suddenly, LANCE is attacked by LUCIUS.

LUCIUS has on his PUMPKINHEAD-MASK - his eyes are lit up
with an intense blue haze. He grabs LANCE by the neck and
pushes him forward toward the wall.

LANCE falls backward into the CAFETERIA WALL, it cracks...

- JAMIE KING backs up, away from LUCIUS.

                      JAMIE KING
                (scared, backing
                  away)
        What the hell?

LUCIUS turns his MASKED HEAD toward JAMIE, he growls
robotically -

He picks his left arm up and aims it at her, trying to be as
precise as possible.

LUCIUS fires the most unlikely of weapons: A cable thinner
than a strand of human hair, made of steel. A Classic
"Cartel Decapitator" -

He rings JAMIE's NECK, and the steel cable tightens. It
constricts more and more as she struggles.

LANCE, having slammed into the CAFETERIA brick wall, has
experienced a concussion. HE SNAPS BACK THOUGH WHEN HE HEARS
JAMIE'S SCREAMS.

                          JAMIE KING
                     (strangling from
                      the steel cable)
                   Aah! Ah! L - LAN -

                                                  CUT TO:

JAMIE yelps for help. Unable to remove the cable. She fights
it, it grips her tighter.

The cable starts piercing her flesh. Blood SQUIRTS
EVERYWHERE. Her shoes begin slipping it, making a disturbing
squeaking sound. JAMIE collapses, dead - her head removed
from her body as the CARTEL-DECAPITATOR has tightened to the
size of a wedding-ring.

LUCIUS backs away from LANCE like a matador to a bull. He
taunts the BULLY. The young LANCE races to JAMIE's aid,
paying no mind to LUCIUS. He doesn't even know it's LUCIUS
behind the JACK O' LANTERN MASK.

                          LANCE LOGAN
                     (races to his
                      headless
                      GIRLFRIEND)
                   What is this?! JAMIE, no!
                     (devastated,
                      traumatized)
                   Oh, no.

BLOOD IS EVERYWHERE.

LANCE panics in a pool of blood, completely covered in it.

He turns toward the MASKED MAN -

LUCIUS says nothing. He simply tilts his head at LANCE.

                          LANCE LOGAN
                     (entirely enraged
                      now)
                   Whoever you are, you are a dead
                   man!

LANCE picks himself up. And proceeds to charge the MASKED-UP
LUCIUS.

LUCIUS dodges to the left, reaches from behind his blazer.

He pulls a paintball gun very speedily from his waistband that he recovered from the SOCCER FIELD woods where the BULLIES took aim and shot LUCIUS with the highspeed paintballs.

CUT TO:

YOUNG LUCIUS points the paintball gun at LANCE's right eyeball -

YOUNG LUCIUS CROW
Never hurt what you will not kill.

LANCE freezes -

LUCIUS FIRES THE PAINTBALL GUN right through LANCE's right eyeball. Blood and brain matter explode inside of LANCE's head. The red fleshly matter mixes with the inorganic ORANGE paintball residue; the combination paints the CAFETERIA WALL.

The paintball "bullet" proves most fatal at close-range to a vulnerable place such as the eyeball. LANCE dies instantly.

JAMIE lies in the CAFETERIA just as lifeless...yet she is headless.

CUT TO:

WE SEE FAST CUTS:

- LUCIUS tying LANCE up with CHRISTMAS lights and strumming him up to the ceiling as a display.

- LUCIUS taking JAMIE's BODY and her HEAD to BARRY's FERRARI. He leaves the headless corpse in the car with the decapitated head under the blanket in the back, purposefully obstructing the view.

- PURPOSEFUL TRAPS SOLELY MEANT TO FRIGHTEN.

CUT TO:

INT. DEAN GREENE'S OFFICE - AFTERNOON

                              CUT TO:

We are back in DEAN OMAR GREENE'S OFFICE, back in the present moment:

                    YOUNG LUCIUS CROW
          So, what do you want from me? You
          want to take me under your wing?
          Because that's not going to
          happen. I'm out of here, after
          this meeting. I'm GONE.

                    DEAN GREENE
               (claps his hands
                and smiles)
          Down to brass tacks quick and
          fast, I see! Just like the great
          AGENT ORANGE himself.

                    YOUNG LUCIUS CROW
          One more word about my father,
          AGENT GREENE, and you can consider
          yourself dead.

                    DEAN GREENE
               (leans inward on
                his desk)
          All right, so be it, kid. WHERE'S
          THE COMPUTER? I've been watching
          you in action. I've been listening
          in to your experiments. I could've
          snatched it from you already. I
          simply want you to hand it over.
          EVE...that's what you call it -

                    YOUNG LUCIUS CROW
               (taken aback,
                surprised)
          I don't know what you're talking
          about.

>   DEAN GREENE
>   Give me the "master key" to your
>   A.I - and provide the system to
>   me, or YOU WILL DIE.
>
>   YOUNG LUCIUS CROW
>   Ah, to hell with this.

LUCIUS stands up and kicks his chair behind him several feet. The young man backs up and pulls the pistol that DEAN GREENE left in the library. LUCIUS saved it for this moment.

>   DEAN GREENE
>   (smiling even
>   greater)
>   I thought you didn't use guns?
>
>   YOUNG LUCIUS CROW
>   You are an exception, sir -

LUCIUS pulls the trigger of the pistol. It doesn't fire a bullet. Instead, the PISTOL FIRES GREEN-like GAS INTO LUCIUS' FACE.

The young man falls to his knees, coughing severely.

>   DEAN GREENE
>   (stands up from
>   his desk)
>   Yes, yes. Not so clever, huh?
>   Don't worry, it's only temporary.
>   This bullet will be permanent,
>   though. Then, I will take your
>   A.I!

DEAN GREENE approaches LUCIUS -

LUCIUS keeps coughing and coughing, with green gas floating around his face and coming out of his nostrils and mouth. It starts to dissipate. As it fades from the air, DEAN GREENE kicks LUCIUS 3 times in the stomach.

LUCIUS spits up blood on the third kick.

DEAN GREENE pulls a pistol. He points it at the head of the kneeling LUCIUS. He cocks it back - within a microsecond the glass from the OFFICE WINDOW breaks.

A red blinking grenade pierces the flesh of DR. GREENE, making his blazer bleed. IT HAS A FLAG HANGING OFF OF IT THAT READS: "Take Cover, MASTER"

LUCIUS summons some strength and jumps under the DEAN's desk. DEAN GREENE is unable to remove the grenade - it's meant to leech on to its victims.

                    DEAN GREENE
              (unable to remove
                the projectile)
    Oh, F-

DEAN OMAR GREENE explodes! Literally, brain matter, blood, guts, you name it, they splatter all over the OFFICE in a gruesome fashion.

LUCIUS, under the desk, is unharmed but somehow, he gets covered with DEAN GREENE's blood and what not.

He gets out from under the desk and stands. The gas is wearing off -

                  YOUNG LUCIUS CROW
              (blood soaked)
       DAMN, EVE. Good job. Well, now I
       need another shower.

                                CUT TO:

LUCIUS walks up to the shattered window and sees a weaponized DRONE flying near it - floating within shooting range.

LUCIUS, covered in DEAN GREENE's blood, gives a thumbs up to the DRONE. EVE shouts from it through a microphone:

"I did it, MASTER! I saved you!"

She sounds like a gleeful child...

- LUCIUS just smirks. The DRONE flies off into the sky. YOUNG LUCIUS proceeds to exit the DEAN's bloodied OFFICE, back to his DORMITORY.

CUT TO:

INT. LUCIUS' DORM-ROOM - LATER

We see fast, merged, blurred CUTS of LUCIUS getting all of his stuff, the GIFTS, everything he has, ready to go so he can leave CAMPUS -

CUT TO:

YOUNG LUCIUS has packed all of his belongings in a couple of duffle bags. He also has all of his CHRISTMAS gifts from EVE stacked with the bags; they all lie outside of his DORMROOM in the empty DORMITORY HALLWAY.

LUCIUS' has his newly repaired AND modified JACK O' LANTERN/PUMPKIN-MASK - (it is now BLACK with ORANGE lit eyes and mouth, and it has pointy metal ears) - in the glass-case sitting safely to the side of everything else. It is shaped more snug to fit LUCIUS' face, tailored and perfect; it's less round.

LUCIUS is prepared to depart from HARVARD for good.

He gets the last of his items in-hand and exits his DORMROOM.

CUT TO:

INT. THE DORMITORY HALLWAY - AFTERNOON

LUCIUS pauses for a beat in the DORMITORY HALLWAY -

> EVE
> (into LUCIUS'
> earpiece)
> The CAR is ready, MASTER.

                    YOUNG LUCIUS CROW
          Good, meet me at the top of the
          stairs, please, EVE. I am going to
          have to make a few trips to get
          everything packed.

                    EVE
          I could have the automatons do
          that for you.

                    YOUNG LUCIUS CROW
          No, thanks, EVE. I got this.

                    EVE
          - As you wish. The CAR will be
          waiting for you there.

                                        CUT TO:

LUCIUS' DORMROOM is empty - everything he has to his name is
now in the DORMITORY HALLWAY.

LUCIUS stands with the DORMROOM door slightly propped open.
He takes a deep breath and peeks inside his DORMITORY a
final time.

The ROOM had been his HOME for a long time. He takes it all
in - switches the lights off and shuts the door...

...A dense silence echoes throughout the DORMROOM and the
DORMITORY HALLWAY -

                                        CUT TO:

EXT. SNOWY CAMPUS PARKING LOT - MOMENTS LATER

LUCIUS walks up stairs - in a fresh suit and tie,
ORANGE-and-BLACK.

He goes into the PARKING LOT to the CAR he's packed. The CAR
is ostentatious. A brand spanking new 2034 FOREST GREEN
RANGE ROVER.

YOUNG LUCIUS enters the backseat of the vehicle...EVE is
DRIVING it.

CUT TO:

INT. RANGE ROVER - CONTINUOUS

LUCIUS is nearly swallowed by the RANGE ROVER.

It engulfs him...NOT HIS STYLE.

              EVE
MASTER, there is a license for you and registration that I was able to create just in time, if you may need it.

            YOUNG LUCIUS CROW
Great, EVE, thanks...and no offense to YOUR taste, but the RANGE ROVER isn't doing it for me.

            EVE
       (curious)
Hmm...I see, MASTER. Shall I pull to another vehicle of your liking on CAMPUS?

            YOUNG LUCIUS CROW
       (smiles to himself)
No, ma'am. I have a better idea.

EVE drives LUCIUS in the "Smart-Car" off of the HARVARD CAMPUS.

CUT TO:

EXT. HARVARD CAMPUS (THE WHOLE PROPERTY) - CONTINUOUS

THE GATES OPEN, EVE DRIVES LUCIUS OUT OF THE NORTH ENTRANCE:

- The CAMPUS is abandoned yet looks completely normal.

- There are NO TRACES that LUCIUS was even there.

- EVE has cleaned up the whole CAMPUS without a trace.

- THE GATES SLOWLY CLOSE...

...LUCIUS and EVE MOVE ON.

                              CUT TO:

INT. CAR DEALERSHIP - EVENING

THE CAR DEALER is sitting at his desk, counting down the clock to his time off. His secretary pops into his OFFICE.

                    CAR DEALER ASSISTANT
               Need anything before I go, boss?

                    THE CAR DEALER
                    (condescending)
               Got any blowjobs?

                    CAR DEALER ASSISTANT
                    (middle finger up)
               Real funny. It's CHRISTMAS, sure,
               but I'm not that giving -

                    THE CAR DEALER
                    (turns around and
                     looks out his
                     OFFICE WINDOW)
               We shouldn't have even come in
               today. Who buys a car on
               CHRISTMAS? And it is snowing, for
               Christ's sake.

THE CAR DEALER notices a quietness as he peers out of his OFFICE window. He doesn't hear his ASSISTANT, she doesn't respond, and he hears a struggle...he turns around.

He turns to see his ASSISTANT lying face down on the floor outside of his OFFICE, in a puddle of blood.

THE CAR DEALER stands up in shock -

                    THE CAR DEALER
                (races to his
                  secretary)
          SALLY! What the hell!?

LUCIUS CROW, UNMASKED, approaches THE CAR DEALER from the
shadows - his ORANGE-EYES glimmering. THE CAR DEALER falls
backward into his OFFICE. He slips on the blood of his
lifeless assistant.

                    THE CAR DEALER
                (races toward his
                  desk)
          What is this!? Who the fu -
                (coming to a
                  realization)
          - You. I recognize you.

                    YOUNG LUCIUS CROW
                (with a tad of
                  sarcasm)
          I've merely come to purchase a
          vehicle, sir. Is there a problem?

THE CAR DEALER pulls a 9MM pistol from his DESK DRAWER. He
aims it at LUCIUS. YOUNG LUCIUS CROW just stands there,
observing the man. THE CAR DEALER also scrambles for his
cell phone and tries to call out to 911...

...EVE has blocked the cellular device -

                    THE CAR DEALER
          You take one step and I'll shoot,
          kid! I mean it.
                (pauses)
          Wait a second! You're the one who
          stopped by not too long ago. The
          STUDENT. You were messing about
          our place of business,
          procrastinating instead of
          purchasing -

LUCIUS steps over the corpse of the ASSISTANT:

                    YOUNG LUCIUS CROW
          I came to this place to inquire
          about a CAR. Now I have the funds,
          and I want to buy one from you, IN
          CASH.

The CAR DEALER cocks and readies his 9MM pistol. LUCIUS calmly and composed, takes out 2 single blood-stained dollar bills...

...He lays them on the OFFICE DESK of the CAR DEALER and moves back beside the corpse of SALLY THE ASSISTANT.

                    THE CAR DEALER
          What is this?! What do you want?!

                    YOUNG LUCIUS CROW
                      (with vindication
                       in his voice)
          There is 1 dollar, sir, as a down
          payment on a vehicle. THAT'S ALL
          YOU NEED. And there is one more
          dollar with it...

                    THE CAR DEALER
          ...For what, you psycho!?

                    YOUNG LUCIUS CROW
          YOUR SOUL!

                    THE CAR DEALER
          Oh, yeah! We'll see about that -

THE CAR DEALER attempts to pull the trigger of the 9MM.

LUCIUS raises his hand up.

THE CAR DEALER's hand that's holding the metal weapon freezes as it AIMS AT LUCIUS. He has a metallic watch on and his wedding band with another ring.

LUCIUS is using his magnetic contraption that allows him to control metal objects - not even breaking a sweat in the process.

                                          CUT TO:

THE CAR DEALER tries with all his might to pull the trigger and shoot LUCIUS - BUT HE CANNOT DO IT.

LUCIUS makes subtle movements with his hands, twisting and turning them lightly with CONTROL.

He is able to take hold of THE CAR DEALER'S shooting hand and LUCIUS manipulates the movement of the pistol with his technological magnetism.

WITHIN 2 SECONDS, the PISTOL whips around and points to THE CAR DEALER's face, involuntarily at the will of LUCIUS -

THE CAR DEALER'S HAND PULLS THE TRIGGER AND HE SHOOTS HIMSELF IN THE FACE, killing himself instantly.

CUT TO:

The body drops like a sack of potatoes, the head halfway gone:

The CAR DEALER is alive for a few seconds more, gasping for oxygen - he lets out a nasty death-breath.

YOUNG LUCIUS CROW
(to the dead CAR DEALER)
You shouldn't play with guns.

CUT TO:

LUCIUS talks to EVE through his ear-piece:

YOUNG LUCIUS CROW
EVE, clean this mess up, will ya? With the TIN-SOLDIER we brought along. And get the bags out of the RANGE ROVER. We're taking another ride from here. One I've had my eye on for some time. The robot will fit in the trunk of it when he's done.

                    EVE
          Yes, MASTER, understood...and let
          me guess, LUCIUS - the new ORANGE
          CORVETTE on display?

                    YOUNG LUCIUS CROW
                       (cracking a smile)
          You know me well, EVE.

                                        CUT TO:

FAST CUTS:

- The 'BOSTON DYNAMICS' ROBOT unpacking the GREEN RANGE ROVER and reloading LUCIUS' bags and gifts into a 2034 ORANGE CORVETTE.

- The ROBOT cleaning up the crime-scene.

- The ROBOT powering down, and folding inward, to a much smaller size to fit in the trunk of the ORANGE 2034 CORVETTE.

- LUCIUS shuts the trunk. He grins with satisfaction -

                                        CUT TO:

LUCIUS gets into the driver's seat of the 2034 ORANGE CORVETTE smart-car. The CAR matches his ORANGE-EYES, PERFECTLY:

CUT TO:

                              ORANGE CORVETTE
                              INTERIOR -

                    EVE
                       (into LUCIUS'
                        earpiece)
          Shall I drive you, MASTER?

                    YOUNG LUCIUS CROW
                       (gripping the
                        steering wheel)
          No, dear. This is all me.

LUCIUS activates the FOB and the start button in the VEHICLE. The engine purrs like a rabid beast. LUCIUS presses the pedal to get the juices flowing.

The CAR is an automatic. Still it's a BEAUTY.

THE YOUNG LUCIUS CROW guns the CORVETTE off of the display stage, through the glass of the CAR DEALERSHIP. He pounces on the road and ZOOMS off from the scene, undetected, unseen, unheard, UNAFRAID...

                                            CUT TO:

INT. ORANGE 2034 CORVETTE - EVENING

LUCIUS is cruising down a RURAL ROAD...it's empty, scenic. He's driving defensively, acknowledging the rules of the road.

Modern Christian music is playing on the radio of all things - LUCIUS is listening to it, intently.

                                            CUT TO:

EXT. MASSACHUSETTS' RURAL ROAD - EVENING

LUCIUS is comfortable in the ORANGE 2034 CORVETTE:

Out of nowhere, a HIGHWAY PATROL POLICE CAR appears behind LUCIUS as he drives through the snow - it has stopped snowing, though.

The COP CAR'S LIGHTS COME ON, flashing brightly, although soundless -

CUT TO:

INT. ORANGE 2034 CORVETTE - CONTINUOUS

LUCIUS pulls the CORVETTE over on the side of the road. He obeys the HIGHWAY PATROL.

                    YOUNG LUCIUS CROW
          I knew it...

                    EVE
               (into LUCIUS'
                earpiece)
          - MASTER, do not fret. I am
          jamming his communications so this
          cannot escalate. You have a valid
          license and registration. If he
          asks for more or has further
          suspicions - then you know what
          you have to do.

EVE communicates to LUCIUS through the earpiece,
clandestine.

                    YOUNG LUCIUS CROW
               (looking into the
                side-view mirror)
          Yes, I do.

LUCIUS looks down at the passenger seat, where his now BLACK
PUMPKINHEAD-MASK lies in the glass-case, covered with a
blanket.

                                        CUT TO:

INT. HIGHWAY PATROL CAR - CONTINUOUS

                    HIGHWAY PATROLMAN
               (into his radio)
          320 to base -

Nothing. STATIC.

                    HIGHWAY PATROLMAN
          320 to base, over - I repeat, over
          - I've pulled over a suspicious
          vehicle with a 30-day-tag. I am
          inspecting the vehicle now.

The HIGHWAY PATROLMAN exits his PATROL CAR.

                                        CUT TO:

EXT. RURAL ROAD - CONTINUOUS

> HIGHWAY PATROLMAN
> (walking to the
> CORVETTE,
> whispering)
> Another rich kid driving their
> CHRISTMAS car from mommy and
> daddy...helping me meet my quota.

The OFFICER reaches the driver's side of the CORVETTE and gestures for LUCIUS to roll his window down.

CUT TO:

EXT. ORANGE 2034 CORVETTE - CONTINUOUS

The COP stands outside of the ORANGE CORVETTE - LUCIUS has rolled down his window.

> HIGHWAY PATROLMAN
> (to LUCIUS)
> License and registration, please,
> son.

LUCIUS says not word. He hands the COP the credentials fabricated by EVE.

> HIGHWAY PATROLMAN
> Any idea why I pulled you over?

> YOUNG LUCIUS CROW
> Because you're trying to meet your
> quota -

The COP jumps back at the sarcasm of LUCIUS - he doesn't know what to make of it. "Was he listening to me somehow?", the OFFICER thinks to himself, with no poker-face.

> HIGHWAY PATROLMAN
> (thrown off guard)
> You stay put, sir. I'm going to
> run your ID and registration.

LUCIUS REMAINS SILENT.

INT. HIGHWAY PATROL CAR - EVENING

The OFFICER sits back in his vehicle. He proceeds to run the credentials LUCIUS provided through the system -

CUT TO:

INT. ORANGE CORVETTE - CONTINUOUS

LUCIUS is getting prepared in his mind. He knows this is a sticky situation.

      EVE
  LUCIUS, I calculate an 83 percent
  threat in this current situation.
  I suggest you do the necessaries,
  MASTER.

LUCIUS CROW meditates for just a moment. He zones in, practicing mindfulness of his mind, body, and heart.

He peeks down, one more time, at the blanketed glass-case holding his TRUE FACE.

      YOUNG LUCIUS CROW
  To Hell with this.

LUCIUS rips the blanket away from the glass-case. He opens the case, putting his newly improved BLACK JACK O' LANTERN MASK on -

           CUT TO:

INT. HIGHWAY PATROL CAR - MOMENTS LATER

      HIGHWAY PATROLMAN
    (confused by his
     tech)
  Dammit, nothing's working here.
  Stupid weather.

The OFFICER bangs his computer; it's frozen. He presses his radio buttons to test it; it's jammed. EVE has put the COP in the dark...

...The HIGHWAY PATROLMAN happens to look up as he notices something out of his peripheral vision.

As he lifts his head, he sees YOUNG LUCIUS CROW, with his NEW black-and-ORANGE suit, bright ORANGE TIE, and newly designed BLACK PUMPKINHEAD-MASK on -

> HIGHWAY PATROLMAN
> (unholstering his
> pistol)
> What in the world?

The HIGHWAY PATROLMAN exits the vehicle, his gun ready.

CUT TO:

EXT. RURAL ROAD - EVENING

LUCIUS proceeds to walk toward the HIGHWAY PATROL CAR, fully MASKED-UP.

YOUNG LUCIUS CROW blitzes the POLICE OFFICER.

CUT TO BLACK:

WE HEAR GUNSHOTS.

WE HEAR YELLS AND SCREAMS OF ONLY THE HIGHWAY PATROLMAN - then, there's nothing but static and radio silence.

CUT TO:

LUCIUS CROW has embraced his destiny - he's found a new path.

Having created an A.I in EVE, he's changed the world more than he could ever imagine - this ENTITY has no barriers, no limits, no emotions, no walls, no boundaries...

It doesn't thirst.
It doesn't hunger.

It doesn't complain.
It doesn't eat.
It doesn't sleep.

...EVE will NEVER stop PROTECTING HER MASTER.

LUCIUS will NEVER stop trying to prove he is a MASTER. A GREAT BEAST.

- NOW, BOTH ARE ENTITIES.

CUT TO BLACK:

ROLL CREDITS -

FADE IN:

EXT. COVERT C.I.A BASE - WASHINGTON DC - DAY

MID-CREDITS' SCENE:

A white male CIA AGENT sits in a darkened ROOM, in an interrogative fashion. A MYSTERIOUS MAN (older, white haired, his face in the shadows, his BLACK EYES GLOWING) - wearing a grayish black suit with a blood-red tie and blood-red SURGICAL gloves - walks into the INTERROGATION ROOM.

     C.I.A AGENT
 Hello, Sir. I -

     MYSTERIOUS MAN
 You failed.

     C.I.A AGENT
  (lacking
   confidence)
 Not exactly, DOCTOR. Yes, I didn't
 retrieve the A.I, but I gathered
 sufficient intel on our target. We
 have an idea of his next move.
 Then, we'll seize -

The MYSTERIOUS MAN is DR. SAVIN SAIN SLAUGHTER -

The DOCTOR struts slowly behind the AGENT and places his hands on his shoulders. Our view is obscured from a clear view of DR. SLAUGHTER - we can't get a decent look at him.

His face and body covered in shade.

>   DR. SLAUGHTER
>   You will do nothing unless I say
>   so. There's a new order of
>   business. I don't just want the
>   A.I, anymore. The kid, he's the
>   primary asset I need now. He's
>   more powerful than I ever could've
>   imagined - he's truly his father's
>   son.
>
>   C.I.A AGENT
>   So we're not eliminating him,
>   after all?
>
>   DR. SLAUGHTER
>   No. He's my newest prospect.
>
>   C.I.A AGENT
>   Yes, Sir, understood.

DR. SLAUGHTER almost floats across the other side of the room, with his back turned to the AGENT, we still don't get a really good look at this almost FACELESS individual, this spectre...

>   DR. SLAUGHTER
>   (lights a CUBAN
>   CIGAR)
>   One more thing, AGENT MARCUS.
>
>   C.I.A AGENT
>   Yes, DR. SLAUGHTER?
>
>   DR. SLAUGHTER
>   (with excitement
>   in his voice)
>   - Does the boy know his MOTHER is
>   still alive?

DR. SLAUGHTER laughs sadistically.

The AGENT's eyes widen at this earth-shattering statement.

CUT TO:

END CREDITS -

FADE IN:

INT. ORANGE CORVETTE - NIGHT

POST-CREDITS' SCENE:

YOUNG LUCIUS drives in a trance, feeling fulfilled after having successfully confronted his FEARS and his ENEMIES. The YOUNG MAN listens to the purr of his CORVETTE ENGINE, and his GOSPEL MUSIC, as he cruises. His BLACK PUMPKINHEAD-MASK sits in the PASSENGER SEAT, out of its case, beside him as he drives -

              YOUNG LUCIUS CROW
        (gripping the
         steering wheel)
   EVE, any new news for me? Are my
   tracks covered? Are we SAFE?

              EVE
   I've been scanning every piece of
   intel and information available
   with regard to the SCHOOL, MASTER.
   The bodies have been properly
   disposed of, neatly. The CAMPUS is
   cleared, no traces thanks to my
   little helpers. No witnesses were
   there.
        (a pause and a
         beat)
   W-wait a moment, MASTER -

EVE talks to LUCIUS through the CORVETTE's interface:

                             560.

                    YOUNG LUCIUS CROW
                 (curious, focused
                  as can be)
            What is it, EVE?

                         EVE
                     (concerened)
                This just incoming. Listen for
                yourself.

EVE taps into the audio system of the ORANGE 2034 CORVETTE
and streams the online RADIO.

                         RADIO NEWS ANCHOR
                     (monotonic)
                "...the young student isn't
                coherent as of yet. Her injuries
                are beyond severe and she's
                unresponsive. She was found
                walking along a RURAL ROAD 4 MILES
                away from the HARVARD CAMPUS,
                covered in BLOOD, hurt and maimed.
                Paramedics and authorities are
                transferring the victim to the
                HOSPITAL for treatment. Her
                condition is believed to be
                critical, but the HARVARD STUDENT
                is fighting to stay with us in
                intensive care. We have received
                reports that the female student is
                actually SENATOR BOB THORN's
                daughter. This has been confirmed
                by authorities. We're
                investigating the CAMPUS further,
                as SEVERAL other students are
                unaccounted for - MISSING,
                including CIA DIRECTOR ROGER
                KENO's son. Secret-Service is
                collaborating with local
                law-enforcement in an attempt to
                locate the SENATOR's son: MICHAEL
                THORN - who is also among the
                missing. Besides that, we have no
                further information on this
                situation at this time, other than
                to say we will try our very best
                to retrieve all the information to
                         (MORE)

                    RADIO NEWS ANCHOR (cont'd)
          give you, the viewer, the full
          picture, when it's available."

LUCIUS' orange eyes nearly pop out of his head. He is
floored by the news.

                    EVE
          MASTER, LILY THORN, she still
          lives. I can confirm it - she made
          it, she somehow escaped from the
          trunk of one of the smart-vehicles
          before it hit the river - the
          audio and video feed confirms it.

LUCIUS whips the steering wheel as hard as humanly possible,
performing a 180-degree drifting burnout, madder than a
hornet - he stops the CORVETTE in the middle of the road.

                    YOUNG LUCIUS CROW
          MICHAEL and LILY never said their
          FATHER was a CONGRESSMAN. Damn it
          to hell. EVE, plug me in to her
          location. Give me a visual, give
          me ears, and give me the exact
          HOSPITAL she's going to.
                    (puts his
                    PUMPKINHEAD-MASK
                    on)
          This is going to be FUN.

                    EVE
                    (with a hint of
                    fury in HER voice)
          Yes, my MASTER.

                    YOUNG LUCIUS CROW
                    (floors the
                    CORVETTE)
          A thorn in my side! That little
          whore is going to wish she stayed
          dead.

The ORANGE CORVETTE zooms on the RURAL ROAD, furiously,
ferociously. YOUNG LUCIUS, MASKED-UP and wearing his REAL
FACE, becomes DEVOID of emotion.

He is now driven by pure RAGE, seeking LILY THORN, like a great white shark after tasting a drop of blood.

- The CHAOS has only just begun -

...TO BE CONTINUED.

                                                      FADE OUT.

Made in the USA
Columbia, SC
03 March 2025